CONTENTS
UNDER
PRESSURE

CONTENTS UNDER PRESSURE

EDNA BUCHANAN

HYPERION

NEW YORK

The author gratefully acknowledges permission to reprint the quote from Isaiah on the epigraph page from J. Barrie Shepherd's *Encounters*, published in 1983 by Pilgrim Press.

ISBN 1-56282-932-7

Do not cling to events of the past or dwell on what happened long ago. Watch for the new thing I am going to do. It is happening already—you can see it now!

ISAIAH   43:18-19

CONTENTS
UNDER
PRESSURE

ONE

I stopped to listen. So did a detective and several patrolmen, frozen in motion. One cocked his head and held his walkie up to his ear. The morning had started out as a slow news day, but that could change in a heartbeat. It was happening now.

A radio in the heavy leather belt of a patrolman at the front desk had spit out a rush of static as I walked through the lobby at headquarters after reading a stack of routine police reports from the night before. A high-pitched emergency signal had followed, then the clear-as-a-bell disembodied voice of a dispatcher giving the location, Suwannee Park Elementary School. An armed abduction. Possible machine gun involved.

Children and guns: The combination raised the hairs on the back of my neck.

The victim was a woman, the dispatcher announced, abducted at gunpoint after dropping her children off at school. A domestic, I thought, maybe an irate estranged husband or boyfriend. I had covered countless stories about women murdered by men who "loved" them.

The address hung on the air—precisely enunciated by the coolly impassive dispatcher. The cop grounded by desk duty looked wistful as I quickly pushed through the heavy glass door into the sun-blasted parking lot, already eighty-five degrees at 8 A.M. The cloudless sky was a cruel and brilliant blue. Carloads of commuters swooped by on the elevated Metro Rail tracks across the street as I scrambled into the front seat, hit the key on my dashboard scanner, and peeled out of the parking lot. The dispatcher was reporting that the suspect had forced the victim to drive him away in her own small, white, American-made car.

The crime scene was on the move out there somewhere, rolling through Monday morning rush hour traffic. I tried not to think about what had to be going on in the woman's mind. An all points was out on her car, but nobody knew the exact make or tag number yet. Suwannee Park Elementary was the place to start. I drove, scanning oncoming traffic for a small white car with a terrified woman at the wheel.

A Miami patrol car passed me like a heat-seeking missile, siren wailing, lights flashing. I hit the gas and stayed on its tail, accelerating past startled motorists who pulled to the side. I love it when the cops and I are bound for the same destination. There is no risk I'll be stopped for speeding; their goal is to answer a call for help. As a reporter on the police beat, mine is to write about what happened, how they handled it. Or didn't.

I swung in to the curb behind him, across the street from the school. A child was crying, and I feared at first that students were hurt. But the piercing sounds came from one of two small girls who stood on the sidewalk. About six and eight years old, they clung to one another, half-surrounded by several men in uniform, a disheveled civilian, his white shirt torn open at the front, and a taller man, probably the principal, sweating in a suit and tie. I recognized Officer Ted Ferrell, tall, thin, and wiry, hunkered down in front of the girls. The little one wailed, while the other, wide-eyed and solemn, tried to answer the policeman's questions.

Ted got to his feet and passed me on the way to his patrol car.

"Thought you worked midnights," I called out.

"Hi Britt. I did, until today. Rotation."

I had forgotten this was the first Monday of the month. Shift change. Officers transferring from one shift to another work both.

Ted, I knew, had worked midnights and was now doubling back onto days.

"What happened?" I asked him.

"This is a crazy one, Britt. Woman drops her kids at school and stops to talk to a teacher. He's standing at her car when this guy charges up with what looks like a machine gun, grabs the teacher by the shirt, yanks him away from the car, jumps in the backseat, threatens to blow off the woman's head, and orders her to drive away."

I looked up from my notebook. "Her kids see it?"

"The whole thing."

"Somebody they know?"

"Nope." He reached for his radio mike. "Total stranger."

Ted reported that the eight-year-old said her mother's car was a Chevrolet, a Nova. He asked dispatch to send a patrolman to the family home in search of a relative or a neighbor who knew how to reach the woman's husband at work, then he turned back to me. The gunman appeared to be the same man who had run amok a few blocks away. He had tried a robbery, Ted said, but his victim ran. The would-be robber confronted several strangers on the street, but they stampeded away also. Then he tried to force his way into a house. "People started calling us. He evaded the first units by running through backyards to the school here, where our victim was sitting in her car. Looks like she just happened to be there when he needed a ride."

"Did the teacher give you a good car description, or the tag number?" I asked.

"He was so scared that he fell down and tore his pants trying to get away. I feel sorry for the little girls. I've got one her age." He pointed to the smaller child.

"Mommmeee!" Twin cries rose from the sidewalk. A white car, a Chevy Nova, had turned the corner, a woman at the wheel. The two little girls broke and ran. They attached themselves to her before she emerged from the car.

I joined the circle that quickly formed around her. She was about thirty-five and pudgy, with short dark hair, and wore a slightly rumpled flowered housedress. "I was scared to death," she said, eyes watery. She held her youngest girl tightly in her arms, while the other clung to her skirt. "But I tried to stay cool. That man is crazy . . . when

I told him my gas tank was on empty, he said I was his hostage, and if the engine died, so did I. He made me take him to N. W. Third Street and Twenty-seventh Avenue. That's where he got out and told me to keep driving. I came right back here, to my girls."

The cops were shooting questions as I scribbled notes. "Last time I saw him," she told them, "he was walking toward a Yellow Cab, with the gun hidden under his windbreaker."

Always be suspicious of men wearing windbreakers in Miami during the blistering heat of early September, I thought, taking down a brief, relieved quote from the woman, who praised the Lord, and a number where I could reach her later.

The cops fanned out in their cars to hunt the gunman down. I followed, cruising the neighborhood where he was last seen, hoping to be in the right place for any action.

We zoomed in all directions, passing each others' cars, scouring the side streets. I was pleased that no TV reporters had picked up the scent. They always get in the way and make the cops crazy. TV cars from two local stations had crashed head-on at an intersection while surveilling a ransom drop in a kidnapping last year. The crews jumped out and began filming each other, instead of keeping a low profile in a sensitive situation. Those guys make it tough on all of us.

Ted Ferrell was one of those cops with an uncanny knack for being where the action was, so I decided to hang in close to him. He was good at catching people. The talent was instinctive, something that could not be bottled, manufactured, or taught. He once approached a man he spotted hurrying away from an office building. The man ran, and Ted chased him. As he caught him a block away, a bomb blast shook the building. The bomber explained: "America is falling like Cuba did, and something must be done!" When examined, his motives proved more personal than political: His wife worked in the building. He was unemployed, and humiliated because she was supporting the family. But if the building blew up, she would lose the job and no longer be the breadwinner. His plan made perfect sense to him, another example of how fleeing one's homeland sometimes skews the thought process. I had also reported the time Ted pulled over a motorist on what began as a routine traffic stop and wound up yielding fifty-six kilos of cocaine, $850,000 in small bills, two silencer-equipped Barettas, and one of the FBI's ten most-wanted fugitives.

Ted's hunches were gold. A reporter could stay busy just following him, which was exactly what I was doing, trailing half a block behind, when a Yellow Cab drove past us, in the opposite direction. The driver, a middle-aged black man, sat rigid in his seat, eyes frozen straight ahead. I had heard Yellow Cab conduct a radio roll call at police request on my scanner. This one, number 87, had not responded, although its driver was not at breakfast or using a restroom. He was driving too carefully, stone-faced, at exactly the speed limit in what looked like an empty cab.

Ted, in his car up ahead, showed no sign he'd even noticed. Come on, I thought, you can't be that tired. His cruiser moved on down the street at a leisurely pace and swung into a slow motion U-turn a block away. I rolled into a corner gas station to turn around, trying to stay inconspicuous.

A red light at the intersection a block away caught the cab, which came to a smooth, perfectly precise stop. Ted's patrol car approached quickly from behind it. Suddenly, the cab's back passenger door swung open and a man bailed out. He was running before he hit the ground. He still had the gun. The cab jack-rabbited across the intersection against the light, the open door swinging, as motorists screeched to a stop.

I didn't even see Ted leave his car; I just saw him sprinting after the gunman, a stick-thin dishwater blond in his twenties. Ted was fast. They both were a lot faster than I would be in the shoes I was wearing. I kicked off my heels and pulled on an old pair of flats that I kept in the backseat, along with a set of telephone books, a city directory, and other such essentials. I tossed my purse in the trunk, locked it and ran after them, just carrying my keys, a notebook, and pen.

My press ID swung from a beaded metal chain around my neck as I pounded after them. The gunman started cutting across back-yards toward the projects, a low income, high crime neighborhood, now mostly black. My intent was not to catch them. Sometimes I am reckless, but I'm not stupid; I have seen what automatic weapon fire can do. I just wanted to keep them in sight. Ted had a radio with him, but I hadn't seen any backup yet. When you are running through yards and vacant lots, it is hard to report exactly where you are.

I lost them momentarily and stopped to catch my breath beside a little boy playing in a scrubby side yard. He didn't say a word; he just pointed. I followed his tiny finger and saw the gunman. He still had the weapon as he scaled a wooden fence. The leap could qualify him for an Olympic team, I thought, my heart racing. Ted went over after him. His movements were controlled, with more strength than panic. I could see him being cautious, in case the man with the gun wheeled to confront him. In real life, there were no dress rehearsals.

Having caught my breath, I explored the fence, trying to find a way around it. From the other side came Ted's raspy shouts for the man to halt. A guttural, muffled yell came in response. I could not make out the exact words, but they sure didn't sound like surrender. Maybe he was cornered. More shouts, different voices. Something was happening, but I could not find a way around the fence.

Damn! I hate to climb wearing a skirt, but there was no other way. I clipped my pen to my notebook, stuck them in my waistband, and looked around for something to stand on. There was nothing. A handful of tiny children had gathered, most of them giggling. I attacked the fence, grabbed the top with both hands, and tried to pull myself up. My sunglasses skidded off my sweaty nose as I strained, then lost it, picking up a splinter in my palm on the way down. The kids, now joined by a few adults, were raucous and hooting, doing nothing for my vanity.

"Out of my way," I muttered, and retreated for a running start. Two little boys were jumping at the fence in exaggerated imitations of my poor showing. This time I hit the fence with my right foot first, grabbed the top and walked up the side on the balls of my feet while pulling up with both hands. I grunted as I pushed myself up waist high, swung my left leg over the top and flung the rest of myself after it. Something gave way in my panty hose as I landed, staggering, on my feet. The kids on the other side cheered and clapped. I didn't know whether they were applauding my success or the sight of my bloomers as I sailed over the top.

Neither Ted nor the gunman were in sight. I took a deep breath, then trotted into the project complex, a labyrinth of connected apartment buildings surrounding cluttered courtyards.

People in various stages of alarm were emerging from all three levels, and kids were collecting in the breezeways. I followed their eyes. Ted and the gunman had each taken cover behind concrete stairwells in the same building, about fifty feet apart. Each held a gun. Ted yelled for people to get down, out of the line of fire.

"Go home, go inside," I told the gaggle of children nearest me. None listened, or even looked at me. Their dark faces were intent, aglow with curiosity.

An apartment door opened, four or five feet from the crouching gunman. An elderly lady in house slippers stepped out, her expression irritated, peering uncertainly through her spectacles to see what the commotion was about. The gunman seized the moment, darting past her into her apartment. I held my breath but no shots rang out. He slammed the door behind him. The man was armed, had already committed a good six or seven felonies today, and seemed to be trying for an even dozen. Ted would have been justified had he opened fire—some would say he should have—but shooting was too risky, with all the women and children around.

The elderly woman looked dazed, and started to protest. A young mother who had been herding toddlers into an adjacent apartment took her arm and led her inside to safety. I joined them.

From their open door, I could see both Ted and the apartment sheltering the gunman. Burglar bars protected the windows. The only other way out of that apartment, I realized, was another door in full view, eight feet down the corridor. The man with the gun had boxed himself in.

A half hour ago this seemed to be the slow news day I needed to work on my weekend feature. Now I was two miles from the office in the middle of the projects, in what could be a shoot-out. That is one of the things I love and hate about this job: News always breaks when you least expect it. I couldn't see Ted's expression in the long shadow of the stairwell, but I was certain he was thinking of his own children. Damn, we needed a photographer. I turned to ask to use the telephone when, like an answered prayer, I caught a glimpse of frizzy red hair and cowboy boots across the courtyard. It was Lottie Dane. The cavalry had arrived.

Slung over her right shoulder was her Canon EOS automatic focus with a long telephoto lens, for shooting from a distance. A second camera was slung over her other shoulder, a wide-angle lens with a flash, to use when it was all over, as she elbowed her way in for a close-up. She had already spotted me, sized up the situation, and was scanning upper levels of the buildings for a good vantage point to shoot from. Lottie was the best photographer I'd ever worked with and the best friend I'd ever had. As I watched, she scampered up the outside stairway of the next building and out of my view.

I glimpsed Ted's face as he shifted position. No fatigue there; he looked sweaty but sharp, and as serious as a stroke. The door to the apartment flew open and I saw the gun thrust out, then leveled toward Ted. Involuntarily, I held my breath and squeezed my eyes shut. No shots. Ted held his fire. "Come on out," he called, managing to sound almost friendly. "Throw out the gun." The door slammed.

Twice more, the man opened the door, then slammed it.

"It's okay," Ted said calmly. "Slide out the gun and nobody will get hurt. Do it now." The door slowly opened.

"Take it easy. You won't be hurt. I promise."

"Don't shoot," the gunman croaked.

"Slide the gun out slow, butt first, keep your hands up in front of you. You'll be okay."

The man crouched, then shoved something out the half-open door. Metal scraped on concrete. He straightened up and emerged, skinny and scared, palms open in front of him.

Ted had him spread-eagled against the wall and handcuffed in seconds. Cheers and applause rang out. I heard the whir of an automatic shutter over my shoulder. "Where've you been?" I asked Lottie.

"You might have called," she sniffed, still shooting, never taking her dark eyes off the subjects. "Luckily I stumbled on this myself, on my scanner. Just missed you at the school. Got the woman and her kids."

The bad guy was bundled off in the backseat of a patrol car. His weapon turned out to be a mean .30 caliber sawed-off carbine, loaded for bear.

Residents crowded around Ted, relieved that no one was hurt. Somebody offered a beer, which he declined, though he looked like he could use one. He did accept a cigarette. He allowed the donor to light it. I was betting his own hands were shaky; mine were. I felt elated. For once, my timing had been right; everything had clicked into place. A good story. I got through the crowd to Ted.

"Why did you handle it the way you did?" I asked him, knowing the answer but needing a quote.

"There were women and children on three tiers of the apartment house in the courtyard behind me. If he had opened up with that weapon, a lot of them could have been hurt."

"How dangerous was he?"

"He had abducted two people, Britt. He was committed to getting away. Because of that, he may have been one of the more dangerous men I've encountered in ten years on the department." God bless Ted. He knew how to answer a reporter's questions, none of that monosyllabic crap you get from some cops.

"Last question. I saw your face when you were back in that stairwell, when it was a standoff. You were thinking about your family, your kids, right?"

"Nope." Ted paused, then grinned. "I was wishing I'd worn my bulletproof vest."

Later I sat at my desk after writing my favorite type of story for the early edition. A hero, a satisfying ending, readers happy at getting their money's worth from a dedicated public servant, cops happy at getting good press. Lottie's pictures helped it get prime display on the local page. What more could a reporter ask for?

HERO COP NEVER FIRES A SHOT. RESIDENTS APPLAUD, in 60 point Bodoni. By Britt Montero, *Miami Daily News* Staff Writer. That's me.

Before going home that night, I plugged the culprit's prior police record, which was impressive, into the story, and added a quote from the mother of the accused, who swore her boy must be the victim of mistaken identity. I was headed home, stepping into the elevator, when the city desk clerk yelled that I had a call. I sighed and turned back, determined to keep it brief.

The caller had a tip: D. Wayne Hudson was in the hospital.

"I'll pass it along to the sports department," I said breezily.

"You don't understand the situation," said Rico, one of my sources, who works as an intensive care nurse.

"How serious is it?" I asked warily.

"As serious as you can get. His organs are about to be harvested for transplant."

Hudson was dead, or about to be, of unnatural causes.

"Oh, no," I whispered, and sank into my chair.

Everybody in Miami knew D. Wayne Hudson. Quarterback for the University of Miami Hurricanes, all-American, first-round draft choice, he led the LA Raiders to a national championship and starred for six successful seasons until knee injuries cut short his career. But he did not rest on his endorsements or break into the movies, though he had the talent and the smarts. He came home.

Unlike so many who fight their way out of the ghetto and never look back, he reached down from the top of the ladder to those at the bottom. He tried to make a difference, coaching and working with disadvantaged youngsters to keep them in school, out of trouble, and off drugs.

He was thirty-eight years old.

"He came in by ambulance during the night, a few hours before dawn," Rico continued. "Car accident, unconscious, but expected to recover. A few hours later a nurse on routine rounds called a code blue; he'd stopped breathing. The team managed to restart his heart and breathing and hooked him up to life support, but he was brain dead. They are keeping his vital functions going long enough to take his organs for transplant. He was carrying an organ donor card."

Phone tucked under my chin, I was scribbling notes and groping for the phone on the desk behind me. Ryan Battle, the general assignment reporter who sat there, had gone home, and I needed to call the library for D. Wayne's clip file. I did all this while also trying, without success, to establish eye contact with the assistant city editor in the slot, forty feet away.

"How was he injured?" I asked. "This was an accident?" I rolled my chair up to the video display terminal next to my desk, punched out the password, and slugged the story, taking notes as we talked.

"Apparently, he was running from the cops; they were chasing him."

"Why would Hudson run from the cops? On foot?"

"Nah, if it was on foot, they never would have caught D. Wayne, even with his bum knee. The cops said they were chasing his car when he wrecked it. I was in the ER when they brought him in."

"What cops? Miami? Metro? What kind of injuries? Did he ever say anything? Was he drinking? Any drugs? What was he wearing? Where was he coming from? Where was he going?"

"You always do that, Britt. All I know is what I said."

"What cops? Come on, Rico, you saw them."

"The cops wore blue shirts, Miami." Miami cops wear dark blue; Metro police and highway patrolmen wear brown.

"Miami . . . on the midnight shift. How come I didn't hear about it? I was at the station this morning."

"Well, D. Wayne didn't take a turn for the worse until after the cops left. That's all I know. You got to get everything through official channels, Britt. We didn't talk."

"Right." I thanked Rico and glanced at the clock, stomach clenched like a fist. We had forty-five minutes until deadline for the final. I stepped quickly up to the city desk. Bobby Tubbs was in the night slot, responsible for the news that went into the local section in the final edition. Not a job for someone who hates change. He looked apprehensive at my approach, anticipating what was coming. When I said I had a story, his chubby face took on the look of an evil Muppet. What a newsman. Bobby was famous for becoming apoplectic when his carefully laid out pages were messed up by something as intrusive as breaking news. He was beginning to hyperventilate until I explained what I was working on. If this tip was true, his page would not be torn up after all. The story would go out front, on page one. D. Wayne Hudson was *news*.

Tubbs informed the national desk, and sports, to start somebody on a sidebar with D. Wayne's stats and playing field achievements. I hit the phones, working with a receiver to each ear. At one point, both the police department and the hospital had me on hold. Breathing deeply, I stared at the relentless hands on the big clock mounted over the city desk, then closed my eyes for a long moment. The best years of my life have been spent on hold.

The hospital reluctantly confirmed that D. Wayne Hudson was a patient. I had to go three rounds with an administrator to drag out more details. Meanwhile, the police department's accident reports had been locked in an office until morning. I reached a public information officer at home. He promised to do some digging, then called back with a bare-bones account. A BOLO (be on the lookout) had gone out for a stolen late-model Lincoln Mark VII. The driver was described as armed, dangerous, and fleeing a felony. Officers spotted a car fitting the description and tried to pull it over, but the driver fled at high speed. During the chase he lost it on a curve, crashed into a bridge abutment, and careened into a ditch. He was arrested for fleeing the police and sent to County Hospital for treatment of his injuries. Police confirmed the identity of the driver: D. Wayne Hudson, black male, aged thirty-eight. They had no information on his present condition, dead or alive.

"What was the felony?" I asked. "Was there a gun? Was the car stolen?"

"We have no further information at this time," he said obliquely. "Try again in the morning."

Butterfly wings beating in my chest, I called D. Wayne's home number. The last time I had seen him, he was speaking at a fundraiser for a halfway house for youthful offenders about to be paroled back into the community. He had been an earnest and eloquent advocate. His pretty wife, Alma, gracious and elegant in white silk, and their twin boys and baby girl were with him. How could D. Wayne have been dirty?

A woman answered on the second ring. It was Alma's sister. She was crying; it was true. Alma was at the hospital. A second brain scan had shown identical results, and they were about to pull the plug. All the sister knew was that there had been an accident. "Does he drive a Lincoln?" I asked gently.

"Yes," she answered, sounding puzzled by the question. At midnight I was able to get through to the intensive care waiting room. All Alma could tell me through her tears was that it was over. He was dead.

We put a new top on the story minutes before the presses rolled at 1 A.M. Details of the accident were vague; why he'd tried to outrun police was unclear. Cause of death: pending an autopsy.

The adrenaline rush of deadline was over, leaving me drained and dispirited. The high of the earlier story, the abduction at Suwannee Park Elementary, was gone. But I could go home, at last. Tubbs reminded me to come in early to follow the story. Even though I was the only passenger, the infuriatingly slow elevator still stopped on all five floors before sluggishly descending to the huge lobby where every sound echoed in the emptiness. I stepped out the back door and drank in the warm moist heat of the late summer night, the Miami Beach skyline stretching across the eastern horizon, lights reflected in dark water. Driving my five-year-old Thunderbird east across the causeway, I remembered promising to meet Lottie at the 1800 Club for a drink and some food. But that had been about eight o'clock. By now, she had surely given up on me and gone home.

I was weary, I hadn't eaten since breakfast, and my panty hose were torn. I reminded myself to put an extra pair in my ladies' room locker at the office, along with the change of clothes I always kept there. Billy Boots greeted me with eager mews as I unlocked my apartment door. He was hungry, too. I opened a can of chicken and liver cat food and spooned it into his dish. I wished dinner for me was as simple. The refrigerator yielded a bar of guava paste and a bowl of leftover picadillo covered with a fine, fuzzy mold. In the vegetable bin were a lone boniato and a mango, both withered and shriveled until one could not be distinguished from the other. I had forgotten to grocery shop again. The choice was either corn flakes or soup. Since I was out of milk I opted for the soup. The hour was too late and I was too tired to cook, so I ate it out of the can with a spoon as I listened to the messages on my telephone answering machine.

Calls had come from my mother ("I know you're always busy, Britt, but so am I. We're having a huge sale, thirty percent off. Come take a look. Your wardrobe could certainly use it. Call me"), a Hialeah cop griping about politics in his department, a lawyer eager for publicity about a big win in court, and my mother, again. She sounded peevish this time.

"Where *are* you, Britt? Why is it that *I* must always do all the calling?"

Larry Zink, an insurance salesman I met on a story last month, had left the remaining message on the tape, inviting Lottie and me to meet him and a friend for drinks after work. Too late now to call any of them back.

I am not like my mother, but I am her only child. My dad was Cuban, though I barely remember him. He died when I was three. He didn't die, actually; he was killed, stood against a bullet-pocked wall on San Juan Hill and executed by a Castro firing squad. My mother never forgave him. She was the daughter of Miami pioneers and never understood why he let his dream of a free Cuba become a fatal obsession. His face is not precisely clear in my conscious mind, but in many ways his presence is always with me. *Estamos Juntos*: We are together.

After his death, my mother was ill and depressed and found caring for me difficult. I was farmed out to various relatives on both sides of the family. Small and bewildered, I felt strange and alone, more an outsider than a part of my father's outgoing, passionate, and sometimes volatile Cuban family who all talked at once in noisy Spanish or a part of the more reserved Episcopalians on my mother's side who took turns speaking precise English and never, ever, interrupted one another. My father's family laughed at my Spanish. My mother's criticized my English.

It didn't help that the families were usually at odds, with me, the only link, straddling two worlds, yet not quite at home in either. My father was considered a hero, a patriot, a martyr by the Cuban community and his relatives. My mother and most of her family thought him reckless, a man who had foolishly gambled his life and lost. I did not permanently rejoin her until I was twelve. By then we didn't know each other well, and had little to talk about. We still don't. When I persisted in studying journalism, she encouraged me to attend Northwestern, away from the Miami influences that she considered unfavorable. The school was wonderful, but the Chicago winters were cold and long. I spent the two most miserable years of my life there.

My clothes were never warm enough, my shoes skidded on the ice, and I hated it. I yearned for the musical sound of spoken Spanish, the taste of Little Havana's food and drink, the warmth of Florida and its vivid colors. Chicago was a gray and lonely place. I escaped and finished my last two years at the University of Miami, home at last.

From the stories I have heard about him, and what little I remember, I think I am very much like my father. If I was not, I would believe that I am the victim of a maternity ward mix-up. My mother and I are that different.

I was incredibly lucky to land a job on one of the best newspapers in the nation. My good fortune was more fluke than anything else. Because I was a Miamian with a Hispanic surname, the paper's minority recruiters assumed I was bilingual and hence fluent enough to report for the paper's Spanish language section. Not so. They discovered their mistake when, in my first story, I referred to Miami's vice-mayor as the *alcalde de vicio*, the mayor of vice.

By chance, a city desk post for a police reporter, a job no one else wanted, was open. The editors doubted a woman could endure the work. They expected dead bodies and shoot-outs to quickly gross me right out of the job. That only steeled my resolve to master the beat and make it my own. I was determined to be successful at it.

The job is exciting and enjoyable most of the time. It is almost always a comfort. The newspaper is something I can count on, a constant in a world full of uncertainty. It publishes every day, rain or shine, in peace or war. The newspaper will outlive all of us and record our history, our beginnings and endings. No matter what happens, the newspaper will come out tomorrow, like the sun. People will wake up in the morning and find it on their lawns. One of the few sure things in life, it is something to hold on to.

I had finished the soup. It was vegetable; not bad, actually. Nutritious, I told myself. Before dropping the can into the recycling bin I read the label. "Stir in one can of water and heat." I wondered if I should drink a can of water. I had a glass of wine instead and went to bed.

TWO

I awoke in the dark at 5:30 A.M., wondering if some chronically ill recipient was lucky enough to be waking up with D. Wayne Hudson's donated championship heart. Still weary and let down, I needed to work out the kinks, mental and physical. There was no time for an aerobics class at the Spa, so I pulled on shorts and my favorite T-shirt, sent by a friend in the Salvadoran press corps: ¡Soy Periodista! ¡No Dispare! (I am a Journalist! Don't Shoot!) I clipped my beeper to my waistband and walked two blocks east. From a half-block away I heard the ocean, and, as always, it made my pulse beat faster. A shrouded moon and two morning stars hung high above the stairs to the boardwalk. The eastern sky had paled to lavender above the rim of the sea. Dark purple clouds stacked above it in deranged shapes, like the shadowy skyline of some wild and alien city that exists only in troubled dreams.

The lights of half a dozen ships at sea still dotted the vast horizon. I broke into a slow jog, heading north on the boardwalk, reveling in the refreshing sea breeze, as the lavender brightened to pink and then to orange neon with charcoal smears. A scrawny gray striped cat sat alone on the sandy beach, eyes fixed on the same heavenly spectacle that took my breath away.

I thought of Billy Boots, fat and glossy, and regretted not having a pocket full of cat nibbles. The black sky to the west faded to navy, and then cobalt blue. Two joggers passed briskly on the beach below, running on hard-packed sand, as the steps of others thudded on the boardwalk behind me.

Images of D. Wayne Hudson, his wife and children, and the eager faces of youngsters at the project, where Ted Ferrell and the gunman had played out their taut drama, intermingled in my mind as yellow replaced the orange neon to the east, and the ships' lights began to fade from the horizon. Violence and bad news always seem more shocking when they take place in paradise, I thought. One swimmer was already bobbing out beyond the breakers. Pale blue and pink streaks stretched north and south, a giant finger painting framed by soft billowy clouds. The palms made whispery sounds in the breeze, and crickets still chirped in the sea oats and oleander bushes as I passed the still-sleeping beachfront condos and hotels. Sea gulls soared and swooped over the shoreline, and a pelican skimmed hard-edged surf the color of gunmetal. We were all waiting for the same moment. The playful breeze suddenly ceased, as if in a dramatic pause. The radiance behind the clouds burst into a great blaze of fire as the sun emerged. First a dazzling sliver slid into view, then a quarter, then half and then the brilliant ball of flame broke free, sailing into the morning sky. The ocean instantly changed to a sea foam green fringed by silver.

The gulls cried out a greeting. I wanted to, too. Another South Florida day had been born.

I picked up a quart of milk at the Mini-Market on the way home, and carefully scrutinized my stories in the final edition, over cereal and coffee. Ted Ferrell looked good, surrounded by a sea of admirers, young and old. He sounded even better in print on the local page. He might even make Officer of the Month for this, I mused. Lottie's telephoto lens had caught the suspect in the doorway brandishing his wicked-looking gun before he gave it up, pretty much shooting holes in his mother's mistaken identity theory. The morning's radio news had picked up both my stories, leading with D. Wayne's death, reading them almost verbatim. It was 7:30 A.M.

I showered, dressed, put on some lipstick, ran a comb through my hair, and headed out. Helen Goldstein, my landlady, was watering her flower beds with a hose.

"You came home late last night." She smiled playfully, her face hopeful. The Goldsteins had been married for nearly sixty years, and she was always asking when I would bring home a nice man. I always replied that I would have to find one first, and that was not easy because she had apparently snatched up the last one.

"I know, I worked late," I called, as I hopped in my car. She looked disappointed, and waved me on.

Miami police headquarters squats like a fortress at the edge of Overtown, a mammoth five-story rectangle, its concrete facade covered by red clay colored tiles. Local law mandates that a percentage of the cost of all public buildings be set aside for artwork. As a result, a huge and colorful abstract, handpainted by a French artist on Italian tiles, dominates the gradually escalating walkway to the main entrance. The cops hate it. They favor artwork that is more humanistic and easier to understand, like sculptures of policemen helping little children or of fallen heroes. Squinting at the colors, painfully bright in the glare of the morning sun, I understood their objections.

The accident bureau was an L-shaped office tucked into a corner of the main floor. An officer I didn't know was manning the unit, seated at a desk in front of a giant street map of the city pricked by red pins marking the sites of fatal accidents, yellow pins indicating injuries, and blue pins denoting hit-and-run investigations. Huge clusters of multicolored pins at certain intersections were enough to make me want to change my usual driving habits and detour for miles if necessary. This office was devoted to the deadliest and most destructive force in South Florida, the motor vehicle. Here, the officers had selected their own artwork. Framed photo enlargements of the city's most spectacular smashups hung from every wall, impossible to ignore. The motorist impaled on a pipe when he smashed into a plumbing truck was my candidate for the photo most likely to stimulate the use of bus passes.

I identified myself and asked to see a copy of the report on D. Wayne's accident.

The officer in charge shook his head, eyeing me lazily up and down. "I'm not authorized to release information," he said, as if I should know better than to ask.

This was ridiculous. "Accident reports are public record," I explained.

He was unimpressed. A small, self-satisfied smile played around his lips as he shook his head again, slowly this time, for emphasis. "My sergeant is at a staff meeting. I do nothing without his say-so. You'll have to wait until he's here."

"Okay, I'll be back." I crossed the lobby to the Public Information Office for my usual check of the log and a computer printout of police reports from the night before. When the new station was built, public information was on the fourth floor near the chief's office. But allowing reporters access to the fourth floor to obtain their bleak one-paragraph press releases full of mindless police jargon gave them the opportunity to detour to more interesting upper-floor offices such as Robbery, Homicide, and Internal Affairs—where real news, juicy stories and good quotes could be ferreted out. The brass caught on fast, lopped off part of the vast lobby and converted it into a PI office. They hoped that reporters grounded in the lobby would remain content with what the department chose to tell them. Some actually are.

On the left side of the PI office was a media room, furnished with two desks, telephones, and stacks of police reports and arrest forms. A huge replica of the Miami police uniform shoulder patch dominates one wall. Blue-bordered, with a palm tree at the center, it is a favorite backdrop for TV reporters who like to shoot their interviews in front of it.

I settled down at a desk and sighed. Police reports were far more fun to read when the officers wrote them by hand. Computer programs do not provide for unusual color, details, or theories, or the personalities of the writers. These reports all read alike, gray and uniform. What a pity.

Several still managed to pique my interest. More Miamians had been left in the dark by people who stole the copper wiring out of streetlight poles. The thieves invaded the maintenance boxes, snipped the wires, did the same at the next light, and pulled the loose wires through the underground tubes between the poles. Then they stripped off the insulation and melted down the copper wires to sell to scrap metal recyclers. You would think thieves so savvy and industrious would be capable of landing real jobs, I reflected as I read. But more than $154,000 worth of wiring had disappeared, and nothing seemed to cut the losses. As a last resort, city administrators had ordered the streetlights left on all day—a shocking waste of city money, I thought. But forcing the thieves to tamper with hot wires seemed to be the only way to stop them.

There were reports of more robberies by police impersonators, which was old news by now. The criminal element among the most recent tidal wave of refugees was thrilled to discover that police supply stores would sell uniforms, walkie-talkies, and handcuffs to any one who walked in off the street.

The most intriguing overnight robbery report was a new assault by the biting bandit. He had struck again, savagely tearing off a victim's right ear with his teeth as he robbed him. The MO was familiar. In at least twelve attacks in recent weeks, victims had lost wallets, jewelry, and chunks of arms, hands, and shoulders. One lost a ring finger.

I called upstairs to robbery. The detective was still there, with an artist who was preparing a sketch of the bandit. If it looked good, we could have it for the early edition, he promised. The investigator sounded grim. "He's still out there, and we think he'll bite again."

They had a few new clues. A forensic dentist had examined the victim's wounds, and concluded that the robber had a severe overbite. He would be able to match the bandit's incisors to tooth marks he left behind, but they would have to catch him first—then pry open his mouth to take a wax impression. Little tasks like that make me glad I'm not a cop.

I foraged around and found the Sunday night log. The entry for D. Wayne Hudson's case looked ordinary. A 317 (an accident with injuries), involving one car. A black, male motorist fled from the police, crashed and was taken to County Hospital for treatment of his injuries. He had been charged with traffic offenses and fleeing the officers. Curiously, the log didn't mention any stolen car or "armed and dangerous felony suspect."

I returned to the accident bureau, still manned by the same officious cop, and asked again for a copy of the report on D. Wayne Hudson. "As I told you before," he said, "I'm not authorized to release a thing."

"Can I talk to your sergeant?"

"He's still unavailable."

"When will he be back?"

"No way to tell." The smile lurked on his face. He was enjoying this: Some people love to say no. I stomped heatedly out to my car in the parking lot, fished a public records request form from a folder I keep handy in the backseat, filled in the blanks, and stalked back inside. "This is for you," I said, presenting it to him with a smile of my own.

He looked puzzled, studied it, and no longer seemed so pleased with himself. Florida has one of the best public records laws in the nation. Bureaucrats who refuse to provide documents that are public record face suspension, removal, or impeachment, and can be charged with a first degree misdemeanor. The language on my form said as much, and definitely captures the attention of recalcitrant recordkeepers.

Police records can be withheld during an open criminal investigation—but in this case, I figured, the only potential suspect was deceased and would therefore never be charged with a crime, if one had occurred.

"I'll be back in an hour or so to look at the report," I told him.

He shrugged nonchalantly, but something in his eyes had changed. I saw him reach for the phone as I flounced out the door.

I drove over to Esquina De Tejas for Cuban coffee and a *pastele de guayaba*, a crisp flaky pastry with sinfully sweet guava and cream cheese filling. Another plus about this job is that when I lack enough sleep, I can eat anything without gaining weight. The first swallow of thick black Cuban coffee sent a shudder through me, and suddenly I felt truly awake and full of fire.

Maggie, the comfortably plump and motherly waitress, kept up her usual chitchat, all the advice any one could want, and more. "Such a pretty girl, with that face, that blond hair, those green eyes, but too skinny. You should eat more."

Luis, the young counterman, shimmied to the internal rhythm of a merengue beat and began the usual questions. "When will Fidel fall?"

"I wish I knew," I said, shrugging.

"How do you think it will be?" he said eagerly.

"Maybe it will be a bloody coup, like in Romania."

He liked that one, slicing a forefinger across his throat as he nodded, looking pleased. "I hope they cut off his head." His eyes then took on a wary expression, I knew what would come next; the question I hated.

"Why is the *News* so anti-Cuban?" His expression was intent, accusatory.

"I'm Cuban and *I* work there." Why me? I wondered, irritably. "Maybe the people who say those things are the anti-Cubans."

"You hear it every day, on the radio, the *News* is soft on Castro. You print only what the Cuban government feeds you. You do not do enough to expose the atrocities . . ."

"Don't believe everything you hear on the radio, Luis. You think I would work there if the paper was soft on Fidel? My father . . ."

"Don't listen to him, Britt," Maggie interrupted. "He's been running around the Everglades in the hot sun too long, training for the invasion. Too many guns were fired too close to his head, and now he is loco."

I bought another sweet pastry to go, and made my getaway, back to the paper. When I arrived, I stopped in at the photo department.

"You know I'm on a diet," Lottie wailed when I placed the paper bag in front of her. Her protest finished, she eagerly unwrapped it. "What, you only brought one?" She plugged in the kettle she kept on her desk. "Tea?"

"No thanks, I just had two cups of Cuban coffee."

"Gawd." She wrinkled her nose, teeth on edge. "I wouldn't sleep for five days. Only Latinos can drink that stuff. Your stomachs must be stronger than anybody else's. Well, Britt, you missed it all last night. I finally met Steve, your friend Larry's buddy, and I think I'm in love. We *have* to date these guys. We've been putting them off for weeks."

She pulled a mug from her desk drawer, poured boiling water over an herbal teabag, and stirred in a spoonful of honey.

I was not enthusiastic. I had met Larry while working on a story. One of his clients had heavily insured and then murdered his bride, hardly the sort of first encounter that leads to romantic fantasies. Besides, his favorite topic of conversation was tax-deferred variable annuities. My personal life is a battlefield littered with the corpses of once-promising relationships, casualties of my job. I had come close to marriage once, with Josh, the college sweetheart who had followed me home from Chicago. But he disliked Miami, and sharing me with the police beat. Somehow the job, with its deadlines and long, unpredictable hours, always interferes with romance. The two seem unable to peacefully coexist. So right now, I give work priority.

"You know how tough it is for us both to be off at the same time," I told her, "and, anyway, I don't think I'm interested."

"Well you sure put a rise in his Levis."

She daintily polished off the pastry and licked the flakes from her fingers.

"It's bad policy to date men you deal with on the job," I said righteously, my usual response.

"Get real, it's not like Larry's a source or somebody you work next to every day of the world. That was a one-shot story. Simple. He sold the life insurance policy; you covered the murder."

Lottie shrugged it off as though it was the most natural equation in the world. Two plus two, life insurance equals murder. Her tea smelled like orange peel. As she sipped it, I could read the lettering on the side of her mug: "Make a Cop Come. Dial 911."

"Hell-all-Friday, you'd think that rascal would have waited more than two weeks after the policy was signed a'fore he killed his wife. His IQ must be the same as his shoe size. What is really amazin' is that he nearly got away with it," she continued, brushing crumbs off her blouse. "All Larry did was confirm that spanking-new insurance policy. Your story and the arrest saved a bundle of his company's money. He *owes* you a few big nights on the town. Besides, you're always working. If you don't date anybody you meet on the job, you'll die an old maid. That's what it will say on your tombstone, 'Single But Successful.' I bet you were here 'til one o'clock this mornin'. Nice stories, by the way."

"Nice pictures." We grinned at each other.

Whatever else we share or don't, we are both news junkies, hooked on adrenaline. Lottie is divorced, and has been for years, no children. At age thirty-nine, she is eight years older, almost four inches taller, and twenty pounds heavier than I am. Fearless and dedicated, with a Texas twang in her molasses-smooth voice, she has covered Colombian earthquakes, fire fights in El Salvador, and, wearing a scarf across her face against the stench, photographed the endless corpses in Jonestown. Lottie captures the heart-stopping moment, the football at the fingertips, life and death in America's most violent city. Nobody does it better.

Lottie is funny and full of life, more outgoing than I am. I always wished that I was taller, like her statuesque five-eight, that my hair was thicker, my hips thinner, and that I had a more ready laugh, like hers.

"Let's make a definite date with these guys," she was urging.

"What does his buddy do?"

"Something in sales and marketing. They actually seem normal." She raised an eyebrow significantly and leaned back, her hand-tooled leather cowboy boots up on the desk, red hair unruly, her smile smug. "I feel like a whole woman again. I got my IUD put back." Her drawl became more pronounced when she was relaxed.

"Normal guys . . . I wouldn't know what to talk to them about," I said. "Pete Zalewski is the only man who has been calling me lately."

Lottie frowned. "I thought he was in jail."

"He is."

"Gawd, that looney tunes. Why do you waste your time talking to him?"

I had no answer. Feeling wistful, I sighed and glanced restlessly at the clock. Lottie picked up on my anxiety.

"Bummer about D. Wayne. I photographed him once at the Orange Bowl; nobody else could scramble the way he could. He completed thirty-one out of thirty-nine passes that day. What the hell happened to him?"

"I don't know. I'm going back over there now to see the accident report. Some guy at the station really jerked me around this morning, until I laid a public records request on him."

"Good for you. Go get 'em, Britt. I've got something you can take along. I made extra prints of Officer Ted in action yesterday." She handed me a manila envelope. "Give Ted my best when you give him these, or maybe I'll do it myself. Is he married?" she asked slyly. Lottie is a survivor, full of hope. Ready to settle down and have children, she is impatient. If the right man doesn't come along soon, she might just start without him.

I told her Ted was a family man.

"Heeelll," she said, the only person I know who regularly wrings two syllables out of that word. "Well, his wife and the kiddies will love the pictures, and he will, too. Hee, hee, it doesn't hurt to have a friend over at the Miami Police Department."

It sure didn't. Lottie is savvy about cultivating sources. Unlike most photographers, she is as interested in the story as the picture. She always wants to know everything. If you don't know the story, you don't know what the picture is. She is always optimistic and re-sourceful, a woman who, if cast ashore alone on a desert island, would build a house with a guest room. I promised to think about us seeing Larry and Steve, and checked my desk on the way out.

The usual melange of messages waited, from sports fans wanting to talk about D. Wayne and from unhappy inmates at the Dade County Jail, including two from Pete Zalewski. He was eager, no doubt, to unload on me more of his tearful talk about Patsy, the lost love of his life.

Many people I meet are fascinating in the way that something ugly or evil fascinates. I often talk to criminals even when not working on specific stories about their crimes. We each satisfy a need in the other: theirs is to be listened to, mine is curiosity. How did they get that way? What overpowering force drew them to disaster and will continue to do so, no matter what? Were they born with it, or was it something that overtook them along the way?

Our talks are often disturbing, but I learn a great deal from them. Yet it is never enough. I guess my hope is to one day ask the right question and hear the answer that somehow makes sense out of all the terrible things people do to each other—and themselves.

In the meantime, patient listening occasionally paid off with a good news tip from behind bars. However, Pete Zalewski's poor-pitiful-me refrain was growing a bit thin. If Patsy was the light and great love of his life, he should have refrained from choking her. Now he was growing increasingly apprehensive about his upcoming murder trial, with good reason; I doubted a jury would buy his defense—that he only killed Patsy because she wanted to be put out of the misery of her life, on the streets since age fifteen. Pete wanted assurance that his day in court would turn out fine. He would not get that from me. I never lie to anybody behind bars, or to any source, for that matter. I am straight with them, and expect them to be straight with me.

At police headquarters, I spotted Ted in the parking lot and over-took him. It looked almost as though he tried to avoid me.

"Is everything okay?" I asked.

"Sure," he said, squinting into the sun. "In fact, the mayor called me at home this morning, to congratulate me. I thought it was a put-on at first," Ted said gruffly, "some of the guys horsing around. But it was really him. I never talked to the man before."

"Neat. I guess he does read the newspaper, despite the big deal he makes out of canceling his subscription every time he doesn't like a story."

"Well, I liked your story, Britt. My family was proud, although my wife is on me now about wearing my vest." Ted's words were friendly, but he seemed strangely guarded and uneasy, in a hurry to get away. I gave him Lottie's pictures, and he drove off without even opening the envelope.

Instant celebrity, no matter how brief, often affects people in odd ways. Other cops may have been teasing him about the publicity, I decided.

The same officer was at the accident bureau. He greeted me like an old friend. "Nothing personal, you know," he said cordially, handing over a copy of the accident report. "I just didn't want to cross my new sergeant. He never told me what I could and couldn't release."

Sure, I thought, but I just nodded and took the report. I moved away from his desk and began to read.

The report on D. Wayne's accident was written by a veteran patrolman named Lou Carpenter. It had been a one-car accident, witnessed by at least five officers in pursuit of the vehicle. The chase began on Biscayne Boulevard at 1:08 A.M., after the BOLO went out, and ended after the car veered off into the city's fashion district, blocks of warehouses and manufacturers' outlets, deserted at that hour. He may have been trying to reach an expressway entrance ramp, but missed the turn, struck a concrete abutment, and skidded into a drainage ditch that bordered the highway. The officer had checked off the box that indicated the driver was not wearing a seat belt.

The report said that Hudson's car had been hauled out of the ditch by a Double Eagle truck, one of the towing firms with a city contract. It could still be there, I mused; Alma must be exhausted, with more important things on her mind today than reclaiming her dead husband's car.

I continued reading the stilted police jargon, which said that the driver, bleeding from a head injury, semiconscious and combative, had to be restrained by the officers and fire department medics. Then I did a double take: One of the pursuers, listed as a witness, was Badge Number 262, Officer Ted Ferrell—yesterday's hero.

Why didn't he mention it then, or just now in the parking lot? I wondered. That could explain his uneasiness, his rush to leave before I started asking questions about D. Wayne Hudson.

I studied the names of the other witnesses listed: Officers Manuel Machado, José Estrada, and the Blackburn twins, Roscoe and Roland. I was surprised at the latter two. The twins had a reputation for high-spirited exuberance. If there was a chase, they led the pack; in a manhunt, they ran the bad guy to earth; in a brawl, they won; and if there was an outrageous practical joke, they were usually responsible. I knew them by sight, and had heard they were being kept apart after some of their prior escapades. Yet there they were, out riding midnights together, involved in the same call.

I did not know Estrada or Machado well, except as bulky, overly muscled weightlifter types who spent a great deal of time working out.

The report concluded that the driver of the car had not been involved in a felony after all. No wonder they had been reluctant to release the report—the cops had chased the wrong car. But why had D. Wayne run?

I left messages for all the officers listed to call me, then headed for Number One Bob Hope Road. The site is not what it sounds like. It is not show biz; it is the morgue.

The medical examiner's brick and concrete complex is conveniently adjacent to the county hospital.

Actually, the morgue is more modern and comfortable than the hospital. A stranger might mistake it for a hotel. There is ample parking and well-manicured landscaping. Wall-to-wall mauve couches fill a huge lobby, carpeted in muted forest green. The futuristic building incorporates the latest in technology, including a system borrowed from the airport's method of dealing with jet fuel odors. Molecules that create odors are constantly broken down and filtered out by air handlers, making the atmosphere smell, for the most part, springtime fresh. With its pastels, warm lighting, and cozy family rooms, this is a place you might have liked to visit had you not known its purpose.

Dr. Vernon Duffy was temporarily in charge while the chief medical examiner accepted honors at an out-of-town conference. I was first introduced to Duffy out in an Everglades hammock full of rare ferns, air plants, and orchids. We shook hands over the skeletal remains of a slain drug courier discovered by bird watchers a few hours earlier. It was one of my first murder scenes, and I will never forget it.

Duffy began his career as a sheriff's deputy in rural New Hampshire. His father had been a funeral director, and Duffy always had a preoccupation with death. He decided to go to medical school, where he realized that the only doctors who ever know what really happened, albeit too late, are pathologists. So for the past twenty years he had elected to be the last, rather than the first, responder to the scenes of unexplained deaths.

He caught the eye of Dade County's chief medical examiner in a hotel bar during a convention nine years ago. The chief liked Duffy immediately because he told great stories, despite coming from small-town New Hampshire, where not much ever happened. In fact, Duffy's only cases of consequence were carbon monoxide deaths caused by sex in the snow. Impassioned young couples parked in freezing lovers' lanes always left the heaters running.

Duffy wanted to work where the action was, so he quickly accepted the offer to come to Miami, a long way from snow-driven New Hampshire.

I hoped to find him in his office, but the acting chief was busy in the ground-floor morgue, which resembles a gleaming stainless steel kitchen so shiny and immaculate that you could eat off the floor— except that you wouldn't want to.

A visit to this place, in fact, is enough to convert one to vegetarianism. It does that to me, sometimes for weeks, until I am overcome by yearnings for roast pork or a palomilla steak.

Dr. Duffy, slightly built and stooped in his surgical greens, was working on a case. Occasionally he turned to scribble with a felt-tip pen on a wall board behind him. The object of his attention was an older man with wispy gray hair. Age seventy-three, I saw, peering at his chart. The doctor acknowledged me with a nod as he continued, intent on his work. I stood behind his elbow and watched. The dead man's pale arms were blackened by soot, and the left one bore a strange pattern of scrapes. His front teeth were broken, and he had big raccoon eyes, darkened by skull fractures. His head lolled at an odd angle.

"What happened?" I asked.

"Traffic," Duffy said. "Didn't stop at a red light and got walloped by a dump truck. Broadsided."

"What time of day?"

Duffy ran the back of a wrist across his creased forehead and grimaced through his bifocals at the paperwork. "At 1:47 P.M. on Coral Way, the 2400 block."

The gas tank had ruptured, and the man's car had burned, which explained the soot on his arms. The grillwork of the dump truck, which had smashed into the driver's side, left the pattern on his left arm.

No one, according to the police report, knew where the dead

driver had been coming from or the destination he had never reached. His back and neck were broken and his aorta ruptured. "Did he slump over before he ran the light?"

"No, no heart attack here, Britt. He'd had prior, successful heart surgery and was in relatively good shape. Why he didn't stop, I don't know."

"Strange neighborhood?"

Duffy glanced at the paperwork again and shook his head. "Nope. Lived right nearby."

Not unusual, I thought. Most fatal traffic accidents take place within a few miles of home. That might also explain why he had not worn his seat belt. Motorists buckle up as they head for the highways, but often don't bother for a drive to the corner store for a quart of milk. The man with the wispy gray hair had undergone heart surgery to prolong his life, then failed to fasten his seat belt. "Small car?"

"Big four-door sedan."

Swell. Sometimes I think about trading in my T-Bird for a tank. Miami traffic teems with lost tourists, illegal aliens, bewildered senior citizens, crazed crack addicts, and aggressive gun owners, many of them fugitives with short fuses, automatic weapons, and extra ammo in the glove compartment. But this man drove a tank, and it didn't save him.

Dr. Duffy plopped the man's liver onto a scale. I stepped back, but not quickly enough; droplets spattered the front of my print challis skirt. "Oh," Duffy said, seeing my expression as I wondered how to explain this to the dry cleaner. "Excuse me."

He scooped the internal organs into a plastic bag and tucked it back into the canoelike cavity in the man's body. Then he began to close the incision. His needle, about five inches long, was S-shaped and stainless steel; his thread was thick twine, and the stitch he used was a running figure eight.

"What brings you here today, young lady?" he asked as he worked.

"Another traffic," I said. "D. Wayne Hudson."

He nodded. "We already did that case." He motioned for me to follow him. Bodies enter the morgue very much like they do the jail, photographed, weighed in, and then stored in a cold room. The doctor opened the walk-in cooler and indicated the second from the end in a row of occupied trays on wheels. "Here he is."

I wished I was not seeing D. Wayne like this. Though slightly sunken due to the transplant team's organ removal, his body was as well muscled and impressive in death as it had been in life. He had been an amazing athlete. Swelling on one side of his face gave him an almost whimsical expression. His head had been shaved in the hospital, I assumed. He had not been circumcised.

"What are all those marks?"

"Extensive evidence of resuscitation and medical attention," Duffy said slowly. "Needle injections. He came in with a Swan-Ganz catheter, which monitors blood pressure, an endotracheal tube to provide air to his windpipe, a Foley bladder catheter to drain urine, and a nasogastric tube so he wouldn't aspirate his stomach contents. The other injuries were apparently sustained during the fatal event."

I grew queasy counting the cuts on Hudson's head, and had to turn away for a moment. It is easy to maintain a professional distance from a dead stranger, but there is no way to remain impassive when the body in the morgue is someone you know. A cut less than an inch long angled his right eye. There was another about two inches above the brow, one over his left eyebrow, and one between the eyes. The longest measured two and a half inches. Five in all. He must have gone through the windshield, I thought. Feeling light-headed, I took a deep breath and fought the desire to sit down.

"He was in otherwise good health?" I scarcely recognized the sound of my own voice.

"Oh yes, Britt, excellent donor. All there is of note is scarring from old knee surgery."

"What about alcohol or drugs?"

"Blood alcohol measured .01, taken shortly after arrival at the hospital," Duffy said, glancing at the chart. "Equivalent, I would say, for a man of his size," the doctor half-closed his eyes as he calculated, "to about one highball or shot of whiskey consumed in the past two hours."

That was well under the limit: Florida's legal definition of an intoxicated driver was one with .10 blood alcohol.

"Drugs?"

"Still running tox, but nothing discernible. Apparently, this is what did the job," Duffy said, his gloved finger indicating the cut over D. Wayne's half-open right eye. "Depressed skull fracture. Although it doesn't appear that deep, it had to have caused the brain swelling that proved fatal."

"Anything unusual?"

Duffy peered over his eyeglasses and shook his head. "The head injuries are consistent with a traffic accident."

I nodded, thanked him, and stumbled out into the sunshine and untreated fresh air. Driving back to the paper, I realized with regret that I would now find it difficult to remember D. Wayne any other way.

My mail and a stack of phone messages were waiting back at the newsroom. None of the calls were from the cops I wanted to hear from. Two were from Pete Zalewski. I harked back nostalgically to the days when inmates were allowed only one phone call. Now all Dade County Jail prisoners had phones in their cells, with free local and 800 calls. I was out when he called, but there was no escaping Pete Zalewski today. Among my mail was a bulging envelope bearing his return address. The word "legal" was scrawled in the upper right hand corner, in place of postage.

Jail mail from the accused to their attorneys was free, courtesy of us taxpayers. So inmates now seemed to be marking all their mail "legal," with no questions from corrections or postal authorities. It was not surprising; no one questioned another inmate who had operated a gigantic nationwide $2 million credit-card scam from behind bars, while he awaited trial for murder. More than a thousand credit-card numbers and hundreds of 800 numbers were found in his six-by-eight cell, but police were powerless to stop him because taking his telephone away would violate his rights. No wonder no one bothered to question mere postage.

The envelope from Pete contained a dozen sheets of lined yellow legal-size paper, each covered on both sides and in the margins with his tiny, cramped handwriting. I pushed it aside to read later.

The scrawled address on another envelope looked dishearteningly familiar. The letter inside was neatly printed:

Dear Miss Montero, Since you have not shown me the courtesy of a reply to my most recent letter, I must introduce myself once more. I am the one about whom the late President John F. Kennedy spoke in his televised inaugural address in January 1961, in Washington D.C. He later said that "we must prepare World History for the next 10,000 years," or "we might become extinct like the dinosaur." He was referring to my mind.

Let me explain. In 1959 I separated my psyche (soul) from my head. My psyche stared me in the face. It was round and yellow and disappeared. Later on, in 1960, I was hospitalized and had some electroshock treatments which electrified my mind and sent it into outer space, in orbit around the planet, among the Russian and American satellites. Since then, my mind has been monitored by the satellites orbiting earth and by Russian and USA computers on the ground. Sincerely, Martin T. Rodgers

P.S. I am radioactive.

I closed my eyes for a moment, and the image of D. Wayne Hudson appeared. I shook it off and looked at the letter again. Why, I wondered, did the crazies seem to single me out?

The voice of Ryan Battle broke into my thoughts. He was aglow, though not radioactive, at his desk behind me, telling someone how his feature story about the need for more mommies to lead Girl Scout troops had been read into the Congressional Record by Congressman Lewis Black. Ryan had curly, chestnut-colored hair and big, soft brown eyes with lashes that any woman would kill for. He looked like a young Lord Byron, and was a talented writer and an aspiring poet. A gentle, sweet soul, he was far too nice a person to be a reporter.

"Guess what, Britt?" I turned toward his smiling face. "The Kiwanis is giving me a plaque for the series I did on parents without partners."

"Nice," I said.

"What's wrong?"

"You get plaques and I get jail mail—and this." I thrust Martin T. Rodgers' missive at him.

Ryan read the first line and looked up, frowning slightly. "He says you didn't answer his last letter."

"Of course not."

"You saw the memo. You're supposed . . ."

These are lean times for newspapers, and our publisher, Harvey Holland, had recently launched a campaign to make the *News* more "reader-friendly." Part of his strategy was to torment reporters further by instructing them to answer all reader mail.

"Read on. Encourage somebody like him, and he bombards you with a dozen more. I don't have time to be Radioactive Man's pen pal. I'm polite; I answer letters. But some mail begs to be ignored."

"He won't like it," Ryan murmured, rolling his eyes toward the sixth floor, where the publisher lurked in his spacious penthouse office.

"Never mind," I snapped. Ryan didn't get it. Even the nicest guy in the newsroom was irritating me now. I was having a bad day. The sight of a dead hero on a slab kept surfacing in my mind like a nasty headline.

I tore open another fan letter.

Dear Miss Montero, Someone should knock your depraved brains out for printing the name of the man charged with raping that slut in the Flagler Plaza parking lot. Since when are you the guardian of morality and ethics in Miami? How do you get your kicks, through sadistic perversion, like hurting and destroying harmless normal men with your degenerate newspaper? Bravo, you castrating Cuban bitch! Is this your contribution to the feminist movement? Congratulations, you sick broad.

Sincerely yours, Randall Woxhall.

I could not believe this one. The arrested man had had a history of violent crimes. The "slut," a medical secretary attacked while walking to her parked car after working late, was still hospitalized, a cheekbone and both arms broken. I crumpled the letter and wondered if there was a full moon.

"God, Britt, I love it when you open your mail," Ryan said. "Let's see."

I flipped the letter onto his desk, then rolled a sheet of paper into my typewriter. "Dear Sir, Thought you should know that a deranged person is writing me crank letters and signing your name. Sincerely, Britt Montero, *News* Staff Writer." I tore it out of the typewriter, signed with a flourish, and passed it back to Ryan. "What do you think?" I said, addressing the envelope.

Ryan read it in silence. "I doubt this is what Holland had in mind," he replied solemnly. I took it from his hand, stuffed it into the envelope, marched into the glass-walled wire room, and flung it in the outgoing mail basket as he watched.

I returned to my desk, ignored Ryan, flipped open my notebook, and started work on the D. Wayne Hudson follow-up for the early edition.

"Britt?"

"I spun in my chair. What *is* it, Ryan?"

"Where's my phone?" he asked softly.

I couldn't help laughing. "Sorry, I needed to use it last night." I pawed through the debris on my desk: long computer printouts of D. Wayne's football career, Styrofoam coffee cups, old newspapers, notes, messages, mail, and copies of my own stories. I unearthed Ryan's telephone and plunked it back onto his desk.

"You can use it anytime, when I'm not here. Just try to put it back," he said. There was no way you could take offense at Ryan.

I promised. Moments later, "Britt?"

"Yesss."

"What's that funny smell in here?"

I glanced down at my clothes. "Something splashed on my skirt this afternoon."

"What?"

"Ryan. You. Don't. Want. To. Know."

I focused on the screen in front of me as I tapped words into my computer terminal, watching my story grow.

"Britt?"

I cocked my head in his direction, my eyes still on the screen.

"You are a beautiful woman."

In spite of myself, I smiled into the green glow in front of me. Ryan always knew the right thing to say.

I ended the story with the time and place of the funeral service. It was annoying that none of the officers had responded to my messages. I glanced at the time. Ted Ferrell would be off by now, and had gone home without calling me. Damn. The Blackburn brothers and the weightlifters were still on midnights. They wouldn't arrive until 11 P.M., if they worked tonight. I had left both my home and office numbers. I wondered if they would call.

I knew I might never find out why D. Wayne ran. His license was clean and valid. Perhaps he simply wanted to avoid a ticket that might spoil his driving record. Maybe it was his competitive spirit. The movies often make outrunning the cops look like a challenge. Maybe, though this seemed unlikely, he was simply speeding and didn't see them until too late. Maybe it was something else. Why did this story trouble me so? I made a note on my calendar to check the tox report when it came back in a week, then began work on the stolen copper wire story.

When my phone rang I snatched it, hoping it was Ted or one of the other cops. But before a word was uttered, I knew the origin of the call. The background noises were unmistakable—the echoes, the yells, the slams of metal doors. "Hello Britt, this is Pete."

"I know."

"You've been busy today. I tried calling you a couple of times."

He spoke very slowly, as though heavily medicated or deeply depressed. His sonorous voice was sad, like his long, pebbly face. I had seen Pete only once, on the Sunday he killed Patsy.

The murder scene was the shabby room they shared in a six-story hotel. The cops in the lobby refused to tell me which floor it happened on, and wouldn't let me go upstairs. Even usually talkative officers were inexplicably surly. They ordered me not to talk to hotel employees, and sent me outside to wait. I was on deadline and couldn't understand why they were being so secretive since the case was no whodunit. The suspect was in custody; in fact, the killer had summoned police himself. The cops were pissed off, I soon realized, because it was Super Bowl Sunday. They all wanted to be holed up with a TV set back at headquarters or some other air-conditioned hideout. The cops in the lobby were all clustered around a set in the corner.

So they never noticed when I slipped in a side door and went up the fire stairs. I popped the door open on every floor and found empty hallways. When I opened the sixth-floor door, breathing hard, there was Pete, hands cuffed behind him, sitting on a bench right outside the stairwell. He was a tall, skinny sad sack with a scruffy mustache and a hangdog expression. His short-sleeved shirt hung open, his stringy hair was askew.

Cops and ID techs were assembled in and just outside of the room across the hall. The body was still there, so was a TV. Somebody had turned it on and it was tuned to the game.

"Hi," I said, and smiled at Pete.

"Hi," he answered, his dark eyes watery and bloodshot.

I was delighted that he spoke English. Despite my last name, my Spanish is not that good. I asked what happened. He told me, and had been telling me ever since, more than I needed or wanted to know. Pete wanted to be punished. That was why he called the police to report what he had done. That was why he called again, impatient, when they did not come. He was waiting, eager to tell all, when they finally arrived.

Cops are usually happy as hell to see a killer who waits beside the body and confesses to the first officer at the scene. But they were furious at Pete, clod that he was, mad as hell that he had strangled Patsy during the third quarter of the Super Bowl. At any other time they would have treated him like a long-lost buddy, plying him with cigarettes, coffee, and sandwiches and listening raptly as he talked all night. But not during the Super Bowl. "It's enough to piss off the pope," one of the cops snarled, not for attribution. "The son of a bitch could have waited 'til the game was over."

Pete was a loser. After nearly seven months in jail, he had lost his desire to be punished and was even more depressed. Now he wanted my critique of a poem he had enclosed with his letter. I had to confess I had not read it, and explained that I was on deadline. That didn't stop him; he slowly began to explain his complex new legal defense. His sluggish voice was deep and dreamy. "What if . . ."

I stifled the desire to moan aloud, and politely feigned attention while continuing to pound out my copper wire story, and the one after that.

THREE

Despite his friendly, easygoing demeanor, when Fred Douglas stops by your desk, he is never there for just a casual chat.

"You covering Hudson's funeral tomorrow?"

"Nope, it's my day off," I told him.

"Never knew that to stop Britt Montero from covering a story," he said heartily.

Uh oh, I thought. Fred is smart and creative, the best there is at the *News*. While some editors give you nothing but grief, Fred gives nothing but support and ideas that make you wonder, "Why didn't I think of that?" It is impossible to say no to Fred.

But I tried.

"There must be somebody else who can go . . ."

"Hell," he said, grinning, "it's your story! You broke the thing, got the jump on everybody. And you know the widow, which gives you a leg up."

"I only met her once or twice," I grumbled. I hate covering funerals. I am embarrassed when the media pack stampedes through churches and cemeteries, shoving microphones and cameras in the faces of the bereaved. People in pain deserve some privacy. When I had covered newsworthy funerals with Lottie, she, at least, had been discreet, dressing in subdued fashion and shooting from a distance with a long lens. But few TV journalists show any respect. That is what gives reporters a bad name.

"Show 'em how it's done, Montero," Fred urged. "It could be a nice piece.'"

I frowned. I had laundry and grocery shopping to do, and needed some time off. "What about Janowitz, can't he go?"

"Ahhh, he's tied up on some weekend story, and besides," he leaned forward, lowered his voice, and triggered both barrels of his famous persuasion, "he doesn't have your touch." He chuckled, his bow tie bobbing.

"There must be somebody," I said, frantically scanning the huge newsroom.

"The city desk is shorthanded, as usual. You know how it is."

Sure, I thought, the general assignment reporters always manage to look too busy on other projects when it comes to covering something nobody wants to do. Still, I began to waver. The story could be a good one, if done right. Hudson's death was a big loss to the community. The man should have a decent send-off, a story his kids could read years from now, when they were grown up.

I left the office on time for a change, to have dinner with my mother, who had been complaining about "never seeing me." We arranged to meet in my favorite neighborhood, South Beach's Art Deco district, a treasure trove of architectural confections in pastel pinks, blues, greens, and white. For decades, the eccentric hotels of the 1930s housed only elderly retirees who drowsed and daydreamed in the sun. Then, like Rip Van Winkle, South Beach rose from its slumber. The neighborhood sprang to vivid new life with miles of hot pink neon, back-lit glass brick, wraparound porches overlooking the Atlantic Ocean, and chic sidewalk cafes frequented by beautiful people from all over the world.

In one respect I'd liked South Beach better before it became the in place to be—at least you could find a parking space back in those days. My T-Bird crept along Ocean Drive, caught in a traffic jam of stretch limos, Porsches, Cadillacs, Mercedes, and BMWs. A dazzling long-haired model wearing short shorts swept by on roller blades, making far better time than we did along a two-block stretch of palm-fringed oceanfront streetscape.

The rediscovery of South Beach was due primarily to a small band of preservationists who fought to save Art Deco from our city fathers who, given the chance, would have eagerly leveled it all to make a buck—and to a TV show about two Miami cops who dressed to kill and busted notorious drug lords and psychotic mobsters without ever messing up their perfect hair. Ironically, Miami city officials had strenuously objected to the television concept. They refused to cooperate with the production, insisting that it would further damage the city's image, already tarnished by crime and violence. The successful show, now long dead, had left a legacy.

In its first season, the series showcased the glamorous discos, terrific-looking nightspots, and swank restaurants of Miami Beach. Such places were strictly fiction, of course. In reality, Miami Beach had become a ghost town after 10 P.M. A bowling ball rolled down Ocean Drive after sunset would not have hit a thing. But life gradually began to imitate art. Within months, such nightspots did begin to open, and they were mobbed by the beautiful people. Where had they come from? I wondered. Where had they been hiding? Now we had traffic jams on Ocean Drive at 1 A.M.

Since valet parking began at five bucks, I left the T-Bird at the new Miami Beach police headquarters on Washington Avenue and walked the short blocks to Ocean Drive. The city's new cop shop is another prime example of the TV show's style and influence. All the police stations built in Dade County since the sixties are formidably constructed fortresses. Not so the new Beach headquarters, built several seasons into the show. The structure is white and full of windows, balconies, and glass brick. The show's producer shot an episode there before the cops even moved into the building.

In a later season, one plot had revolved around a fictional place called The Sex Club, a Miami Beach nightspot that headlined simulated sex acts on stage. I had joked with Lottie about it the next morning.

"Did you see that?" I said. "I bet some tourist from Kansas City will arrive at Miami International Airport any minute now, jump in a cab, and say, 'Take me to The Sex Club.' " We shared a laugh because no such establishment existed.

Months later, Lottie received tickets to the opening of a new night-spot in Miami Beach. She invited me along. The name was different, but the concept was The Sex Club. Again, life imitated art.

Walking over to Ocean Drive was no problem. The evening was balmy, and television had even made the streets safer. If you and a sinister stranger are the only people on a dark street, you might be in trouble. But when you are part of a crowd headed for a trendy South Beach club or restaurant, there is safety in numbers.

Television had even performed its own brand of urban renewal, I thought, passing by the candy-striped awnings and arched windows of a small hotel, once crumbling, but now fully restored. When pro-ducers shot scenes at abandoned gas stations or aging hotels, they spruced up the places first, painting murals, installing neon lights, and leaving behind much improved properties. They had certainly done a better job at it than our local politicians.

I turned the corner onto Ocean Drive and spotted my mother's convertible, parked at a meter in front of the classic Deco hotel where we planned to dine. How she does it, I will never know. When I found her inside, she already had us on the waiting list for a table in the subtly lit dining room. I would have liked to sit outside, next to a lavender keystone pillar, under the curved, overhanging porch roof. A jazz band was playing out by the pool, but my mother pre-ferred air conditioning.

Small and neat with ash blond hair in a becoming Dutch girl cut, she wore a stylish dark suit, probably purchased at a generous dis-count from the upscale fashion house where she had been manager for the past fifteen years. She was smoking a long brown cigarette.

"I thought you quit," I said in greeting.

"Britt, smoking is one of the few vices I have left in life. Indulge me."

"Sure," I said.

We waited at the black and green bar, once the hotel's reception desk, for our names to be called. She ordered a Manhattan and raised her finely penciled eyebrows when I asked for a mineral water. "I have to make a few calls on a story later tonight," I explained.

"You should have said so, I wouldn't have ordered a drink." She looked annoyed.

"No reason why you shouldn't have one, just because I'm not."

"Well, I'm uncomfortable . . ."

"Okay, okay. I'm having dinner anyway, so I guess it's all right." I hailed the bartender and changed my order to a Dubonnet, red, on the rocks.

"Maybe I should have wine," my mother said.

"I thought you wanted a Manhattan."

"What are you having?"

"A Dubonnet."

The young, slick-haired bartender stood poised, the soul of patience though the bar was crowded.

"Okay," she smiled brightly, as though doing me a favor. "A Manhattan."

Nothing with my mother was ever easy.

We got our table, covered with pink linen, and our menus. "Now tell me," she said, leaning across the place settings and patting my hand. "Why in the world are you working so hard? You spend too many hours at the office. I hope they pay you lots of overtime."

"Not really, they say to take comp time, but you never get the chance. In fact, I'm working tomorrow."

"Your day off?"

"It's an important story, and it could develop into something."

"Tell me all about it, dear."

As I did, I saw her eyes glaze over and slowly wander the room. They came back when I got to the part about something just not being right about the police handling of the Hudson case.

"Britt." She looked at me, lips pursed in disapproval, making me feel like an errant child. "You mustn't antagonize the police department. They are the people you deal with every day, though God knows why you don't try to get off that depressing beat."

"It's not depressing." The waitress appeared with her pad.

"Why don't you go ahead and order," I told my mother.

"What are you having?"

"I'm not sure yet."

She waited, watching me over her menu and the little half glasses she had put on to read.

"Okay," I said, feeling slightly irritated. "I'll have the *ropa vieja*."

My mother did a double take and wrinkled her nose. "This is not a Cuban restaurant, Britt," she whispered, as the waitress wrote.

"No, but it's on the menu." I had always loved my Cuban grandmother's version of shredded beef stew with tomatoes, peppers, onions, and wine.

"It's not smart to order fish in a steak house, or beef in a seafood restaurant," she said, trying not to move her lips as she spoke.

"Indulge me," I said, and smiled at the waitress.

My mother closed her menu with a snap. She ordered the special, grilled tuna, with minted baby peas and a baked potato, then looked at me expectantly. "Shall we have another drink?"

"Would you like one?"

"Are you going to have one?"

"I'd rather not, but don't let that stop you."

She fidgeted with her silverware.

I ordered her another Manhattan.

She was saying, "You give them enough time, they're not treating you fairly. You should find a job with decent hours. I hear there is an opening in the better dress department at Jordan's. With your way with people and your figure . . ."

The dress department! She brought it up at least once a week. Because she adored fashion, she thought it should be my life's calling, too. "C'mon, Mom, I love my job. I'm lucky to have it."

"Think of the commissions, and the discounts. I mean, Britt, you're so pretty, but look what you're wearing. You never think about your appearance."

I looked down at my crinkled cotton dress. I *liked* it. "It's supposed to look this way, and I don't have to iron it. The wrinkled look is in, Mom. I'm finally in style, after all these years."

She did not smile. Instead, she leaned across the table and lowered her voice. "Where did you ever find it? Those pooched-out pockets." She made a wry face and then looked away quickly as though the sight was too ghastly to behold. "It's a white summer dress, Britt, and this is September, after Labor Day."

"I need pockets, and it's eighty-five degrees outside. It's absurd to dig out fall clothes and dark colors because of the calendar. This is Miami. It's crazy to let the New York fashion world dictate what we wear here."

"It's that job," she hissed. "You never have time to dress properly, shop, or visit. The girls in my building would love to see you, but no, you're always too busy. And when's the last time you had a decent date? You're past thirty, Britt. Didn't you read that report that says a woman past thirty is more likely to be killed by terrorists than find a husband?"

"I think I missed that one." Mercifully, she stopped as the waitress delivered our salads. They looked good, but I was rapidly losing my appetite. Now I remembered why I had not gone out to dinner with my mother for several weeks. Why did I always think it would be different?

"Look Mom, someday, when the time comes, I'll meet the right guy. And my job means a lot to me, a lot more than selling clothes would."

She rested her fork on her plate and looked wounded. "Now you're putting down how I earn an honest living. It raised you and put you through school." She fumbled for a handkerchief in her neat little purse with the designer's name on it, and appeared on the verge of tears.

I got scholarships and worked my way through school, but I didn't want to mention that and spoil a good meal. I tried to remember how our conversation had taken this turn, to figure out how this always seemed to happen to us, despite my best intentions.

"You don't just wait for a man to come along," she said. "You don't wait for your ship to come in. You have to swim out to meet it. But you don't make any effort. Instead, you're too busy with other things, like this story. What you are doing," she accused, jabbing her cigarette in her best Bette Davis imitation, "is pushing your luck and making strangers hate you. You have no idea how dangerous some people can be. You persist in taking risks, taking chances, with no regard for me."

I never should have told her about my friends on the bomb squad, and that bad night when we nearly got blown up. My first inkling of trouble was when I saw the experts summoned to dismantle the device running for their lives. What would have been my last thought, had the thing actually exploded, was how furious my editor would be when I failed to come back with the story.

"How are you ever going to meet a decent man like this?" she demanded. "Why must you throw your life away? Yours is just beginning. Mine is ending."

"What do you mean?" I felt a stab of fear. "Is anything wrong? Is there something I should know?"

She shook her head and looked noble. "At my age anything can happen."

"Mom, you're only fifty-two."

She bit her lip and glanced around us, lowering her voice. "Britt, I've told you before that age is a personal matter. I would appreciate it if you respected that."

I whispered back. "I don't think anyone overheard us. Nobody's about to print it in the *Enquirer*."

"Don't be sarcastic. I didn't bring you up that way."

I wanted to say that she didn't bring me up at all, that my grandmother was the one there for me when it counted. Instead, I said, "It's just that selling designer dresses is not going to help change the world."

"Neither are you, my dear. Neither are you." She sipped her drink, then lit another cigarette. When I didn't answer, she perked up, her eyes softening into hopeful expectation. "Would you please just consider that job at Jordan's? I could put in a good word for you."

"Mom, you know how I feel about my job." My stomach was beginning to churn. "The world is full of poverty, ignorance, crime, and corruption. I do what I do because I think I can help change things."

"You know who you remind me of?" she said bitterly. She leaned back in the booth, inhaled deeply on her cigarette, and glared at me across the table.

I knew, and I was proud of it.

FOUR

I had hoped to spend my day off at the beach, basking, restoring my tan and my spirit, swimming with my back to the shoreline, the city and its troubles. Instead, I went to a funeral.

Since the service would not be until eleven o'clock, I stopped by Youth Hall first, to gather some background about the man. I knew D. Wayne Hudson had volunteered here to work with the facility's young offenders.

Dade County's juvenile justice system had been designed decades ago for kids who stole hubcaps and skipped school. Now it housed delinquents whose crimes would have landed them in the penitentiary if they were adults. A jail disguised as dormitories, it was attached to courts, holding cells, and visiting rooms. The place was as gloomy and sterile as ever, echoing the same wails and yells as the downtown lockup for adults.

Linda Shapiro, the director of Youth Hall, understaffed and overwhelmed as usual, agreed to see me for a few minutes. Her spartan office was cluttered with paperwork. On the desk was a paperweight that said: "Sometimes the best man for a job is a woman."

Linda wore a rumpled black linen suit and little makeup except for a pale lip gloss and a touch of blusher high on the cheekbones of her broad face. Her hairstyle and eyeglasses were severe and no-nonsense, like the woman herself. She was very much the tight-lipped bureaucrat, and we had clashed at times over the release of information. I believed that if a kid was old enough to rape and rob, he was old enough to have his name published in the newspaper. The law, and therefore Linda Shapiro, said that he was a child who must be protected. She looked more serious than usual when I mentioned D. Wayne Hudson.

For the first time in the five years I had known her as she battled crisis after crisis in the system, she looked close to tears.

"You don't know what he did for the kids, Britt. He was our best artillery."

"How so? As a positive role model?"

Linda clasped her hands on the desktop in front of her, her mouth drawn up in a sad pucker, eyes brooding.

"Better than that. You know that most of our mothers come here faithfully, grandmothers, too. But rarely did we have fathers visit their sons, until D. Wayne Hudson. When they heard he would be here, fathers showed up en masse."

"You mean they weren't really coming to see their kids, they just showed up to meet the football star?" I asked.

"You've got it. He knew it, we knew it, but it brought them out, Britt." Her voice grew intense. "Some of these boys had never even seen their fathers before. You don't know what it meant to them. D. Wayne didn't simply stand around posing for pictures or signing autographs. He had a way of getting these men involved. They played father-son ball games, had barbecues, watched tapes of championship games." She waved one hand hopelessly, then rubbed her temple. "He was the best thing that ever happened here."

This was as talkative as I had ever caught Linda Shapiro, and I was busy scribbling notes. "So you actually saw a positive effect on the kids?"

"Disciplinary action, escapes, fights, they were all down by more than half after he started visiting once a week. And he personally followed up on some boys after their release. He went to court to speak up for others. He took boys to the library every Friday afternoon. Did he make a difference? I would say that the man made a major contribution." Linda removed her glasses and flicked something off an eyelash with a pudgy forefinger.

I made a sympathetic sound, then asked, "What's been the reaction here to his death?"

"He was irreplaceable. The staff is totally disheartened, the kids are devastated and angry. We're taking a busload, those who have been on good behavior, to the funeral to pay their final respects." She slowly polished her lenses with a tissue. "It's unprecedented, but the staff thought it was important for them to say goodbye, to provide them with a sense of closure. And the promise of going helped keep them under control. Look here." She removed a thick, battered file from a desk drawer. "Clarence Overholt, in and out of here since age seven." Her mouth had become rigid, her words clipped. "Hard-core case. Prime candidate for maximum security at Raiford. All he lacked was the age. It wouldn't have surprised me to see him on Death Row some day. Would you like to know where he is now?"

I nodded. "Tell me."

"Attending the University of Miami on a full scholarship. That is what a few years of D. Wayne Hudson's influence accomplished. He even took the boy on a mountain climbing expedition, one on one, to North Carolina."

She dropped the battered file onto the desk in front of her, papers spilling out every which way, and leaned forward on her elbows, eyes bright. "What happened? Why did we lose him, Britt? You're in a position to find out. He never let anybody down. The man was world class all the way."

"I don't know, Linda. One mistake, maybe." I shrugged, feeling uncomfortable, wishing I had an answer. "The best of people do stupid things sometimes. I'll try to find out more. Let me know if you hear anything."

She picked up the file containing the success story of Clarence Overholt and briskly replaced it in her desk, staring bleakly at me as I left, as though somehow I had let her down.

The church was jammed, the mourners a mix of blacks, whites, hulking football types, weeping relatives, saddened fans, and a battalion of shiny-faced young people in their Sunday best. There were simple working folk who took pride in D. Wayne Hudson's accomplishments, community leaders who served with him on charitable and civic projects, and, in the back, two pews of ragtag kids from Youth Hall, along with Linda Shapiro and several social workers and corrections officers.

The dead man's mother was inconsolable. Short and heavyset, she had spent most of her life as a day worker, cleaning other people's homes. D. Wayne had been her only son, and the pain of losing him was too much to bear. She sagged into the arms of relatives several times before the service even began.

D. Wayne's father, a tall, gray-haired retired sanitation worker, seemed in a trance, unable to comfort his wife. He rarely lifted his eyes from the coffin, and when he did, he looked bewildered.

Alma remained ramrod straight, reaching out to those in pain around her. Her twin sons, aged six, were solemn and well behaved. I choked back a few tears myself when one boy cried out, "Daddy!"

Former linebacker Bernie Howlett began the eulogy, talking about a championship season he and D. Wayne had shared. Sure enough, a TV cameraman in a garish Hawaiian shirt and blue jeans climbed up onto one of the wooden pews and turned on his lights. I was delighted when some beefy football players I didn't recognize hustled the TV crew out a side door.

We sang and prayed, and amens and sobs filled the church. I strongly related to the second verse of "What a Friend We Have in Jesus," the one that asks: "Is there trouble anywhere?" That is a question I get paid for asking every day.

The rest of the overflowing crowd, who had listened to the service over outside speakers, parted for the husky pallbearers and the casket. The funeral cortege, an endless procession of slow-moving cars, detoured en route to the cemetery in order to pass the Orange Bowl, where D. Wayne had made a few great plays in his prime and later coached underprivileged kids. As the motorcade snaked through a bleak and aging neighborhood, old black men on the street doffed their caps, and I saw one sad-faced shabby woman place both hands over her heart.

During the burial, friends formed a protective barrier around the widow. It surprised me when Alma approached me afterwards, took my hand, and said she wanted to talk to me back at the house.

The Hudsons lived in artsy Coconut Grove, on a residential street shaded by ancient ficus trees. The house was attractive but not ostentatious, the long driveway flanked by lush and well-kept flower beds, impatiens, and zinnias. Their bright blooms seemed inappropriate, given the somber tone of the day. Like many Florida homes, there was a screened-in pool and patio with a barbecue and hanging plants.

The inside of the house was high-ceilinged with skylights, the floors shiny white Cuban tile, and the airy rooms were filled with light and people speaking in hushed tones. D. Wayne's father sat at the dining room table like a blind man, seeing nothing around him. His wife had retired to a bedroom.

Alma sat, her hat removed, hair in a neat chignon. The top button of her high-necked dress was undone, and the chubby baby sat on her lap. I sat next to her, declining her offers of food and drink, saying I had to get back to the paper soon. I had learned earlier that D. Wayne had been returning from a community action meeting the night he died. Circuit Court Judge William Randolph and several city commissioners had attended, along with Major Francisco Alvarez, a high-ranking cop who had represented the police department in a discussion on how to combat juvenile crime.

Alma handed her bright-eyed baby off to a cooing grandmotherly woman and leaned forward. I expected her to divulge something and was ready, notebook open in my lap, pen in hand. What she wanted, however, was to ask what I knew, if I had learned anything more.

"Britt, I know my husband," she said quietly, her eyes soft liquid pools. "He obeyed the law, even when he didn't respect it. I can't believe we lost him because policemen chased the wrong car. He was not a stupid man. He would never, ever run from them. He had no reason to do so. Why?"

"I thought you might have some idea."

Alma shook her head. "I haven't slept, trying to understand what happened. He had attended a dinner meeting. He drank nothing but coffee," she said, as though anticipating the question. "He did stop for a drink with three other committee members, to discuss matters that came up at the meeting. I am told that he consumed one scotch and water. *One*. My husband was not a drinker or a wild carouser out to party. He was a responsible man who cared for his family and his community. Have you spoken to the police officers who chased him?"

"I left messages, but they never returned them. That's not unusual. One of them is Ted Ferrell, the man who was a hero in the projects the other day. I know him to be a good cop."

"They're all white?" Her dark eyes held mine, intent.

"The ones listed on the accident report as witnesses, yes. White and Hispanic." I was beginning to feel uncomfortable, hoping she would not put a racial spin on what had happened.

"They mistook my husband's car for one driven by a criminal and chased him?"

"Apparently, that's what happened."

Alma shook her head in confusion. "Britt, I don't understand any of this. I don't believe that he wasn't wearing a seat belt . . . My husband was extraordinarily safety-conscious. He always buckled up and made sure the children were strapped in. He even insisted on a car with air bags."

I nodded. "But a number of people have been killed because they relied on air bags to protect them and didn't fasten their seat belts. It's important to use both." It sounded inane when I said it.

"Britt." She reached for my hand. "All this is so uncharacteristic of him. All I know for sure is that he's gone. What do I tell our children?" The classic cheekbones seemed to crumble, her composure cracking for the first time. A bevy of murmuring women closed in, as if on cue, surrounding her with hugs and hankies.

Alma shook them off to see me to the door. "I'm glad you're the one who wrote the stories," she said softly. "You're smart and thorough. We've always admired your work. I hope you keep reporting and get to the bottom of it. If you learn anything more, I'd like to know. It would give me great peace of mind."

"I'll find out what happened," I said boldly, startled by my own words, knowing that so many things people do are never explained, and that this could well be one of them. During the drive back to the office, I thought about Alma. She'd be all right, eventually; she was strong, and the needs and energies of her children would help her to survive this. But the boys, already scampering playfully through the hallway as I left, were too young to grasp the finality of death. They would know their father only in memory. His daughter would not remember him at all. They would miss the guidance he had so freely given to other children. I felt unutterably sad for them all, and I wondered how I could find out what had really happened to D. Wayne.

After writing the funeral story, I called police headquarters and asked to hear the radio transmissions of the chase and the earlier BOLO for the car the police had been seeking. The transmissions are continuously recorded, and the tapes are changed every twenty-four hours, stored for ninety days, and then reused. The voice on the line told me it would take a day or so to pull that particular tape; not an unusual delay.

I couldn't shake my thoughts of the tapes and the cops out there on the midnight shift, so I called Francie Alexander from home that night, and we agreed to meet for lunch. Francie stood not quite five foot one and weighed about 105 pounds, all muscle and guts. She worked midnights, on patrol. Francie's only problem, if one can call it that, was sometimes tending to overcompensate for her size and sex by acting braver and tougher than cops twice her size. When she worked the hooker detail on Biscayne Boulevard, some of her would-be johns later complained that she was rude, even verbally abusive, when handcuffing them. They dropped their complaints, however, after hearing the playback of their lewd propositions to her. She had been wired for sound, somewhere under the little tube top and mini-skirt she wore for the detail.

Dispatched to back up a male officer in a major barroom brawl, she hadn't hesitated to wade right into the melee—and a mean drunk hadn't hesitated to break her nose. You could hardly see where it was fractured. I liked it better now; it gave her character.

It was already 10 P.M., so I stayed dressed, napping atop the flowered comforter on my bed for a few hours. My portable police scanner usually sat silent in a battery-charger on my nightstand while I slept. But tonight I left it on, the volume a low murmur. Police calls broadcasting on the edge of my consciousness kept me from falling into a deep slumber, and I had become fine-tuned to the point where only a three, an emergency, signal would penetrate and instantly jolt me awake. Piercing beeps from my alarm clock roused me at Francie's "lunchtime"—3 A.M. I lay there for a few minutes in the dark, listening. The scanner crackled with a constant stream of routine dispatches. The night seemed calm and quiet, which meant Francie would have time to break for lunch.

I carried my gun outside with me, its cool weight reassuring in the shadows. I slid it into the glove box of the T-Bird, and left the compartment unlocked in case I needed it in a hurry. It was a blue steel Smith and Wesson revolver, a .38 with a personalized sight and grips that fit my small hands.

I favor revolvers, as they are more reliable. Automatics sometimes jam, and when fired, they spit out hot shells. That didn't faze me until a mishap at the range where I practiced. A young couple who looked like newlyweds were using a small automatic. As he was teaching his bride to shoot, an ejected shell flew down the front of her sundress. She reacted with a squeal, inadvertently squeezing the trigger of the gun still in her hand. Her husband dropped like a rock, hit in the groin.

The newspaper fiercely editorializes against handgun ownership, and I am loyal to the people who pay my salary, but the highly paid executives who write editorials don't keep the hours or go to the places that I do. Like a hurricane tracking chart, a gun is something you hope you will never have to use. But if you live in Miami, you can be damn well sure that you will need them both someday. It is a fact of life.

The drive to the Pelican Harbor boat launching ramp took about twenty minutes. I looked forward to seeing Francie. She always looked like a fresh-scrubbed teenager, a teenager who wore on her hip a Glock 17, a semiautomatic pistol loaded with eighteen .9mm full metal jacket hollow point rounds. She carried another loaded magazine in her heavy leather belt, along with a buck knife snapped into a patent leather case. Another accessory was her PR-24, the modern version of the old-fashioned nightstick. It has a crossbar handle called a Yawara grip, the Japanese word for striking implement, and a twenty-four-inch extension to use when needed.

Most professional women carry a little bag of essentials. Mine includes my press ID, a police whistle, my book of important unlisted telephone numbers, notebooks, pens, a candy bar, and a small, unassuming tear gas grenade. Francie's contained a gas mask, a helmet, a Plexiglas shield to deflect rocks and bottles, and a bundle of plastic flexicuffs to use when making mass arrests.

Francie was a paradox, a Miamian who rarely saw the sun.

I would have thought it was swell to work midnights and snooze on the beach by day, but Francie found that, for her, the only way to adjust to midnights was to completely reset her body clock and keep it that way. She ate supper in the morning after work, and breakfast at night before reporting for duty. Because most night shift cops joined their families and the rest of the world in normal daytime activities on their days off, they constantly reversed their sleep-wake cycles and spent much of their lives in a state similar to jet lag. Not Francie. She stayed on the midnight shift, working or not. She grocery shopped at 3 A.M. at a twenty-four-hour market, then visited the all-night laundromat. Blackout drapes shut out the subtropical sun while she slept, and she emerged fresh and alert, ready to face each new day, in the dark. No doubt this limited her social life—but who was I to criticize?

We became instant friends after she got in trouble and I interviewed her. Cops were prohibited from using choke holds because that method of subduing a suspect had resulted in several unintentional deaths. But how else could a 105-pound cop stop a violent, drug-crazed felon? Some very mean people inhabit our world. They are almost always large, and become nasty at the most inconvenient times.

Survival is the name of the game. Francie diligently pumped thirty-five-pound barbells, building the strength to apply the pressure just right. Her bicep cut off the artery on the right side of the neck, her forearm squeezed the artery on the left, and the trachea remained unscathed, tucked safely inside the crease of her elbow.

Francie knew how to dive onto a running suspect, crawl up his back, and apply the choke hold to stop the flow of blood to his brain. At times, fleeing suspects smirked at her efforts, then blacked out, often while still running. The lone drawback was that they fell so fast that the momentum carried them forward, often injuring her knees as she broke their fall.

But all in all, her technique made sense. The trouble came when a violent suspect, once dropped, never woke up. His family, who had called the police themselves because he was brutalizing them, yelled, "Foul, illegal choke hold," and hired a publicity-hungry lawyer. Francie was in trouble big-time, until the chief medical examiner ascertained the real cause of death—cocaine psychosis—which also accounted for his raging-bull imitation before Francie took him down. I interviewed her in midcrisis, when her career was on the line. We had stayed in touch ever since.

Tonight she was riding with her favorite and only partner, and I looked forward to seeing him again, too. Some cops share their homes, lives, and patrol cars with huge slathering monsters, highly trained K-9s who track fugitives, sniff out drugs and explosives, protect their handlers, and attack bad guys.

Francie's secret partner, Bitsy, was a toy poodle. Francie had acclimated herself to midnights, but Bitsy refused to accept the long nights home alone. Her howling, whining, and wailing riled the neighbors. More for the dog than to appease them, Francie smuggled Bitsy onto her beat. Only a few friends and fellow cops knew her secret. Who wouldn't break a few rules for a best friend?

How did she do it? Francie would attend roll call, pick up her assigned cruiser, then stop at her own car where Bitsy was patiently waiting. She'd open the door to her sporty Datsun, and her partner would scamper out and into the patrol car, eager for the adventure ahead. Most police dogs loved their work. Though she was undercover, on no official roster, Bitsy enjoyed her life as much as any canine officer. She rode patrol in the passenger seat and crouched on the floorboard as Francie handled calls. No one would ever know she was there.

The night people Francie arrested wouldn't tell. They were embarrassed enough at being busted by somebody who looked like a cheerleader, much less sharing the ride to the slammer with a white toy poodle wearing a red silk ribbon in her top knot. Some of them probably thought it was all a bad dream.

Francie was waiting, standing next to her patrol car. She looked pale, as usual. She smiled, as Bitsy bounced around my ankles, wagging her tail furiously.

"Hey officer, you two catch any crooks tonight?"

"We were holding back until the press showed up to cover it."

Francie had picked up sandwiches, and I brought a thermos of Cuban coffee and plantain chips. "What's this, Britt?"

I was unwrapping a napkin full of herbs to liven up the fast food. "Yerba buena, it tastes like peppermint, and there's parsley and basil, from the herb garden in my kitchen window box. They're good for you."

Francie gingerly held up a green sprig for closer scrutiny. "Sure this isn't some controlled substance? Or poison oak?"

"Trust me, I'm a farmer at heart. My dad ran a sugar plantation in Cuba."

"Somehow I just can't see you behind a plow."

We dined at a rough wooden picnic table near the boat launching ramp at Pelican Harbor, under a brilliant three-quarter moon that seemed to sail across a star-swept sky. The boat ramp occupies a spit of land that juts out into the Bay from the northern most causeway linking Miami and Miami Beach. This vantage point, only a mile from the steamy nighttime streets populated by prostitutes, drug addicts, and hustlers, commands the view that made the cities famous. The wraparound skyline looked crystalline and pure, Miami Beach glittering to the east, Miami to the west. The night was still, with a soft breeze and lights glistening off the water.

Life at that moment felt good and serene in the warm night. Overwhelmed by a sense of well-being, I thought of D. Wayne Hudson's family and realized how lucky I was.

"Most people who 'do' lunch would have difficulty with this concept," Francie laughed, placing her walkie on the table. Bitsy sat on the wooden bench next to her, immaculate paws up on the table, using her nose to carefully separate the meat from the bread on her sandwich.

"You don't miss the daytime world?"

"What's to miss, Britt? Miami never sleeps. There are late-night movies, all-night restaurants and department stores with midnight sales, and no traffic jams. Just wait and see, some time in the future, as the world becomes more and more crowded, we'll all have to live on proscribed shifts. Our circadian rhythms will be orchestrated by science or biology. It's the only way to avoid global gridlock."

Her expression was serious; she had obviously given the matter a lot of thought.

"Busy out there tonight?" I asked.

She shook her head. "My only calls so far have been malfunctioning burglar alarms, prowlers in the old city cemetery again, some drag-racing teenagers, and a woman in labor whom I sent off with fire rescue. What about you?"

I told her about my stories, and mentioned that I had requested the taped transmissions of the D. Wayne Hudson chase. Francie grew unusually quiet. "Were you working the night it happened?" I asked.

She nodded.

"Were you there?"

"No, but I heard some of it go down on the air."

"You didn't go by?" I asked.

"Nah, I wouldn't unless I was dispatched to assist. I tend to stay away from those guys."

"Why?"

She shrugged and looked out over the water, her fine brown hair ruffled by the breeze. Francie was quiet, somewhat shy, and a loner. I could see why she might avoid the raucous, joke-playing Blackburns and the brawny Latinos. It could not be easy for a woman in a department as macho as Miami, and she wasn't the type to huddle with the other women to complain or gossip. She just liked doing her job.

"Steroids."

"What?"

"The body builders, Estrada and Machado. They're on steroids. Makes 'em act crazy and aggressive. I rode with one of them one night and said never again. It's too easy to get in trouble around those guys."

"Why would they be taking steroids?"

"They like to bulk up, to look good. They get carried away in the gym with that macho weight-lifting stuff. Lots of guys, mostly the Latinos, are on them. We must have thirty or forty of them on steroids in the department."

"How can you be so sure?"

Francie looked at me as if I wasn't very smart. "They go from in shape to Conan in three or four months. It's obvious. They look good, but once they pump up on that stuff they turn into walking time bombs. They take nothing from nobody. Anything sets them off, and they start smacking people around."

"Whoa. Aren't steroids illegal?"

"Right, possession without a prescription is against the law. But they bring home fistfuls of gold medals from the Police Olympics and they fit the image, they look good, so nobody seems very concerned."

"I had no idea."

"The Blackburns don't need steroids," she said. "They were born crazy. I backed them up on a tenants' dispute one night. Guy on the fourth floor gave them some lip, so one, Roscoe, Roland, I don't know which, starts tuning him up in the kitchen and the other one goes in the bedroom and uses his pen to punch holes in the guy's waterbed. Damage to the apartment and the ones below it was more than $10,000."

"Did you report it?"

"Are you crazy? I didn't need to; the guy reported them. IA investigated and called the complaint unfounded." Francie looked down at her knuckles, then back up at me. "I need to survive this life, this job, this shift."

"Sounds like the wild bunch on midnights." I shook my head.

"People behave differently on this shift," she said slowly. "Not just because it's dark. It's an entirely different world, a different mentality. You don't know it, Britt. You've been out here, sure, but not all night, on patrol. You should see what it's like. The real night doesn't start at dusk, or even later when we come on duty. A lot of people are still moving around the city until midnight. It really changes when the last late workers have gone, and people leave the restaurants and the clubs. Then we're all alone out here. It's just us and them." She slipped the last of her sandwich to Bitsy. "A lot of times, I'm more afraid of us."

"What are you talking about?" I asked. I wanted to push for more on D. Wayne but sensed that Francie had to be eased into it.

"Most people with lives and families want to work days. Only a few want midnights, some of them for all the wrong reasons. Then, too, the brass dumps a lot of screw-ups on this shift, sometimes as punishment, more often, just to get them out of their sight." She leaned forward, her blue eyes earnest.

"After a while on midnights, a lot of patrolmen develop the attitude that anybody out on the street is a bad guy. Policemen tend to wolfpack. A lot of times you see them traveling together or radioing each other so they can do things in twos, threes, or fours. Everyone wants to be cuter than the others."

"Why on earth do you work it?" I asked.

Francie thought for a moment. "I stay away from the pack and do the job. The nights are cooler. Money is a big motivation. We all spend a lot of time in court, but if you work midnights you go to court on overtime. The money adds up, and I'm saving to buy a townhouse."

"Wow, a townhouse, that's great." I could empathize with her desire to own a place. We'd told each other our life stories, and they were similar in many ways. Francie's father took off for parts unknown before she was born. Her mother died when she was eight, and she spent much of her adolescence in foster homes. "You know," I said, "we grew up okay for little girls without daddies."

We smiled and clinked our coffee cups in a toast.

"You really think so?" she said. "What would they say if they could see us now? Lunching at a deserted boat ramp at 4 A.M. in Crime City, USA?"

"Survivors," I said. "We're survivors."

Bitsy was running in circles, nose to the ground. She found a suitable place to squat, did her business, and scampered off to explore one of the ramps. After we cleared the table, Francie used a napkin to pick up after Bitsy and deposited it all in the trash receptacle. "Don't want to leave any little time bombs for boaters to step in in the morning."

"Such a good citizen." I laughed.

"Hey, there's a five-hundred-dollar fine for littering."

"You're lucky you have a small dog."

She whistled and Bitsy came at a gallop, red ribbon flying.

We got into our cars, my T-Bird facing south, her cruiser north, our windows open. As we said good night, I finally asked, "Any idea why D. Wayne Hudson ran?"

"If Machado, Estrada, and the Blackburn twins were after me, I'd run too," she said. "If you really want to see the midnight shift, Britt, why don't you sign up to ride with me some night as an observer? You'll see. It's like another planet."

The idea appealed to me. "That would be fun. Maybe I'll do it."

Francie spoke into her radio mike, checking back into service. She pulled out onto the empty causeway, waved, and headed west, back into the city. Pondering the midnight shift, and cops pumped up on steroids, I drove home to catch a few hours' sleep.

FIVE

The late-night coffee, and the knowledge that I could sleep only a few hours, kept me restless and awake, so I was irritable when my day got off to a bum start, stonewalled by the cops. They said they were shorthanded on the bridge—the department's communications center—and had no one to pull the radio transmission tape of D. Wayne Hudson's pursuit and arrest for me.

I had little time to argue, as the day brought problems more serious than mine to a lot of people, many of them kids. Playful small boys found a dirty, discarded hypodermic needle near their school and used it to chase, jab, and terrorize fellow fourth graders. Seven pricked children now faced AIDS testing.

By the time I arrived, most of the little victims had dried their tears and were back at play. It was their parents who were tearful, scared, and upset.

Then I interviewed a homicide detective about a baby girl found drowned in a freak accident that morning. Her family's tropical fish aquarium had sprung a leak during the night, dripping water into the plastic-lined crib where she slept.

Before noon, patrolmen had rescued three grimy and underfed little boys from a rat-infested crack house their parents were operating in government-subsidized housing. From there, I drove to another elementary school, where second graders had seen their teacher robbed at gunpoint in the classroom.

I learned from a detective there that a popular day-care-center operator had just been arrested for molesting half a dozen youngsters over a period of months. He had warned his young victims that if they told anyone, their parents would die. Growing up isn't easy any more, if it ever was, I thought.

Victim profiles run in cycles. Today it was little kids, tomorrow might be open season on senior citizens, cabbies, convenience-store clerks, or even cops. Whenever a police officer was shot, another police shooting seemed to follow within forty-eight hours, as did selections from the usual assortment of other misfortunes, freak accidents, crashes, and random assaults. During the most recent streak of bad luck, two good cops had died in sky- and scuba-diving accidents, and a third was crushed in a train wreck. All were off-duty, and presumably safer than when patrolling Miami's mean streets.

Not only was it a bad day to be a kid in Miami, it was a tough one to be a reporter, thanks to the assistant city editor on duty, Gretchen Platt.

Women striving in this, or any, male-dominated profession should be supportive of one another. But in Gretchen's case, I had seen the enemy and she was us. Ambitious and eager to be one of the boys, she was tougher on women than the men were.

A vocal supporter of the Chamber of Commerce types who ran the city and strongly influenced our editorial board, she complained bitterly about "too much negative news" in the paper, and regarded my beat with contempt. She believed that the less the public knew about danger and crime, the better, especially in a resort city dependent on tourist income. This was the ignore-the-monster-and-it-will-go-away theory. I believed that when ignored it flourished into something bigger and more dangerous, but that informed people could protect themselves. However, Gretchen wanted Chamber of Commerce–approved puff pieces and stories on cultural topics and education. Her talent was for gutting stories of their best quotes, along with anything else that might be funny, meaningful, or dramatic.

Reporters were not her only victims. She cropped photographers' work so that it lost all impact, form, and composition, reducing carefully thought-out photos to mug shots.

Her only talent that I could see was getting her hair to look great no matter what the weather or how high the humidity. Gretchen was in her early thirties, and beautiful. Her blond hair was blunt-cut, smooth and sleek, with feathery bangs, and ultrastylish like her sophisticated designer suits. Always as polished as the cover of *Vogue*, she looked like Ms. Perfect. In reality, she was Perfectly Awful. Recruited out of the Medill School at Northwestern, she appeared to be ascending the corporate fast track to the top as rapidly as her exquisitely fashioned Italian-made high-heeled pumps could scramble—and pity the poor soul, man or woman, who stumbled into her way. Married to a wimpish schoolteacher, she reveled in her assertiveness training and arrogantly ordered us around in a voice that sometimes shrilled to a nasal pitch when she lost control and forgot to "modulate." You might get the impression I disliked her—I did.

Partly to escape the office and the chance that Gretchen's eyes (set a wee bit too close together, by the way) would focus on me and trigger some cockamamie assignment, I finished my stories on the day's disasters for the early edition, eased out of the newsroom, and drove out to Double Eagle towing for a look at D. Wayne Hudson's car.

Even mild-mannered motorists become enraged when their cars are towed, and pitched battles, often with automatic weapons, erupt as a result. Taking someone's car stirs the same primal emotions aroused in olden days when somebody stole a horse—and you know what they did to horse thieves. Towing is a dangerous business. Several companies held contracts with the city, and their home bases looked like armed camps, surrounded by tall barbed wire fences and protected by guard dogs. They were so tough that one firm refused to give a patient her insulin from the glove compartment of her impounded car because she was ten dollars short of cash for the towing fee. Not even a diabetic coma changed their minds. Motorists redeem their wheels at small, barred windows, cash only, in small denominations, no checks, no hundred-dollar bills. There seem to be more counterfeit than real hundred-dollar bills circulating in Miami. Even the post office refuses to take the big bills any more.

I was trying to explain to the woman behind the bulletproof glass that I was not there to bail out a car, I just wanted to *look* at one, when Lucas Taylor, one of the owner-operators, saw me and stepped out of his well-fortified office. We knew each other from many an accident and/or homicide scene where he had hauled cars out of the ocean, the bay, rivers, waterways, and canals, out of swamps, airport parking lots, and the woods, often with bodies in the trunk, bodies in the backseat, and bodies still strapped behind the wheel, some for years before being discovered. The highest count was eight bodies, almost nine, in a car; one was a pregnant woman.

"Hey, Britt!" He grinned. "You got a car here? You and Lottie wreck another one?"

"No," I said, irritated. "That only happened once." It wasn't our fault. Who could know that a four-car crash up on the expressway would grow into a nine-car pile-up, with a truck spinning out of control and onto the shoulder where we had parked to cover the initial wreck? Or that the automobile we had just left would cartwheel down a highway embankment and explode? It was Lottie's company car, and there was hell to pay in the newsroom. (Photographers are provided with take-home cars; reporters use their own wheels and are reimbursed at twenty cents a mile.)

"I want to have a look at D. Wayne Hudson's car. It's a Lincoln, a dark blue Mark VII."

"Sure, come on back." He unbolted the steel door and led me through the office into the storage lot. Lucas was in his mid-thirties, hard-boiled, and husky, a guy that irate motorists should not tangle with. They usually tried anyway, and regretted it. He wore the blue twill uniform of Double Eagle towing, and a smear of grease across one bronzed cheekbone. When he reached for a clipboard hanging from a hook on the wall, I noted his impressively muscular arms. Have I become so desperate, I wondered, that I feel the urge to let Lucas tow my T-Bird? Maybe Lottie was right, maybe we should go out with Larry and his friend Steve.

The Lincoln was parked out on the lot and already wore a coating of dust. The headlights were smashed. Both fenders and the top of the hood were dented, though not seriously, and the windshield, though still intact, was an intricate spiderweb of cracks. Oddly enough, the taillights were also smashed.

According to the paperwork, which Lucas left on the hood when he went back to the office to take a call, the car had no police hold on it. The accident investigation was complete, and the car was currently accumulating forty-five dollars a day in storage fees. I opened the door and peered into the driver's compartment. The interior still seemed to have a new-car smell. Maybe I noticed it because my car definitely did not.

D. Wayne Hudson's Mark VII *was* almost new, with 5,784 miles on the odometer. There was a baby seat in the back. My beeper went off, with a message to call Gretchen at the city desk. I ignored it. I could see no bloodstains or damage inside the car. I assumed D. Wayne's head had broken the windshield; the shatterpoint was on the driver's side, but there was no physical evidence that I could see. Something about the car bothered me. The beeper went off again, and a voice instructed me to call Gretchen, immediately. Irritated, I ignored it. If some emergency had occurred on my beat, she would have said so. She was just checking up on me. The glove compartment contained the owner's manual, warranty papers, a baby's pacifier, a map, and a flashlight. I'd never seen a pair of gloves in one yet.

The beeper chirped for the third time and I switched it off, then began to worry that perhaps there was some question that, unanswered, might keep one of my stories out of the early edition. Reluctantly I wandered back to the office and asked to use the telephone. Gretchen answered with: "Where are you?" I explained, and she sounded annoyed. "What's the point?" she demanded.

I didn't want to go into it with several people listening to my end of the conversation. "We can talk later," I said, "I'm tying up a business phone here."

"You shouldn't have gone out there without checking with me first," she snapped, then put me on hold, interminably.

I was tempted to hang up but still thought she might have an important question. The woman cashier sulked, picking impatiently at her chipped vermilion nail polish as though waiting to use her own phone. Gretchen eventually got back to me, brisk and officious.

"I want you to check in with me once an hour, so I know where you are."

No other editor had ever demanded such a thing. Swallowing my anger, I took a deep breath and tried to speak calmly. "Any questions about my stories for the first edition?"

"They didn't make it," she said lightly. "I haven't looked at them yet. We had too much other breaking news."

"Oh?"

"The new United Fund campaign, appointments to the Cultural Affairs Council, the groundbreaking for the Performing Arts Center, the Jewish Libraries Convention on the Beach, and a public hearing on the special taxing district." She sounded pleased; it was her kind of newsday.

"I think what's happening to kids in our inner city, the robbery in the classroom, and the children stabbed by the hypodermic needle, is important." My stomach knotted.

She sniffed. "You can speak to whomever is on tonight."

I knew I would have to go back and lobby to get my stories on the budget for the morning paper. As day slot editor, she would leave the proposed budget for the night slot editor. Stories not on the budget stood far less chance of making it into the newspaper.

"Since I didn't know where you were and you didn't answer your page, I had to assign a good story to someone else." Gretchen actually sounded regretful. "Get your ass back in here," she said, and hung up abruptly.

I was still seething when a thought occurred to me: the air bag. What happened to the air bag in D. Wayne's car? Once deployed, air bags deflate and lie there limply, like used parachutes. But it wasn't there. Alma had said the car had an air bag.

I went to Lucas, who checked, then wrinkled his tanned brow. "Funny," he said. "The thing never deployed. Guess there wasn't enough impact."

"It was enough to kill him!"

We stared at each other. His deep-set eyes became a trifle wary.

"Was D. Wayne still there when you got to the scene?"

"They were just putting him in the ambulance," he said, then threw up one hand as though I was a hoodlum aiming a gun. "Don't you drag me into nothing, Britt. That city contract is the lifeblood of my business."

"Of course I won't. I'm only trying to find out what happened."

"Whatever it was, it was all over by the time I got there." His expression was defensive.

"Isn't it odd that the air bag didn't inflate?"

"I dunno," he mumbled. "Maybe it's defective, maybe the car skidded sideways. The collision has to be head-on for the bag to deploy."

"There is damage to the front." I looked at him questioningly. "Did you see skid marks?"

He hesitated. "It was dark." His lips tightened and his eyes focused over my shoulder at nothing that I could see. "Talk to the accident investigator. He's the man with the answers."

"Okay," I said, then gave him a sweet smile. "But if you think of anything that will help me put it together, you know where to find me." I handed him my card.

"Sure," he said. As I walked away, he called after me. "Hey Britt, you and Lottie should ride together more often. We can use the business."

On the way back to the paper I stopped at headquarters to request the tape of the chase again. The public information officer, usually a nice guy, was snotty. "We take more than fifty thousand calls a week from the public. That's our priority, not catering to your whims. You'll get it, if and when we find the time to track it down for you."

I wasn't sure if taped transmissions were public record, so I didn't lay a legal request on him. I left messages for Ted, Roscoe and Roland Blackburn, Jose Estrada, Manuel Machado, and Lou Carpenter, the cops who had chased down D. Wayne, and the officer who wrote the accident report, to call me.

Back at the paper, I stopped first at our attorney's office. Mark Seybold looked unassuming and stodgy, but beneath that business suit beat the heart of a tiger, and cops who caught him by the tail were in for a wild ride. He had kept me out of jail when a judge had instructed me to reveal a source and had come to my rescue when prosecutors tried to seize my notes in an attempt to get me to do their investigative work for them. I was relieved and immensely grateful each time. The law scares me. Each time Mark saved me, he disappointed the members of our editorial board. They would have been delighted to see me jailed, giving them the opportunity to fiercely editorialize about freedom of the press. If it ever came to a showdown, I would refuse to reveal a source, but I sure as hell would hate to hear cell doors clang shut behind me.

Mark and I shared something in common. His desk also looked like a dump truck had backed up to it and unloaded. Not quite middle-aged, he was confident and attentive, with intelligent eyes that looked huge behind the magnifying lenses of his gold-rimmed glasses. An avid train buff, he was wearing his favorite tie, navy blue stripes with an embroidered locomotive, the Southern Railway's #1401. To anyone who complimented him on it, he would rattle off the engine's history, built in '26, retired in the '50s, and now on view at the Smithsonian. I didn't; I was in a hurry. I asked a simple question instead, hoping for a yes or no answer.

"Are the taped transmissions between dispatch and police officers in the field public record?"

Mark clasped his hands together behind his head and looked thoughtful. "Good question," he said. Oh Lord, I thought, to a lawyer is there ever a simple answer?

"It's a gray area," he said. "They would say it's not, we would say it is. That's a fair assessment."

I sighed, knowing that Gretchen, upstairs in the fifth-floor newsroom, was probably dissecting my stories at this very moment.

"Transmission between cop cars and base is exempt from the public records law if it is part of an active criminal investigation," he continued. "The key question is: Are the tapes part of an active criminal investigation?"

I explained the situation.

"What do you hope to find on the tape?"

"I'm not sure until I hear it or read a transcript."

"A fishing expedition?"

"More or less."

"We should probably save an all-out battle for a worthwhile cause, when you know you have a story there."

"Any investigation of D. Wayne would logically conclude with his death, right?" I leaned an elbow on his messy desk.

"Yeah, but if there is an internal affairs investigation into the conduct of the cops that night, that would make it a gray area," he said. "If an internal affairs investigation began after the tape was made, then the tape was obviously not compiled for that purpose. If the investigation began on day five, for example, that doesn't mean they can retroactively place public record under a veil of secrecy. Of course," he shrugged, "they won't agree, and not every judge will buy our version, either."

Public records requests from the media were usually run by a police legal advisor who might argue the point. Since my request had not been flatly refused, I agreed that it would be wiser to continue pursuing the tape on my own, without making it a legal issue just yet, saving the big guns for war. Mark relished a good fight but chose his battles. I couldn't argue with that.

I found my corner of the newsroom in chaos. Lottie, another photographer, several reporters, a librarian, and a clerk were clustered around Ryan's desk. Gretchen sat up at the city desk looking prim, purposefully working on something, her perfectly outlined lips curved into a smirk. Ryan must have inherited the assignment she meant for me, I thought as I approached them.

As it turned out, Gretchen had indeed had a brainstorm. It had been triggered by the hordes of Cuban rafters, nearly 2,000 so far this year, who had braved the Florida straits in inner tubes and rafts to escape Castro's Cuba and come to Miami. Many were found by the Coast Guard or Hermanos al Rescate (Brothers to the Rescue), a volunteer search group of Cuban exile pilots, of whom I knew a few; one of my father's cousins was a member. Others, their homemade rafts or small boats treacherous and unseaworthy, were lost forever at sea.

The newspaper, Gretchen had decided, should cast a reporter adrift for a first-person account of what it was really like out there on an inner-tube raft in shark-infested waters, facing strong currents and fifteen-foot waves. She chose Ryan for the job. He told her he was too busy working on his conservation series. When Gretchen insisted, Ryan confessed that he had never learned to swim. "Whether one can swim or not really doesn't matter out at sea," she had said. She had a point. Ryan explained that he was easily seasick. "All the better, to make your account more realistic," she had answered.

Ryan was no survivalist or Outward Bound enthusiast; in fact, he tended to be a bit of a hypochondriac. Other reporters, pretending to commiserate, had gathered like sharks, thoroughly enjoying his plight.

Lottie was to shoot pictures of Ryan on his raft from a Chalk's seaplane, which would ultimately pick him up if the Coast Guard, a freighter, or Brothers to the Rescue did not find him first.

"Or the sharks," Howie Janowitz, a general assignment reporter, said happily.

"Is she serious?" I asked. "This sounds like some tabloid TV stunt."

"She's serious," Ryan said glumly. He already looked queasy.

"We must congratulate her. This has to be the first genuinely original or dramatic idea the woman has ever had in her entire life," said Eduardo de la Torre, our society editor. Impeccable as usual, with his aristocratic profile, gold-buttoned navy blue blazer, and a perfect manicure, he smiled at Ryan and sighed. "If only she had chosen me." We all laughed.

The raft would be authentic, borrowed from the Coast Guard, who had either rescued the occupants or found it empty and adrift.

"I just hope it doesn't have bad karma," Ryan fretted.

"You live in South Florida, surrounded by water, and you really can't swim?" I asked, when most of the crowd had drifted back to work.

He gazed balefully at the city desk. "I never could put my face in the water. Besides, Britt, you know yourself, whenever you cover a drowning you always quote the survivors who describe the victim as a good swimmer. They *always* say that. Something happens. Good swimmers get cramps, their feet get tangled in underwater vines, they go out too far, they get overconfident. You almost never hear of a drowning victim who couldn't swim. When you can't swim, you're safe. You know enough to stay out of the water." It made perfect sense to him.

"And you'll never die in a car crash if you never get into a car," I said. "But you'll never go anywhere, either."

"And you never get pregnant if you don't have sex," Lottie added. Ryan's face settled into a pout. Even his pals had turned on him.

"You've got to learn to swim," I said. "Look at all the cars that wind up in the water around here."

"I don't have time now," he said miserably. "She wants this for Sunday's paper."

"What if there's a storm? This is hurricane season, for God's sake. How long are you supposed to stay out there?" I glared across the room at Gretchen, her glossy, golden head bent over her terminal.

"Twenty-four hours."

"I'll take such great pictures of you," Lottie said soothingly, "on your flimsy little raft, out there alone, man against the sea. In color, front page. You'll be famous."

Ryan looked slightly happier. "Look at it this way," I told him. "No phone, no pager, you'll get a great suntan out there on the water. No noise, just the birds, the fish, the sea, and the sky. It'll be like a vacation, a day on a sailboat."

"I don't sail. I get motion sickness on buses. I get nauseous standing on a dock looking at the waves." Ryan already looked a bit green, but the promise of fame was beginning to look attractive. "What if the Coast Guard tries to rescue me before you take the pictures?"

"Don't go," Lottie said quickly. "Just tell them you're out there waiting for somebody."

"Sure, in the middle of the Gulfstream. Britt," he turned to me, his brown eyes imploring. "You love this kind of stuff, you're even half Cuban. If you volunteered . . ."

"No thanks. It's not on my beat. I'm working on something, and besides, I like boats with bathrooms."

"Don't forget sunscreen, shark repellent, and Dramamine," Lottie said, tallying them on her fingers. "And don't worry, I've got nautical maps and the tide tables. We won't lose track of you."

Ryan began to clear his desk, which was as neat as mine was messy. "I'm going home," he said. "I think I'm coming down with something." He sniffed several times, blew his nose, and left the newsroom like a man walking the last mile.

"It'll be a great adventure, something to tell your grandchildren about," I called after him.

"Poor thang," Lottie cooed.

I sat at my computer terminal and scrolled the edited versions of my stories. As I had feared, Gretchen had gutted them, changed the leads, and hacked them by half. The editors had already conducted the last news meeting before the final edition, and Gretchen would soon go home. I slipped into an empty chair up at the city desk, called up my stories and rapidly restored them to their original versions. There were only so many times one could get away with that. I prayed fervently for Gretchen's future success, a golden opportunity in a distant city, like Peking. Soon.

Bobby Tubbs took over the night slot, and I made my pitch. I hated to do this, but Tubbs grew enthusiastic when I hinted that the competition was also at work on the story about the kids jabbed by the hypodermic needle. By the time I left, my stories were on the budget and bound for the morning edition unless big breaking news bumped them out.

What a way to earn a living, I thought, fighting the world to get the news, and then sparring with co-workers to get it into the paper.

Lottie's wine-colored Chrysler was parked outside the 1800 Club, so I stopped and went inside. The place was dark and crowded as usual, but I spotted her red hair right away in a backroom booth. Ryan hadn't gone home sick after all. "You have to watch out for seabirds," she was saying as I joined them, "they'll try to peck your eyes out."

He responded by draining his wineglass.

I frowned at Lottie. No point in adding to his anxieties. "How many of those has he had?" I asked when he went to the men's room. "Has he eaten anything?"

Ryan was no swimmer and no drinker, either. At newsroom parties he usually got sick, then fell asleep. I ordered a hot roast beef sandwich for him, a dinner salad for me.

"The Bermuda Triangle has got him as worried as hell with the hide off," she said.

"The way to calm his fears is not to tell him about birds that will peck out his eyes."

Lottie looked miffed until I agreed to join her, Larry, and Steve one night later in the week. Then she perked right up. Ryan came back and claimed he wasn't hungry. "You need some blotting paper, pal," I told him. He began to nibble at his food as I changed the subject from his upcoming ordeal.

"Can you believe how the department of health and rehabilitative services mixed up those babies?" I asked.

Howie Janowitz and another reporter were working on a story about an unknown number of infants taken into custody by the state at birth and apparently inadvertently switched by foster parents and social workers during the months that followed.

"They never would have known it," Lottie said, her fork in my salad, "if they hadn't tried to return that white baby to a black couple."

"Our tax dollars at work," Ryan sighed.

The black couple, now capable of caring for their child and eager to take him home, protested that they were being given the wrong baby, but state officials insisted the infant belonged to them. Two other mothers then complained that babies returned to them were not the same ones taken by the state. Only after they repeated their stories to a reporter did state officials begin to acknowledge the possibility of a mix-up. None of the infants' footprints matched those taken at birth, but it was also discovered that footprinting is not a priority to delivery room nurses. Most prints are too smeared to match to anything. Now other mothers were suspiciously scrutinizing the babies returned to them by child welfare. The scandal was burgeoning, and there was talk of mass DNA testing—at major expense to the taxpayers—in an attempt to sort out the whole mess.

"A baby is a baby is a baby," Lottie said dreamily. "Hell-all-Friday, those people should just be grateful and love the little 'un they've got."

"You wouldn't say that if it was *your* little 'un," I told her. "Imagine raising the wrong child."

I left Lottie and Ryan just before 11 P.M. and drove to police head-quarters. At the public information office, I made another request for the tape, thinking I might have better luck with a different shift. The man on duty promised to look into it. The Blackburns, Estrada, and Machado were all off, I was told, but in the lobby I spotted Lou Carpenter, arriving for duty. Weathered and slightly paunchy, he was a soft-spoken veteran cop, never a standout but never a total screw-up either, just a man putting in his time.

"You didn't return my call," I accused him, trying to look wounded.

"Uh," he said, surprised to see me. "Sorry, uh, I was off. Got to get to roll call."

"I have some questions about D. Wayne Hudson's accident," I said, falling into step beside him.

"See my supervisor." He kept walking. So did I.

"You wrote the accident report. You were there. I'd rather talk to you."

He stopped, inflated his cheeks, and blew out a puff of air in exasperation. "What do you need to know?" he said brusquely.

"What exactly did the car hit?"

"It's on the report. He did a head-on into the bridge support, then skidded into the drainage ditch beside the road."

"How fast was he going?"

"It was a high-speed chase, but he slowed down on the curve and was trying to brake when he lost control—probably doing about forty-five."

"How'd he get hurt?" I continued.

"Bouncing around in there, hitting his head," Carpenter said irritably, shifting his weight from one foot to the other, his eyes darting around the lobby.

"How did you know he wasn't wearing his seat belt?"

"Usually you ask the driver, if he's conscious, but he was gone from the scene when I got there. The witnesses told me."

"Witnesses?"

"Right. The officers who were first at the scene."

"Uh huh. Did you figure out his speed by measuring the skid marks?"

"Nah, it was dark . . ." He shook his head and extended one hand in an entreating gesture. "It didn't look like a fatality. At that point I didn't think his injuries were serious. It didn't seem like a big deal."

"So where did the estimate of his speed on impact come from?"

Carpenter glared straight into my eyes, his voice slowing down and taking on a hard edge. "From the visual observations of the officers in pursuit."

I nodded and scribbled in my notebook, then without looking up, casually asked, "How fast does a car have to be going on impact for the air bag to deploy?" Carpenter froze for an instant, a cornered look in his eyes.

"Depends on the make and how sensitive the sensors are. On the average—about thirteen miles an hour."

"Did the air bag in Hudson's car inflate?"

"I dunno, did he have one?" He tried to sound breezy, but didn't quite pull it off.

"That's what I understand." I watched his eyes. He began to waver. I felt a sudden stab of pity for this lump of a man past his prime, smelling optimistically of aftershave, his leather belt bulky and weighted down, his uniform shirt too tight, knowing that his life would never become much better and could get a helluva lot worse.

His voice became weary and resigned. "The car was still in the drainage ditch when I got there. I didn't climb down to take a look. It was dark, it started to rain, and I didn't have to," he shrugged apologetically. "They gave me everything I needed for my report."

"Who, the officers who had been chasing him?"

"Yeah," he said, my tone putting him back on the defensive.

"Did you examine the car after the tow truck took it out of the ditch?"

"Nah, that wasn't necessary."

"Then you would expect that the air bag did deploy?"

He shrugged again. "You tell me. I guess you know, you seem to know everything. I got to go to work, lady."

He picked up his gear to rush to roll call. Was he concerned about his sloppy accident investigation, or covering up something else? Heading out to the parking lot, I glanced back into the lobby. He hadn't hurried off to roll call after all. He was at a pay phone, punching in numbers.

SIX

M y conversation with Lou Carpenter kept replaying in my mind as I drove. Did he kiss off the accident investigation because he was lazy and inept, or deliberately dishonest? The expression in his eyes when I mentioned the air bag was more sick than surprised. He had seemed so desperate to end the conversation and get away.

The night felt charged with a peculiar electricity, making me too restless and energized to go home. It had to be the weather. The early signs of fall are unmistakable to a Miami native: The temperature had not exceeded ninety for two consecutive days, and an almost indiscernible breeze faintly stirred the steamy air. Meteorologists were monitoring a tropical depression a thousand miles east of Venezuela. Here in Miami, the mold and pollen counts had soared to new highs, with ragweed at its peak and melaleuca trees pollinating early. I had been listening to poor Ryan, who was prone to allergies, sniffle and sneeze all week.

The tides, the changes, and the atmospheric pressure make a lot of people itchy. The police scanner pulsated with steady action. A shooting at the Reno Bar caught my attention; a man down, people running from the scene. Homicide and patrol were en route. Gunfire erupted with regularity at the Reno, only a half-dozen blocks west of where I was now. They'd had four or five shootings in the past six months alone. Should I go home, feed the cat, and go to bed, or should I go see who was shot at the Reno? No contest.

Rescue and a police unit were already there. So was homicide. I recognized the hot-looking detective standing at the door talking to a wizened barfly, and was glad I'd come. I slipped my khaki blazer over my cream-color T-shirt. The oversized jacket and matching trousers had several pockets, a prerequisite for my work clothes. Lots of pockets meant not having to carry a purse in neighborhoods where it would be an invitation to trouble.

Homicide Sergeant Kendall McDonald acknowledged me with a lifted eyebrow and half smile. Good, I thought, hoping to pump him later about the Hudson case. Unafraid of the press, never hostile, wary, or combative like so many cops, his attitude toward me had always generated sparks that left me flustered. He was lean and long-legged with a strong jaw, a cleft chin, and metallic blue-gray eyes. I felt a sizzle whenever they met mine, and wondered if he had the same effect on every woman. He was smart, sexy, and dynamic, and probably should be avoided at all costs.

McDonald was busy and did not try to stop me, so I stepped gingerly past him. Inside, the jukebox was blasting out "I Shot the Sheriff." The Reno was one big room with a square mahogany bar that had rounded corners and a hardwood dance floor to one side. The place was dark, dreary, and uninviting—yet always crowded with hell-raising customers, until the gunfire started.

This shooting was a variation on the usual theme. The victim was usually a customer; the shooter most often another customer, punctuating a drunken argument with bullets. Sometimes, however, a robber would gun down a customer. And on occasion, it was the owner doing the shooting, with his target a robber or a rowdy patron.

This time it was the owner, Max Pickard, who lay in front of the bar in a puddle of blood, a white apron still tied around his ample midsection, the toes of his black shoes pointing straight up. He was still alive. Medics were cutting away his shirt and exclaiming about what they found under it. I assumed it was the bullet wound and looked away. I had talked to Max after each of the other shootings. It was a shock to recognize the face on the barroom floor as his. I walked back toward the door.

"Where the hell is Max's gun?" Sgt. McDonald was saying.

The little man he was talking to shrugged. "Somebody picked it up."

The shadowy interior of the Reno looked like a *Twilight Zone* set with all the characters suddenly disappeared, sucked into another dimension or vaporized by some cosmic ray. Sweating drinks sat on the bar, smoking cigarettes in the ashtrays, a half-eaten sandwich on a paper plate on a small table. A game of pool had been interrupted, solids and stripes still scattered across the table in a lousy break. The cuesticks lay on the floor where they had been dropped. The song on the jukebox ended, then the same one began again.

"Somebody unplug the fucking jukebox," McDonald's balding partner, Dan Flood, said, then stomped over and yanked the cord himself.

Flood was a grizzled veteran detective who had seen everything during his thirty years on the job. He projected a bored, obnoxious attitude, which I was convinced was a put-on. He had to love his work, because most cops could retire after twenty years, and he was still there. I had glimpsed a few cracks in Flood's hard-line facade, especially when he reminisced about old, unsolved cases. They haunted him. Beneath that gruff exterior, he cared. Though he would surely deny it, I suspected him of being a good man, dedicated to the job.

The medics worked on Max, who seemed conscious but increasingly pale, with a grayish pallor. "Is he gonna be okay?" I asked Flood.

Flood glared, going into his act. "Who invited you here? Whaddaya want?"

"What happened? How is he?" I continued, determined not to be put off.

"Whaddaya think happened? This is the Reno Bar, you've been here before. Dust off your last story, change the names, and save yourself some trouble."

"The owner never got shot before," I pointed out. "Where's his gun?"

They lifted Max onto a stretcher and wheeled him out. I felt better when he looked my way and waggled some fingers at me. He looked as if he wanted to say something but couldn't because of the oxygen mask over his face.

"He'll be okay," Flood said. "He was wearing a vest. It stopped the one that wudda nailed him. The other one looks like a through and through to his left side, just below the vest."

"A bulletproof vest? Since when does Max wear a bulletproof vest?"

"Since about two shootings ago. Makes sense."

In an only-in-Miami way, it did. Max had seen, or been involved in, so many shootings it was probably routine by now for him to don a bulletproof vest when going to work. Now it looked like what Max really needed was full body armor, maybe riot gear, to tend bar at the Reno, I thought. Perhaps the entire bar should be enclosed in bulletproof glass, and he could shove drinks and collect tabs through little windows, like the ones in self-service gas stations.

McDonald joined us. "Brenda Starr," he said with a smile, standing close to me. "You come here all the time? I always wondered where you hung out."

"I just got here," I said stupidly, as he turned to Flood.

"Max says the shooter is a regular customer, one Placido Quintana. A dispute over the jukebox. Quintana kept playing 'I Shot the Sheriff,' over and over. Everybody started to complain, Max threatened to unplug it, and the guy drew on him. Max pulled his own gun but never got any shots off. Evidently one of the witnesses picked it up and took it with him," he winked in my direction, "for safe keeping." Though talking to Flood, he kept his eyes fixed on me until I felt flushed and distracted.

McDonald broadcast a description of Placido Quintana, short, squat, and wearing a bright yellow guayabera, as I checked the jukebox. Motive for the crime was selection C-7. I wrote that down, then strolled to the pay phone outside and scanned the directory in the yellowish glow from the anticrime lights. It would be a long shot, but the Reno was an English-speaking neighborhood bar. If Quintana was a regular, it probably meant he spoke English and lived nearby. The Quintanas took up four columns, with a Placido on Fourth Avenue near Twelfth Street, about six blocks away. I scribbled the address in my notebook and turned toward my car.

"Going somewhere?" McDonald was strolling after me.

"There's a Placido Quintana in the phone book. The address is just a few blocks away."

He raised his eyebrows. "Then let's go over there."

He and Flood left uniforms to secure the bar. I got into my car and followed them, heart pounding. It was always this way on a breaking story, the action, the anticipation, the high of chasing it down. *This* I knew must come from my father, who carried out clandestine missions against Fidel Castro's communist government, who had even engineered a prison break to free political dissidents from the infamous Isla de Pinos.

I parked on Fourth Avenue, got out quietly, and joined McDonald and Flood at their unmarked car, parked in front. The small wooden frame house was set back from the street; the yard was mostly weeds and gravel, the lights were out.

Other police quietly surrounded the place, guns drawn.

"He's drunk, armed, and dangerous, and just shot somebody, and you were about to visit for a little midnight tête-à-tête?" Flood shook his head sadly. "They never used to send women out on the police beat."

I batted my eyelashes at him, then stared at the darkened house.

"Should we call out SWAT?" a young patrolman asked eagerly.

"Not so fast. We don't even know if our guy is in there," McDonald said. "Let's see."

He stepped carefully up the path to the front door, patrolmen standing by, alert for any movement from inside. A car suddenly squealed to a stop behind us, and the darkened front yard was instantly bathed in blinding light, illuminating McDonald, caught halfway up the path. He was a perfectly silhouetted target for any gunman lurking inside.

Piling out of the car, Minicam rolling, TV lights blazing, was a Channel 7 news crew. They had no idea what was happening but were determined not to miss it in the event it should be newsworthy. Angry cries came from the cops, curses from Flood. "Cut those lights! You crazy bastards!"

The yard plunged back into darkness so suddenly that it made me blink and see shadows that weren't there. McDonald was on the front porch now, staring reproachfully over his shoulder. He stood prudently to one side of the door frame, rapped hard on a wooden panel, then did it again. Nothing happened. Some cops in uniform moved swiftly up onto the porch beside him, guns in hand. McDonald pounded the door once more, and a light bloomed inside. After a moment the door inched open. The Channel 7 lights blazed again, focused on a dazed man who stood there in his underwear blinded by the brilliance. From somewhere inside came a woman's querulous voice and a baby's wail. Soon the woman appeared, wearing a shapeless pale green cotton nightgown, hair in curlers. McDonald spoke briefly to the couple, the exchange ended cordially, and he came striding back to his car.

He wrenched open the door, slid behind the wheel, then looked up at Flood and me. "Wrong Placido Quintana. This one's been home all night with his family. Let's go, Dan."

The TV crew pressed in. "Who are you looking for, Detective?" the reporter asked, shoving a microphone in front of Flood.

"Gitoutdahere, you scum," he snarled, squinting into their lights. "You cudda got somebody killed."

As the TV news car zoomed off, police radios bleated reports of another shooting. "What is this?" Flood said irritably, climbing into the unmarked.

The scene was just eight blocks away at a bar called the Velvet Swing. It looked like the start of a long night. I was already overtired, and had to go to work early in the morning, but I was game. It would be nice to start the day with a story already in the bank.

McDonald radioed that they were on the way. "Well, Brenda, you gonna meet us there?" He looked up at me.

"Sure thing," I said, as if it were an invitation to Buckingham Palace. Some single women do meet men at bars, I thought, hurrying to my car, but not like this. Nearly 1 A.M., and I was racing around downtown Miami, making eye contact with a sexy detective at sleazy bars with blood on the floor. I should know better.

My scanner said the shooter was GOA, gone on arrival of the first police unit. Medics and uniforms were already inside. The door to the Velvet Swing hung open. From out on the sidewalk we all heard it at the same time: "I Shot the Sheriff," blaring loudly, from the juke-box inside.

A young officer with a notebook in his hand hurried out to meet us. His expression said he had important information to report. Before he could speak, McDonald said, "Short, squat, yellow guayabera?"

The cop looked up from his notebook startled, mouth open. "Yeah, how'd you know?"

"Put out a BOLO for Placido Quintana, then check every jukebox in the city. No telling how many quarters he has left."

The layout was similar, except for the picture over the bar, a laughing dark-haired woman in a velvet swing. This victim was a cus-tomer who'd lacked the foresight to don a bulletproof vest before objecting to the gunman's obsessive taste in music. He had done a lot of bleeding and was unconscious as medics bundled him into a MAST suit (military anti-shock trousers) that forced blood up toward the heart, elevating blood pressure that had dropped dangerously low. A tired, middle aged barmaid wearing a low-cut black blouse and purple lipstick crinkled her face in concentration, pretending to speak no English. When a young officer offered to translate, she scrunched up her face even further, pretending to speak no Spanish either.

I had had no chance to ask Sgt. McDonald about D. Wayne Hud-son, and was beginning to think about how much I would hate myself in the morning. Though I wanted to follow the manhunt, I knew too well what would happen. Stay out all night, and without fail the fol-lowing day would erupt with news that required a minimum twelve hours on the job.

I had to catch some sleep. "Can I call you guys first thing in the morning, before you go home, to find out what happened?"

"Crapping out on us, huh?" Flood said. He was politely giving the tired barmaid a seat in the back of a patrol car until she could decide what language she did speak.

"No way," I said, "but I have this editor who wants me to be in early."

"Call me anytime. Better yet, come by for coffee," McDonald said, radiating that personal one-on-one smile, amid the chaos and confusion of organizing a manhunt.

I entertained salacious thoughts about him on the way home. The police scanner stayed busy, and the FM station I punched into the car radio began to play "I Shot the Sheriff." I had not heard that song in years, and now, all of a sudden . . . Wondering if the spin was a request, I waited for the disc jockey to dedicate it to Placido Quintana and laughed myself halfway across the empty causeway.

SEVEN

Billy Boots and I were still huddled under the comforter when the alarm woke us at 6:55 A.M. I rolled over, reached for the telephone, and called homicide.

McDonald answered. He sounded wide awake and alert.

"Did you find Placido Quintana?" I yawned.

"You sound all sleepy and cuddly," he said.

"Did you find him?" I mumbled, conscious of how groggy I sounded.

"He's right here, want to talk to him?"

"Yes!" I sat up quickly, disturbing Billy Boots who mewed in annoyance, as I scrambled for my bedside notepad and pen.

There was fumbling as the telephone changed hands. I heard McDonald say, "Somebody wants to talk to you."

"Hullo."

"Mr. Quintana?"

"Who's this?"

"Britt Montero, from the *Miami Daily News.*"

There was an awkward silence. Damn that McDonald, I wished he had filled me in first on how Quintana was captured and the conditions of his victims. Was the one from the Velvet Swing still alive? Had there been any more?

I didn't want to spook the shooter by asking him, as it might make him reluctant to talk to me.

"Mr. Quintana?"

"Yeah, what do you want?"

"Are you okay?"

"Yeah."

"You went out last night?"

"Yeah."

"To some bars downtown."

"Yeah."

Shoot. I should have had coffee before I called, I thought numbly, rubbing my eyes.

"You ran into some trouble?"

"Yeah."

"How did it happen?"

He sighed. "It's a long story."

"I have time," I tried to seem awake and cheerful.

He sounded confused and hung over. "I don't know. Those guys . . . you know how nobody's polite anymore? They show disrespect."

"I know what you mean."

"And I had a few drinks."

"What were you drinking?"

"Cuba libres."

"How many?"

"I dunno."

"Any drugs?"

"I don't smoke crack."

"Marijuana?"

"A little."

I decided to try learning more about him, and then work my way up to the shootings.

"Do you have a job?"

"Yeah." His voice was low and mumbling now.

"What kind of work do you do?"

"Auto mechanic."

"Where?"

"Vinnie's Garage."

"You married?"

"Yeah."

"Does your wife know where you are? Have you called her?"

"No," he sounded glum. "I'm not sure where she is, we're sort of separated right now." I could hear him take a long drag on a cigarette.

"Do you have children?"

"Two. They're with her mother."

"Why do you like that song you were playing on the juke box so much?"

A long pause. "I dunno."

"Have you ever shot a policeman?"

"No!" He seemed shocked at the suggestion.

"Did you know Max who tends bar at the Reno?"

"Yeah, nice guy."

"What about the other man, at the Velvet Swing?"

"I seen him around, but I don't know him to talk to." There was a pause. "I think they want me to go now."

"Is there anything else you want to tell me?" I said miserably.

"Wha's your name again?"

"Britt Montero, from the *Daily News*."

"Nice talking to you, miss."

"Okay," McDonald was back on the phone. "How was that? Don't say I never did you any favors."

"I need one more. What's the scuttlebutt on D. Wayne Hudson?"

There was a pause. "I know nothing. We were off that night. Besides, you've got your big story. Exclusive interview with my man Quintana."

"It was awful," I moaned.

"I heard," he said chortling.

"You were listening in?" I said, indignant.

"Sure, he's my prisoner."

"How did you catch him? Why did he do it? Are the victims alive? What set him off?" I was beginning to wake up.

"Two of our guys stopped at Gordon's all-night drugstore, on Seventeenth Street, for coffee. You know the place, has little jukeboxes along the counter and in each booth?"

"Yeah."

"They're eating raisin danish, shooting the breeze, and guess what starts playing?"

"You're kidding."

"Nope. There he is, short, squat, in his yellow guayabera, hippity hopping in time to the music, dropping quarters in the jukebox. It was G4. I got that piece of information just for you," he said, his voice dropping to a deep pitch. "Saw you check that out at both places last night."

"You should be a detective." I found it easier to talk to McDonald on the telephone without the distraction of his magnetic eyes. "Did he give them any trouble?"

"Nah, they didn't try to pull the plug on his theme song. The gun was in his waistband, but he gave it up nice and easy. He was sobering up. I think he was glad to see them."

"Does he have a past for violence?"

"*Nada*. A few misdemeanors, drunk and disorderly, that's it. Thomas, the guy from the Velvet Swing, is in intensive care, but he'll probably make it."

"Where'd Quintana get the gun?"

"Bought it four years ago for home protection. Flood just took him down to booking, charged with two counts of attempted murder and carrying a concealed firearm."

"What happened? Why did he do it?"

"At this moment, the silly son of a bitch doesn't even know himself."

"It's all so stupid."

McDonald stayed silent for a moment. "It's not unusual," he finally said. "It's common. That's how it is. Most violence grows out of anger and frustration. If you've been taking a lot of shit all day, every day, and you can't dump on your boss or your wife, especially if you can't find her, and you can't dump on the government or the police, it's easy to dump on some guy in a bar. It doesn't take much."

What he said sounded right, and so sad.

McDonald's tone suddenly changed. "Now I have a question." He spoke softly, urgently, his lips close to the mouthpiece. "What are you wearing?"

I laughed, threw a pillow over the phone, and plodded into the kitchen to make coffee.

I went by the cop shop midmorning, hoping to find the D. Wayne Hudson tape, or a transcript, waiting. Instead, the public information officer left me waiting, sitting in the media room while he went off to investigate the status of my request. He was gone for a long, long time. The frigid air conditioning made my head ache. It had never been this tough before to get the cops to cough up a reel of tape from communications. I was sure they hoped I would grow tired of waiting, or become involved in some other story and go away. But it only made me mad, and more determined.

All my life I have had the feeling that something big is about to happen, perhaps tomorrow, or tonight, and that I must be ready. That is why I keep a comfortable set of clothes, dark trousers, a blouse, and a lightweight bomber jacket hanging on the back of my closet door, for the nights when I have to fight my way out of a sound sleep to rush out into the dark to cover a crime or disaster. Nothing is worse than groping sleepy-eyed through a cluttered closet for something to wear to a multiple murder at 4 A.M. Often I lie awake in the dark, waiting for the sound of the pager or the phone, feeling somehow that tonight is the night. The paper's lawyer, Mark Seybold, carefully chose his battles, but I tried to hang tough and fight them all. I might be wrong, but it is a matter of principle for a woman in this business. One small sign of weakness or lack of resolve and you are lost.

Officials who succeed in withholding information always celebrate by withholding something else. They continue to further block the free flow of facts until they are operating the way they like best, in secrecy. At least that had been my experience. Letting them know that you never surrender, give up, or go away is the only way to be sure you are not shut out when the big story breaks.

Danny Menendez was the sergeant in charge of the PIO, a reasonable and competent man who used to be a robbery detective. He had been very good at his work. I covered the story when he was shot and nearly killed in a robbery stakeout that went awry. His wife, Sarita, wears the bullet doctors dug out of his body on a gold chain around her neck.

"It's been three days since I made this request," I complained, plopping into the chair facing his desk in a small cubbyhole office. "It's starting to look like a cover-up."

Menendez did not swallow the bait. Ignoring my accusing eyes, he checked his watch and grazed through paperwork on his desk, trying to look busy.

"Is the chief in?" I shoved back my chair and rose to my feet, as though ready to march into the man's office, which was next to impossible since the department installed its new security precautions. I would need a key card to even reach the fourth-floor office by elevator, plus a SWAT team to get by the chief's protective executive staff.

I liked this chief, who'd been in office for two years now. He seemed honest and fair but was far less accessible than the former chief, a born leader who'd risen through the ranks and was regularly seen out on the street, in uniform. Tough and feisty, he had been a cop to the core, and his men had loved him. He had died in uniform, in fact, red in the face as usual and railing at the mayor at a city commission meeting, demanding a bigger budget, more cars, more equipment, and more money for his troops. Heart attack.

The current chief was more colorless administrator than flamboyant die-hard street cop. He had neatly trimmed gray hair, wore well-cut gray business suits and steel-rimmed spectacles, and was into modern policing and scientific detection. He was what the department needed but was highly unpopular with the rank and file who bitterly resisted change and would never forgive him for being an outsider, recruited from New England after a nationwide search for a new top cop. With no old ties, friendships, loyalties—or skeletons—he instituted many changes, which, of course, made the troops resent him even more.

"I should speak to him before we get the lawyers involved." I flounced toward the door, as though about to hop on the elevator and actually get it to go somewhere.

Menendez stood up, his eyes stone cold. "You shouldn't get so pushy, Britt, it will only defeat your purposes here in the future. The chief is in conference, but I'll see that he gets your message."

"Okay, but I need the tape or transcripts today, otherwise the lawyers will probably put the department on notice by 5 P.M. and ask for an emergency hearing. Nothing personal," I said, smiling, "I'm just doing my job."

I thought about his implied threat while driving back to the *News* and considered stopping by the legal department to fill in Mark Seybold. Instead, I decided to wait and see if the cops called my bluff.

Gretchen Platt wrinkled her pert nose in apparent disgust as she read my story on the screen in front of her. In her classic suit, worn with effortless elegance, she looked as though she had stepped off a fashion-house runway. I always felt shabby and rumpled sitting next to her, which meant I began our encounters at a disadvantage. "Barroom shootings?" she asked, her voice sliding up the scale to a pitch that would repel attack dogs. "You were out covering barroom shootings? Nobody even died." She stared at me as though gravely disappointed, her face an exaggerated question mark.

"Admittedly this is not front-page news," I said carefully, "but it has its place, Gretchen. When people are being shot for such trivial reasons, when a barkeep in downtown Miami must resort to wearing a bulletproof vest on the job—and is still shot; when half a dozen people have been gunned down at the same location in the past several months—that, I think, is worth reporting. It says something about our quality of life. The newspaper should be a mirror that reflects the community and what happens in it and, like it or not, this is our city."

I looked earnestly into her china blue eyes and saw nothing hopeful.

"Barroom shootings?" she repeated, shaking her head. "Sit," she commanded, motioning toward another chair. I had seen Francie Alexander use the same tone and gesture with Bitsy. Bitsy, however, was better trained.

"I'd rather stand."

"Britt, Britt," she sighed, twisting a strand of shiny hair around a well-manicured finger. "You need some direction, stories to take you onward and upward, out of this rut you seem to be in. I am thinking of your best interests. All of these policemen *friends* of yours are not going to enhance your career."

"Friends?"

"You know what I mean . . ." She lowered her head as though amused, then came up with a knowing smirk. "Because you're young and unmarried . . ."

"Britt," somebody shouted, "Sgt. Menendez on the telephone!"

I stared in open anger at Gretchen, then turned and stalked back to my desk.

The sergeant's voice was cool and distant. "We have a transcript of that tape you requested."

"Great," I said. "I'll be right over."

Fred Douglas walked by my desk just then. "Hey Britt, I love your 'I Shot the Sheriff' story. Just saw it in the system."

"Do me a favor," I pleaded, snatching up my purse and a notebook. "Say that in front of Gretchen, will you?"

He understood instantly and nodded. "She giving you problems? Sure thing. Where you off to?"

"Cop shop," I said, heading for the elevator. As news editor, Fred outranked Gretchen and carried major clout. What she had said about direction worried me, as though she planned to take me on as a project. No way, I thought.

Lottie stood at the elevator, looking flushed and impatient, jabbing the button again and again. "I'll be go-to-helled! What is wrong with this dadblasted thing?"

"What's your hurry, something happening?"

"Gretchen is what's happening," she muttered. "I'm trying to escape before she captures me."

"Me too," I said.

"You won't believe what she . . ." we said in unison.

"You first," I said.

"The assignment she gave me!" She pretended to shove a finger down her throat.

"That bad?"

"She wants me to make individual color portraits, and then group pictures, of Miami's ten best-dressed society women for a special section to kick off the fall season. She said it will be a good change of pace for me. I'm working with Eduardo."

"What's hard to take?" I said, as the doors finally opened and we boarded. "You'll see a lot of beautiful clothes, pick up some fashion tips . . ."

Lottie shot me a dark look. "That's just what Gretchen suggested I need. Do you know what it's like to set up photo sessions with those piss-ass women?" Her voice rose. "Each wants her own hairdresser, make-up person, and designer to be there. You know what it's like trying to schedule that? Ten times over? And then get all of them and their entourages organized for a group shot, while making sure they don't wind up in a cat fight? They all loathe and despise one another. I swear, Britt, I'd rather shoot pictures of a wreck or a plane crash or a dead body. One best-dressed has already changed her appointment three times. I want to strangle that woman. She has so many designer ball gowns that the overflow is hanging from the shower stall in one of her half-dozen bathrooms. Her furs have their own locked room down the hall. Furs? In Miami? You know how I feel about wearing poor dead critters."

"Me, too. What are *you* going to wear?"

"The usual. My L. L. Bean shirt, jeans, and cowboy boots," she said. "What else?"

"At least make it designer jeans."

Lottie glared and punched the lobby button impatiently, as the elevator made grinding sounds, its door moaning open at every floor even though no one was waiting. "I cain't see how this assignment is gonna change the world and benefit mankind. This is not why I got into photo journalism."

I made sympathetic noises. "How is Eduardo to work with?"

"Oh, he's in hog heaven, mingling with high society and going to their big charity balls and fashion shows. I wish to hell he would butch up."

"You think he's . . ."

"Nothing would surprise me. How did Gretchen do you?"

"Insinuated that I am sleeping with the police department."

"All of them? Even the SWAT team, and the vice squad?"

I nodded glumly.

"I hope you told her to eat shit and die."

"I wish I had, but one of my stories was in front of her at the time. What is wrong with that woman?"

"If we had the answer to that we could take it on tour. That woman is mean enough to steal from her daddy. Just remember, leave time for Larry Zink, we're fixing to have supper with him and Steve tomorrow night, so you make sure you don't get involved in a story that keeps you late."

The elevator doors parted, at long last.

"Try to come to the 1800 tonight for drinks with Ryan. It could be your last chance," she said. "We're launching him tomorrow. Gretchen wants the story for the weekend. We borrowed a used Cuban escape raft from the Coast Guard."

We rolled our eyes at each other.

It took me twenty minutes to park at headquarters. I circled the lot endlessly, waiting for a space to open. Gretchen beeped me twice, but I ignored her. Finally, I nabbed a spot and hurried inside.

Menendez looked like he'd been waiting. He handed me a manila envelope.

"It's a transcript," he said, then stepped back into his private office.

"Danny, wait a minute. I need the paperwork to ride as an observer, on midnights, with Officer Francie Alexander." Civilians have to sign a release absolving the department from liability when they accompany officers in city vehicles, a mere formality.

He turned back to me, his eyes expressionless, as though I was an unwelcome stranger. "I don't think so," he said, shaking his head.

"What do you mean? Is this some change in policy? I've ridden before, on days. It's never been a problem."

He shrugged and looked distant. "I'll have to see if the major approves." His expression said he knew damn well the major would not approve.

"Last time I signed up and rode the same day. It was no hassle."

"Things are different." He closed his office door.

What *is* this? I thought. I sat down at an empty desk in the media room and opened the envelope to look at the transcript. I scanned it and knew what was wrong.

There it was, cops radioing that they were in pursuit, dispatch asking if they needed additional backup. Negative. Other units appearing to join in anyway. Officers broadcasting their swiftly changing locations as the chase progressed. Then a delay, followed by a unit requesting rescue and an ambulance for the subject. Then a request for a wrecker.

What was missing was the most important, right at the start. No be on the lookout by the dispatcher for a car that looked like D. Wayne Hudson's. No radioed description of an armed and dangerous suspect in a similar car, no reason for the fatal chase.

Menendez saw me approach his glassed-in office and picked up his phone as though making a call. I knocked anyway, then opened the door. "Danny, this isn't complete."

He stared, the phone in his hand. "Yes, it is."

"Where is the BOLO the dispatcher put out for a car like Hudson's?"

"There's nothing like that on the tape."

"But that was the reason they chased him."

Menendez cradled the phone. His mouth was rigid, spitting words out rapid fire. "They went over the tape forward, backward, and upside-down. It's not there."

"Why would they lie about it? Why did they chase him?"

"I wouldn't be calling anybody a liar, Britt. You'll have to talk to them."

"Is there an internal affairs investigation?"

He jerked back in his chair and thrust out his chin. "Why should there be? The case is cut and dried. The man ran from police and cracked up his car. What are you suggesting?"

"I'm not suggesting anything. I just don't understand . . ."

"You have to talk to them."

"They're not returning my messages."

He shrugged. "I can't force them to talk to you. There is still a policeman's bill of rights." He picked up the phone again, dismissing me.

I was stunned. I sat down and reread the transcript. The chase ended at 12:58 A.M., when one of the units said, "We got 'im," and gave the location.

That must have been the time of the crash. It wasn't until 1:06 A.M., eight minutes later, that rescue and an ambulance were requested. The call for a wrecker followed, six minutes after that, at 1:12 A.M. That was the first mention of a 317—a traffic accident with injuries. I began to think about the air bag, and got a sick feeling in my gut.

The most obvious conclusion was too outrageous to be true. There has to be an explanation, I thought. Please let there be an explanation.

I left messages again for the cops involved, slid the transcript back into the envelope, and went back to Menendez, who looked exasperated.

"I want to ride on the midnight shift as soon as possible."

He shook his head. "Sorry."

"What do you mean?"

"I just talked to Major Alvarez. He said no."

"Why?"

"He doesn't have to explain why. He's the major—observers ride at the will of the department. The major said no, and he's the man in charge."

"What's his number?"

He told me, and I heatedly called it from one of the media room telephones. A secretary took my name and pronounced the major busy. I asked if she could be sure to have him return my call. All she could do, she said, was give him the message. She did not sound encouraging. Even if I did reach him, my chances of changing his mind seemed remote.

Francisco Alvarez had arrived in Miami as a teenager, in the sixties, during the first wave of Cuban immigration. About five feet, ten inches tall, he was solidly built and sullen-looking with dark tangled eyebrows and slick black hair. He carried a gold-plated automatic and rarely talked to reporters. Years ago he was linked to a big *bolita* scandal and never forgave the press, especially the *News*, for reporting it. One of those cops who liked to walk the cutting edge, he socialized with questionable people who invariably got into some degree of trouble, yet he always seemed to emerge all right.

Alvarez was never indicted in the *bolita* case but was summoned before a grand jury. He had always aspired to be chief, and felt that the news stories undermined his chances. Perhaps they did, then, but they were old news now, and next time the chief's job opened up he would probably be among the top candidates. In fact, the politicos would probably select from inside the department next time, after all the flak from the police union and the troops for bringing in an outsider. As a Latino, Alvarez's chances were excellent, if he was still around when the time came. Personally, I dreaded the possibility. If it was sometimes tough to dig a story out of the department now, it would be a heckuva lot harder with him as chief.

My problem now was how to get myself into a police car on the midnight shift. I had wanted this simply for background and atmosphere, and perhaps a glimpse of the troops in action, but being refused made me want to ride with them even more. I could ask Francie to smuggle me along like Bitsy, but she could wind up in trouble. That wouldn't be fair. Homicide detectives, however, did their own thing. They were the elite, and were known for having an attitude; their positions were more secure. Maybe Sgt. McDonald liked me well enough to do it.

He liked me well enough to return my call at eleven o'clock that night. "Couldn't stay away, could you?"

"Is this the recorded line?" I asked.

"Obviously not. Why?"

"You're right, I can't stay away. I want to ride with you guys as an observer."

"Sure, Britt. No problem. You just have to call PIO and sign a release."

"There is a problem. I was there today, and the major said no."

"How'd you piss him off?"

"I guess he's in a hate the media mood."

"He does have fits of that from time to time. Why don't you just talk to him?"

"Why don't you guys just let me go with you anyway? We don't need a release. Nothing will happen. I'm not gonna sue if I stub my toe."

I could almost hear him thinking, and see his face, serious and thoughtful. "It's against policy. Is there something here you're not telling me?"

"I just want a look, for background purposes, at what it's like out there on midnights. I didn't think you'd mind showing me."

"Background for what?"

He wasn't stupid. "Whatever stories I do in the future that concern midnights." That was the truth.

"My partner would not be crazy about this. We'll both step in it if anything happens. I can't do that to him."

He was saying no and laying it on his partner. "What could happen? Who would ever know? The brass isn't out there on midnights. If something big goes down, I'll act like I'm not with you."

"When did you want to come?"

"Tomorrow night?" I tried not to sound too elated.

"Fine with me."

"What about Flood?"

"He'll be okay."

I agreed to meet them at the station just after eleven. This would be interesting.

EIGHT

Ryan wore cut-offs, sneakers without socks, and a fluorescent flaming orange life jacket over a loose white cotton shirt. There were seasick bands on his wrists, and a jaunty wide-brimmed straw hat on his head. His luggage included a duffel bag, several large plastic grocery sacks full of supplies, a big blue cooler full of sandwiches, soft drinks, and beer on ice, and a small tin pail for bailing. I had driven down to the Miami Marina to bid him bon voyage. The weather was grand, chamber of commerce perfect, sunlight dancing like diamonds on the water. The seas were flat; all systems were go. His raft was constructed of three Soviet truck inner tubes reinforced by canvas and lashed to a wooden framework. The lower frame was crisscrossed with chicken wire to keep out the sharks. The inventive homemade craft was spacious compared to some of the contraptions used by the *balseros,* runaway Cubans, to attempt the ninety-mile open-sea journey to Florida. Ryan had selected from what the Coast Guard had on hand. His other choices had included a block of Styrofoam with a single seat hollowed out and oars strapped to the sides, and a tractor inner tube equipped with homemade oars.

Seeing the flimsy weather-beaten raft made me respect even

more the desire powerful enough for people to brave such leaps of faith, flinging themselves into the ocean on anything that might float them to freedom. Seven Cubans had put out to sea from Santa Fe, a coastal town about forty minutes west of Havana, on the raft Ryan chose. Eight days later the five survivors were rescued about ten miles off the coast of Islamorada. Two had lost their lives in pursuit of freedom, like my father. But there was a difference; I felt mixed emotions accompanied by a surge of pride. My father had returned to Cuba to fight for it.

The captain of the *Vagabond,* a local deep-sea fishing boat, had agreed to ferry Ryan down to the Keys, then east to the Cay Sal Bank, above the reefs, where his raft would be launched in relatively shallow water, twenty to thirty fathoms as opposed to thousands. Years ago the Navy used the same area, south of the Bermuda Triangle, as a bombing range.

The *Vagabond* would remain in the general vicinity, just out of Ryan's sight in the interests of authenticity but close enough to rush to the rescue in case of trouble. He would be picked up after twenty-four hours. In the interim, his raft would drift up through the straits, the escape corridor parallel to the Keys used by both Cuban and Haitian boat people and rafters.

Lottie would spend the night aboard the *Vagabond,* keeping in touch with Ryan via portable hand-held radio. In the morning, a seaplane would skim out over the water for Lottie, who would shoot aerials of Ryan. Then the *Vagabond* would bring him back in.

Swim fins and a spear gun protruded from one of Ryan's bulky bags. He appeared well prepared, a little plastic nose guard fastened to his sunglasses, his face smeared with sticky white sunscreen. The six-packs of Coors in his ice chest concerned me, and I warned him to go easy on the beer out there in the hot sun. "Remember the blotting paper," I said, as I hugged him goodbye and resisted a sudden wicked impulse to hum the theme from *Jaws.*

Lottie, wearing jeans, boat shoes, and two cameras, leaped gracefully aboard the *Vagabond.* Ryan followed, a little uncertain on his feet as the boat rocked gently at the dock. Lottie reached out to steady his arm, glanced my way, and we both smiled. Ryan did look like a tenderfoot.

We had had to cancel dinner with Larry and Steve, who had made reservations at a famous French restaurant. Lottie was disappointed, but I was secretly pleased that her assignment, and not my midnight shift plans, was the official reason for postponing our dinner date. I did not want to be accused of ruining her love life, when I was already to blame for ruining my own. She did not seem depressed at the moment, probably because the captain of the *Vagabond* was blond, Nordic-looking, and husky.

The *Vagabond*'s twin engines thundered to life, and the handsome blue and white vessel began to slip away from the dock. Lottie stood up on the tuna tower, hair streaming in the wind like a Viking princess. Ryan stood on deck surrounded by his belongings, ready for adventure. He gave me the thumbs-up sign, and I waved as the captain steered smoothly out toward Government Cut and deep water.

A visitor was waiting back at the office. She rose from her lobby chair outside the newsroom and stepped forward when Gloria, the receptionist, greeted me by name. Long, lustrous brown hair framed a heart-shaped face that looked eager, though shadows smudged the skin under her eyes. Her figure was slim except for the swelling that filled out the front of her maternity jumper. She held out a hand and introduced herself as Betsy Ferrell, Ted's wife.

"I'm sorry. I know I should have called first, but I just happened to be in the neighborhood," she said.

I invited her into the newsroom, a little embarrassed about my grubby desk, and asked if she'd like to go to the cafeteria for coffee. "Not unless you really want some," she said. "I just need to talk." The look in her eyes told me that she didn't just happen to be in the neighborhood.

Ryan's chair was available, so I wheeled it around his desk and parked it next to mine. She sat down, clutching her purse. "I didn't know you guys were expecting again," I said cheerfully.

She started to say something, gulped, and her eyes brimmed with tears. Embarrassed for her, I took the box of Kleenex from my desk drawer and handed it over. She plucked one out, then kept the box balanced on her lap. Naively, I figured there must be trouble in paradise, that Ted had been acting up. Some men did when their wives were pregnant, but I was surprised at Ted.

"Britt, I want you to know we've always been grateful. Putting Ted's name in stories in the past, the story last week . . ." Tears overflowed and she pressed a tissue to her eyes. Her fingernails were neatly trimmed and immaculate. I became conscious of my own fingers, stained with ink from the cheap ballpoint pens the paper issued to us. "It's meant a lot . . . We're so proud of him." She sniffled, struggling to continue.

"Mrs. Ferrell, what's wrong?"

"Please call me Betsy."

I nodded.

"This story, the story that you're working on, please let it alone. Don't write it." Pink blotches had appeared on her cheeks as she dabbed at her eyes.

"What do you mean?"

"You know what I'm talking about," she gulped. "D. Wayne Hudson."

"Why are you so upset about this story? Look, just catch your breath and tell me what we're talking about here."

"You know why," she said, then leaned back in a determined effort to regain composure. She sniffed and made an attempt to smile. "You know we're a SITKOM family."

"Excuse me?"

"Single Income, Two Kids, Outrageous Mortgage," she placed her left hand, with its modest wedding band, on her swollen belly—"except soon it will be three."

Not living out in suburbia, I guessed I wasn't caught up on the lingo.

"I have never wanted Ted to work midnights," she said cryptically. "He never liked working with those guys; they're always in trouble. But he wanted the extra money, with the new baby and all. He swore he'd never let them drag him into anything. That was why he switched back to days. If only he'd done it sooner." She leaned forward, eyes pleading. "We can't afford to have him get in trouble and lose his job. It's not just losing the paycheck, or even the house with a baby on the way. It's the job." Her voice was low and intense. "He loves it so much." She looked ready to weep again, and I felt like shit.

"What makes you think Ted is in trouble?"

"He won't be if you just let it go. Let it go, Britt."

I was confused. "How do you know what I'm working on? I haven't even talked to Ted about it."

"They know, Britt. They all know you're on the story."

"Who is 'all'?"

"Ted, the Blackburns, Manny Machado, Estrada, their families, Carpenter. Everybody's upset."

Her words were chilling. While I'd been piddling around, unaware, my lame efforts had been agitating a lot of people.

My face must have telegraphed my feelings. Betsy looked apprehensive. "Ted doesn't know I'm here," she whispered. "But I thought if I appealed to you, woman to woman, you wouldn't do this. There are so many other stories. I'm sure they'd be eager to help you with some of them. You've been so good to us, so fair in the past." She shredded a tissue nervously.

"I've never been good to you and Ted, Betsy. I wrote stories about him because he deserved them. All I can tell you is that I'm as fair as I can be, and I do care. Did Ted do something wrong?"

"He never would!" she cried vehemently.

"So what is there to be upset about?"

"You don't understand . . ." she stopped, her eyes changing. "You're going to keep working on it," she said slowly.

"Sure, and it would make everything a lot easier if Ted would just give me a call and help me piece together what actually happened that night."

"I have to go now." She stood abruptly, placed the box of tissues on my desk, and turned to leave. Unconsciously, she was clutching her purse to her bosom, like a baby. "Thanks for talking to me. Please don't tell anyone I was here."

So something ugly did happen between the cops and D. Wayne Hudson, I thought, watching her walk away. I bet I knew what it was.

Somebody had lost control, and the others were covering up for him. I wondered which of D. Wayne's injuries had come at the hands of a brutal cop? Or did they all? Only one thing was certain—nothing would keep me from this story now.

NINE

Parking at the police station was a pleasure at eleven o'clock at night. What a difference twelve hours made. I dropped my car keys, a comb, and other essentials into the deep pockets of my navy blue cotton jumpsuit.

McDonald had not forgotten. When I mentioned his name at the front desk, the officer said I was expected, and handed me a clip-on visitor's pass. He escorted me across the empty lobby, past the stainless steel memorial to the thirty city officers killed in the line of duty since 1915, inserted his key card into the elevator slot, punched five, and returned to his post.

The fifth-floor halls were deserted; few people were on duty, and I liked the freedom of not having to look over my shoulder for Major Alvarez or some other officious supervisor eager to challenge my presence.

Robbery and homicide shared a big open office with picture windows looking out on Overtown, a high-crime ghetto neighborhood. McDonald, Flood, and two other detectives were huddled at desks at the homicide end of the room. They were handling their mail and paperwork, returning phone messages, and monitoring their radios all the while. McDonald broke into a big, slow smile when he saw me wending my way toward them, and I couldn't help smiling back. He spoke to his partner, and Flood's head spun around. "What!"

"Britt's with us tonight," McDonald repeated.

Uh oh, I thought. No wonder everything was okay with Flood, until now. He didn't know I was riding with them.

Ignoring Flood's scowls, I browsed the homicide board, which spanned an entire wall. The board listed each of the current year's murder victims in numerical order, revealing at a glance the number of killings inside city limits so far this year, 121. Although most of those whose names were listed there did not lead orderly lives, their deaths were neatly catalogued. Each entry, precisely printed in black grease pencil, included the date, time, the name of the victim, the location and manner of death, the lead detective on the case, and the killer. Many of the killers, as well as occasional victims, were described simply as UNK. The worst possible case scenario for an investigator was a homicide in which weeks or months have elapsed with both victim and killer still listed as UNK. Where did you start when one unknown human being was murdered by another?

Other suspects' descriptions were brief and basic enough to fit thousands of South Florida residents, such as W/L/M (white Latin male), age 20s to 30s. Those known by name were identified, along with their DOB (date of birth) and the charges filed against them.

Most of the names seemed like old acquaintances. That was because I had covered their cases.

Another detective, whom I knew only slightly, was on the telephone at a nearby desk. His end of the conversation sounded like he was pacifying a citizen unhappy about an unsolved case. He looked bored and slightly sullen, gazing blankly out the window as he mostly listened. Suddenly he leaped to his feet with a shout.

"Holy shit! Gotta go now!" He slammed down the receiver and sprinted across the office toward the hall.

"What the hell?" Flood muttered, rising from his desk.

"A 330, just down the street, corner of six and two," the detective shouted breathlessly. "Some son of a bitch just shot a guy right off his bicycle. Right in front of me. Out there!" He was pointing and talking rapidly into his radio.

We ran to the window. A block-and-a-half away, a man lay

sprawled in the street under a bright anticrime sodium vapor light. His bicycle was already gone. The killer had pedaled away on it.

One reason for building the new station in this neighborhood was so its presence would cut crime and upgrade the area. Some people didn't get the message.

"He won't even need a car," Flood said. "He can beat feet to the scene."

We heard the detective on the radio, reporting the shooting to dispatch. He had seen two men, one on a bike, apparently arguing under the streetlight. The other had pulled a gun and shot him.

McDonald picked up his radio and spoke laconically to the detective, who by now had reached the lobby. "I guess we can assume you're handling this one," he drawled.

We all stared out the window. Several youths had appeared and approached the body. One crouched beside him.

McDonald radioed what was happening to the detective who was on the way. "We've got some bystanders, looks like one of them is taking your victim's pulse—or his wristwatch. Hell, dammit! He's got his watch! Tall black kid, wearing jeans and a dark-colored muscle shirt. Headed west on Six. He's running."

A patrol car skidded around the corner, lights flashing. The bystanders scattered.

"Nothing good ever comes out of Overtown," Flood grumbled, turning back to his desk.

I continued staring out the window at the growing tableau below. "Something did once," I said quietly. "D. Wayne Hudson."

The radios stayed active with the manhunt and with street patrolmen frequently raising detectives for advice or to report incidents or injuries that might develop into something serious. Homicide detectives hated surprises, like people who died in hospitals weeks after minor crimes that were never properly investigated and were now murders.

Flood was discussing a mugging victim on the radio. "How bad was the hit on the head?"

"Apparently it was some object, maybe a pipe," the tinny voice of a young patrolman answered. "Knocked the victim to the ground. He was hit from behind, then fell forward and struck his face on the pavement."

"How many stitches?"

"About twenty-one in the back, six in the front. His nose is kind of bloodied, and it may have loosened a couple of teeth."

"Was he ever unconscious?"

One could hear the officer conferring with someone, perhaps the victim, in the emergency room. "He's not sure, maybe briefly. He crawled to the corner gas station where somebody helped him and called us."

"How old is he?"

"Seventy-two."

"Talk to the doctor and see what he says. Lemme know if they decide to admit him."

"QSL."

McDonald was responding to an officer handling a robbery on NW Twentieth Street at Twelfth Avenue, a rental car attacked by street people who smashed the windshield with rocks, then robbed the occupants. "Are the victims local?" McDonald said.

"Negative. Tourists, a family from Ohio."

"Okay, get them down here to talk to robbery. Now."

Had the victims been Miamians, a report would have been filled out and a detective may have contacted them eventually, if he found the time. But tourists took priority. Their cases carried a sense of urgency. Criminals loved to stalk them, like hunters stalking their prey, because of the scant chance that an out-of-towner would return to testify against them in the unlikely event of an arrest. In fact, there was a strong possibility that the victim would leave town before an investigation could even be launched. Most traumatized tourists fled at once. That, of course, left city officials and chamber of commerce types wringing their hands and ordering the cops to give their cases top priority, even if it meant ignoring the local tax payers who got mugged.

McDonald motioned me to help myself from the coffeepot set up near the interview rooms. The muddy brew looked like it had been made earlier in the day, perhaps even earlier in the week, but if the night stayed relatively quiet, I would need the caffeine. It was murky and lukewarm, but I poured some into a Styrofoam cup and stirred in sugar with a plastic spoon.

A hoot of jubilation came from McDonald, and I moseyed over to his desk. He'd received a positive ID from the lab on a print lifted from a detective's car. The crime had been one of deception on both sides, a narcotics reverse sting gone awry ten days earlier. The "drug sellers" were really cops, the "drug buyers" were really robbers. The playacting ended when the robber ringleader pulled his impressive new gun, a European model fitted with extra safety features. He had never fired it before and forgot to release the safety before trying to kill the cops. As he wondered why his expensive new gun wouldn't work, they shot him dead and his accomplices scattered.

Police shootings are more sensitive than they once were, and are now investigated like homicide cases. It is important to interrogate all participants. Police had had no luck until now—the Rockwell computer had matched a single thumbprint lifted from the roof of the undercover car to a man by the name of Rodney Williams.

He may have been one of the conspirators. All of the robbers had leaned on the detectives' car at some time during the negotiations.

McDonald called records for Williams' rap sheet and copies of all his prior arrests. We all pulled chairs up to the same desk, searching the paperwork for the dead man's name as a prior codefendant or relative. We found no link between Williams and the man police shot. Williams did have a number of arrests on drug and robbery charges, which looked good, but none were in the Brownsville neighborhood where the shooting went down. That looked bad. Criminals are creatures of habit.

"Uh oh," McDonald said, scanning A-forms. "Unless he's doing something new, or his cousin or somebody lives in this building, he may have left his print on that car at some other time, some other place." He looked disappointed.

"When's the last time they washed the car?" I asked.

"Good question," Flood said.

"Probably impossible to find out, but worth asking," McDonald said.

"Would the undercover officers recognize Williams' mug shot?" I asked.

"Maybe, maybe not," he said. "They were dealing mostly with the main man, the guy they shot."

"Thing to do," Flood said, "is to go roust Rodney and ask him what the hell happened that night. That could solve our problems. He might tell us." He looked at me. "That's the secret, never ask *if* he was there, ask him what happened *when* he was there."

"I do that all the time," I told him, chin on my palm, elbow on his desk.

"Don't ever try it on me," he growled, but he cut his eyes at me with a grudging look of approval. I did like him.

Since the city seemed quiet, with no major chaos in the streets at the moment, we studied Rodney's most recent mug shots and set out to hunt him down at his usual haunts.

I was glad to be alone with McDonald and Flood in their big unmarked Chevrolet Caprice, in a more private setting, without others overhearing our conversations. McDonald drove, with Flood in the passenger seat, me in the back.

We drifted through neighborhoods unsafe for motorists in broad daylight. There was a great deal of movement on the street given the hour, which was almost 1 A.M., and our plain, unmarked four-door car fooled no one. People lounged comfortably on corners and in doorways as though in their living rooms. The downtown foot traffic was constant, homeless people pushing shopping carts full of aluminum cans, piled high with their possessions, stacked with merchandise they had stolen. Others dragged their beds, huge pieces of folded cardboard as big as refrigerators, looking for their spot. Most wore layers of clothing, carrying their entire wardrobe as they moved about.

"They're younger than the hobos and bums of yesterday," Flood pointed out. "Drinking has stayed about the same, but a lot of these people are strung out on crack."

"It's the drug addiction of the poorest of the poor," McDonald said. "If they're young they're usually addicted to crack. They drink wine too, but just to stay numb. When they do get their hands on a few dollars they buy crack first, then alcohol, then they try to *get,* not buy, food. That's the order of their priorities."

We rolled through the streets staring, watching for a face, as eyes watched us from the shadows. Nothing in this city where I was born and raised looked the same as it did during the day. Miami's blue vistas seemed shrunken, as though a lid of darkness had been clamped down, cutting off the vast horizons and shrinking the city. I felt a strange intimacy between us, out there together, sharing a metal cocoon moving through a strange and surrealistic landscape. I could see how police partners who worked this shift could become closer to each other than to their families or spouses.

Alone in the backseat, I eased out my notebook. Flood was reminiscing about the bad old days, the year of the big gasoline shortage. The long lines at the tanks sent the city murder rate skyrocketing while the county's dropped, when killers stopped dumping dead bodies out in the remote countryside. Short on gas, they left them lying where they fell, inside city limits, unfortunately.

Flood folded two slices of chewing gum into his mouth. "Trying to quit cigarettes," he explained, as he chomped and offered the pack around.

During a lull in conversation I asked, "How does this shift affect your home lives? How do your wives cope?"

"She's used to it," Flood said, and shrugged.

"Not married," McDonald said. "A few close calls, but I'm still a free man. It would be a lot to ask of anybody. Quite a few of the guys have marital problems. What does your significant other think of your job?"

Yes! He is single, I thought, glad he couldn't see my expression. "Oh, it keeps me too busy to really get involved with anyone," I said, trying to sound casual. "Why do you guys like midnights?"

"We're the warriors of the dark," McDonald said playfully. "The white hats out here to save the innocent. Also, the station is empty and you don't have to put up with any shit from management. No traffic, no staff meetings, no ass-kissing. Things are simpler. We also don't have to deal with people who walk into the office wasting our time with complaints that their neighbor is threatening to kill them over some backyard dispute."

He occasionally glanced at me in the rearview mirror as he spoke. "It's easier on this shift to deal with witnesses, perps, people on the street. We can persuade people to cooperate without getting tough. At night people feel that it's just between us. They also seem to think that if they don't cooperate, and try giving us some lip, we're gonna kick their asses. During the day they've got options: They can call their boss, their lawyer, or their neighbors who come out and start hassling the police. You don't have much privacy dealing with people during the day."

"Yeah," Flood said, snapping his gum. "You can't do anything during the day, without catching flack. At night you can scare 'em shitless. And perps are a helluva lot easier to catch at home at about 5 A.M. We can just go put the grab on 'em, snatch 'em out of bed. We don't have to play hide-and-seek on the street or drag them off their jobs."

"It's also unpredictable," McDonald said, slowing to scrutinize a gaggle of beer drinkers outside a small, all-night grocery store. "The night has a definite mystique, the feel, the air, the lighting, the smells, the attitudes, the people. Work it awhile and it gets in your blood. You learn to expect the unexpected. It makes people behave and feel in a different way."

"How so?" I had stopped taking notes and just sat, listening. I liked the sound of his voice and what he said, and the way he could drive, search the streets for a face, talk, and turn me on all at the same time.

"Criminals fear the police more at night, even the hard-core guys hanging out on street corners and at poolhalls. Except for really dangerous, crazed bad guys, most criminals are easier to deal with at night. They figure that we're bound by law and order, that society's rules keep us from doing anything crazy during the day. But at night the image people have is different, they think we're capable of much more. The atmosphere changes, not just because it's dark, but because the night is a whole different ballgame. We're all alone out there. It's just us and them."

I remembered Francie Alexander saying the same thing.

"Maybe people have good reason to be more afraid of police on midnights," I said. "Don't a lot of cops get in trouble on this shift?"

Flood swung around in his seat. "You're not quoting us?"

"Nope," I said, "just background."

"Some of the uniform guys shouldn't be out here without stronger supervision," McDonald said mildly. "They tend to act up and horse around more at night than they do in the daytime. Sometimes they badger and bait people into problems."

"What about the Blackburns?"

Flood snorted. "Not for quote? Always said they'd wind up sharing a cell."

"They are a couple of wild guys," McDonald agreed.

"They get away with a lot," Flood said, "screwing each others' wives and girlfriends . . ."

"You mean their wives can't tell them apart?"

"Maybe they don't want to," McDonald said.

"What about José Estrada and Manny Machado?"

"Steroid freaks," McDonald said.

"They really use the stuff?" Francie was right.

"Ever notice their faces? That's not teenage acne. You should see their backs in the gym," he said.

"Real aggressive and real irritable," Flood said. "They've got no kids and probably won't. I hear it shrinks their nuts."

"What about Ted Ferrell?" I asked, glad to change the subject.

"Good policeman," McDonald said, glancing at Flood, who nodded.

"First-rate, probably wind up in the detective bureau one of these days." Flood turned and frowned at me. "I'll tell you one thing, Britt. I've got a daughter about your age. I'd never let her run around the city doing what you're doing."

"What do you mean? My job?"

"Damn right. Girl like you don't belong out here on the street in the middle of the night. Running around at homicide scenes. I've seen you, snooping around neighborhoods where a cop ain't safe. You oughta watch it."

"What does she do?" I asked. He looked blank. "Your daughter, what does she do?"

He turned back around, settled in his seat, and stared at the windshield, chewing his gum in silence.

"Go ahead, Dan, tell her. You brought it up."

"What does she do?" I coaxed.

"Tell her Dan. You know what Britt's like, a pit bull. You've said it yourself, she never lets go until you tell her what she wants to know."

"Marine," he mumbled, looking straight ahead.

"Marine?" I said. "As in leatherneck? As in U.S.?"

He nodded. "And damn proud of it."

"But you'd never let her be a police reporter?" I couldn't help but laugh.

"Damn straight," he said, but didn't bring it up again.

We stopped at an all-night gas station–convenience store. McDonald asked the proprietor if he had seen the man we were looking for, and I asked for the restroom key. "Again?" Flood said pointedly.

I ignored him. I had visited the restroom at headquarters before we left, but here I was again. I have to be a candidate for the *Guinness Book of World Records*—the world's only woman who puts out more fluids than she takes in.

One reason I am not fond of small boats and planes, and hate murder sites or plane crashes in remote and inaccessible areas of the 'Glades, is because once out there, I always have to pee. My life sometimes seems an eternal quest for a bathroom. In that respect, men and women will never be equal. Tipped in advance, I can go easy on the Cuban coffee, but breaking news has little regard for Mother Nature.

This dank, low-ceilinged, and unpleasant restroom had no ambiance at all. Not even room to turn around. How would a guy stand back and hit the mark? Some hadn't. The comfort of a jumpsuit paled when struggling in a closet-sized space trying to keep it from dangling in unspeakable debris. I wished they had drop seats, like Dr. Denton's.

I heard the three signal, meaning "officers need help," through the flimsy door. Flood pounded on it until the boards rattled and I burst out, still pulling the jumpsuit up over my shoulders.

Uniforms were involved in a fight and yelling for emergency backup. We scrambled back into the unmarked Caprice. Fewer people work midnights, so there are fewer to help fellow officers in trouble. McDonald plunked his portable Kojack light, a blue strobe like the wingtip flasher on an airplane, onto the dashboard and floored it. We all flew back as though slammed against our seats by g-forces in a fighter plane. I peered over and saw the needle jump to ninety.

We seemed launched into the night, the wailing siren and blue flasher propelling us, leaving a wake of sound and light in our path. I braced at every intersection, anticipating the drunk driver who ignored stop signs and traffic lights. We roared up the feeder ramp off LeJeune to the Airport Expressway. At the curve onto Thirty-seventh Avenue, we all swayed to the right. A mile later, at Twenty-seventh Avenue, we were slung to the left. McDonald jogged over to Twenty-second, hitting the brakes to veer around a confused motorist who stopped dead in front of us instead of pulling over. My head snapped back as he floored it again, north for three blocks and then right for another two. We covered four-and-a-half miles in less than three minutes.

The address was at NW Twentieth Street and Seventh Avenue, a rundown house with a screened-in front porch. We were the first backup to arrive. Two empty patrol cars sat outside, whirling gumballs casting eerie shadows off the walls and trees.

McDonald and Flood were out and running, their doors slamming. "Stay in the car!" McDonald yelled. "And lock it."

What sounded like a major brawl was going on inside the house. Shouts, cries, crashes. My mind raced. I had promised to follow their instructions, but waiting in the car was no way to observe what happened on the midnight shift. I watched McDonald charge through the door first. Flood followed, then was propelled off his feet, out of my sight by a blow from one side.

Three shots rang out, and I was out of the car and running toward the house without even thinking about it. Screams came from inside. I saw people moving about as I approached the front steps. A huge police officer, a gun clenched in his raised fist, stood atop a coffee table, bellowing like a bull. My eyes were lifted, looking through the window, which is why I did not see what was coming until it hit me below the knees, almost knocking me off my feet. At first I thought it was a dog, then realized it was a tiny, terrified person. A little boy about four years old.

He was sobbing, eyes wild with fear. He clutched me around the knees for a moment, then realized I was a stranger, let go with a scream, and tried to elude me. I snatched him up as he kicked and flailed, struggling in my arms. He was barefoot, in a T-shirt and underpants. His nose was running and his face was wet with tears.

"Hey, it's all right. It's all right." I tried to soothe him. "You don't want to go out there by yourself. It's too dark."

Another gunshot resounded inside. "Mama! Mama!" he screamed. He stopped struggling after a moment and hung on tight, wailing his heart out in open-mouthed despair. I stepped back into the shrubbery, out of the line of fire. Instinctively I rocked him while staring, trying to make out what was happening. I was afraid to let go because he might dart out into the shadows and become lost or hurt. From the shouting inside, it sounded like the cops had the upper hand and were forcing people to the floor. I turned my body so that his eyes were averted, and peered in a window.

The cops were handcuffing several black people who lay face down. One was a thin woman in a print housecoat. McDonald was bending over someone near the door. I stood on tiptoe. Oh, shit. It was Flood, still down. I watched him move slowly and painfully into a sitting position, both hands to his face.

Moments later they emerged, McDonald helping his partner. "Let's go," he snapped abruptly as they brushed by me. I hesitated; if the parents were being arrested, the cops would put the youngster in state custody. God only knew what would happen to him there.

Cops inside were bullying and shoving their handcuffed prisoners, radioing for a wagon. Neighbors began to gather outside. An older woman in a bathrobe emerged from the house next door. I made an instant judgment call and started toward her, still holding the child tight.

"Listen, sweet boy," I whispered, my mouth close to his ear. "Everything is okay. My name is Britt." I slipped a business card out of my pocket and pushed it into his small wet hand. "You keep this. Do you know this lady?"

He raised flooded eyes. "Miz Lucille," he moaned.

"Does she know your mama?"

"Yes," he said shyly.

"Okay," I said. "What's your name?"

"Darryl," he whispered.

"Ma'am," I said to the woman, "can you keep Darryl for a little while?" I fished another card from the half dozen or so that I keep in my pocket. "Just 'til his mom can pick him up." I leaned forward and whispered, "I'd hate to see the state take him."

"Come here, baby." She opened her arms and he went to her.

"If there is any problem, please call me." I handed her the card, hoping I had done the right thing, then ran for the unmarked, which was already moving. McDonald slowed down as I dove into the back, then he burned rubber.

He was cursing. At first I thought it was at me for being out of the car and getting involved. It wasn't.

Flood sat quietly, slightly slumped. His face was already puffy and swollen. He muttered something unintelligible.

I put my hand on his shoulder. "Are you okay?"

"His jaw's broken," McDonald said bitterly. "He got sucker-punched coming through the door. Damn. It could have, should have, been me. I was first in, never saw the son of a bitch standing on the sofa next to the door. I heard Dan hit the floor. I've worked with him long enough to know that he's too tough to go down and stay down unless he's hurt bad.

"That's when one of the uniforms fired a couple of rounds into the ceiling to stop the whole fracas." He glanced at Flood, who was holding his jaw with one hand and signaling that he was okay with the other. There was blood on his shirt.

"We can get him to the hospital faster than rescue could get here," McDonald said. He radioed ahead to Cedars Medical Center that he was bringing in an injured police officer, then punched the steering wheel.

"What set it off?" I asked quietly, hoping not to infuriate him any further.

"Nothing but a goddamn domestic. Guy comes home drunk. Fights with the old lady. The rest of the goddamn family gets involved. Somebody waves a butcher knife. She calls the police, and then they all fight the cops. The usual shit."

Flood mumbled something.

"Those goddamn muscle freaks are never happy until they wind up in a fight, busting heads. They coulda handled it better. That son of a bitch Estrada!" McDonald gave the steering wheel another bruising wallop.

"Was Estrada the one up on the coffee table?"

"You guessed it," he swiveled his head around, taking a corner at forty-five miles an hour, blue flasher spinning.

"Will they arrest the little boy's mother?"

"Knowing them, they'll arrest everybody and sort it out later."

He hit the brakes and skidded to the curb two blocks from the hospital.

"This is as far as you can go, girl. The acting lieutenant is gonna show up at the hospital. No way I can explain what you were doing there. There's a cab stand on the corner."

"Sure," I said.

He turned as I climbed out of the car. "Sorry about this, Britt. I'll make it up to you. I promise."

"It's okay," I said, and smiled, taking in the dark, deserted intersection around me. "The story of my life." I shrugged, then glanced at Flood. "Take care of him."

He nodded and hit the gas. The sleepy cab driver showed no surprise when I walked up to his taxi at 3 A.M. and asked to go to police headquarters, where my car was parked.

TEN

The next morning started out like a runaway freight train, careening downhill fast, picking up speed as it went.

Thoughts of everything that had happened kept me from sleeping. I called headquarters at 7:45 A.M. McDonald was still there. Flood had been hospitalized after doctors wired his shattered jaw together.

"It's broken in seven, eight places. The guy swung on a downward angle. It had to be a powerful blow with all his weight behind it." He sounded grim.

"Hey, it could have been worse," I said gently. "The guy could have had a gun, or a tire iron. Thank God it was just his fist."

"Yeah," McDonald said wearily. "Thank God for small favors. Sorry we had to dump you off like that. Regulations. I said I'd make it up to you, Britt. How about dinner sometime? No sirens, no shootings, no busted bones."

"Sure," I said. "Call me." I hung up the phone, shocked that saying yes came so easily. Where was all my firm resolve about never mixing business and pleasure? What had happened to my irrevocable decision to place work above my personal life? I had tried but found no way to juggle both. I didn't like disappointing people or the guilt at letting someone down. I would never forget Josh's face when he finally gave up on me and Miami, and left town for the last time.

I scooped Billy Boots into my arms and curled up, stroking his chin, to sort out my thoughts. I had never dated anyone I dealt with on the beat; I knew of other reporters who had got into real jams by becoming involved with sources. Yet, instead of considering whether it would be ethical to go out with McDonald, I found myself wondering dreamily about what to wear when I did. Billy and I were both purring and half dozing when the phone rang again.

"Britt, we messed up," Lottie said. Though I was drowsy, the urgent sound of her voice pierced my consciousness like a dagger. "We lost Ryan."

"What do you mean lost?" I shot upright in bed, bouncing Billy to the floor.

"We cain't find him," she muttered. "Him and his damn raft are gone."

She was calling from a pay phone on a dock in Marathon, and spoke in a low pitch as though trying not to be heard by anyone around her.

"You just mean you lost sight of the raft, right?" I tried not to panic, visualizing Ryan's trusting puppy dog eyes. "I was afraid you meant he was dead, drowned or something."

"Well, he may be as good as. He's long gone, since midnight."

"Shit, have you called the Coast Guard, the Army, the Marines?"

"No," she said sharply, as though that was understood.

"Well, why the hell not?" I said. "Get the damn Coast Guard to launch a search!"

I could feel her frown. "We're trying to hold off on that," she muttered. "They're not gonna be happy. Eric, the captain of the *Vagabond,* is worried, he could be in deep shit for this. I already had a huge fight with him. Britt, don't you give me no ration of shit, I'm in no mood. I'm calling you for help. It's been a bad night."

"Mine was no picnic either, Lottie. My God, Ryan could be dead. What could you be thinking, not calling the Coast Guard?"

"You try explaining this stunt to them."

"You didn't file a float plan?"

"Heeelll no. They thought we just were taking the raft somewhere to shoot pictures in an authentic setting."

It had not occurred to me that the plans to set Ryan adrift were never shared with the Coast Guard, but it made sense, now that she mentioned it. The Coast Guard oversaw huge numbers of drunken, amateur, and ill-equipped boaters out on the water, all emergencies waiting to happen. And then there were the rafters, and sinking sailboats loaded with Haitians. Throw in the smugglers, poachers, and pirates, and they had more than enough to handle. Gretchen's scheme would have been officially frowned on from the start. The Coast Guard sure as hell would hate it now.

"Eric estimated the raft's speed at about two-and-a-half knots," Lottie was saying, "so we went up ahead and anchored, out of sight, to keep it authentic. I checked in on the radio with Ryan every hour. Reception wasn't too good. Those things always work better when you test them on land. He was drinking beer and slurring his words a little, but he sounded fine.

"I was a little late for the midnight check with Ryan. No answer. We kept trying—nothing. So we pulled up anchor and started circling, with a searchlight. Nothing. I kept trying the radio and we kept looking. The Coast Guard doesn't search at night, so there was no point in calling then. We thought we could spot him after daylight."

"Christ, Lottie, you should have called last night. The Coast Guard would have had a chopper in the air at dawn. We've lost a lot of time." I imagined a small raft, circled by sharks.

"We've been looking all over hell-and-a-half for hours, but all we found were some Coors bottles floating."

"That's his brand. Did you pick them up?"

"This is not the time to worry about the environment, Britt!" She spat the words out furiously.

"No, dammit, maybe there was a message inside," I said impatiently. "That's the sort of thing Ryan would do. You know he's a romantic. He might have left his course, or a message on what went wrong."

"How the hell would he know his course? He had no idea where he was. Eric thinks he was swept north by the Gulfstream."

"God," I said. "Where would that take him?"

"Palm Beach, I guess. New England, Newfoundland eventually."

"Jesus." The operator interrupted for coins, and I told her to charge it to my number.

I pinched the bridge of my nose. A headache was beginning to throb behind my eyes. I couldn't resist being a bitch, though I knew it would piss her off. "You were partying," I accused.

"What was I supposed to do, sit there and stare at the water? One of the crew plays guitar, so we were singing and had us some wine."

"Okay, okay. We have to find him. Have you called Gretchen?"

"Heeelll no. Why don't we just call Fred Douglas? He's the news editor."

"This whole fiasco was her idea, she's Ryan's editor on the project. Why should we be the only ones in a panic? Call the Coast Guard now," I said, trying to sound logical and in control. "I'll call Gretchen in half an hour. If we talk to her first, she might tell us to wait. Once they launch a search, there's no way to keep this quiet. It could embarrass the paper. But we don't care, right? Finding him is what counts."

"Right. I'll feel like a fool if we spot him five minutes after the Coast Guard launches ships and planes." Lottie paused. "But I'll feel worse if we don't. Damn, Britt, what if we don't find him at all?"

"Lots of Cubans float around out there for days and make it," I said unconvincingly.

"Yeah, and a lot of them don't. And Ryan ain't Cuban."

"Ryan is no commando, but he's smart." A pang of fear clutched at my gut, and my eyes blurred for a moment. Ryan. Alone at sea. Oh God.

"If he dies, Britt, I'll feel like shit. Has he got somebody we should call?"

I thought for a moment. "His latest crush is that new intern in the arts department, the pretty one who writes movie reviews. But she didn't come to see him off, so I guess it's not serious. His parents live in Ohio someplace. I could get their number, but I think it's too early to scare them."

"Well, I'm sure scared. If he's dead, we're in trouble."

I wanted to say "What do you mean *we*, kimosabe?" but decided against it. "Think positively. He'll really have an authentic story now," I said with a sinking heart.

"Let's pray he's alive to write it."

I needed something strong, so I filled my two-cup Cuban coffeepot with water and took a can of Bustelo and a jar of sugar from a cabinet shelf. Maybe he drank too much, rolled off the raft, and the sharks got him, I thought, spooning coffee into the pot. The strong aroma of the boiling brew soon enveloped my small kitchen. I drank half a glass of cold water first, then filled my pint-sized coffee cup, savoring its rich, black contents as I tried to scan the morning paper. How long before you die of exposure? I wondered. The coffee cleared my head. My heart beat faster as I reached for the phone to call Gretchen at home. I wasn't sure if it was the caffeine rush or my fears for Ryan.

Gretchen sounded perky and in command, even before reaching the office. I hate consistently cheerful, perky people. People who are bouncy and perky all the time obviously don't have the faintest idea what is really going on.

"There's a problem," I told her.

She sounded patronizing and pleased, as though I was calling to say I was in jail. "What's wrong now, Britt?"

"Ryan's lost at sea."

She sounded less pleased on hearing that her front page weekend project might be sleeping with the fishes.

"What went wrong? Have Lottie call me, at once!"

"She's too busy with the Coast Guard search."

"The Coast Guard has been informed? What the hell did you do that for?"

"That's what you do when someone is lost at sea and in life-threatening danger." I emphasized the last three words.

"Of course," she said, most of the perk gone out of her voice. "I just thought that it might be premature to call them in at this point."

"It's too dangerous not to," I said, then tried to sound breezy. "Just thought I'd let you know since you are his editor and this is *your* project." She didn't sound worried enough. What was Ryan to her? Just another reporter to step on as she clawed her way up the ladder.

"I just hope the Coast Guard doesn't file charges," I added.

"Charges against whom?" Gretchen said warily.

"The paper, I guess, and the person responsible for sending him out there. I think there are both civil and criminal penalties, and if the captain loses his charter license—he'll surely sue us because we hired him."

"Penalties?" Her voice faltered for the first time.

"Sure, as well as assessing us the cost of the Coast Guard search, tens of thousands of dollars a day. You know what it costs to operate a helicopter? The search planes, cutters, rescue boats and their crews? It's against federal law to deliberately endanger a life on the high seas. The searchers themselves could wind up in jeopardy out there. Anything can happen. You better get on the horn with Holland, Douglas, and the paper's attorneys."

I hate lying, but when I do it, I am creative. All that kept me from loving this was that Ryan was really missing.

For a day I took part in the search, flying with a photographer in a Chalk's seaplane, skimming in ever-widening circles over the Great Bahama Bank, eyes straining, squinting into blinding sunlight reflected off the sea, scanning green water and the Gulfstream, that swift blue river that flows through it. Under other circumstances, I would have thrilled to the endless rhythm of the ocean and the beauty of the limitless horizon, but not when searching for a tiny speck it seemed to have swallowed up.

No luck. Ryan was gone.

I was ordered back to the newsroom the next day. Stories still had to be written and deadlines met. Lottie stayed out with the *Vagabond,* an assignment I did not envy. Over ship-to-shore radio I discerned that although she and the skipper had been hitting it off until Ryan vanished, now they were furious at each other. Only Ryan's speedy return in good health and good spirits could save that foundered flirtation.

An endless parade of gray suits marched somberly through the newsroom; *Miami Daily News* executives and lawyers, gathering for meetings in the big glass-enclosed office of managing editor John Murphy. The Coast Guard district commander arrived for some sessions. Gretchen, attired in a navy blue power suit with a little tie, sat in on all of them, trying hard to look innocent, her darting eyes giving her away.

Fred Douglas, the news editor, stopped and parked his lanky body on the corner of my desk for small talk and a few questions. He was casual, but I sensed that my answers would go directly back to a meeting. He wondered aloud if Ryan had volunteered, and if the rafting story was his idea.

"No way," I said. "Like any good reporter he followed orders when Gretchen gave him the assignment, but he dreaded it. He wanted to stay here and work on his conservation series." Douglas looked thoughtful, his eyes serious. God knows what Gretchen was saying in there, trying to cover her ass.

By day three, updated notices were still being posted on the newsroom bulletin board every few hours. They detailed the progress of the search—basically, none. There were a few flurries of excitement; the Coast Guard and the brothers spotted two Cuban rafts and a Haitian boat—but no trace of Ryan. The Cubans were rescued and greeted like heroes. The Haitians, poor souls, were interdicted and sent back to Port au Prince, and who knows what fate.

I was troubled by thoughts of more than Ryan and D. Wayne Hudson during my first full day back at work. Something drew me back to the house at NW Twentieth Street and Seventh Avenue. With its peeling green paint and sagging porch, it looked different, more innocent, by day. Darryl was playing out front.

He looked up as I approached, his mouth dropped open, and he scrambled to his feet. He wore brown shorts, sandals, and a yellow T-shirt with turtles on it.

"Remember me?" I didn't want to mention the night that must have traumatized his little heart. He nodded shyly and ran inside, then stood behind the screen door holding it open. I knocked, then followed him into the room. The furniture looked scarred, as though from more than one all-out family brawl, and was covered with a pale powdery dust, which I realized came from the bullet holes in the ceiling plaster.

Darryl's dad, cousin, and uncles, one of whom had landed the bone-crunching blow to Dan Flood's jaw, were still in jail, charged with resisting arrest and aggravated assault on police officers. His mama, Onnie Gilmore, had been released by a judge at a bond hearing. She was in the kitchen, a tall, angular woman, all cheekbones, sharp elbows, knobby knees, and collarbones like bird wings. She looked to be in her late thirties, though the arrest reports I had seen revealed her age as twenty-nine. Seated on the only undamaged chair, she regarded me with suspicion.

"I was worried about Darryl," I said lamely.

She tossed her head back, barely moving the tight cornrows in her hair, and scrutinized me, her dark arms crossed protectively across her small bosom.

"You the newspaper lady who gave Darryl over to Miz Lucille the other night?" She spoke slowly, her voice weary. When she got to her feet it was slowly and stiffly, as though both body and spirit were bruised.

I nodded.

She carried what must have been Darryl's lunch plate to the sink and rinsed off the sticky residue from a peanut butter and jelly sandwich. "I saw you," she said, "at the funeral."

"The funeral?"

"For Mr. D. Wayne Hudson." She nodded, her eyes empty.

"You knew him?"

"No one but God knows what that man did for my boy . . ." her voice trailed off.

"Darryl?"

"No. Darryl's brother, Randolph. He's still in Youth Hall." Something sharp came back into her eyes. "What were you doing out here the other night?"

"I just happened to be an observer with some police officers."

"You *observe* what they did? You saw how they beat up on his daddy?" she said, jerking her head toward the room Darryl had disappeared into, "and all of us? Then they arrested everybody, even me, and I was the one who called 'em. I called 'em for help, and they busted in here like wild men, smashing furniture, beating on everybody."

"It sounds like things got out of hand," I said. I meant it, but still felt defensive. "I don't know what happened before we got here, but the detectives I was with came to help, and now one of them is in the hospital. They had to wire his jaw together."

Her eyes showed no response.

Darryl marched out of the bedroom as though on an important mission, carrying something to show me. She started to wave him away, but I said I'd like to see it.

He had crayoned drawings on both sides of a brown paper grocery sack. I was no judge, but I thought they were excellent, considering that the artist was not quite five years old. I said so, exclaiming over the composition and colors. A leafy green tree dominated one picture, with an abundant crop of round red fruit hanging from the branches. Darryl watched expectantly as I studied it. "Are those apples or cherries?" I asked.

He pressed in eagerly at my elbow, scrutinizing his own handiwork before committing himself. He regarded it intently, lips pressed together. Then he looked up with his answer, big eyes serious. "They are whatever you want them to be," he said, melting my heart.

"That's great," I said, hugging him. "That's what all the famous modern artists say about their work."

He ran for his crayons, to produce more. What chance, I wondered, does a darling child like this have? I turned to his mother, who stood at the sink, watching. "He's really good, so smart," I said.

"I know," she said quietly, fingering a bruise above her left eyebrow.

"If you and Darryl need a place to go, there is a shelter for battered women." I looked around the room with an appraising eye. What was worth taking would probably fit in the back of my car or in a small U-Haul trailer.

Her eyes showed a faint flicker of interest, but she shook her head without explanation. She didn't know me. I knew little about her life, and was certainly in no position to push. I just wanted her to know that she had options. I scribbled the referral number for the shelter on the back of one of my cards and handed it to her.

"My number is on the front. Please call me if I can help you or Darryl."

She took the card and studied it without a word. Before leaving, I fished a fresh notebook from my purse and gave it to Darryl to draw in, along with one of those cheap red pens issued us at the office. I hate taking notes in red ballpoint, anyway. The newspaper's bean counters probably buy them by the gross because reporters are less likely to glom them for use at home. Who wants to balance their checkbook in red ink?

Darryl watched from behind the screen door, one hand shading his eyes, as I got into my car and drove away. Talk about a Prozac moment. I wanted to cry—for Ryan, for Darryl and his mother, for the late D. Wayne Hudson, his widow and children. I almost never weep; I guess it was for the little kid and all little kids like him. And Ryan. On this job, I make new acquaintances every day but have only a few real friends and can't afford to lose any of them. Guilt settled behind my breastbone like a bad case of heartburn for telling Ryan that it would be an adventure, instead of helping him find a way out of the assignment.

The longer he was missing, the less chance we had of finding him. The paper had notified Ryan's parents, and they were on their way. All that TV had reported so far was that a search was underway for a *News* reporter who had become separated from a charter boat while working on a story about rafters.

The newspaper constantly accused others of cover-ups and withholding information, yet our brief stories, put together by editorial committee and overseen by lawyers, were deliberately vague. A short on page two of the local section identified Ryan's raft as a "small craft." No other news agency so far had had the smarts to ask specific questions about the craft or the precise purpose of his story.

My mailbox contained a half-dozen letters, including two thick ones from Pete Zalewski, and an assignment from Gretchen. She wanted me to take over Ryan's conservation series, a suggestion I found both rude and insensitive. I found her at the city desk and said that though I was all for conservation, it was not my beat.

"The change of pace will do you good," she said flatly, turning away as if to dismiss me, shiny gold earrings catching the light.

I might enjoy a change of pace some other time; not now. "I need time to work on the Hudson case."

"What for?" she turned brusquely toward me, frowning as though my continued presence was annoying.

"He may have died of injuries inflicted by the police."

She looked at me skeptically, her pink tongue flicking across her creamy cotton-candy-colored upper lip. "Can you prove that? Are you sure you can pin it down?"

"Not yet. I'll have to talk to a lot of cops, but there does seem to be a pattern of brutal behavior on the midnight shift . . ."

"How much time would this take?" she snapped.

"No way to tell, but I'd like a few days to work exclusively on the story."

She shook her head, her perfectly cut hair swinging gracefully with the movement. "We're shorthanded. We need you to cover the daily stories on your beat while you finish the conservation series." She opened a desk drawer and withdrew a press release from a tickler file of upcoming events. "There is also a town meeting I want you to cover in Miami Beach tonight, on the anti-noise ordinance." She smiled archly, flashing her even teeth. That would teach me to give her an argument.

If Ryan's disappearance had raised her sensitivity toward reporters, I sure as hell could not discern it. There was no point in arguing. I didn't even return to my long printout of phone messages. Instead, I retreated to the library, hoping that the Vu/Text, a database from newspapers all over the country, was not in use.

No one was at the terminal, and the screen was empty except for the cursor, blinking invitingly. I rolled up a chair, sat down and typed in the key words, POLICE and BRUTALITY. A list began to appear on the screen before me, all the articles on the topic published by major papers around the nation in the past twelve months. It was longer than I had anticipated, and I spent the next hour-and-a-half calling them up on the screen.

Then I burst into Fred Douglas's tiny glass front office for help. He has the best view among the midlevel editors, a panoramic vision of sky and Biscayne Bay behind him.

"This," I told him, "could be a major story. There is a chance, a good one, that one of the cops killed D. Wayne Hudson . . ."

"Uh-hmm," he said, looking doubtful and leaning back in his chair. "What makes you think so?"

I told him everything I had. "I've also been reading clips about major police brutality cases from all over the nation. The Rodney King case that was caught on videotape in LA, the ones in Texas, New Orleans, and Boston—all of them happened on the midnight shift. Those hours seem to be a dumping ground for violent, trouble-prone cops. The officers who need discipline the most are allowed to roam their cities at night with little or none."

He was silent for a moment. "Do it," he said, dropping his pencil on the desk. "Go get it, and take all the time you need."

"Will you spring me from Gretchen's clutches? I'll keep an eye on my beat," I promised, "and do any daily stories that need to be done while I'm working on this."

"Sure thing, but if you get backed up and want to hand some stories off to another reporter, let me know."

All right! I thought. My steps bounced as I returned to my desk, mind racing. My phone was ringing. I reached for it with misgivings, glancing at the clock and hoping fervently that it was not Pete Zalewski, who often called at about this time. An old axiom warns to be careful about what you wish for, because you might get it.

The caller was not Pete.

"Hi, Britt, I'm so glad I caught you."

"Hi, Mom."

"Are you busy?"

"Sort of."

"Did they find your friend yet?"

"Ryan? No."

She made tsking noises. "Too bad. I like reading his stories. They aren't always full of crime and violence."

"That's because he isn't on the police beat like I am, Mom." I rubbed my forehead, suddenly realizing how weary I was. "The search is still on," I said. "We still have hope."

"I've got a surprise, something that will cheer you up."

"Oh?" I said warily.

"I asked a friend over at Jordan's to put away the perfect handbag for you."

"I really don't need one, Mom."

"That awful big thing you carry around is just too much. It makes you look like a bag lady, Britt. You'll love this one. It's precious, and it's on sale. My friend can use her discount, and it will be a great buy."

"Does it have the designer's initials all over it?" Her silence told me it did. "I don't know, Mom. I just have this thing about carrying a purse with initials on it. I want them to be mine."

"You don't understand designer quality," she said, a chill in her voice.

I sighed. Maybe it was nice. "How many sections does it have? Does it have an outside pocket for my beeper?"

"No. There's a pocket inside with a tiny mirror."

"It's not very big, is it, Mom?"

"That's what we're trying to get you away from."

"But I need something roomy, with lots of compartments and outside pockets."

"That's what you have now, dear. It's not the look for you."

"I don't care about the look, it doesn't sound like what I need."

"Nothing I try to do for you is good enough, is it?"

"It's not that. I appreciate you thinking of me, but it just wouldn't be practical. I wouldn't use it."

"All I'm trying to do is help you to properly accessorize . . ."

Call waiting kicked in with a click. Perfect timing.

"Somebody's trying to get through to me, Mom. I better take this call. Talk to you later. Bye."

With relief I hit the button and greeted the new caller. No one answered. "Hello?"

At first I thought no one was there, but then I heard breathing and the faint sound of music in the background. "Hello?" I said again. "This is Britt Montero."

"Dead," whispered a voice so low that I was unable to discern whether it came from a man or a woman. "You are dead."

"You have the wrong number," I said emphatically, and hung up, shaken.

The phone rang again almost immediately. Steeling myself, I answered. To my relief, this time it was Pete Zalewski.

ELEVEN

All I wanted was to go home alone, mope a little, and get to bed early. I needed the rest, which is why it is difficult to explain how I wound up dining on smoked salmon and red snapper and sipping a 1986 Chardonnay in an intimate and elegant little restaurant on a side street in Coral Gables, with Sgt. Kendall McDonald.

He had fought his way through to me on the telephone, no easy feat when competing with tips on stories, the calls from my mother, a deeply depressed Pete Zalewski, and whoever was trying to scare me. Like me, McDonald hated the voice mail systems. My line was constantly busy, so he finally called the main newsroom number. Phyllis, the city desk clerk, waved that I had an emergency call on another line, giving me a good reason to escape from Pete, just in time. I usually tried to cheer Pete up; this time he was dragging me down with him into his own bottomless depths of despair. I simply could not accept the general newsroom consensus that Ryan was shark bait.

I told McDonald that I was feeling punk and sad about Ryan, was getting threatening phone calls, and wanted only to go home and await news from the Coast Guard. Yet somehow, minutes later, I was giving him directions to my apartment.

By the time I had thrown the unsightly stacks of newspapers that pile up in my kitchen and living room into the bottom of a closet, showered, and slipped on a pale lavender silk shirtwaist, he was at my door.

He stood there, removing his sunglasses, looking handsome in chinos, a pale blue oxford shirt, and a navy sports jacket. *Buenisimo.* It had been a long time since a man had stood in my living room, waiting to take me out.

"Very nice," he said, glancing around the apartment, then resting his eyes on me. "Very nice."

Billy Boots greeted him with friendly curiosity, as though they were old acquaintances. "I hope you're not allergic to cats," I said.

"Nope. So are you the watch cat here, big fella?" McDonald said soothingly, scratching under Billy's chin, while I picked up my purse and pager. "Do you chase away all the bad guys?"

Billy purred loudly and rubbed against his pants leg.

"Looks like love at first sight." I was surprised. "He usually ignores strangers."

"He must smell Hooker."

"Excuse me?"

"Hooker, my dog. She got the name because I found her on the street, on the Boulevard, up near Seventy-ninth."

This was a good sign, I thought. I have never trusted men who didn't like animals.

He was studying a framed photo on an end table. "Who's this dude on the horse, a Mexican bandit?"

"No, a Cuban freedom fighter. My father. That was taken on the *finca* where he grew up."

"Ah, I can see the resemblance now."

"You can?"

"Sure, the jawline, the eyes." He glanced between me and the photo. "No denying you're his daughter. What does he do now?"

"He doesn't. Castro killed him."

"I'm sorry."

"I was just a little girl at the time." Suddenly I wanted to prolong the moment. "Would you like a drink before we go?" I had a bottle of vodka in a kitchen cabinet, and chilled white zinfandel in the refrigerator.

The phone interrupted before he could answer. The new city desk clerk was very young and very serious.

"You've got a call," she said urgently. "I've got him holding on the other line. Sounds important. Says his name is Pete Zalewski. Want me to put him through to you?"

"No," I said, annoyed. "Tell him to call me tomorrow, when I'm in the office."

"I didn't give him your home number," she said quickly. "Even though he asked for it."

"Thanks," I said. "You did the right thing. You never know when it could be important. This one isn't."

McDonald was scrutinizing the Winslow Homer prints on the wall. "These are nice," he said, smiling.

"I like his later stuff the best, the watercolors in Bermuda and Florida," I said, realizing too late that I sounded pretentious.

McDonald nodded. "Did you know that before Homer became known as a painter, he covered the Civil War? Did sketches from the front lines for the newspapers of the day. Actual battle scenes. Can you image Eddie Adams, or some other famous war photographer, being sent to the front with a sketchpad instead of a camera?"

"How did you know that?"

He shrugged. "Civil War buff. I read a lot on that era."

"Your drink . . ." I remembered, as the telephone rang again.

We stared at each other. "You're a popular girl."

"Only with people who want their names in the newspaper, or find themselves in forced confinement." The answering machine kicked in after the second ring. The voice of the caller resounded loudly in my small apartment. It was my mother.

"Where are you, Britt? If you're not there, I can only hope to God you're out on a date. But that's probably too much to expect . . ." Face burning, I rushed to lower the volume on the machine.

I turned back to McDonald. "About that drink . . ."

He was grinning and pacing near the door, graceful, long-legged, and athletic, like a racehorse eager to run. "I've got a better idea.

Let's beat it out of here. I've come to take you away from all this. You work too hard, you need escape, a few laughs, a little cheering up." He touched my shoulder lightly as we went out the door, and ushered me to his car, a shiny black Jeep Cherokee. I saw when he removed his jacket that he wore his off-duty gun, a short-barreled revolver, in a shoulder holster. A police department pager was clipped to his belt. I stifled a laugh. I also wore my pager, and carried a notebook in my purse. So this is how we get away from it all, I thought. Though neither of us was on the job, we weren't quite off, either.

I am an edgy passenger with most men, watching the traffic and itching to take the wheel myself, a trait that I'm sure does not enhance my social life. But now, I relaxed. I liked the confident way he drove. Usually watchful and alert, I had forgotten what it was like to really wind down when I was out and about in Miami.

Perhaps I knew the dark side of the city too well. I guess we both did. When a figure approached the car at a red light near an overpass, I stiffened in my seat. "It's only a window washer," McDonald said, noticing my reaction. The bearded street person vigorously smeared the windshield with a dirty rag.

"I always watch out for these guys; some of them are okay, but others . . ." I said, as McDonald passed the man some change.

"I guess it's scary for a woman driving alone," he said as we pulled away from the light.

"It doesn't scare me," I said quickly.

"Oh I know, you never get scared," he said, sneaking a sidelong glance out the corner of his eye.

"I don't. I just try to avoid trouble by using common sense."

"Not an easy thing to do sometimes," he said.

"Right, if you drive the expressway you run the risk of being nailed by the highway robbers." Modern-day highwaymen, they hurl heavy objects into traffic, disable passing cars, and attack the occupants. "So to avoid the x-way, you stay on city streets and wonder about that stranger lurching toward your car at traffic lights. It may be somebody who just wants to wash your windshield, or a robber ready to put a brick through it to get your money, jewelry, and maybe even take your car."

"Yep," McDonald said. "But what you should watch out for, since you're usually where the action is, is the sudden civil disturbance. Those things erupt so fast, without warning."

"I know, I once interviewed a woman horribly burned by a Molotov cocktail hurled into her open car window for no apparent reason."

"It's hard to believe," he said, "that there are still towns where a driver's biggest concern is watching out for potholes. Here we have vandals dropping cinder blocks from overpasses . . ."

"And police impersonators who pull over cars to rob or rape the drivers," I chimed in.

"Robbers who deliberately rear end other cars, then rob the motorist who steps out to check the damage," he said.

"The deranged drivers with guns . . ."

"Ready to kill for a parking space," he finished. "I've handled a couple of those."

"The Beach has had some driveway robberies. The guys follow motorists home and pull guns on them as they get out of their cars," I told him.

"I know what job you'll never be offered," he said. "Writing brochures for the chamber of commerce."

"I bet they'd like to muzzle us both. It is sad," I said. "I can remember when driving used to be fun. When I was a teenager and first got my license, my friends and I would just go out for rides. We'd cruise up and down the beach, and then go all the way out to the Monkey Jungle."

"Driving through Miami now is like the Grand Prix," he said. "You win if you make it to where you're going."

"The prize," I said, "is keeping your wallet."

"Is this a great town, or what?" he asked, and we both laughed.

I watched with fresh eyes the scenery flashing by. I was in someone else's hands, being driven to an unknown destination by an armed and well-trained man who could handle any crisis. Nobody dared mess with him, and that made me feel safe and cared for, instead of alone and on my own in a mostly hostile world, the way I usually was.

The music on the radio ended, and a weather report followed, warning of squalls and fifteen-foot seas. Sick at heart, I had a vision of a tiny raft surrounded by black sea.

"They've got to find Ryan," I burst out. "I hate to think of him lost out there."

"Tell me about him," McDonald said, turning onto Ponce de Leon, a broad European-style boulevard in Coral Gables.

"He's a sweet, gentle guy," I told him. "A young twenty-six, just a kid, but a good writer. He's sentimental, and he's had a crush on every woman in the newsroom."

"Including you?"

"That was over in two weeks. He's like a younger brother. His desk is right behind mine, and we talk all the time. It's almost like being roommates. He must be scared to death out there. And I'm afraid we'll never see him again. That he'll just be lost in limbo, one of those unsolved mysteries of the sea. I feel so guilty. Somehow I should have kept him from going."

"You can't beat yourself up over this, Britt. He's an adult; he could have said no. It sure as hell was a dumb idea. That editor who sent him sounds like living proof that a mind is a terrible thing to have."

"You wouldn't say that if you saw her," I replied.

"She good-looking?"

"The kind of face men write poetry about."

"Brains turn me on before beauty." He turned to look at me. "But real dynamite is a woman with both." He made a left onto a small side street. "Don't write this Ryan off so fast. Some people are born survivors."

"You usually see the ones who aren't," I said glumly. "So do I."

"There's nothing we personally can do about it tonight, so block it out for now." He reached for my hand and squeezed it. "Worry about it tomorrow," he said, and winked.

Inside the bistro, fresh flowers adorned the table and an attentive waiter hovered over us like a helicopter. The staff seemed to know and like McDonald; our table was quiet and candlelit.

"The special here is always superb, something that will make you want to junk your stove and make a standing reservation," he confided.

The waiter told us about the special, and I shook my head. "I never eat veal," I said quietly. He backed off while I studied the menu. I intended to spare McDonald the story, but his eyes were questioning.

"The baby calves," I explained. "Do you know they snatch them from their mommies?"

He rolled his eyes. "You, uh, have personal knowledge?"

"As a matter of fact, I was there a couple of years ago when a hijacked truck was recovered. The hijackers took it at gunpoint and forced the driver out in the Everglades. They must have thought he had a load of whiskey or VCRs. They abandoned the truck later, left it parked in the hot sun. When the police opened the back a day-and-a-half later, there were all these adorable, glossy baby calves, big-eyed and hungry, and bawling for their mothers.

"I was new on the job at the time, and thrilled that they had been rescued. It was a happy ending. Then I asked a policeman what would happen to the calves next. He said the owners were dispatching a new driver to deliver them to their original destination—the slaughterhouse." I took a deep breath. "I will never forget that scene, or eat veal again."

"I swear, I have never harmed a baby calf in my life." McDonald solemnly searched his menu, then his eyes lit up. "How do you feel about baby fish? They don't have to bite that hook if they don't want to. They never cry for their mommies."

We both ordered fish, and McDonald sat back and smiled. I wanted to relax and unwind, but as I gazed across the table into the endless depths of Kendall McDonald's silvery blue eyes, a loathsome question gnawed at my consciousness: What if Gretchen could see me now? Her implication that I fraternized with the cops was insulting and had infuriated me, yet here I was, big as life and twice as sassy, doing exactly that. I glanced guiltily at the door, expecting her and her schoolteacher husband to walk in, catching me in the act, proving that she was right. This is a big city with lots of restaurants, but stranger things happen all the time. It would be just my luck to see her, or someone else from the newspaper. I bit my lip and scrutinized an arriving party of four.

"Somebody you know?" McDonald asked.

"No," I felt startled. "But I was just thinking that it could be awkward if someone from work saw us together. You know, there could be a conflict because of our jobs."

"Don't think that hasn't occurred to me. I don't think I'd be a happy camper if some of the brass caught us with our heads together."

"Maybe we should blow out the candle," I said, laughing as I glanced around the softly lit room.

"Don't," he said. "I like you in candlelight. And I can take the heat if you can."

The snapper was fresh, moist, and sweet with the crunch of slivered almonds, and doused with the tangy juice of key limes. I began to feel much better after the third glass of Chardonnay.

"How do you know baby fish don't scream when they're caught?"

"My dad used to take me fishing, and I never heard one. Although it was probably too cold to scream in Lake Superior."

"So you're a Yankee?"

"I was. Marquette, Michigan, until my folks moved down here during my first year in high school. My mom couldn't take the weather anymore. Frostbite didn't help her arthritis."

"So they retired?"

"No, he taught science, she taught history. She still does. He retired two years ago and became a naturalist; takes people on nature walks and bird-watching expeditions in the 'Glades."

"That's great. It must be fun."

"He loves it. My sister teaches phys ed in Bonita Springs; my older brother is a computer analyst for Florida Power and Light; and my kid brother is a lifeguard out at Crandon Park, living out all his fantasies. His sole ambition is to meet 'babes.' "

"It must be nice to have a big family. I'm an only child. So was my mother, and she doesn't get along real well with my dad's family. In fact she and my aunt Lourdes haven't spoken since I was fifteen. That was when my mother refused to give me a *quince,* you know, the big traditional formal fifteenth birthday party for Cuban girls. You wear a big *Gone With the Wind* type dress and have two thousand pictures taken.

"My mother insisted that I would have a traditional sweet-sixteen party the next year. My father's family was furious, of course, and wouldn't come."

"Which one did you want?"

"Actually, I was shy and didn't want either one. All I wanted was my driver's license. I felt guilty, though, because I wanted to please them all. At the *quince,* your first dance is with your father. My uncle Julio would have taken his place, but my mother wouldn't hear of it because of the scandal. You see, Uncle Julio had been arrested, for building bombs."

"How did they catch him?"

"Apparently, he didn't do it very well and blew off his left hand."

"Jesus, Britt. Well, at least they're family."

"Yeah, like the Mansons." Leaning forward, over my crème brulée, dead serious and, to my surprise, slightly slurring my words, I said, "So, you've been a homicide detective for six years now, and a cop for eleven?"

McDonald nodded, his sensual mouth gently curved, as though secretly amused.

"Tell me the best, most memorable last words that you've heard," I said. "The ones you can't forget that were brave, poetic, or inspiring." Was I thinking of Ryan? Or my father? Or maybe Uncle Julio. I had been trying to remember the last thing Ryan had said at the dock. I believed it was something about his beer supply.

McDonald laughed, a nice sound. "Another reason to wonder what our country is coming to." He raised his coffee cup. "Another sign of the sad state of education in America, or at least in Miami. We're not turning out a lot of Nathan Hales, or even W. C. Fieldses these days." He shook his head. "Let's see, from victims of homicides, construction accidents, traffic wrecks, and natural disasters, the most common last words I have heard or have had repeated to me by witnesses are: 'Oh, shit.' "

"Nothing more profound than that?" I laughed.

He thought for a moment. "I don't seem to recall any that were brave, poetic, or inspiring—only stupid. 'Go ahead, I dare you,' is a popular phrase. You hear that one a lot in homicides, Russian roulette, and in a few traffic fatalities." He put down his cup and signaled for the check. "There was the hit on Vito Cuccinella," he said thoughtfully, slipping a credit card out of his billfold. "The Mafioso gunned down back in eighty-six. He was ambushed outside a restaurant, shot nine times with a high-powered weapon. People heard the shots and came running. He was lying in the street, mortally wounded, full of bullet holes, and with his last breath, he gasped, "Don't call the police. I'll handle it myself.""

I laughed. "That case was never solved, was it?"

"Nope. OC hits rarely are. It still bugs Dan. He was the lead on it. He hates open cases with his name on them. We heard that it was professional, a hit man out of Boston."

"You know what I hate? These over-educated pseudo-intellectual criminologists interviewed on TV every time there's a mass murderer or a serial killer at large. The interviewer always asks for a profile of the perp, and the expert always ponders for a long moment and then comes up with this stunning revelation: 'He's a loner.' They *always* say that. All sorts of degrees, years and years of study and analyzing criminal behavior, and *that's* the best they can do?"

McDonald smiled. "Of course they're loners, they've killed everybody they knew."

The valet brought the car. The Cherokee looked shinier and newer, the night darker, and the lights brighter.

"Where are we going?"

He shrugged. "Let's just cruise and schmooze." He headed north on Lejeune, east on the Dolphin Expressway, then across the MacArthur Causeway to Miami Beach.

"Do you know that more accidents happen on this causeway than on any of the others?" I said, suddenly too talkative, the wine and the night making me giddy. "I used to think there was something about the surface that made tires skid and drivers lose control and slide all over the place." We were approaching the entrance to Palm Island. "That," I said, as we whipped by, "is crash corner, the most dangerous intersection in the city of Miami Beach." I looked back, trying to fathom what sinister forces lurked there.

"They've resurfaced the roadway several times since I've been on the beat, but the accident rate stays just as high. Now I think it's the distractions, the city skylines, the big cruise ships passing so close in the narrow channel and the little go-fast boats speeding by, trailing those monster wakes. It's so beautiful that drivers can't help but take their eyes off the road for an instant and land upside-down in the drink or up against a palm tree. Or an Australian pine."

I knew I should shut up, but couldn't seem to. Being alone in the car with McDonald at night was making me babble.

"That's why I hate cars with power windows. They short out when you hit the water and you're trapped. I've covered a couple of those. One was a young insurance salesman. Do you know that hitting one of those old trees is like hitting a stone wall?" I babbled on.

"Do tell." He looked at me quizzically. "You're full of cheerful small talk. You're right about the windows, though. We handled that guy. He had just sold a policy to a couple in that condo complex on the island and was trying to drive back to the mainland during a thunderstorm. Nobody saw his car slide off that little bridge. His power windows shorted out. Even when the car settled on the bottom and the pressure equalized, he had no way out. He had a gun in the glove compartment, and he emptied it through the windshield. It made neat little bullet holes, but the glass wouldn't shatter, and he couldn't break it out. Funny you should remember him."

"I remember all the people I write about," I said ruefully.

"Bummer," he said.

"I bet you do too," I told him. "And so does Flood, the way he's always talking about unsolved cases. That's what we do. You guys clean up the mess, and I tag right along with my little notebook."

"But we love it," he said. "I never dreamed I'd stay with it this long. I'm hooked."

"So am I, but I never wanted to be anything but a journalist. What did you plan on before police work?"

"Law, but I ran out of bucks a year into law school. Figured I'd wear a badge for a year or so and go back. But somehow I took to being a cop and got a little disenchanted with the legal profession."

"How so?"

"Ohh, I just didn't want to spend the rest of my life talking out of the side of my mouth. You know what it's like in this town. The judges are the best that money can buy, and the lawyers all resemble Pinocchio."

I laughed at the image.

"I'll probably go back and finish some day, then practice after I've got my twenty in with the department. But I've found that I like the action more as a police officer. Every day you feel a second closer to solving a problem. A lot of what lawyers do is mental masturbation; it's not something real. Instead of resolving problems, they make them more complex."

"True. I agree with that bumper sticker: Help Save America, Shoot a Lawyer."

"You're not so bad," he said. His eyes left the road and gave me an appreciative sidelong glance. "Do you realize that a lot of people on the police department think you're ten feet tall and green, with a tail?"

"What?" I said, embarrassed.

"Sure. You scare them. You and your stories. They have a totally false image of who you are and what you're like. The only thing green about you is your eyes."

I felt flushed. Thank God it was dark. "But they must know that I'm always fair."

"Hell no. You know that cops are paranoid. They all think you're out to get them."

He slid the Cherokee into a parking space on Ocean Drive at Tenth Street. "Let's walk," he said. "You could use some air."

"I know, I've been talking too much," I apologized. "I drank so much wine. I haven't been this relaxed in a long time." The music from a live band at the Tropics wafted across the street as we strolled out onto the open sand. When I stumbled over the remains of somebody's castle, he took my arm. His hand felt smooth and warm.

The water was as black as an editor's heart, and I thought of Ryan. I wanted to yell at it to give him back.

McDonald caught me staring at the ocean. "I know what you're thinking about, your missing buddy."

I slipped off my shoes and carried them as we strolled north along the waterline, the wind whipping at my hair and skirt and the surf lapping at my stockinged feet. A walk alone on the beach or with any other date at 1 A.M. could be tantamount to suicide these days, but I felt safe with McDonald. The wind was warm, but carried the smell of fall. We stopped at the Twelfth Street lifeguard stand, then climbed up and sat inside, sheltered and close together, watching the ocean tumble toward us as the tide came in. I trembled slightly, not due to the temperature, but I did not resist when he put his jacket and then his arm around me.

His natural male heat and magnetism drew me to him like the tide, but also made me nervous. I hadn't been with a man I was really attracted to in a long time. And when I got nervous, I tended to talk. "What you just said about police perception of the press might explain why Danny Menendez is acting so weird these days."

There in the cozy confines of the covered lifeguard stand, I told him about the D. Wayne Hudson story and how, before leaving the office, I had called PIO to request the personnel files on the Blackburn Brothers, Estrada, Machado, and Lou Carpenter. The on duty PIO man had referred me to Sgt. Menendez. Still apparently in a snit, curt and unlike his usual self, he had grudgingly agreed to provide them to me in the morning. "His attitude was unsettling, because I know Danny. We always had a good professional relationship," I concluded.

McDonald was silent for a long moment, then shook his head. "Look at this from his standpoint, Britt. He's a man caught in the middle. His job, no matter what the title, is not to inform the press but to polish the department's image. If he pushes to get you the information you want, he catches heat from the people he's pushing, many of whom outrank him. If he doesn't, he catches heat from you and the newspaper. He's in a no-win situation. And, speaking about being caught in the middle . . ." He took his arm from around me and half-turned to face me, his tone serious.

"Now I know why you asked about those guys the other night. We need to get something straight between us. Our jobs could create a problem. If we keep seeing each other socially, that's exactly what it has to be, strictly social. No shoptalk, no questions, no gossip. You can't use me as your pipeline into the department."

I felt flushed in the darkness. "Tonight was your idea."

"Don't get hinky, now."

"If cops are really so paranoid, maybe they sent you to find out how much I know about this case." I knew that was absurd the moment it came out of my mouth, but I couldn't stop myself.

"Oh sure, I'm spending my only night off this week trying to pick your brain for the department." He was beginning to sound angry. "Yeah, maybe I'm wired for sound, too."

I suddenly realized that I was blowing this whole night and that was not what I wanted to do. "Maybe you are," I laughed, "so I guess I'll just have to find out. Spread 'em, Sergeant."

I saw the surprise in his face as I started to frisk him. I even shocked myself; had it not been dark, I never could have done it. But I patted him down, gingerly in places, but all the way down. Hell, I'd watched cops do it a hundred times, and had been frisked a few times myself when visiting prisoners or entering high-security court-rooms. I did a pretty good job.

"Watch it, I'm ticklish," he yelped. We were both laughing uncontrollably. By the time I found out he wasn't wired, he was. So was I.

"Don't stop now." He closed his arms around me. "Just when I'm beginning to like it. Well, you find anything? Any devices or dangerous weapons?"

"Just your gun."

"Then I think you missed one."

"One what?"

"Dangerous weapon."

"No comment." The amount of heat our bodies generated in such close quarters left me breathless. I backed off and pulled my shoes on, needing to regroup a bit. "It's getting late."

"Yeah, and it sure is warm in here," he said, as the chill night wind blasted through our open-sided little shelter.

We drove the short distance to my apartment in relative silence, the air between us charged. He walked me to the door. Once inside, he kissed me, long and slow. I felt myself starting to melt, but something held me back. Why is this wrong? I asked myself.

He reminded me.

"You know that story you're so intent on doing?"

"Hummm?" I murmured into his chest.

"You should drop it." He released me and stepped back.

"What about you?" I asked.

"No comment," he said, and let himself out, but his eyes were smiling.

TWELVE

The morning started out fast and furious. A thirty-ton crane being used to remove a forty-five ton metal sign over the Palmetto Expressway toppled over, and the sign crashed onto the roadway. Thousands of overheated motorists and steaming cars were trapped in a six-hour traffic jam that spawned three heart attacks and numerous fistfights. The official temperature was 92, but out on the sun-blasted pavement it had to be 110. I parked on a side street that flanked the Palmetto and climbed the embankment to the x-way to interview the unhappy workers, hassled highway patrolmen, and melting motorists. Lottie was up in a rented chopper shooting aerials of the mess, when more bad news broke out ten miles away at the toll booth to the Rickenbacker Causeway.

Midday temperatures had triggered a battle in which a pregnant woman and an eight-year-old boy were injured, and three other motorists shot. When the car in which the woman and child were riding overheated and stalled, enraged drivers behind them attacked. When one waved a knife, the woman's brother-in-law pulled a gun from the glove compartment and shot him. Half a dozen other motorists drew their weapons. A police officer on patrol nearby had already radioed that a fight seemed to have broken out at the toll plaza, but by the time he could cross six lanes, motorists had already taken cover behind their cars and were trading shots. "They wanted to kill us because our car broke down," the pregnant woman sobbed when I got there.

It was a bad day to be a motorist in Miami. I called in the stories for the street edition, learned that there was no news on Ryan, and then went to headquarters to look at the cops' personnel files. Unfortunately, Menendez was on his toes. Though the files were public record, the cops' home addresses and phone numbers were not, and he had meticulously gone through and whited them out. It only made my job slightly more difficult; nothing is ever simple.

Recalling McDonald's description of Menendez as a man caught in the middle, I tried to give the PIO sergeant a friendly smile, but he remained aloof, avoiding eye contact. I sat at an unoccupied desk in the media room and leafed through the files. Each contained the essence of a policeman's career; all the excitement, boredom, danger, and routine reduced to impersonal sheets of paper.

I started with Ted Ferrell's. It was sterling, packed fat with accolades. He had been honored as Officer of the Month several times, and was once nominated for Officer of the Year. He had enough endorsements and grateful letters from citizens to run for office. He was kind to little old ladies who were lost, and even had a letter praising his sensitivity from the foreman of a jury he had testified before in a rape case. He qualified as an expert marksman, and his evaluations consistently ranked between good and excellent. There were also numerous letters of commendation from other agencies he had assisted in investigations, including the Drug Enforcement Administration and the Florida Department of Law Enforcement.

The Blackburns' files were equally fat, but the contents more spotty. Even city file clerks seemed to have trouble telling the brothers apart. Some of Roland's files were in Roscoe's folder, and vice versa. I automatically sorted out the misfiled papers as I read through them, replacing them in the correct jackets.

Both had reprimands for off-duty bar brawls. Roscoe had forfeited three vacation days for reckless handling of a shotgun that had apparently killed the plumbing in the third-floor men's room. He claimed that the weapon had toppled over and discharged while he used the john. Clues between the lines suggested horseplay. His records also reflected several visits to the city doctor for temporary hearing loss, apparently caused by the blast in such close quarters. Roland had drawn a two-day suspension for challenging a downtown security guard to a quick-draw contest. The guard took him up on it, and accidentally shot himself in the shin. Both Blackburns had been warned to stop teasing and hassling the transvestite hookers on Seventy-ninth Street. Their six-month evaluations from supervisors ranged from poor to excellent.

There were also letters commending both for fixing flat tires for elderly motorists, assisting lost tourists, helping citizens locked out of their cars and their houses, and praise from downtown business-men who were pleased that the Blackburns were cleaning up the city by sweeping the homeless, the panhandlers, and the free-lance win-dow washers away from their establishments. There was also a flood of letters dated around the same time from angry advocates for the homeless, accusing the brothers of hassling the street people and trying to drive them out of downtown. They had shared Officer of the Month honors for an exceptional run of good felony arrests, and received citations of appreciation from the department of corrections for quickly recapturing half a dozen jail escapees, including a murder suspect who had shinnied down sheets from a third-floor cell block.

The Blackburns had been reprimanded over the years for being late to roll call, making bathroom sounds and burping noises over police frequencies, failing to show up for traffic court, and occasion-ally losing their police radios, which cost about $1,500 apiece. Sev-eral letters from jailed felony suspects and their lawyers accused the Blackburns of overzealous tactics that encompassed both mental and physical cruelty. Both had been injured several times, either in fights while making arrests or in accidents during pursuits. Both seemed to suffer another occupational hazard of police work: the names of their wives, beneficiaries on their departmental insurance forms, had changed over the years, after divorces and new marriages. All in all, the angry complaints and pats on the back seemed to balance out.

Carpenter's file was slim by comparison, though he had more time on the department than all of them. That is exactly what he appeared to be, a civil servant putting in his time, a veteran cop who would not leave a ripple when he retired. No bad marks, no good marks; a career characterized chiefly by inertia. In six months no one would remember he'd ever worn a badge.

Manny Machado's evaluations ranked high on appearance and low on attitude. He had received reprimands for tossing a snotty motorist's car keys off the Brickell Avenue bridge into the Miami River; for refusing to speak English to non-Spanish-speaking citizens, though he was born in this country; and for the use of unnecessary or excessive force. He did a brief stint as a K-9 officer, cut short because his partner bit too many people, including innocent bystanders and other police officers. The K-9 sergeant wrote in one evaluation that Machado did not have the temperament to work with a canine, and spent too much time agitating the animal, something he seemed to enjoy. During that same period, it looked as though Machado would have done better had he let the dog drive; they had been involved in seven on-duty auto accidents, most of them minor, except for one in which he had suffered head injuries and a dislocated shoulder.

Most interesting was that he and Estrada had both been reprimanded for a brawl with fellow officers, including a captain, over the use of weights in the police gym. Denying a captain a turn at the equipment had been a mistake.

Estrada had graduated in the same academy class as Machado, and also seemed short-tempered with the public. One man complained that when he had called police to report a noisy party next door at 2 A.M., Estrada had arrived and pistol-whipped *him*. A woman said he had broken her jaw when arresting her for quarreling with a taxi driver about a fare. On the other hand, he had positive letters for his outstanding appearance in the honor guard when the president visited Miami, and for his playing in the Pig Bowl, the hotly contested annual football game between the city and the county police departments.

Menendez did not look up when I left. Next stop was the Dade County Courthouse. The swallows return to Capistrano, and the turkey vultures come back to Miami, I thought. They arrive every year to glide and wheel in the wind drafts above the Courthouse, a towering twenty-eight-story, four-tiered granite wedding cake built in

1925. Spreading six-foot wings, the buzzards ride the northeastern breezes and sun themselves on the silver pyramid atop the building. I love the neoclassical columns, the broad stone steps, the high ceilings, and the secrets inside, just waiting to be ferreted out.

The civil court index, the key to the legal battles, the frivolous and the frauds, the dreams and divorces, the torts, the scams, the tortured truths and all-out lies, is contained in a revolving cassette holder in a public viewing room in the recorder's office. Each cassette contains a spool of microfilm listing the alphabetized names of plaintiffs and defendants. Under Ferrell, Ted, for example, you would see all the local civil suits in which he was named, either as plaintiff or defendant, including divorces. Ted had once sued a realtor and some people named Warren.

Both the Blackburns and Estrada had divorces. The Blackburns together and independently were listed as codefendants with the city in a half-dozen lawsuits. Estrada, a cop only six years, was codefendant in nine cases, Machado in eight. I didn't bother with Carpenter since he was not present when whatever happened to D. Wayne Hudson took place. I listed all the case numbers in my notebook, and took the ornate elevator down to the first floor to pull the files.

Fred Douglas had evidently done right by me with Gretchen; either that or my beeper battery was dead. I had no desire to hear from her, unless of course a major story broke on my beat, or news came from the Coast Guard.

I wrote the case numbers on slips of paper, passed them to a clerk and waited at the counter. Lawyers, law clerks, and private detectives occupied four large wooden tables, scribbling notes and examining files. I was glad no other reporters were present. They usually nosed around to find out what I was working on. I did the same when I saw them, out of curiosity and the worrisome fear that perhaps they were on to something I'd missed, something major, the big one. Thank God for competition; it keeps you on your toes.

The clerk, a slim, fortyish woman named Bev who had been there for years, came back with an armload of files. "This is enough to keep you busy for awhile, Britt. Tracking something, huh?" The eyes behind her fashionable eyeglasses were as bright and as alert as a bird's.

"Yep," I winked.

"I'll watch the front page," she said.

I carried my stack of files to one of the tables and settled in a corner chair, facing the door. This was an old habit; I hate having anyone peer over my shoulder while I am poring through the public records of other people's lives.

Ted and his wife, Betsy, were the plaintiffs in his lone lawsuit. When they had bought their home, the sellers and the realtor claimed it had a new roof. The Ferrells learned it was a lie the first time it rained. The old roof had simply been whitewashed, and leaked like a sieve. The Ferrells sued and settled for the cost of a new roof. Good for them, I thought.

A chilling pattern emerged from the other men's lawsuits. Virtually all the most serious incidents had taken place between midnight and dawn. The cases had been filed by people who did not simply write letters to the department; they hired lawyers. Some did so from hospital beds, others from jail cells. Most people claiming abuse by the Blackburns appeared to have a reason for being stopped, such as jogging in a residential neighborhood at 2 A.M, but not for what they claimed happened next. Physically assaulted, battered by fists, night-sticks, and heavy metal flashlights, the plaintiffs said that numerous unidentified cops witnessed, took part in, or ignored the attacks on them.

A burglary suspect caught red-handed said that he was captured and cuffed with unnecessary roughness, his face pounded on the pavement, his nose and a cheekbone broken. I had seen another side of the same case in the Blackburns' personnel files, a letter from the neighborhood homeowners' association, applauding them for this very arrest. I took a break to stretch my legs and go to the water fountain. This burglar could be a savvy criminal trying to evade jail by blurring the details of his arrest, I thought. But what about the fifty-nine-year-old stockbroker whose arm had been broken in two places after he was stopped on suspicion of drunk driving? He claimed he was cold sober, returning home from a financial seminar in Boca Raton. He alleged that he was unable to pass the roadside sobriety test due to recent hip surgery, and that he was beaten when he tried to explain.

Estrada's cases were even more frightening. A woman motorist said he stopped her for failing to signal a turn at an empty intersection at 3 A.M., grabbed her by the ankle, and dragged her from her car, bouncing her head on the concrete and the curb. She suffered a skull fracture. She claimed he also damaged her car by jumping up and down on the hood.

I remembered that night at little Darryl's house, Estrada atop the coffee table.

Another motorist, a doctor on his way home at 1 A.M., after being called out to attend a patient at the emergency room, was pursued into his driveway by Estrada, who accused him of making "a wide turn," then struck him with a heavy metal flashlight that broke his glasses and his nose. The physician had then been arrested for resisting arrest.

How can somebody be arrested only for resisting arrest? I wondered. Few cases had gone to trial. The city had settled most out of court with relatively modest cash awards. Some were still pending, like the case of a waiter, stopped after exiting the expressway on his way home from work, assaulted and beaten with nightsticks. His wrist and two fingers were broken, and he lost some teeth. His offense: a burned-out tail light. Machado was a codefendant on that one, along with the Blackburn brothers.

Stiff, chilled by the air conditioning, and eyesore after shuffling papers for hours, I walked down the courthouse steps in brilliant late-afternoon sunshine, crossed the street to the towering new government center with its lobby full of shops and potted palms, and rode the elevator to the tax assessor's office. It was almost closing time, but what I needed would not take long. I found the Blackburns, Estrada, Machado, and Carpenter all listed as homeowners on the Dade County property tax rolls, and copied their addresses. The Blackburns lived in modestly assessed houses in South Miami. Roscoe had a pool; Roland did not. Carpenter lived in a Miami Springs condo. Estrada and Machado lived in the same subdivision, a block-and-a-half apart. That would make it easier when I went out to knock on their doors.

I felt a sense of accomplishment driving back to the office. Nothing conclusive; from what I'd read, almost any one of the cops involved could have attacked D. Wayne Hudson. But at least I'd done a good day's work. Using public records sometimes gave one a sense of invincibility. People could slam doors, refuse calls, stonewall, and run, but in today's world of computers, one thing they couldn't do was hide.

The stack of phone messages on my desk contained none from Kendall McDonald, leaving me vaguely disappointed. Several times that day I'd thought about laughing with him, and his goodnight kiss. Was I crazy to be thinking this way about a cop?

Lottie was back, and had left me a note. The *Vagabond* had abandoned the search, leaving it to the Coast Guard. Ryan's parents had arrived in town. She was with them, and invited me to join them for dinner, not an event I looked forward to. I began to organize my notes, typing them on sheets of yellow paper torn from a lined legal pad instead of tapping them into the computer terminal. Call me old-fashioned, but I still love typewriters, empty sheets of paper waiting to be filled with words, and the privacy of one, lone, hard copy of a file. Worse than having somebody look over your shoulder while you work is to have them do it electronically. Anyone at the *News,* if clever, could access whatever anyone else entered into the VDTs, which are all linked to a central computer. Editors snoop on reporters; reporters snoop on editors and each other. That is their business, it is what they do. With the right equipment, they can even do it from outside the building.

I opened a file for each of the cops. The best time to catch them at home would be in the hours before they left for work. I hoped to hit them all the same night; I didn't want to give them the chance to match notes on my questions and rehearse their stories. Taking people by surprise, I'd found, usually resulted in the most truthful answers, or enough devious confusion to make the lies obvious. At least that was my experience.

Needing to map out an itinerary, I went up to the city desk to get a fix on the cops' neighborhoods from the big blue city directory. Getting lost is easy in Dade County. I've lived here all my life, and I do it all the time. Streets to nowhere end in canals, waterways, farm fields, or swamps. The secret is in knowing the through streets and the grid pattern, which divided into northeast, northwest, southeast, and southwest. Flagler Street is the north-south dividing line, and Miami Avenue divides east from west.

Unfortunately, all the municipalities didn't follow the system. Miami Beach has no NE, NW, SE, or SW designations, and wealthy Coral Gables reflects old Spain, with Ponce de Leon Boulevard, Alhambra, Segovia, and Aragon, names found only on short squat curbstones, unlit and impossible to read after dusk. That upscale bedroom community favors the attitude that if you do not know the exact location of your destination, then you are not welcome in their city.

No wonder bewildered tourists keep stopping to ask directions from strangers who draw guns and rob them.

The big Bresser's City Directory lists the intersecting streets and landmarks around any address. My phone rang as I was running my finger down Machado's block, checking for a through street. I sighed impatiently, tempted to let it ring until the caller was switched to voice mail. I felt an undercurrent of urgency, like a bloodhound on the scent. But the call might be important, so I marked the page with a scrap of paper, plodded dutifully to my desk, and unenthusiastically answered. It took a moment for what the caller said to sink in, then I shrieked as though I had won the lottery.

"Ryan! Is it really you? Where the hell are you?"

"Mexico City. At the airport, Britt."

"Mexico City?" I was laughing, although tears stung my eyes.

"Look Britt, I don't have much time. They want to put me on a flight to Toronto."

"Toronto?" I repeated, dimly aware that a crowd had begun to form around my desk. "It's Ryan!" I cried, nodding at them, and cupping my right hand over my ear to block out their applause and cheers. Getchen lingered on the fringe, and I saw a look of relief in her eyes. I couldn't even feel angry at her at that moment.

"Yeah, I don't have a passport or any papers with me," Ryan was saying, "so they won't let me stay here. And I can't prove I'm an American citizen . . ."

"How did you get to Mexico City?"

"From Cuba, on Mexicana Airways."

"Cuba!"

"Yeah," he said sheepishly. "Where was Lottie? She didn't call at midnight, so I thought my radio was malfunctioning. I'd had a couple of beers, and when I stood up to get better reception, it slipped out of my hand. Sank like a rock."

"Oh Ryan, they were singing and playing the guitar . . ."

"I got swept south, past the reefs, by the current. I saw sharks. Big ones, Britt. I give them all my food to keep 'em happy. I threw out messages, in Coors bottles."

"I knew that was you! I told Lottie she should have checked them!"

"I ran out of sunscreen, and the batteries in my portable TV got wet. A Cuban fishing boat finally picked me up. They saw the Soviet inner tubes and thought I was trying to escape from the island, so they turned me over to a patrol boat. They took me to Mariel. I finally convinced them I was a gringo, but the military thought I was CIA, or a drug smuggler. They questioned me for twelve hours and finally let me go, but the tide wouldn't quit pushing me back along the coastline. I kept getting picked up again by other boats and taken back to the same military guys. They finally gave up pushing me off the coast and put me on a plane for Mexico City. Put Lottie on."

"She's out to dinner, with your folks."

"Mom and Dad? What are they doing there?"

"Getting ready to plan a funeral, Ryan. We've all been so scared. We thought you were lost at sea. The Coast Guard is still searching for you. Geez, you would have loved your obit. They've had three people working on it."

"Ha, ha, ha. It had better be good. Hey, Britt. Can somebody go by my apartment and get my passport and a credit card?"

"Ryan, wait! Don't get on the plane to Toronto." Word of mouth had already reached the executive offices, and gray suits were joining the crowd. One had snatched up the phone on Ryan's desk and already had lawyer Mark Seybold on hold.

"Call the Czechoslovakian embassy," somebody had directed, after hearing me mention Cuba. In the absence of diplomatic relations with Cuba, cases involving Americans were handled through the Czechs.

I handed the phone off to Fred Douglas, and sat at my desk laughing in sheer delight and relief. I caught sight of Gretchen shaking her head in exasperation, as if to ask what that pesky Ryan would do next, and managed to totally dislike her again.

Lottie and I went to meet him at the airport before dawn. She was sunburned and peeling, mad as hell at Eric, and disappointed that we had not seen Larry Zink and Steve, who had been put on hold during the crisis. "What kind of sunblock do you use?" she demanded as we waited.

"I don't use any," I said truthfully. "I never burn, just tan."

"I do hate you," she grumbled. "Blond hair and green eyes, and you never burn."

"Hey, I always wished I had red hair and fair skin, like yours, but I take after my dad."

Ryan came home on a 6 A.M. flight, wearing a camouflage shirt and pants, sunbronzed, aglow, his eyes filled with the excitement of the adventure he had to write. He pressed his lips to the tarmac like all the Cuban refugees.

We hugged him off his feet.

I envied his brief sojourn, or several brief sojourns, in Cuba. I yearn to travel there someday, to trace the roots and the steps of my father, to walk up San Juan Hill, and stroll the beaches of Veradero. But, for now, I go there only in dreams, and they will have to suffice until the man who ordered him killed is no longer in power.

It felt so good to have Ryan home. You never realize how much you cherish your friends until you are afraid they are gone.

THIRTEEN

The message from Officer Francie Alexander was left in the daylight. Unusual for her. I dialed the number, and imagined her answering in the darkness of her blacked-out apartment in the middle of a brilliant South Florida day.

She sounded as though I had roused her from a sound sleep. "It's me, Francie. I'm sorry. I should have waited until tonight. I'll call you later."

"No, Britt, this is important," she mumbled. "I left the phone on, hoping you would call." I could hear her work herself into a sitting position, trying to sort out her sleep-skewed thoughts. "Listen, last night, I heard somebody run you on the radio."

"What?"

"Right after roll call, I heard somebody ask what kind of car you drove. I didn't say anything and couldn't see who asked the question, but it sounded like one of the weightlifters. The room was full of people, but it was low-key, a one-on-one question as we were moving out. I didn't hear the answer, but later, around 2:30 A.M., somebody raised the dispatcher and ran you. To see if your license was current, if you had any wants, warrants, outstanding tickets. It was as though somebody had you pulled over on a traffic stop."

"I was home asleep at 2:30."

"I figured. What's going on Britt? Whoever did that has your age, your license number, your home address."

"Goddammit, what's going on?" I remembered the threatening phone call, and my hand holding the receiver trembled. I felt indignant and, I had to admit it, a little scared.

"Maybe one of the guys has a crush on you?"

"You don't think that's it, do you?"

"Do you?"

"No."

"It's about D. Wayne Hudson, isn't it," she said, more statement than question. "There has been some grumbling, more than usual, about the paper and you. The guys were just beefing and mouthing off. I defended you a few times, saying you were just doing your job, but they're really pissed off."

"Hey, Francie, act like you don't even know me with those guys. They're your backup. Don't catch any crap because of me. I'll fight my own battles. I know you're my friend, you don't have to prove it. I'm really glad you told me about this. Give me a call if you hear anything else."

"Sure."

"Go back to sleep, Francie."

"Britt?"

"Yeah?"

"Be careful."

"You know it. Give Bitsy a hug. See you soon. Pleasant dreams."

The best recourse for me now was to work like hell on the story, put it in the newspaper, and get it over with. Nothing is older than yesterday's news. No matter what the result, things would get back to normal. People forget fast.

My mother had also left a message. Her voice was excited when I returned the call. "I've got a surprise for you, dear. Can you meet me on your way home?"

"I wasn't going home. I'm working tonight."

"Well can you spare a few minutes?"

"Sure," I said, hesitantly.

"We're working late, too. Inventory. Then I'm meeting one of the girls from my building for dinner. But I have just got to see you first!"

"Okay." The surprise part worried me. "I was going to stop by La Esquina for a bite. Want me to bring you anything from there?" I didn't know why I bothered to ask.

She hesitated before saying no, as if bewildered by the offer.

We agreed to meet later at the bar in a restaurant in her neighborhood, up on Biscayne Boulevard. I drove to La Esquina first. The meat empanadas were hearty and the advice free, as usual. "Regardless of anything," Maggie said, "family and your children, they are the most important. You are so young, you should get married. The streets are so hard, it is not easy to find a nice man. Aren't you afraid to write stories about violence? That should be left to the men. It would be nice if you wrote pretty things, society things." Her eyes brightened with an idea. "Interview Julio Iglesias!"

"Why," Luis, the counterman, demanded, "does your newspaper call Fidel 'president'? Why not tell the truth and call him the tyrant or the dictator who covers the island in blood?"

"President," I said patiently, "is his title. We only report the news. It's not up to us to give our opinions of him. All the world knows he is a dictator."

Luis glared. "How will he fall?"

"Perhaps," I said, "he will kill himself, when he knows the end is near."

Luis didn't like that one. "Fidel is too much of a coward to commit suicide!" he cried. "You work for an anti-Cuban institution, a tool of the communists!"

I escaped into the night, clutching my cardboard take-out container of Cuban coffee. I would need it, I thought. This would be a long evening.

Driving north on the Boulevard, I passed the run-down motels that once drew free-spending tourists and businessmen but were now frequented by hookers and transients, stopped at the out-of-town newsstand on Seventy-ninth Street, bought a *New York Times*, and continued north, through the residential neighborhoods of Miami Shores and the condos of North Miami.

My mother's convertible was in the parking lot. She was smoking and sipping a Manhattan at the bar, wearing a classic navy blue blazer with a matching skirt.

Her smile faded when she took in my attire. I had forgotten what I was wearing.

"Isn't that the same white dress you had on last time I saw you?" she said, incredulous. "With those awful pockets!"

I smiled gaily and perched on the stool next to her. "I washed it between wearings, Mom. I've been busy this week, and it's easy."

"People will think it's the only thing you own."

"I'm sure they're all alarmed," I said, and ordered a Perrier.

"Well, anyway, that's not why we're here. This," she said proudly, "is for you." She presented me with a shiny, lacquered shopping bag. Something inside was wrapped in layers of tissue paper. Oh, no, I hoped fervently, as I unwrapped it, it couldn't be the handbag, it was far too small; it couldn't be. It was.

"I just couldn't resist. It was far too fabulous a buy. Now Britt, I know you said you didn't want it, but you'll love it. Look, it's just absolutely precious," she trilled.

"It is beautiful," I said sadly. That was the truth. "But I don't think I can use it." I opened it, then closed it again with a smart snap. "It's way too small. No place for my beeper, or a notebook. Look, it's even too short for my comb."

"Carry a smaller comb, Britt. Or get one of those little folding combs."

"It's far too expensive to just sit on a shelf in my closet," I said, shaking my head and folding it back into the tissue paper.

"Just try it for a few days, Britt. That's all I ask. You'd be amazed at how the right accessories spruce up your wardrobe."

"If I used it, Mom, I'd have to carry the rest of my stuff around with me in a shopping bag. How stylish would that look?"

"It can't be returned," she hissed. "It was on sale. I'm trying to help. You will never meet a suitable man running around like that . . ."

I almost told her about Kendall McDonald, but held back. Just as well, I thought, as she went on. "Miami is full of doctors, lawyers, and businessmen, but you don't meet them covering the stories you do, and you never have time to socialize."

She wouldn't consider McDonald suitable, I thought. Of course she had married a man who was either a terrorist or a guerrilla fighter, depending on which side you talked to. Why did everybody seem to think that the solution to all life's problems was a man? I had always found that they just seemed to complicate your life.

"Take tonight as an example," she said. "What is it that you're working on?"

"It could be an important story, Mom."

She sighed, savagely extinguishing her cigarette in the ashtray. "It's the one you told me about, isn't it, the one that's antagonizing everyone?"

I nodded. "Mom, think back. When I was a baby, was I ever in state custody, at any time, for any reason?"

"Of course not," she said, annoyed. "What kind of a mother do you think I was? Why on earth would you ask such a thing?"

"I dunno."

"You do come up with the strangest ideas."

FOURTEEN

S o far it was unanimous. Nobody wanted me working on the D. Wayne Hudson story: not Kendall McDonald, Gretchen Platt, the police department or my mother. Maybe somebody else, too. When I left the restaurant and walked into the parking lot, the two right-side tires on my T-Bird were flat.

I tried not to be paranoid. Maybe it was something I had run over; maybe it was the restaurant valet, offended that I had parked the car myself; maybe it was random vandalism. Maybe not.

My mother had driven off in a snit while I paid the bartender. She had snatched up the tiny purse and departed after I declined to go out with her best friend's visiting nephew.

Since I had only one spare tire, I needed help. Service station lights beckoned from the other side of Biscayne Boulevard, about three blocks south. It seemed quicker to walk there than call, and perhaps I could work off the empanadas that now resided like rocks behind my navel.

This stretch of the boulevard was not pedestrian-friendly, with no sidewalk and no crosswalk. Cars whizzed by, catching me in the glare of their lights. Lucky I was wearing my white dress; less chance of being hit, I thought, as I darted across four lanes.

The station was spacious, bright, and clean but only open for self-service gasoline. The lone attendant, a cashier, was crouched behind bulletproof glass.

"Exact change only. No mechanic on duty after 6 P.M.," the sign said. I asked anyway, but there was no one to help me. I used the outside pay phone to check the office for messages.

Kendall McDonald had called right after I left. I didn't recognize the number, so it had to be his home. I fished for another quarter. He answered on the first ring.

"You called?"

"Yeah," he greeted me. "A complaint. My newspaper didn't arrive today. I checked the roof, the hedges, nothing."

"Sorry," I said. "My bicycle broke down."

A semi rumbled by about ten feet away, and I couldn't hear his response. "Where the heck are you?"

"By the side of the road on north Biscayne Boulevard. It's a long story."

A carload of boisterous teenage boys hooted and howled as they rolled by.

"Give me the short version."

"Came out of a restaurant and found two flat tires. Hiked to a gas station, but nobody's on duty after six. So here I am."

"What's that location again?"

I told him.

"I'll be there in ten minutes."

"You don't have to do this," I said, hoping like hell he would.

"I know. Stay right there. See you in a few minutes."

Stay here, I thought, how could I go elsewhere? I sat down on a wooden bench in front of the useless service station, watching for McDonald and smoothing the skirt of my much-maligned dress. Hell, this had been my favorite, packed well, no-iron, washed like a handkerchief.

In less than ten minutes, the Cherokee swung off the roadway in a cloud of dust and pulled right up in front of me. He wore white cotton twill pants and an open-necked shirt, and looked like the best thing I had ever seen.

He asked for my keys when we got back to the restaurant parking lot, walked to the rear of my car, and then just stood there, without opening the trunk. I got out of the jeep and joined him.

"When did you wash your car last?"

"Okay," I said. "I'm embarrassed. I know it needs it, but that's the least of my worries at the moment."

"Look," he said, his expression odd.

I followed his eyes. At a certain angle, in the dim light, it was easy to make out. In the thin coat of dust on the trunk lid of my T-Bird, somebody had scrawled: BRITT, WE WERE HERE.

"Could that have been there before tonight?"

"Maybe. I'm not sure," I said. "I haven't been in the trunk for a couple of days. But considering the circumstances, I tend to doubt it."

"Me too."

I suddenly felt uneasy, as if we were being watched.

He worked silently and efficiently, putting the spare on one wheel and removing the other flat. He tossed both tires into the back of the Cherokee and drove us to a garage in North Miami. The owner removed a three-inch rivet from each tire and patched the holes, warning that I should replace both. We returned to the restaurant where McDonald put one on the car and the other in the trunk to replace the spare.

Too late to go back to work now.

"I'd like to buy you a drink," I gestured toward the restaurant, "but somehow I suspect it's not a swell idea to leave my car parked out here."

"Good thinking." He wiped his hands on a rag, scanning the traffic and the buildings around us.

"Let's get out of here."

"I've got to wash my hands and clean up somewhere."

"I have soap, hot water, and cold wine at my place."

He hesitated, his gaze intense. I could feel my hormones slam-dancing. "I'll follow you," he said.

I could swear I felt it physically when I wrenched my eyes from his. I kept the Cherokee in my rear-view mirror sights all the way home, alternately asking myself, "Are you crazy?" and answering, "Go for it, Britt."

My landlady, Mrs. Goldstein, was out front. I introduced them, trying hard to look innocent.

"Sorry," he said, to explain his appearance, which still seemed swell to me. "I just changed some tires and need to wash up."

She nodded, her expression coy. When I glanced back from the front door of my apartment, she was smiling and giving me the thumbs-up sign.

"Nice lady," he said, as I used my key.

"First rate," I agreed. "She keeps an eye on my apartment when I'm out of town, and lets me putter around in her garden whenever I get the urge. You would love her husband; he was a prosecutor in New York until he retired. A man after your own heart."

"I prefer a woman after my own heart." He stood just inside the door, watching me.

"Sit down, I'll get you a drink."

"Forget it," he said.

My heart sank. I thought he was leaving, then saw the glint in his eyes.

"That's a beautiful dress."

I grinned like a fool and almost laughed. "You really like this old thing?"

"It makes you look like an angel."

"I'm not."

"Good."

He moved toward me, then stopped. "I better wash my hands."

They were grimy from tossing my tires around. So were his white trousers. I didn't care.

"Oh, no, you don't," I said, and hugged him, pressing my cheek against his shirt.

"Ummmmm," he crooned, arms folding around me. I felt the wall hard behind my back as he pressed forward, his mouth on mine.

"I warned you," he whispered huskily. "Now look at that." A dark smudge on my right sleeve.

I whispered in his ear. "Then I guess we'll have to wash it, and your pants, too."

"You've got a washing machine in here?" he murmured, between kisses.

"Outside the back door. Just big enough for my dress and your pants to get all sudsy and swirl around together."

He raised his eyebrows. "I guess that means we have to take them off."

"I guess it does."

Our bodies moved together again as he kissed me. We were making the framed print behind me hang crooked; in another moment it might fly off the wall altogether.

"Did I ever show you the rest of my apartment?"

"No," he sounded breathless.

"Like to see it?" My lips felt swollen, my bra too tight.

This was not exactly a guided tour. We walked together like some clumsy, four-legged creature. I backed up and steered in the right direction, his mouth on mine all the while. We landed on my flowered comforter, me fumbling with his trousers, he fumbling with the buttons on my dress.

A soft tropical breeze billowed the sheers at the windows, and the room was filled with the scent of fragrant night blossoms. I had one last sharp moment of reservation. "The department? Our jobs?" I mumbled against his throat as he kissed my ears and my forehead.

He was not so swept away by passion that the thought did not penetrate. His eyes locked onto mine, and at that moment we both knew that this could be a big mistake—but it sure as hell was not going to stop us.

The slow-moving ceiling fan paddled over my bed, making me dizzy. My dress was bunched up around my waist, then around my neck. I leaned forward and was soon free of it.

So we did what Gretchen had suspected all along, and it was wonderful. Then we did it again. And then we discussed it.

"The chief always says he wants better police-press relations." He lay naked and relaxed, with me curled up inside the curve of his arm.

"I can tell you for a fact, this is not what he had in mind," I said, raising up on one elbow and pushing back my hair. "What if he could see us now?"

"Hate to lose another chief to heart attack. We could plead insanity."

"Or just say we took him literally."

Eventually we traipsed out to the kitchen, weak and exhausted, and opened the refrigerator. A gloomy sight. McDonald peered over my shoulder at the half-empty can of cat food on the top shelf.

"Don't even think about it," he said. "I would know it wasn't tuna."

"Moldy cheese?" I said, sliding open the bin.

"Just what I love," he said, his finger lightly skating figure eights down my spine until I shivered.

Billy Boots had responded as usual to the sound of the refrigerator door and curled around our bare legs. I found some ham, fresh lettuce, and tomato. McDonald sliced the bread, and I fixed him a sandwich and a glass of wine while his pants and my dress followed our lead, tumbling around together in the washer and dryer. After he finished his sandwich, he led me back to bed and we made love again.

The night sky was wild and wonderful. I opened all the windows and blinds wider, drew back the curtains, and slipped back into bed beside McDonald. The cool ocean breeze caressed our bodies, carrying in with it the music of wind chimes and the exotic haunting perfume from the ylang-ylang tree outside. We were lulled to sleep, our bodies tangled together as though bedded down in a windblown meadow full of flowers.

There was a faint light in the sky when something woke me. McDonald was moving quietly about the room gathering his scattered clothing. He had succeeded in finding all but his trousers. He bent to plant a light kiss on my forehead.

"They're in the dryer," I whispered.

"Ah ha," he said, remembering. "Lucky I didn't have to beat feet in a hurry." He sat on the edge of the bed, stroking my hair.

"Hope nobody stole them during the night. Occasionally that happens, with panties and things," I teased.

"What?"

"Just kidding." I sat up, slipped on his shirt, padded barefoot through the kitchen, and stepped out the backdoor. The sky looked bruised and threatening. I plucked the dress and the trousers from the dryer, shook them out, and ducked back inside.

"Gee, my dress was there, but your pants were gone." I tried to look serious, holding them behind my back.

He took my face gently in his hands, kissed it, and, when I was thoroughly distracted, wrestled away his trousers.

"Hey," he said. "I wish I could stay, but I've gotta get home and change. I've got an eight-thirty bond hearing. Remember Placido Quintana?"

"What? You can't call in sick?"

He laughed. "Mind if I take a shower?"

"Nope."

"Join me?"

"Sure thing." He took my hand.

We splashed each other, wrestled around under the spray, and scrubbed each others' backs while he got psyched for court by singing, "I Shot the Sheriff."

"No, you didn't," I whispered over his slick, soapy, wet shoulder. "You nabbed the police reporter."

He stepped out of my shower, hair damp and tousled, his skin all ruddy and pink. "I wish 'our song' was more romantic," I pouted, as he held the blow drier over my hair.

We slowly sipped coffee and eyed each other across my tiny kitchen table. "What a way to start the day," he said.

"Somebody has to do it. Maybe I should have car trouble more often."

He frowned. "What you had was a lot more than just car trouble."

"I know, I know," I said, wondering if I could somehow factor the cost of two new tires into my expense account. "I'm gonna wrap up the Hudson story and get this thing over with as quick as I can."

"That goddamn story. You never back off, do you?" He put his cup down.

I shook my head and tried to change the subject by plopping myself on his lap and kissing him soundly. He was not placated. "Is all this about getting the goddamn story?"

"You know better," I said, spine stiffening in indignation.

His eyes turned the color of sheet metal. "Be careful, Britt," he said at the door. "Keep turning over rocks, and sooner or later something ugly jumps out at you."

I am never lonely. I love my life and living alone, doing whatever I please whenever I want to, like a spoiled child. But when the door closed behind that man, my apartment suddenly seemed empty. It had been a long time since I'd felt that close to anyone. I tidied the kitchen, thinking about the phone call, the flattened tires, and the message on my car. Suddenly, instead of feeling great, I was bummed out.

Pulling on shorts and a T-shirt, I jogged the two blocks to the beach and ran the length of the boardwalk, turned, and started back again. The heavy tread of another runner thudded behind me. The sound had always been a comfort in the past; someone else sharing the same exhilaration. Now the steps, gaining rapidly, seemed ominous, filling me with dread. I scanned the beach and the boardwalk ahead. Few people were about. No witnesses. The threatening skies had kept most early risers at home. I picked up my pace, but he continued to gain. Heart pounding, I braced myself, my hands balled into tight fists, as the runner neared. And passed. A familiar face, a black boxer in training from the Fifth Street Gym, wearing a hooded sweatshirt and carrying a five-pound weight in each hand. He was out here every morning, rain or shine.

My own angst made me angry, angry that one of my simple pleasures had become a frightening experience. How could I let anyone, any story do this to me? Why, I asked myself, was McDonald so angry? The answer seemed obvious. The cops who had chased D. Wayne Hudson are hiding something terrible, I thought, and he knows what it is.

The sea was shaded tones of gray, green, and silver. Black clouds stacked up on the horizon, and even though the sun was shining, a drenching downpour began to fall.

My mother had told me when I was a little girl that whenever the sun shone through the rain, it meant that the devil was beating his wife. I remembered running out into the backyard and putting my ear to the ground, but I never heard a thing.

FIFTEEN

On my way to work, I stopped at a little art supply store on Lincoln Road and bought a set of twelve jumbo color pencils, easy for little fingers to hold, with thick nontoxic lead in rainbow shades. Then I picked up half a dozen jelly donuts.

Onnie and I devoured donuts and drank coffee while Darryl examined his new art supplies. Though scarred, the place looked much neater and cleaner, even cheerful. Probably because all the men in the family were still in jail.

Darryl and his mom looked pretty good. This woman was no dummy, I learned. She had graduated from Northwestern High and had attended Miami-Dade Community College for a year-and-a-half. I could see where Darryl got his smarts. She had wanted to be a librarian, but her last job was for a firm that cleaned downtown offices at night. It turned out that I had covered the case that put Randolph, Darryl's older brother, age nine, in Youth Hall. He had been with bigger boys who splashed lighter fluid on a dozing wino. Then one of them lit a match. The idea was not original; they had seen a similar scenario in a TV movie the night before.

The lone bright spot in recent memory had been D. Wayne Hudson. He had picked up Randolph and two other Youth Hall inmates on Friday afternoons, driving them downtown to the big public library and cultural center to pick out books and see the displays.

I did not bring up the topic during my brief visit, but as I left, Onnie said, "I still have that phone number you gave me, the one for the shelter."

"If you do decide to do anything, keep me posted. Let me know where you two are." She nodded, as Darryl came running with a new masterpiece he had just dashed off: a house, a sturdy tree, and what could have been a dog, or maybe a cat. "This is wonderful," I said. "Look at these colors!"

"You can take it home with you," he said shyly. "It's for you."

"I would love to hang this on my refrigerator," I said, "but . . ." His eyes grew huge. "The artist has to sign it first."

His mother guided his hand as he solemnly scrawled his name in blue in the lower right hand corner.

Now I had two men in my life, I thought as I went on to work, wondering how long either of them would stay.

It felt good to see Ryan back at his desk, working feverishly on his rafting story—it had grown into an exclusive two-parter on how he had followed the rafters' perilous paths back to Cuba. Gretchen and managing editor John Murphy hovered behind him, reading over his shoulder and congratulating each other. Gretchen glowed, looking very much the fast-track executive in a pale Chanel-style suit with built-up Joan Crawford shoulders, as she accepted congratulations for her creativity and enterprise. The woman had emerged smelling like a rose again.

Fred Douglas, my editor on this project, thought that I should not show up at the police officers' homes alone. He suggested that another reporter or a photographer come along. Sounded okay to me, as long as it could be Lottie.

We took her car, equipped with a two-way radio to the city desk, and a police scanner. Anybody who thought my T-Bird was loaded with the tools of my trade had never traveled in Lottie's wheels. She goes her way, and her world goes with her. Stashed in the trunk of her company car are an assortment of cameras, lenses, and film; a tripod; a hard hat; blankets; sunscreen; insect repellent; a bright yellow rain slicker; sunglasses; rubber boots; rope; knee pads; hats; towels; plastic bags; HandiWipes; apples, oranges, granola bars, and bottled water; flares; flashlights; jumper cables; a tire repair kit; road maps; Spanish-language and Creole dictionaries; a police whistle; and an English racing seat mounted on a stake that can be driven into the ground to provide a portable perch for waiting.

Whenever big news breaks fast, Lottie arrives first. Also tucked into the trunk is a brown cardboard accordion folder full of neatly filed plans and diagrams, detailing all entrances to the city's major buildings, hotels, the convention center, and all the runways and terminals at Miami International Airport.

We are each equipped with Q-beams, intensely powerful lights that plug into the cigarette lighter. On a job that is unpredictable, they come in handy. The late nights and bright lights of the city are bordered by unlit rural areas as dark as a coal mine at midnight. They stretch out to remote swamps, where a small plane could go down and not be found for years.

We use the Q-beams most often to find street addresses at night, holding it at arm's length out the car window in case somebody shoots at it.

Inside Lottie's Chrysler are packets of pictures she intends to someday deliver to people she photographed. Eventually she spills coffee on them and has to throw them out.

According to my carefully mapped-out route, we would drop in on the Blackburns first, work our way back north to the body builders in a West Dade subdivision, then Carpenter in Miami Springs, and Ted Ferrell in Miami Shores.

"How is Ryan's story coming?" Lottie wanted to know, as we pulled out of the covered parking under the building.

"It's not a story anymore, it's a two-part series," I said, buckling my seat belt. "And guess who is queen for a day in the glass-front offices?"

"Hell-all-Friday! No! It isn't?"

"Yes! Gretchen has more lives than a cat. How many times can she land on her feet?"

"She steps in shit, and it turns to gold," Lottie lamented. "I thought for sure she'd get her ass fired this time."

"No chance. The managing editor took her to lunch today. She'll probably get a fat bonus for her brainstorm."

"It almost would have been worth sacrificing Ryan to get her run outta this town once and for all." Lottie looked sullen.

"You don't mean that," I chuckled.

"I know." She sighed and steered around a carload of tourists, asleep at the switch when the light turned green, and accelerated up the expressway ramp.

Lottie is a great wheel person, another of the few drivers I feel comfortable with. We had both taken police combat driving courses, and our reputation for being hard on the *News*'s cars was undeserved.

We had no trouble locating our destination, with her driving and my navigating. The Blackburns lived a few blocks apart in South Miami, in one of those mazelike residential neighborhoods full of cul-de-sacs and dead ends. There seemed to be no one home at Roscoe's place. We approached the door together, Lottie carrying only one small, unobtrusive camera so as not to spook anyone. In the driveway sat a dusty old Chevie van with a Confederate flag tag on the front. No one answered the doorbell. We gave it some time, in case he was sleeping. The lone sign of life was a liver-colored hound that bayed at us from a wire kennel at the side of the house.

From one side of the front walk we could see a modest pool in the back. It didn't look used much; the whole place seemed to lack a woman's touch.

Lottie was thinking the same thing. "Bet he's divorced, or his current wife has hauled ass." She cooed and talked soothingly to the hound dog, who stopped barking and cocked an ear to listen. He looked neglected. So did the house. I scrawled "Please call me," on the back of one of my cards and stuck it in the door.

We hit Roland's place five minutes later, and had better luck.

Two pickups were in the drive, along with a single-engine bass boat, an eighteen-footer with a narrow draft, the kind you could take out into the flats and swamps. The name DURTBAG was lettered on the prow. The trucks were blue, identical models. Both had Fraternal Order of Police symbols on their tags.

"They're not gonna be thrilled to see us," I warned.

"Is anybody, ever?"

"Occasionally," I smiled smugly.

Lottie cut her eyes at me. "I knew you had somethin goin' on. You can explain later." At the door, she said, "You ring, you're sweet."

A woman answered. Young, blond, and heavily made up, she wore a crop top over skintight short shorts. She couldn't have been more than eighteen, if that.

She looked suspicious at finding two women on the doorstep. Her brow furrowed as she eyed us through the shadowy screen, chewing her lower lip and clutching a Budweiser can in her right hand. Country music was playing inside.

"Hi there," I said cheerfully. "Is . . ."

"We don't want any," she said, then licked her lips and grinned at how clever she was.

"Officer Blackburn," I said, "we're here to see him."

"Which one?" She worked her mouth into a pout, doubtful again.

"Both, if they're here." I beamed, oozing friendly confidence, and reached for the door handle, "Can we come in?"

Looking sulky, she reluctantly shoved the screen door open. I had one foot inside when a man came up behind her. "Who is it, Jaycey?" He wore jeans and a T-shirt. It was Roland, maybe Roscoe. He stopped short. I smiled and offered my hand, stepping forward into the room.

"Jesus," he said, the color leaving his face. "Who gave you this address?"

"Hi," I said. "You remember me, Britt Montero, the *News*. I've been trying to reach you."

"How did you get this address?" he said slowly, emphasizing each word.

His mirror image, minus the T-shirt, had appeared behind him.

"What are you doing here?" his twin said.

"We've been trying to reach you," I said, stepping aside, enabling Lottie to ease in next to me.

"Just one damn minute," the shirtless one said. He turned to his brother. "Are you crazy? Letting them in here?"

"I wanna know how they got this address," the first one said. "And I didn't let them in." He turned to glare at Jaycey, who took two steps back and tried to look innocent.

"You know it's not difficult to get somebody's address," I said quietly. "I need to ask you some questions for a story about the death of D. Wayne Hudson. This is my friend, Lottie. She's also with the *News*."

"Get outta my house and offa my property," the first one said.

"You must be Roland." Lottie smiled warmly, her voice friendly and down-home. "Howdy. I like your music. Charley Daniels, my favorite." She looked at me as though I was a caution. "Don't you pay her no mind; she don't mean to be pushy. She just gives people that impression sometimes. I'm not a reporter; I just shoot pictures."

Out the corner of my eye, I saw Jaycey's hands fly to her hair and begin to primp.

"Out," the first one said, his expression darkening. "Get outta my house."

"I really think we should talk about this. Clear it all up," I said.

"You got no right bothering us at home," the other said belligerently. "We don't have to talk to you. Contact us through the department."

"But you haven't returned my calls," I said patiently. "This was the only way to reach you."

The first one moved toward us, hairy arms spread, as if to sweep us out the door. "Okay, okay," I said, giving him a hands-off sign and stepping outside. "Then it's accurate to say that you refused to comment?"

He hesitated.

"Why don't you come out here and talk?" I invited.

"I sure wanted to hear the rest of that record," Lottie said hopefully.

"Sorry babe," he said, looking at her as though he might be interested, if she wasn't with me and didn't work for the *News*.

The shirtless one said, "Wanna take a picture, take this." He had his hand on his zipper.

"Look," I said, turning to the other one, "there is going to be a story. There are unanswered questions. You guys are career cops, you've won medals, honors. You've got a lot invested in the job. You deserve the chance to tell your side. All I'm trying to do is give you that chance."

He seemed to consider it.

"If you didn't do anything wrong, you oughta tell her," Lottie coaxed.

"What do you mean *wrong*?" he blustered. "We . . .

"Shut the hell up!" The barechested Blackburn stormed forward, chin jutting at an angry angle. "This is your brother talking!" he shouted. "Don't say another fucking word to them!" The screen door swung shut between us. So did the solid oak door behind it. Before it slammed I said, "Give me a call, if you change your mind."

Inside we could hear Jaycey's high-pitched squeal. "Don't you take it out on me! I didn't let them in. They pushed their way inside!"

Lottie and I stood on the stoop, ejected and dejected. "We nearly had him," I sighed. "If only his brother hadn't been here."

"Twin charmers," she said. "Double trouble. Can you tell 'em apart?" she asked, as we trudged back to the car. The sun was dropping fast.

"I hear their wives couldn't."

"That must be interestin' . . ." she said thoughtfully. "One of 'em must have a mole or a birthmark, someplace."

"Let's not even think about it."

"I always meet up with such fascinatin' people when I'm with you."

"I never said this would be fun. Two down, four to go," I said, looking at my watch. "Look at it this way. It can't get much worse."

I was wrong.

Machado lived near Fontainebleau Park, in west Dade.

A flashy red Firebird with custom trim looked like it was doing sixty miles an hour standing still in his driveway. A shiny Harley Low Rider Custom sat in the open garage; boys and their toys, I thought.

Before I even raised my hand to knock, the door was flung open as though someone was expected. No way to slip inside past *him*. He filled the opening, his weight-lifter's body straining against his gray sweats. Half a dozen religious medals hung from two thick gold chains. His swarthy skin was pitted by what looked like a case of terminal acne. He wasted no words on small talk.

"Who gave you this address?"

Funny how the people who are expert at getting *your* address are always so shocked when you show up at *theirs*.

He looked cornered, already agitated. "I just want to talk to you," I said, hoping to sound casual. Braced for him to slam the door, I was stunned when he shouted "I got nothing to say!" and lunged forward, rushing out past us.

Lottie and I, shoved together when he came barreling out, watched in amazement as he bolted to the Harley in the garage and kick-started the machine. It caught on the second try, and he thundered out to the street, nearly lost it at the foot of the driveway, then roared south at a high rate of speed.

I stood there with my mouth open.

"Strong as an ox, with the brains of a tractor." Lottie nudged me with her elbow, as the rumble of Machado's bike faded in the distance. "You must be onto one helluva story. Did you see that man's face? He's so paranoid, he thinks we're gonna chase after him. Bet he doesn't come home for days out of fear of us hidin' in the bushes."

"He's not even wearing a helmet. It's the law."

"I doubt any traffic cop will write him."

"He'd have to catch him first. Where do you think he's headed?"

"Dunno," she said. "Maybe home to his mama—or his lawyer's office."

"Three down, three to go."

Estrada was just a few blocks away. I half expected to see the Harley, but it wasn't there. There was a rice burner—a Kawasaki Ninja bike—and a shiny black Syclone, one of those racy pickups they say can outrun a Porche 911 Carrera on a short course. The tract house was modest, with a small, fenced-in front yard and straggly grass. It was dark now, the vast eastern sky dominated by the great square of Pegasus. We left the car parked on the grassy berm and hesitated outside the gate.

The porch light was on. Something about it didn't feel quite right to me. Maybe I was just spooked by the way the others had behaved, but I wasn't alone in my apprehension.

"Did you bring a gun?" Lottie asked quietly.

"I thought about it, but it seemed ridiculous. What the hell would we do with it? Shoot a cop?" This all seemed crazy, the good guys as bad guys.

Lottie nodded. "Let's do it," she said, and unlatched the gate.

The house and yard were quiet, too quiet. "What do you want to bet he asks how we got his address?" I said softly, pressing the doorbell.

"This is the one that tap dances on automobile hoods and shoots ceilings dead, am I right?"

"You've got it."

I sensed movement on the other side of the door, punched the bell again, and called. "Officer Estrada!"

The wooden door inched open, and I heard a strange snuffling from within, as though somebody or something inside was suffering a severe head cold.

"Who is it?"

"Officer Estrada?" I looked up, toward the voice, straining to see the speaker. "Britt Montero and Lottie Dane here, from the *News*. Can we talk to you?"

"Who the fuck is giving out our addresses?"

"They're public record," I said, weary of the question.

"Well you're on *private* property. I'm warning you once. Get your asses off it."

"You probably didn't get my messages. I need to talk to you about D. Wayne Hudson."

"I got a message for you." He yanked the door open. For one crazy moment I thought he might be inviting us in. He wasn't. He was letting something out.

"Pit bulls!" Lottie shrieked. Two of them burst out, snarling and scrabbling, short legs churning so fast that for a moment they seemed to run in place.

I glimpsed Estrada for an instant. He loomed in the doorway behind them, his eyes alight with malevolent glee. "Toro, Diablo, go get 'em! Get 'em!"

"Call them off! Call them off!" I yelled, as Lottie and I both ran for the gate.

He hooted in laughter as we fled screaming. I swatted the charging brindle across the muzzle with my notebook, the only thing I had to defend myself with. He tore it from my grasp and shook it wildly between powerful jaws. The other dog caught Lottie's ankle as we scrambled through the gate, screaming. "Call 'em off!" I yelled as she clung to the gate to stay upright.

A vicious rumble bubbled from his throat as the dog tried to take her down. He must have weighed sixty-five pounds. "Hold on," I screamed. I lunged toward the animal and jabbed at one eye with my pencil. He yelped and wheeled, snapping viciously as I recoiled. The pencil split in two, splinters flying, as Lottie and I tumbled together outside the gate. I dove at the latch, fumbling to be sure it was engaged as both dogs hurled themselves at it furiously.

"Oh, Lottie," I sobbed, trying to catch my breath. "How bad are you hurt?"

She leaned on me for support as we lurched to the safety of the car.

I heard Estrada's feral laughter as he came down the walk. Fearing he would open the gate, I slammed the car doors and rolled up the windows.

Lottie was wincing but still game. "You wanna try to get your notebook back?"

"No way. There was nothing in it anyhow. Let's get out of here." My hands shook uncontrollably as I inserted the ignition key. Estrada stood at the gate, spewing obscenities and grinning. In the tawny glow from the streetlight, he looked more dangerous than his dogs. He gave us the finger as we pulled out.

"I guess we can put that down as another 'No comment,' " Lottie said, rubbing her ankle.

My knees still rubbery, I pulled over in front of an open convenience store and turned on the interior light so we could examine the damage.

"Thank God for cowboy boots," Lottie said. The dog's teeth had left holes in the leather but did not break the skin. Her ankle was badly bruised, already swelling and discolored.

"He could have crushed the bone."

She nodded. "He was gettin' ready to do just that when you poked him in the damn eye."

"I didn't think he'd let go. They have a reputation for hanging on. They're four-legged land sharks! Remember my story on that woman jogger? Two pit bulls dragged her down and just maimed the hell out of her. She nearly died."

Lottie nodded. "I shot the pictures of Bobby Applegate," she said softly.

Who could forget the four-year-old mauled by his uncle's pit bull? The boy's disfigured face was being painstakingly restored by plastic surgeons in an endless series of operations. They hoped to finish by the time he was twenty-one. I shuddered involuntarily. "How could he do that to us? He's a police officer."

"You'd better hope it's not him they send if we ever need help and dial 911. I swear, I almost peed my pants."

"Want to call the cops and report this?" I asked.

"And say what? That we trespassed on this police officer's property and his watch dogs did their job? They'd laugh their asses off and most likely arrest us for trespassin'."

"Think we should call the city desk and tell them what happened?"

"And have 'em call us crybabies who cain't take the heat?" She turned in her seat and stared at me balefully.

She was right.

"How many more?"

"Two to go," I said. "You feel up to it?"

She nodded, still massaging her ankle.

"I'm sorry I got you into this, Lottie."

"Heellll," she said. "It's still more fun than the damn ten best-dressed women. Who's next?"

Carpenter's condo was a boxy building with designated parking spaces. I asked Lottie if she wanted to wait in the car. She did not. We located Lou Carpenter's name on a metal wall of mailboxes, and took the elevator to the third floor. The hallway was bleak. A vague smell of mildew mingled with combined cooking odors made me queasy.

I knocked, glancing nervously at Lottie.

"What could he have?" she whispered jauntily. "Rattlesnakes? Killer bees?"

During the delay that followed my knock, I had the distinct impression that we were being scrutinized through the tiny peephole. The door opened about two inches, then caught on a metal safety chain.

Carpenter peeped out. The one eye I could see looked weary. "Hey, Britt."

"Hi there," I said, moved almost to tears by any reception not openly hostile. "I need to talk to you about the night D. Wayne Hudson got killed."

"We talked," he said. "Nothing more I can say."

"Open the door," I said. "This is silly. We're not gonna break in and overpower you."

"I wish," he said with a morose smile, and closed the door. We heard the metallic rattle as he removed the chain. The door opened. He was standing on green shag carpet. The furniture behind him was spartan. He did not invite us in.

"What are you doing, Britt?" His tone was accusatory. "You shouldn't have come here."

"I'm writing a story about what happened to D. Wayne Hudson."

"I know." He sighed and seemed at a loss for words, refusing to meet my eyes.

I eased a fresh notebook out of my pocket.

"Tell me about D. Wayne's traffic accident."

He shifted position and shielded his eyes with one hand, as though blinded by bright light, though the hall behind us was dim.

"I'm eligible for retirement in six months, Britt." His voice was a tired monotone. "I've got alimony payments, a kid in college, another one still in high school. Things have changed a lot on the department." He leaned heavily against the doorjamb, as though for support. "Years ago I would have gone out as a lieutenant or higher. But I never even made sergeant. Made the list twice, but they had the mandate to promote minorities. I was still hoping to get stripes before I left, to goose up the pension."

His eyes belied the trace of hope in his voice.

"Years ago nobody woulda cared about something like this. A lot worse went on. A lot worse."

"What about the accident?"

"I wrote an accident report. You saw it."

"But what exactly happened?"

"Why do you ask questions when you already know all the answers?"

My stomach lurched, and I felt Lottie stir beside me.

"How did Hudson get hurt? Who hit him?"

He hesitated. The air felt dense between us.

"I can't, Britt. I don't want to be rude, but I just can't talk to you. Don't do this to me. Not now," he mumbled.

He projected the aura of someone ineffectual and almost helpless, not a man invested with enough power and authority to take away somebody's freedom, or their life.

"You're making a mistake," I told him. "You're the guy who signed your name to the report. There's going to be a story. Count on it. Why should you be the one to catch the heat?"

"Let me think about it," he said. "Let me talk to somebody."

"The FOP lawyer?"

He paused. "You always know everything, don't you? Never miss anything. Young and smart," he said vaguely, as though remembering a time when he might have considered himself young and smart. "I wasn't there when it happened, you know."

"You know what didn't happen."

He said nothing.

"Give me your number," I said matter-of-factly, "and I'll call you tomorrow."

Without argument, he recited his home number as I took it down.

Neither Lottie nor I dared speak until the elevator doors closed. "He's so close to spilling it, so close," she whispered.

I blew out a puff of air to ease the tension. "Just one more to go. One more."

The cops were obviously networking, signaling our visits ahead by telephone. Ted had probably been warned and was unlikely to cooperate, but I nurtured a slender hope because he seemed so decent, and I had difficulty believing him capable of participating in anything more than a cover-up for guilty colleagues.

The house stood on a quiet residential street with well-kept lawns and hedges. Two cars, a small Japanese model and a Buick, neither of them new, were parked in a circular blacktop driveway wrapped around a huge spreading ficus tree.

I rang several times, waited, then rang again. Lights were on inside. Ted finally answered the door himself, moving slowly. At first I didn't recognize him. The man who opened the door was not the flashy spit-and-polish honor cop I knew. This man looked smaller, was pale and rumpled, and hadn't shaved. His eyes were red-rimmed and bloodshot. He had apparently pulled on jeans and a T-shirt to answer our ring.

He simply stood there, his face growing paler.

"I'm sorry, did we wake you?"

"I was having trouble sleeping anyway." His voice was barely audible. He pushed the door open wide, then turned and walked toward the living room, shoulders stooped, running his fingers through his disheveled hair.

Lottie and I exchanged glances, then followed. I closed the door softly behind me, wondering where Betsy was. There were traces of her presence. Wholesome, delicious smells, like meat loaf and apple crisp, came from the kitchen. I inhaled deeply and vaguely wondered when I had eaten last.

Ted just stared, hollow-eyed.

"Betsy's next door," he finally said. "They're making Halloween costumes for the kids. I was trying to get some sleep."

He had not been warned, I realized. "You had the phone turned off?"

He looked up, a distracted look in his eyes. "Yeah." He thanked Lottie for the pictures she had taken that day in the project, and turned back to me. "How's the story coming?"

"Right along, I'm working on it."

His fingers danced nervously along the arm of the sofa where he sat.

"Who else have you talked to?"

"Roscoe and Roland, Estrada, Machado, Lou Carpenter." It was not a lie; we *had* talked to them, albeit briefly, before they slammed doors, ran away, or sicced vicious dogs on us.

He nodded and stared at the floor. "It was one of those things," he said softly. He lifted his eyes and looked directly into mine, his expression earnest, his voice dropping. "Just got out of hand. Beyond belief. Never should have happened."

"Who hit D. Wayne?" I asked, my heart thudding.

"One of the Latins. Estrada, I think, pulled him right out of the car window. He was a big guy, but he got dragged right out through the driver's side window." He tensed and leaned forward. "I can't be quoted, Britt. It's all gonna come down now. But you can't quote me by name, at least not now. Promise me?"

I hesitated, hating to promise, but I sure didn't want him to stop.

"Nobody can know I talked to you."

"You have my word." We both looked at Lottie, who nodded.

Suddenly he seemed talkative, almost relieved that we were there.

"I heard the BOLO go out, and just a minute later the Blackburns spotted him at Thirty-sixth and the Boulevard. They went after him, but he didn't stop."

"Why?" I looked up from my notebook.

Ted looked surprised. "They weren't in uniform; they were in an unmarked. He probably wasn't sure who they were."

Of course. All the police impersonators, robbers posing as cops, pulling people over, committing stick-ups, rapes, kidnapings, even murders. "I didn't realize they were in plainclothes that night."

"Sure." He looked at me sharply as though surprised that I had missed the obvious. "The unit number tells you that. They were supposed to be assisting on a prostitution detail, the john squad up at Seventy-ninth and the Boulevard."

"So D. Wayne Hudson may have thought he was being chased by robbers?" Lottie said.

"Well," Ted shrugged, "he pulled right over when the blue and whites joined in. I pulled up at the same time as Estrada and Machado. They were racing to see who could get to him first. The guy rolled down his window when they came up on him. And Estrada drug him right out that window."

"So there was no accident?" I asked, my vocal cords knotting.

"No," he said, and shook his head.

There was a sound behind us. Betsy stood in the doorway, wearing a black jumper over a white maternity top. She had something glittery with silver wings and a white sheet over her arm. Her eyes were big, her stomach huge. Her mouth formed an O, but nothing came out.

She walked into another room, apparently to hang up the costumes, then returned and sat down next to her husband. He reached for her hand, and she patted his.

"It's been hard to live with," he said softly, his face haggard. "I have kids, a family of my own. When I see mine, I think of his."

"What happened after Estrada got him out of the car?"

Betsy looked as though she wanted to interrupt, but said nothing. He took a deep breath, then swallowed. "The Blackburns were pissed because the blue and whites passed them and got to him first. Everybody just piled on, swinging at him. The Blackburns, Estrada, Machado. Me."

"You all hit him?" My voice was a croak.

Ted nodded, his eyes flooded. "We weren't cops anymore, Britt. We were a mob. It was like a scene out of one of those cartoons where all you see is flailing elbows and knees and feet."

A tear skidded down his cheek. Betsy wept silently with him.

"I hit him once."

"With your hand?"

"Fist, but there were sticks and flashlights and feet flying."

He looked sick, and placed both palms over his eyes, elbows on his knees. "I realized he was cuffed, and I stopped, but nobody else did. I tried to reach in and grab him away from them, but they went crazy. A couple of blows hit my arm and I just backed off."

Betsy looked at us, eyes defeated. "Do you want some coffee?"

"Sure, I'd love some," I said gratefully, looking at Lottie, who said she would, too.

We sat around the kitchen table. The room was warm and cheerful, but Ted looked worse under the bright light. He wanted to keep talking, as though it relieved his burden.

"I swear, Britt, I had no idea he was hurt so bad. He didn't look critical when the medics took him."

"How did his car get damaged?"

"The Blackburns banged it up with their sticks and all. Machado kicked out the lights. They shoved it into the ditch. Figured no one would believe the driver's story, even if he remembered what happened.

"They had his wallet out. That's when one of the Blackburns yelled, 'Oh shit, you know who this nigger is?' That's when they said we had to get our story straight and stick to it. Stick to the story." He repeated it like a mantra. "Stick to the story."

"What about Carpenter?"

"He came up after it happened, but he helped push the car in the ditch, then called the tow truck to haul it out. They figured it would be all right, until you started asking questions."

"Did D. Wayne ever fight back?"

"He never got the chance. Somebody had the cuffs on him right after he was yanked out of the car. Wasn't much he could do."

I felt sick. Ted looked as if he did, too. The muscles in his jaw worked involuntarily.

"I've always tried to do the right thing, Britt. You've been there. You've seen my file."

I nodded.

"I still don't know how I got caught up in it. Those guys have a rep, but I never would have believed that I could be a part of anything like this. I'm still trying to figure it out. Still don't know what happened," he muttered, shaking his head as though bewildered. "It was the excitement, the adrenaline of the moment, like a whirlwind, that's the way things happen on midnights. Everything's different. It's like nobody's in charge. As if the rules change when the afternoon shift leaves."

Betsy stood behind his chair, small neat hands gently massaging his shoulders, as if to absorb the pain.

"What started the chase?"

"The BOLO," he said flatly. "Described the car and him to a T. Fleeing felon."

"There was no BOLO. I got a transcript of the tape from communications. It wasn't on there."

"Sure," he said tiredly. "It was there. Heard it myself, then one of the Blackburns responded, said they had the subject in sight."

I shook my head.

"I swear, Britt. I heard it myself."

I shook Ted's hand and hugged Betsy as we left. So did Lottie. "Thanks," I told them.

"I know you have to do what you have to do," he said, resigned. "But you won't use my name?"

"Right."

Lottie and I turned to each other once the door closed behind us. The night air was warm and soft. "Well, we did it," I said.

"So how come you're not all lit up like you usually are when you nail down a story?"

"Do you feel excited and happy?"

"Don't have the heart," she admitted, "though I'd be delighted to see those others get busted. What I want to know," she said peevishly, as she hobbled to the car, "is why the hell we didn't come out here first?"

We were mostly silent on the drive back to the office.

"He sure talked," she commented. "Looks like his conscience is killin' him."

"Yeah," I said, thinking aloud, "he seemed so truthful about everything else, wonder why he lied about that one thing? There wasn't any BOLO, but he kept insisting."

"Sure sounded like the truth to me. Makes you wonder about cops, don't it? Looks like we got us the scum of the earth runnin' around here wearing badges and playing with guns. Don't it make real guys like Larry and Steve look good?"

"The cops do look bad," I said ruefully. "But don't tar them all with the same brush. There are good cops out there."

She stared at me suspiciously. "Sure, and until tonight, you'd have ranked Ted Ferrell high on that list, right?" She settled back into her seat. "Now spill it. I've been waitin' all evening."

"What are you talking about?"

"You're just lookin' too damn smug these days. Like the cat with her face in the canary cage. Who is this new man? Tell me all about the big romance."

"Well, I have been seeing somebody, but it's no big deal." I thought of Kendall McDonald, naked in my bed, and felt hot all over. "I don't even know if I'll see him again."

Lottie sharply scrutinized my profile as I turned off Fifteenth Street toward the *News* building.

"You will," she intoned. "Who is he? Where'd you meet him? Is he good? What does he do?"

I tried not to look guilty.

"Oh shit," she said. "It ain't a cop? Tell me it ain't a cop." She leaned closer as I wheeled the Chrysler into her reserved spot under the building. I cut my eyes at her, still trying to look prim. "Damn, it is!" she cried. "Are you crazy?"

SIXTEEN

I typed up my notes that night, slept poorly, and went in early the next morning, to meet with Fred Douglas. He called in half a dozen other editors and Mark Seybold. Lottie joined us in the high-ceilinged conference room. We both refused to divulge even to them the identity of the officer who had talked to us. All we would verify was that official police reports had placed him at the scene, and that he had acknowledged participating in the attack on D. Wayne Hudson.

"He's admitting to a serious crime," Mark Seybold said. He was wearing his train tie, tacked down by a tiny locomotive. Leaning back in his leather chair, he peered at me speculatively over the top of his wire-rim glasses. "Why would he tell you this?"

The solemn faces around the conference table awaited my answer. "I think it's because he's basically a decent man who got caught up in something he bitterly regrets."

"His conscience is eatin' him up," added Lottie, slouched in her chair, arms folded across her chest. "You should've seen him. He looks whupped."

"You promised him confidentiality, without consulting first with any of us?" The managing editor formed a pyramid with the fingers of both hands and eyed me, looking faintly troubled, his usual expression when regarding me or Lottie. He came from the old school of journalism, the days before newsrooms began to look like "hen houses," as I once heard him complain to a male colleague. When he broke into the business, women were relegated to flossy features and gardening columns. Few covered hard news, much less the police beat. Behind him I could see the drawbridge on the Venetian Causeway slowly rising to accommodate a huge white yacht northbound in Biscayne Bay.

"It was the only way to ensure that he would talk to us. The others are stonewalling, sticking to their story," I said. I hated justifying myself to these men. Where were they when we were out there in the dark, in strange neighborhoods, dealing with slamming doors, curses, and attacking pit bulls? How long since any of them had been reporters on the street? Most didn't know what it felt like. Most editors are recruited from the ranks of government reporters; most never get their hands dirty. Yet here they sat, in air-conditioned comfort, demanding explanations. By the curve of Lottie's mouth and the guarded expression in her eyes across the table, I could see that she shared my discomfort. She didn't look like she had slept well, either. Would they be this skeptical and question us this closely, I wondered, if we were men?

Common sense fought my feelings of hostility and persecution. Weariness was affecting my thinking; looking at their side, I could see what concerned them. This was a sensitive story. They had to be absolutely sure. They were the guardians of the newspaper's deep pockets. If I made a serious mistake in print, the paper would be the primary target in a lawsuit, not me. I tried to keep my foot from wagging impatiently under the polished oak table and told myself that this interrogation could be worse; Gretchen had late duty today, and hadn't come in yet. Thank heaven for small favors.

"I say we go with it, for tomorrow," Fred Douglas said finally, his hearty voice booming through air that felt thick with doubt and indecision. The faces around the table nodded. Chairs scraped. No one objected.

They wanted the copy early, they said, so it could be read by them and Mark, who would vet it before going home. Though it would be finished in plenty of time, the story would be withheld from the early edition, so the TV competition would not be tipped off before the eleven o'clock nightly news.

It felt good to be out of the meeting and back in the huge, bustling newsroom, working at my terminal. Sometimes I think this job is what I was born to do. I like fighting deadlines. I have always been competitive, and it is exhilarating to race the clock, perhaps because I know full well that all victories are temporary, and that in the end, the only winner is time.

When the story was pretty much put together, I called Alma Hudson to tell her what it would say. I didn't want her to read it first in the newspaper—and I wanted to include a quote from her. She listened so quietly that when I had finished, I wasn't sure she was still there.

"I knew that my husband had done nothing wrong," she finally said, her voice catching, "and I pray for justice in his case. Thank God the truth is finally beginning to emerge. Bless you, Britt."

I used her first two comments. I also called to confide in Francie, swearing her to secrecy until the paper hit the street. Then, heart pounding, I called Kendall McDonald.

"Clark Kent? Lois Lane here."

"Isn't he the reporter who takes his clothes off in phone booths?"

"I know a few reporters who do that."

He laughed. "I was just thinking about you, Britt." He sounded pleased to hear from me.

"We must be psychic—or psycho."

"Probably both," he said. "How's business?"

"I wrapped up the Hudson story."

"That explains all the rumors, huddles, and paranoia among the uniforms on the road last night. When's it gonna break?"

"Tomorrow's newspaper. All but the early edition tonight."

"Front page?"

"Depends on what else is happening in the world. The editors decide that. Want to know what it's going to say?"

"Nope. I think I'd just rather read about it like everybody else. How much hell do you think it'll raise?"

"I'm not sure," I said. "We'll see what happens once the story is out."

"Well, one good thing may come out of all this."

"What's that?"

"Maybe now you can focus more on your social life."

"Meaning you?" I couldn't help but smile, and wondered if he could hear it in my voice.

"Seeing more of you wouldn't be the hardest thing I've ever done."

"Well," I said, "How nice. I thought I'd been seduced and abandoned."

"Not you, lady, not you."

We said goodbye, and I hung up, still smiling. Behind me, Ryan had overheard my last comment and was ablaze with curiosity. "Who was that on the phone, Britt? Who was it?"

"You damn reporters," I said, my face hot with embarrassment. "Is nothing sacred?"

My story shared the front page with part one of Ryan's rafting adventure, the usual international politics, and a weather story. A tropical depression had formed in the Cape Verde Islands off the coast of Senegal in western Africa, 3,424 miles southeast of Miami; ominous news during the Atlantic hurricane season. That would-be storm never appeared, but my story created a whirlwind.

The furor made it a tough time to be a cop in Miami. Events began to move with lightning speed. The Hudson cops, as they came to be known, were relieved of duty, with pay, the same day. The state attorney's office and the police department launched investigations. D. Wayne Hudson's car, now evidence, was seized from a body shop, where it had been about to be repaired. Within twenty-four hours, the medical examiner had classified Hudson's death as a homicide. The police chief was under seige from the press, and was attacked by community groups who accused him of allowing his troops to run wild.

A black church group conducted a mock funeral procession for D. Wayne Hudson, marching slowly and solemnly down Flagler Street to the courthouse at dusk, carrying a black-draped coffin and plac-ards bearing a one-word demand: JUSTICE. Hundreds of strangers, both black and white, joined them in the hazy purple twilight, until the silent marchers were more than a thousand strong. On the steps of the courthouse they held a candlelight vigil.

My story had evidently been fair and well balanced, because my mail was equally divided between venomous hate letters and notes of praise.

Though I had not used Ted Ferrell's name, I did write his account of what had happened. The other officers did not have to be brilliant to figure out which one of them had broken their silence. I won-dered if they were causing him any problems. I felt a sense of relief that their fears and paranoia would no longer be focused on me. They had more important things to worry about now. Staying out of jail was one of them.

I did fight apprehension as I raced out to cover a violent death in Miami police jurisdiction the day after the story appeared. How would I cover my beat if no cop in Miami ever spoke to me again?

The scene was an Overtown street corner. I knew what the smell was the moment I stepped out of the car. Once encountered, you never forget the odor of burned human flesh. The inevitable had happened. The victim was sprawled at the foot of a streetlight pole. The plastic covers on the handles of his wire cutters had melted. Smoke still rose from his hands.

I wondered if his obituary would describe him as an amateur electrician. He looked to be in his late teens, early twenties. Wit-nesses, possibly accomplices, young men his own age who seemed to know him, eagerly described what they had seen.

A short, plump, big-eyed fellow in a baseball cap and ratty shorts was talking to a homicide detective, who nodded when he saw me. Neither he nor the cops conducting crowd control seemed to have any problem with me listening.

"A big, bright flash of fire," the pudgy youth was saying, waving his arms descriptively. His moist eyes kept returning in disbelief to the newly dead man in the street. "Bobby was hunkered down, right here," he demonstrated, squatting beside the pole, "working on the power box, then it flashed and he did a back somersault." The youth got to his feet and stared at the body. "He somersaulted, man. He got blowed about seven, eight feet away. Sparks flying everywhere and his whole body shaking. Smoke coming outta his hands, man, and his shoes and socks was shooting black smoke. Man," he shook his head, "Bobby got hisself fried."

"Bar-be-cued!" hooted one of the group from the sidewalk.

A power company emergency car had arrived, a yellow flasher spinning on its dash. The driver wore a hard hat and a cool, clinical look. "Bound to happen sooner or later," he said laconically. "The current jumped from the line to him. The electrical field is so great you don't even have to make direct contact." While stealing copper wire from a streetlight, Bobby had been zapped out of this world by "7,720 volts, pretty standard high voltage," the company spokesman said.

What impressed me most, aside from Bobby's unfortunate experience, was the attitude of the cops. I had feared that they would all hate me like poison and clam up, but the rank and file exhibited no rancor and treated me no differently than before.

Francie and I discussed it later. Most good cops, she pointed out, are delighted when bad cops get in trouble. The others are simply relieved that it is somebody else who got caught, and not them. Few tears were being shed over the Blackburns, the weight lifters, or even Carpenter. Ted did have a lot of friends and defenders, but few seemed to blame me for his trouble. The messenger had been spared; life for me was business as usual.

At least, until my visit to police headquarters the following day. A parks employee had dragged a dead man out of nine inches of water off Watson Island, on the north side of the MacArthur Causeway. The corpse had a quarter in his pocket and two bulletholes in his chest.

I missed the homicide detectives at the scene and again, by minutes, at the medical examiner's office. At headquarters I was on my way to the PIO office when I passed a small group of people waiting for the elevator. The door opened and they all piled in. What the heck, I thought, and piled aboard with them. A crime lab technician punched five and I stepped off with him. He headed in the opposite direction, toward internal affairs; I made a right, bee-lining down the hall toward homicide-robbery.

Rounding the corner just thirty paces from my destination, my luck ran out. Major Francisco Alvarez was striding toward me. Too late, no place to hide. I was unaccompanied and had no official pass, a plastic clip-on card bearing the number of the floor you had been approved to visit. I expected him to ignore me, and then call PIO to complain about a reporter on the loose. That was his usual MO.

I smiled hopefully as we neared each other. Perhaps he was in a good mood. Even if he did report me, I might be able to work fast enough to gather what I needed from homicide before somebody showed up from PIO to hustle me out of there. Alvarez's eyes narrowed, the fierce bushy brows connecting dead center in an unbroken line, not unlike a black fuzzy caterpillar.

"Hi, Major," I sang out in my most friendly voice, veering to pass him on the right. Deliberately, he blocked my path, rubbing the fingers of his right hand together. With his other hand he removed a cigar from between his teeth.

"Where is it?" he barked.

I blinked innocently.

"Your pass. Your permission to be on this restricted floor."

"Oh heck," I said and patted my pockets absently. Then I squinted and tossed my head like a silly goose. "I forgot to get one."

I was alarmed to see the color mounting on his cheeks. He looked agitated. Very agitated. His mood changes had always seemed lightning fast. Just my luck to catch a bad one, I thought.

"I only need to talk to a detective for a minute, then I'll go get one," I offered lightly. He continued to block my way, eyes smouldering.

"You've got no business on this floor. It's restricted to police personnel. How'd you get up here?" he demanded heatedly, much too heatedly, I thought, given the transgression. I had never seen him get this red in the face, even at scenes of mass murder. And he was only warming up. "You've got no business anyplace but the lobby! You've been around long enough to know the rules. You think the rules don't apply to you?" His voice was rising, booming down the corridor, the tirade causing heads to pop curiously out of the homicide office. People passing by were slowing down to view the spectacle.

"Okay," I said, something in me bent on foolishly persisting. "But can I talk to the detectives for just a moment?" I realized as I said it that no detective in his right mind would acknowledge my existence, much less divulge any information under Major Alvarez's withering scowl. It would be professional suicide.

"Outta here! Get your goddamn ass off this floor and out of this building. Out!" Alvarez continued to work himself up, pointing now in the direction of the elevators, as though I were an unruly child that had seriously misbehaved. My heart was thudding and my face burned, as an edgy fear began to twist at my gut. Three purple veins throbbed in his forehead, and he looked as close to violence as anybody could be without swinging. He wouldn't go that far, I told myself. But hell, I never thought he'd go *this* far. Dozens of eyes were fixed on us now.

"Okay, you don't have to shout about it," I said mildly. Turning, I marched reluctantly down the hall toward the elevators, hoping Alvarez would be content and go on about his business. But he wasn't; he stayed right on my heels, with a mouth that wouldn't quit. Other eyes joined the silent watchers. Some were enjoying it, I'm sure. Others had to be embarrassed for me.

The back of my neck felt scalded and my knees shaky from the sheer intensity of his attack.

"Harassing my men off duty, trying to push your way into their homes. You don't get away with that in this department. You're outta here! Out!"

I tried to maintain my composure, chin up, hoping my hand didn't tremble as I pushed the down button. It worried me that those who witnessed or heard about this scene would be reluctant to talk to me in the future, afraid of incurring his wrath. I dreaded the possibility of him boarding the elevator with me. As it arrived, he stopped his diatribe and picked up the telephone at the reception desk, manned by a goggle-eyed young public service aide, who stood with his mouth open.

As the door closed, Alvarez shouted, "Don't you show your goddamn face up here again!" I blinked hard to avoid tears of anger and self-reproach as passengers boarded at two stops on the way down. A mad bomber could probably roam the station unchallenged, I thought, but not a reporter. Sure enough, Danny Menendez, rousted by Alvarez's call, stood waiting to meet me, his face stony, when the elevator stopped in the lobby.

I smiled, and moved to walk on by, to the media room. He waggled an index finger at me. "This way, Britt."

"What do you mean?"

"The major wants you out of the building. Now. I don't know what you did, but he's pissed off and wants you out." He jerked his thumb toward the big glass doors to the parking lot.

A storm had blown up and the sky was gray and blustery, palm trees bending in a fierce wind. Fast-food wrappers swept by, riding the air.

"He can't do that, Danny. This is a public building, and I represent the public. Besides, it's getting ready to storm out there."

"He can do it. He's in charge."

"Where's the chief?"

"Out of town, took a few vacation days to get away from this mess. People are already signing petitions for his resignation. Alvarez is acting chief in his absence."

"Oh."

Menendez glanced expectantly at the elevator. Oh no, I thought, Alvarez is probably on his way down.

"You better go, Britt."

The doors slid open and Alvarez erupted into the lobby, shoulders rigid, stiff-legged, and angry, like a bull about to charge. The place was full of people, both civilians and police.

"Okay Danny, but you know I'll be back."

"I know," he sighed.

I beat it out the door as Alvarez tore into Menendez.

"You're supposed to control access to this goddamn building by keeping the press restricted to this floor! What the hell was she doing upstairs?"

The sky had darkened and the wild wind had whipped itself into that feverish peak it reaches just before the deluge. A few drops sprayed my face as my hair caught in the blast like a banner. My car was at the far end of the parking lot, and I was only halfway there when it began. Fumbling with my car keys, I dropped them as the cold rain beat down on me. As I miserably groped for them, drenched, the ink running off the pages of my open notebook, I felt eyes watching from the glassed-in lobby.

SEVENTEEN

The Hudson cops were indicted ten days later. The charge: murder in the second degree. With community pressure mounting, investigators had wasted no time. Scuttlebutt from the state attorney's office was that Ted Ferrell had been offered a deal to save himself by testifying against the others. He would never wear a badge again, but he wouldn't go to jail, either.

He turned it down flat.

The state attorney had then made Carpenter an offer. Less culpable than the other officers, he seemed guilty only of assisting in the cover-up and writing a false report. In exchange for testifying for the prosecution, he would not be charged, and would remain suspended until after the trial, when he would be allowed to retire. He snatched the deal that would save his pension like a drowning man lunging for a life preserver.

Permitted to surrender at the county jail in the company of their attorneys, the Hudson cops were spared the disgrace of being arrested in front of family members or neighbors and marched away in handcuffs. The process was still agonizing. They were still police officers suddenly on the wrong side of the bars, though briefly. They endured processing and fingerprinting, and had their mug shots taken. After brief hearings in the Justice Building across the street, they posted bond and were released.

When we heard that indictments had come down and the officers were surrendering, Lottie and I were assigned to stake out the jail. It seemed like poetic justice, sweet revenge, as she captured Estrada, in jeans and a leather jacket, striding quickly out of the jail with his lawyer, trying to duck the cameras and hide his face. No curses or pit bulls this time.

The Blackburns looked grim, eyes downcast, accompanied by a top-flight criminal defense attorney. Machado, religious medals dangling from his gold chains, was accompanied by several family members and a young woman identified as his fiancée.

Betsy had apparently insisted on accompanying Ted through his bleakest hour. Outside the jail he seemed to try to convince her to wait in the car, but she was determined. She looked ungainly and ready to deliver but walked with him, hand in hand, their faces strained and pale, through the gauntlet of TV and still cameras.

All of the accused refused comment.

Betsy spoke to the crush of reporters and photographers around them as she and Ted were climbing into their car. "My husband is a good man. He cares about people and the community." Tight-lipped and tearful, she said nothing more.

As I typed her quote into my story later, I experienced an odd sense of déjà vu. Where had I heard those words before? Then I remembered. Another wife, another mother had said the same thing to me about her husband. Alma Hudson, the victim's widow.

That night, I watched myself uncomfortably on the TV news, on the fringe of the media pack that pushed, shoved, and rushed after each accused cop. It flooded my mind with images of the horrifying scene Ted had described, the wild pack attack on D. Wayne Hudson. I shivered, switched off the set, and took refuge in the warm arms of Kendall McDonald, who had been watching somberly beside me.

The Hudson case continued to dominate daily news coverage for months, as though it, like the voyage of the Starship *Enterprise,* would be never ending. I took little part in that coverage. My job was to report on crime in the streets, and the city had no lack of that. The Hudson case had begun grinding its way through the court system toward justice, and the *News* had two reporters on that beat. They did their jobs well, perhaps too well, for my taste. I would have been content to wait for the trial for new revelations. But competition is fierce—from the other local newspaper, the three network affiliates, the local independent station, which had a strong news department, radio news reporters, and the wire services. All had been burned when we broke the story and were now playing catch-up, trying to be the first to report each new angle or new development, like sharks in a feeding frenzy.

In the process of discovery, depositions taken by the prosecution were made available to the defense, and therefore to the public. Other police officers had joined the chase. They came up just after Hudson was stopped but took no part in the attack. Under oath, they testified to what they had seen. Each day brought breathless coverage of damning new disclosures, along with the painful details. Descriptions of the blows taken by D. Wayne Hudson. How he was hand-cuffed during the beating. How the officers deliberately damaged his car and stomped on his watch, smashing it while it was still strapped to his handcuffed wrist. Each new revelation increased demands from the public that the chief step down.

The Hudson cops were the biggest story in town. I watched, at first with interest, then with a growing sense of discomfort, wondering if the saturation coverage would mean that no impartial jury could be picked in Miami, making a change of venue necessary. For me, life went on; deadlines kept coming. The news never slowed down, especially on my beat. Work had always been my salvation, my solution to everything from a broken heart to a bad cold. But life on my beat and in the newsroom was not the same. Caught in the scalding glare of publicity and public scrutiny, the police department did not perform well. Indeed, it began to resemble the runner who suddenly realizes he is in the spotlight, drops the ball, and drops the ball again and again—or more succinctly, perhaps, the Keystone Kops.

Innocently perusing police reports, I unearthed a story about a man on the outskirts of Liberty City who had lost his house keys and wallet to a mugger. When he returned home, he had to climb in his own window. It made sense to me, but it was dark, and a well-meaning neighbor thought he was a burglar and had called police. The officer who arrived sent his K-9 partner in through the open window after the "burglar."

The dog quickly cornered and chewed on the screaming homeowner. Then the officer thumped the man a few times with his fist and dragged him outside, happily thinking he had nailed a felon in the act. The unfortunate resident had been mugged again, this time by the cops. It was a good story.

The homeowner happened to be black, the officer happened to be white. Suddenly race was relevant. Angry black groups charged racism. I wasn't so sure. The same mistake might well have occurred had the homeowner been white and the officer black, or if both had shared the same color skin. To a reporter like me, accustomed to leaving any mention of race out of a story, it seemed odd that it suddenly took on so much importance.

A few days later, a Latin police officer who had been shaking down a Biscayne Boulevard hooker for sex, apparently got too kinky. He had acquired a gynecologist's instruments and wanted to play doctor. Literally. Irate, she refused to play and turned him in. She called me first. Her chief complaint, aside from the rubber gloves, the speculum, and uteroscope was, "He ain't even a member of the vice squad, and he expect me to do him twice a week and now this shit?"

We had a nice long chat, and I referred her to internal affairs. An investigation was launched, with the officer relieved of duty after she passed a polygraph.

Though she did not mention it initially, once the story appeared, she bought into the rhetoric of a vocal group of angry black activists who insisted that the cop did what he did because she was black. I thought the situation seemed more sexual than racial, but there it was again.

A few angry letter-writers accused me of fueling racial tensions in an already divided community, my regular correspondent Randall Woxhall accused me of being a sexist bitch, and I was bombarded by love letters and admiring phone calls from Pete Zalewski and his cellmates. They loved the stories at the jail. I made their day.

None of the above was my intention, but you can't ignore a legitimate news story. Other readers praised my "crusade" to bring injustices to light. This was no crusade; I was just reporting the news. And to tell the truth, writing these stories didn't make my job any easier. I would have been a lot happier if the police had quit dropping the ball and getting themselves into these situations.

But they didn't. It didn't keep raining, it poured. Cops on the midnight shift stopped a trio of unruly, smart-ass teenagers who became belligerent and mouthed off at the wrong moment. Rather than take them in and endure the inevitable hassle of paperwork and juvenile court, the officers decided to simply teach them a lesson, by dangling them over an expressway bridge by their heels. A set of parents reported the incident and a brutality investigation was launched. The teenagers were black, the officers white.

Another midnight shift officer chased down a teenage burglar on foot, then recognized him as a burglar he had arrested just twenty-four hours earlier. The frustrated cop forced the cocky thief to "walk the plank" into a murky canal, then hauled him off to jail sopping wet and blubbering. He claimed the youth had jumped into the canal in an escape attempt. Witnesses said different. The burglar was black, the officer white.

What the hell was going on here? It got so that I almost hated finding these stories. But there they were.

With half a dozen groups clamoring that he resign or be fired, the beleaguered chief raised the drawbridges and refused to talk to the press about anything. He came down hard on the miscreants among his men, but it seemed that the more his troops were publicized, scrutinized, and criticized, the more they fouled up. It suddenly seemed like they couldn't do a thing right. I knew the feeling well myself.

Everybody was supersensitive. When I wrote about a robbery at a CenTrust Bank and routinely described the robber as black, thirty to thirty-five years old, five feet, ten inches tall, with a neatly trimmed mustache, glasses, a tan sports jacket and a buttercup yellow shirt, black readers complained that we had stereotypically identified the robber as black.

Gretchen sternly "counseled" me on the matter. Unless, she said, we had a superdetailed description that could lead to positive identification of the culprit, race should not be used to describe a criminal.

"But," I argued, "reporting whether the wanted man is black or white certainly does narrow down the possibilities. What's the point of mentioning his glasses and his mustache but not what color his skin is?"

She was adamant, and not pleased when I asked why, if it was so wrong, had she, as editor on the story, let it get into the newspaper.

A week later, Fred Douglas, whom I always had counted on to be grounded in common sense, left a brief note in my typewriter: "See me, in my office."

I did, and was not crazy about what I saw. He looked uncomfortable, his thin face pinched and serious.

"Britt, I've been asked to discuss this with you because Gretchen felt you weren't receptive to her the last time this issue came up."

What is he talking about? I wondered. What has Gretchen done to me this time? Whatever, my best defense was a good offense. "I'm always receptive to my editors," I lied indignantly, trying to look properly righteous.

Fred toyed with a slim gold pen on his immaculate desktop. "You know that this paper always strives for sensitivity when it comes to minorities?"

"Of course," I said, on the alert. "And nobody is more sensitive than I am on the police beat."

"True, but you have occasional lapses. Like this latest." He leaned forward, opened his desk drawer, and removed a tearsheet of one of my stories.

The story was sensitively written, if I did say so myself. It was an interview with the family of a grocer gunned down by robbers a year earlier. The murder was still unsolved. The man's son had called, asking me if there was any way to revive the case that still haunted the survivors, and perhaps generate some new interest by police. He wanted to know if offering a reward might help. I went to visit the family and wrote about the major void left in the lives of the widow, three sons, and their wives. The victim's first grandchild had been born since his death, a birth he had eagerly anticipated. The closing of his corner store, where he had extended goodwill and credit, had made a major difference to the entire neighborhood. Senior citizens, single mothers, and others on fixed incomes now had to ride two buses to buy and lug home their groceries.

Bewildered, I scanned the story Fred had dropped in front of me. His expression was stern. "What's wrong with this?" I asked. "You're saying it's not sensitive?"

"Catch the second reference to the widow," Fred said, as though I had missed something obvious.

"Sally," I said.

"A reader called, accusing us of referring to her by her first name because she's a black woman. Our style is to use only last names on second reference."

"Except that in this case everybody else quoted in the story has the same last name. All the sons, all the daughters-in-law. Using her first name was the easiest, most common sense way to avoid confusion and make it clear who was speaking. It had nothing to do with race. Oh, for Pete's sake!" I sprang to my feet, too agitated to sit, pacing back and forth in the short space in front of Fred's desk.

"The cops had forgotten this guy's murder. It devastated his family and changed the quality of life in the whole damn neighborhood, and when I try to rekindle some interest in solving it, I'm accused of being insensitive, and racist? Who the hell complained? Not them?" I jabbed an index finger at the tearsheet, at Lottie's solemn group picture of the Anderson family. "They were thrilled and grateful that somebody still cared and remembered the case."

"It wasn't them, per se," Fred said, swallowing a nervous sip of black coffee from a Styrofoam cup, his adam's apple bobbing. "Sit down, sit down." My body language and argumentative reaction obviously made him uneasy. But I stayed stubbornly on my feet. Probably a mistake; our professional relationship had always been good. But what the hell, I thought, this is ludicrous; I don't deserve being jerked around like this. I towered over him, seething. Wedged behind his desk, he was looking more and more like a trapped rat. "It's just that another reader, a black person, called, got the ear of the ME, and complained that it was demeaning."

"Fred, are you saying to me that you don't think that I am personally sensitive to everyone?" Roiling toward a full boil, I leaned across his desk, breathing fire. "I was not assigned to do this. It was an enterprise story. I thought it was a good idea, and I generated it. Nobody in this newsroom could be more sensitive to a family whose father was killed. Perhaps you have forgotten that my father . . ."

"Okay, okay." Hands raised in surrender, he leaned back in his chair, rolling it toward the farthest wall. "I only delivered the message. It's one of these things we have to deal with. These are difficult times, Britt. Just watch yourself in the future."

Has the world gone wacky, I wondered as I stomped out of his office, or was it me?

Luckily, my personal life was on a high, making it easier to endure the temporary vagaries of the job. In November, I took a week's vacation I had to use or lose by the end of the year, and I asked McDonald if he wanted to spend it together. We had seen each other several times a week since our first night together, and I was torn between the pleasure of being with him and dreading the day that my bosses, or his, found out about us. The attraction between us was powerful. I was thinking in terms I hadn't for a long time—and the intimacy was disconcerting. Why do the things we yearn for always scare us the most? I wondered. Maybe, I thought, some time together, away from our work, might give us some insight as to where we were headed. He agreed enthusiastically and took the time off.

McDonald and I drove across the Everglades to Florida's west coast. We set out early on a clean and sparkling day that was awash in sunlight, the pale, innocent clouds of morning etched against a dazzling Technicolor sky.

We drove west on the Tamiami Trail, giddy with the unfamiliar sense of freedom. Bad things might be happening in Miami, probably were at that very moment—but, hey, gun battles, casualties, and crime scenes were none of our concern today. No beepers, no bad guys. We were gone, out on the trail, the Cherokee rolling west through the ancient River of Grass, Everglades National Park.

I had not driven across state for more than a year. Together, we hooted to see that the signs erected by the Micousukee Indians to pitch their airboat rides were now in Spanish. It had come to that; even the Micousukees had had to *habla español*. More signs beat the drums for their alligator wrestling, which I had no desire to see. I always rooted for the alligator—and he never won.

The warm earthy smell of the Everglades surrounded us, and the big broad sky stretched out above for as far as the eye could see. It was heaven, until a giant, ravenous, dive-bombing Everglades mosquito, sometimes referred to as Florida's state bird, zoomed into the jeep, seeking blood. He looked honest-to-God big enough to shoot. We did some fancy gyrations at fifty-five miles an hour, swinging and swatting, and finally forced the critter back out a window.

A big black turkey vulture was tearing apart something dead at the side of the road. A red Porsche zoomed by, flying low, headed east toward Miami. McDonald and I exchanged glances.

"He's probably got a body in the trunk," I said.

"Or at least a dozen kilos of coke."

"Did you get the tag number?"

"Nope," he said.

"And why not?"

"Because, we're on vacation," we chorused.

"It's so good to be away from the rat race," he sighed comfortably. "Especially when the rats almost always win. Out here, you realize that a hundred years from now none of it will matter. We'll all be well-kept secrets, but this place will still be here." His eyes, behind dark shades, lingered on my face, then swept back to the road.

"Don't be too sure," I said. "If the developers have their way, a hundred years from now this will all be one gigantic paved parking lot, surrounded by condos and shopping centers."

Ospreys wheeled lazily overhead as every variation of green flashed by, pinelands, sawgrass, hammocks and tree islands, willows, pond apples, and mangroves. Graceful egrets feeding in a slough. A timeless tableau, all set against a low flat sky of brilliant blue and fast-moving clouds that seemed to sail right overhead. And McDonald beside me. I realized I had never felt so happy and content, and vowed to fix the moment in my memory because I know that nothing lasts forever and the best is always gone too soon.

Our destination was a waterfront room on Sanibel Island. The first time I visited there I was a child, and the only way to reach those pristine shores was by ferry boat. Now the island had a bridge, a three-dollar toll, and traffic jams.

We finally arrived and carried our bags inside. I felt almost shy—here we were, alone together, away from all our familiar surroundings. The room was beautiful—with double French doors opening onto a small terrace as the sun sank into the Gulf of Mexico, its dying rays leaving golden pools and rivulets on the darkening surface of the water.

"It's perfect, McDonald." I walked over and sat on the edge of the bed, where he had stretched out.

"One question," he said, pulling me down beside him. "How come you always call me McDonald?"

I rolled over. "It's your name, silly."

"Why not Ken, like everybody else?"

I hesitated. "It just doesn't feel right."

"Remind you of somebody?"

"Yeah, in a way." I deliberately sounded evasive.

"Who was he?" Curious now, he leaned over on one elbow, those eyes, as silvery as fish scales in the sun, locked on mine.

"Who was this guy?" he said again.

"I was just a kid."

"How involved did it get?"

"I was eight years old."

He registered surprise, eyes urging me on.

"He was actually involved with my best friend. He was married to Barbie." He didn't get it, at first. "I was very lonesome. Only child, shy, moved a lot. Buried my nose in books. Didn't have any friends, but I had Barbie, and she had Ken. I wrote stories, little plays, and they acted out all sorts of fantasy romances."

"Was he anatomically correct?"

"No, but you are, very correct," I whispered, breathing in his ear.

"Toy with me, Britt." My lips brushed his, then gently swept across his chest. "You remember any of your fantasies? I'll play." I unfastened his trousers and he removed them.

"Let me check this out." I touched him lightly and then my fingers roved to a small scar high on his right inner thigh. "How'd you get this?" Round and slightly raised, it was about the size of a cigarette burn.

"I was hoping you wouldn't notice. Gawd, you sharp-eyed reporters . . ." He shook his head and pulled the sheet up to cover it. "That's where I got shot."

I was surprised. "I knew you shot somebody once, but I didn't know you'd ever been wounded." I peeled the sheet back down, leaned forward as if to scrutinize the small circle, then ran my tongue over it. He was beginning to be aroused. "What happened? Was it some major bad guy?"

"You have to know now?" he said.

I nodded, sitting up, one hand resting lightly on his muscular thigh. "A bad guy?"

"Not exactly." He looked sheepish. "No big deal. Actually, it was a woman."

"A woman! Did this happen on or off duty?"

"Very funny." He was no longer aroused, but my inquiring mind was more intent on the story behind the scar at this point. He propped an overstuffed pillow behind his head, pulled me into his arms, and held me while he told it. "Once upon a time, Danny and I went to arrest a guy, a twenty-two-year-old fugitive on an auto theft warrant. This was a favor for Palm Beach. They wanted to question him as a possible witness in a homicide. We did it, instead of warrants, in case the guy opted to talk about the case. No problem. We found he was staying over in Wynwood with a new lady friend. She was older than him, about thirty-five, and divorced. We were pretty thorough; we checked him out. Nonviolent, just a petty car thief, never known to be armed. Our decision was not to go in with guns on account of the kids. We knew she had small children.

"The woman opens the door, we flash the tin. She says what do you want? We say we have a warrant for her friend Buster. 'Sorry,' she says, 'Buster's not here.' We say we know he's here. Dan heads in the back to check out the bedroom, and I'm looking around. All of a sudden, she screams, 'Get out! Get out!' and she's pointing a rifle at me from across the room. It looked like a cannon. I was caught totally by surprise. She's hysterical, protecting her young lover. A little kid is hanging onto her leg, and she's still yelling 'Get out! Get out!'

"She's got me covered, so I say okay, okay and start backing out the door. I was getting the hell out of her way, going outside to draw my weapon and go back in, because my partner's still in there. Just as I'm almost out the door, she goes *pop!* with the gun. It took about ten seconds before I realized she'd hit me. It stung, I reached down, touched myself, and my hand came up bloody.

"Meanwhile Danny had caught the guy hiding in a bedroom closet and cuffed him. He heard the pop, came out, and saw that the weapon was a gun that just fires one shot at a time. I don't know why they even make a gun like that. You have to break it down manually, take out the spent cartridge, and insert a new one. He just reached over and yanked it out of her hands.

"I was lucky, one inch to the right and it would have rung my bell." From the look in his eyes, the thought obviously pained him. It made me wince, as well. "I made a tie tack out of the projectile, a .22. I was embarrassed; it was not exactly my finest hour."

"Did she deliberately aim for your . . ."

"I don't think she knew where the gun was aiming."

"You could have been killed," I said indignantly. "She could have hit you in the head, or the heart."

"Sure." He nodded, as though it was not the first time that thought had occurred to him.

"Was she attractive?"

He looked startled. "Don't know. Nobody's attractive when they're hysterical."

"What happened to her?"

He rolled those blue eyes, now smoky in the waning light, as the room slipped slowly into darkness. "She plea-bargained. The prosecutor asked me to agree to a two-year plea. I said, 'Hell, no, she tried to kill me.' I wanted to go for the max, which would have been twenty years.

"Next I heard, it was all over. He had taken the plea and never notified me. She sent me a Christmas card from prison with a note, apologizing. Far as I know, she was released and lived happily ever after."

My body felt chilled to the bone. I tickled his ribs and kissed his lower lip lightly, straddling him. "How could any woman pull a gun on you, McDonald? You're so cute, so adorable. Such big blue eyes . . ."

He tangled his hand in the back of my hair and drew my mouth back down to his. "My charms didn't stop her for a heartbeat," he said, voice husky. "In fact, she tried to blow 'em away."

"I'm glad she didn't."

"Me too." He cupped my bottom in his hands. "Want to skip going out to dinner and order room service?"

"Sounds good to me."

That week, we swam in the warm Gulf waters at dawn and explored the shell-strewn beach, collecting yellow cockles, shiny lettered olives, swirling scotch bonnets, and angel wings. After breakfasts of fruit and croissants we walked the white sand beach and lazed in the sun. We lunched on coquina chowder and Florida lobster and explored the rest of the island in the afternoons. Our nights were passionate, but as close an emotional connection as we forged, there seemed to be an unspoken awareness that back in Miami there were strong crosscurrents that could sweep us apart. I began to hope, almost wistfully, that what we had would be strong enough to resist them.

On the way back across state we made a pit stop at the Oasis Ranger Station, and I bought a rubber alligator for Darryl.

I was surprised and heartened when McDonald charmed my mother at Thanksgiving. Perhaps our week together was a turning point, I thought. He insisted on taking us both out to dinner. She was delightful, and seemed enthralled, particularly when he flattered and flirted and spoke about his law school plans, as vague and tenuous as they might be. And though her gaze rested sharply on my ensemble, she mercifully made no comment. Instead she told us wonderful stories about what Miami was like when she was growing up.

Howie Janowitz had filled in on my beat while I was gone. Nothing had changed. He covered the story of the all-white police special investigations unit (SPU) that swooped down on the wrong house. They mistook the home of the Rev. Luther Dingle, a black preacher, for the drug den they were seeking. Only in Miami, I thought, reading the story.

The angry preacher had demanded to know why police bashed in his door, and there was a scuffle. Evidently, he was bumped on the head during the melee. It seemed abundantly clear that he was making the most of the wrong-house raid. The police had dropped the ball, so he ran with it.

The Rev. Dingle hired a savvy, publicity-seeking attorney and called numerous press conferences that were well attended by the media. He wore an elaborate head bandage, which he apparently removed in private but could slap back on, like a turban, for the benefit of news photographers. I could not help but suspect that only months earlier, the *News* never would have danced to this man's tune, dispatching reporters and photographers each time he put on his bandage and summoned the press. I said as much in a memo to Fred, who privately agreed. The paper, however, could not afford to ignore the man, since no one else in the media did, and the competition was so fierce.

Besides, ignoring him might appear racist and offend someone. The Rev. Dingle milked it for all it was worth.

The unfortunate error had occurred when the house numbers were somehow transposed on the face of the search warrant; a typo. When they pulled up, the cops had asked their spaced-out informant if it was the right place. He said it was, nodded off, and went back to sleep. Typos happen. The officers were in more trouble for not backing off when the Rev. Dingle told them they had the wrong house. But that is what everybody says when served with a search warrant.

The officers were relieved of duty with pay. If the trend kept up, there would be more officers under investigation than out on the street. Cops are only human. Mistakes happen. But why to us in Miami, and in such rapid succession? What was going on here?

I helped Onnie and Darryl move in early December. The decision was precipitated by word that bond might be substantially reduced for Darryl's dad and uncles because of a delay in their trial date and severe jail overcrowding. Onnie and I had a long talk first. Nothing frustrates me more than women who leave a bad situation and then go back. They lose credibility with the cops, the courts, and those trying to help them, to say nothing of the damage to their own self-esteem. Neither would it be fair to Darryl or his brother. I didn't know Darryl's father, but from what I had seen of him on paper—his police record—he was no prize. Yet he had to have something for a smart woman like Onnie to hang in there with him all this time. Would that something prove irresistible?

Onnie and I browsed the farmers' market, selecting a basket of fresh vegetables, stopped by the marina for fresh grouper right off a fishing boat, and went back to her place, where she whipped up a mean gumbo. While we chopped okra, green bell peppers, potatoes, and tomatoes and then cooked and ate dinner, we talked mostly about her situation. I decided I didn't need to worry about Onnie. She was ready. The numbed weariness and shame that had weighted her shoulders when we first met had been replaced by an unwavering determination and enough driving energy to take action at last. Pert and clear-eyed, in jeans and a red scoop-necked blouse, she had obviously done a lot of thinking about her man.

"What it comes down to," she told me flatly, as she washed the dishes and I dried, "is that he's broken and he can't be fixed. Lord knows, I tried."

Two days later, we attached a U-Haul trailer to the back of my T-Bird, filled it with their meager possessions, and moved them to an efficiency in Liberty City. The new apartment was small, but the building was not bad. It had a tot lot, and was close to a good school where Darryl would start kindergarten in six months. Onnie had landed a temporary Christmas season sales job at a big discount store. When a better, more permanent position came along, she would upgrade to a one- or two-bedroom in the same complex.

I wasn't interested in seeing other men, but agreed to appease

Lottie by going out for drinks with Larry and Steve one Friday night during the Christmas season. Lottie was all bubbly that day, and actually wore a dress. Just before we were to leave the office, a news story broke. A cruise ship bound for the Caribbean was steaming back to the Port of Miami because something had gone terribly awry with the food or the water supply—it was not immediately determined which—and half the crew and most of the passengers were suffering severe cramps and diarrhea.

We left a message at the bar where we were to meet Larry and Steve. Lottie called, turning to ask me how to explain the breaking story we had been assigned. "Just tell them to check the morning paper," I told her, and we rolled.

Lottie and I met the ship as it docked to interview and photograph the passengers off the once-gala holiday cruise. Honeymooners, retirees, and entire families all raced by in a big hurry, not eager to talk as they disembarked.

We could have made a fortune with a Kaopectate concession. They were all mad as hell and looking for a bathroom.

"You can't be glum about our ruined plans when you look at those poor people," I reminded Lottie, who was still cranky, as we got back to the office. "More than eight hundred went on that cruise. Some probably saved for a year, and now it's ruined. You know they won't even find a decent hotel room here this time of year. Look what's happened to *their* plans."

A good news message waited on my desk. Betsy Ferrell had had her baby, a little girl. Six pounds, eight ounces. Her name, given the season, Holly. Holly Ferrell. I liked it.

"Lucky it wasn't a boy," Lottie snapped. "Poor thang probably would've been named Rudolph."

I sat down heavily at my desk, thinking about the Ferrells and the baby, and what was happening to them and Miami, and suddenly felt a hundred years old. "Maybe," I said, "they should have named her Mercy."

EIGHTEEN

The holiday season was not especially jolly. Miamians were jittery, the multi-ethnic community seethed, more tense and divided then ever, and Kendall McDonald presented me with a Black Forest cuckoo clock for Christmas. It was beautiful, with energetic little Tyrolean dancers that burst out tiny doors and spun around every half hour, and its noisy occupants certainly fascinated Billy Boots who stalked it for hours, tail atwitch. But I had hoped for something more romantic. What did this gift say, aside from its timely cries? Was this a joke? Was he trying to tell me something?

Ryan, romantic as always, suggested that McDonald was saying that he wanted our relationship to endure for all time. If the clock had said something other than "cuckoo," I might have bought that. Lottie, always a pal, tried to comfort me, saying that the gift surely indicated McDonald's hopes for a future in which we shared custody of the clock and more.

Worse, McDonald clearly expected me to be thrilled with his gift, and, ace detective that he was, realized that I was not. We did not really discuss the matter, but he exuded a troubled sense of bewilderment that I failed to share his enthusiasm for the clock.

I shouldn't have complained. Many Miamians had it worse. Some were out of work, others were homeless, and it seemed as though the rest had armed themselves for the Christmas season. Perhaps it was just a run of bad luck for gun owners.

I did the story about the woman who slept with both her gun and her asthma inhaler under her pillow. Fumbling around sleepily after her nasal passages clogged during the night, she squeezed the wrong one and shot herself in the snoot. Another woman was gunned down by her own purse, when she carelessly flung it into a supermarket shopping cart, forgetting the small handgun tucked inside for protection. A dry cleaner lost his .9 millimeter when he forgot that he had set the weapon on the roof of his car before driving away from his Westchester home. Another man surely wished he had lost his. He stuck his .25 caliber handgun in his front pants pocket in order to free up his hands to juggle grocery bags from car to house. As he wrestled with two big brown sacks loaded with canned goods, the gun fired. They found him writhing in his driveway, surrounded by scattered groceries.

Made you skittish about owning a handgun. But as long as every madman in Miami had ready access to weapons and as long as I lived solo and traveled tough turf, I wanted mine, too. At least I was careful, and knew how to use it.

The streets were growing more intense. I could feel it as I made my daily rounds, and saw it in the graffiti on the walls of Overtown and Liberty City. "Cops-Killers." "Off A Pig." I would be relieved when the trial was over. Sure enough, the judge did grant a change of venue because of the publicity barrage, and the case was moved to Atlanta.

Ted's stubborn insistence that there really had been a BOLO that sparked the fatal pursuit nagged at me. Why would he admit everything else and continue to lie about that?

The question was still gnawing at my consciousness the day jury selection began in Atlanta. Janowitz was covering the trial for us. Every news organization in town had a team there. I wished I could attend, but it was impossible. Defense attorneys were eager to take my deposition in the case. The prosecution also wanted to talk to me, about which officer had confessed the night I went to their homes. Then, of course, they would call me to testify against him. No way.

Mark Seybold had informed them that I would not reveal my source, and had warned me to watch out for subpoena servers in case they tried to lay the papers on me anyway. Several had either been turned away or referred to him by security in the lobby.

I had also alerted Mrs. Goldstein, my landlady. Knowing her, not only would she tell them zilch, she would run them off with a broom. She was an expert on spotting shady characters and giving them what-for. The dodge had worked well, so when I stepped off the elevator onto the fifth floor, on deadline, riffling through my notes on a story, I was confident and preoccupied. A process server was the furthest thought from my mind.

Ryan was standing over Gloria, the receptionist, at her big desk facing the elevators. She was on the phone and looked tense, with an odd expression on her face. Ryan caught my eye and kept jerking his head. I had never noticed that sort of tic in him before. What is it with them, I thought, almost irritably. With things so weird out on the street, the least my colleagues could do was try to act normal. Ryan stepped toward me. He needed a haircut, but I liked him that way, with his hair curling around the nape of his neck, the sleeves of his light blue shirt rolled up, his tie loosened and askew.

I assumed he wanted me to join him for coffee. "I'm in a hurry," I sang out, "on deadline," and moved to stride on past him.

"Britt Montero," a perky little old lady, a pink-cheeked cherub with fine white hair, hailed me from behind. I turned in surprise; she apparently had been seated in a chair in the conversation pit for those who waited in the newsroom lobby. She walked as though she had had an old hip fracture but stepped lively, in sensible shoes with short stubby heels. Pink scalp showed through her soft perm. She carried a bulky old-fashioned navy blue pocketbook and a sweater over her arm. Somebody's grandma.

I returned her engaging smile. Ryan waved his arms behind her back. What is wrong with that guy today? I thought.

"Yes?" I said to the woman, wondering if I should remember her from somewhere.

"Here you are, dearie," she said sweetly, as though presenting a home-baked treat, and pressed something into my hand.

I looked down, but before my eyes even focused on the subpoena, I had put it together and knew I'd been had.

"You're good, really good," I said bleakly, as she stepped onto the elevator, smiling triumphantly.

"You young people shouldn't always be rushing around the way you do. Take the time to enjoy yourself," she said, as the door began to glide closed. "Smell the flowers," were her parting words of advice. Ryan had clapped one hand over his eyes and was shaking his head. He had tried to warn me.

"Is that security on the line?" I snapped at Gloria.

"No, it's the lawyer, Mark Seybold."

"Okay, tell him they got me. Then call security and tell them to take a good look at her on the way out, so she can't sneak by next time." I bet she didn't even have to sneak, I thought; they probably gave her directions.

"Who would believe it?" I said, to no one in particular. "Nobody is who they seem to be anymore."

"Sorry," Ryan said. "Didn't you see me trying to warn you?" he added, a tad peevishly.

"Yeah," I sighed, "I just wasn't thinking."

I was in trouble now, I thought. If I had to go to Atlanta to testify, I could conceivably wind up in jail on a contempt citation for refusing to divulge my source. With my luck and the state of the system, the guilty would go free and I'd languish behind bars indefinitely. I examined the subpoena, curious to see which lawyer had been clever enough to send that innocent-looking grandma instead of the usual scuzzy characters who served them.

"Hey," I said aloud. "She gave me the wrong one." Nope, it had my name on it. But the case was Bertie McCloud versus the power company and the City of Miami. "What?" I muttered.

This was not the Hudson case at all. This was a civil case, a wrongful death action. A mother was suing the city and the electric company for causing the death of her son Bobby, who'd been electrocuted while stealing copper wire from an Overtown lightpole. Though they were not married, his girlfriend was also a plaintiff, suing on behalf of their two small children, now deprived of a father. The defendants were accused of negligently maintaining an attractive and dangerous nuisance, one that had enticed their son and father to a premature death. The plaintiffs wanted my notes and/or tapes and photos from the scene and ultimately, of course, big bucks to assuage their grief.

"Now that is chutzpah," Mark said, reaching for his telephone.

I stood in front of his desk. "You don't think they can succeed in getting anything, do you? The man died because he was a thief."

"The power company and the city will probably settle with the family," Mark said, "just to avoid the expense of a trial."

"They shouldn't pay a dime," I said, my voice rising. "They should try the case."

"It's just not worth the expense." He shook his head. "Or the risk that a jury might sympathize enough with the mother or the fatherless children to grant some big award."

"So by the same token," I argued, "the survivors of a bank robber killed in a holdup could sue the bank just for being there, with all that money." This was outrageous. The rats were winning.

Mark had his secretary get the grieving family's attorney on the telephone, as I impatiently prowled his office surveying the railroad art on the walls. While I studied a framed lithograph of two locomotives, Mark convinced the man in no uncertain terms that I had no information that could not be obtained elsewhere and that there was no way I could or would be used by him as his free private investigator in the case.

I returned to the newsroom, relief mingled with my sense of outrage. I was not going to Atlanta, or jail, after all. At least not this time.

Poor Bobby McCloud, lured to his death by a seductive streetlight pole. Only in Miami, I thought.

The city's factionalism had even split the police department. The Latin officers' organization was supporting Machado and Estrada. The Anglo officers' association was raising funds for the defense of Ted Ferrell and the Blackburns, and the black officers' group, supportive of D. Wayne Hudson, was rooting for convictions.

I wanted to talk to Francie about what was happening, so we agreed to meet one morning when she had to stay up to go to court anyway. With tension among the cops so thick that you needed a machete to hack through it, she certainly could not afford to be seen with me. Even McDonald was growing reluctant to be seen with me in public. Francie and I arranged to meet at a safe place, the Holocaust Memorial in Miami Beach, where the only other people would be tourists or elderly local residents, with too much going on in their minds and memories to notice us.

Miami Beach has one of the largest Holocaust survivor populations in the world, and one of the most dramatic memorials to the victims. A huge green arm sculpted from patined bronze and tattooed with a number from Auschwitz reaches into the air, tormented human figures clinging precariously to its sides. The hand blindly gropes the sky.

In the original plans, the giant arm was to be taller than a seven-story building, easily seen by air traffic to and from Miami International Airport. Beach homeowners were horrified at the prospect of the arm's grotesque green shadow falling across their pools, patios, and pricey views, and protested. Eventually a compromise was reached. The arm is only four stories tall.

The unique landmark is a place where I often meet sources who don't want to be seen coming to the newspaper.

I waited for Francie in the meditation garden, a sprawling plaza of Jerusalem stone surrounding a huge water lily pond.

The winter day was a tourist's dream, low humidity, temperature in the mid-seventies, an azure sky reflected in the mirrorlike surface of the lily pond.

I recognized Francie's happy, lilting walk from a distance. She had worked all night and spent several hours in court, but looked fresh and energetic, though pale. She still wore her dark blue police-issue trousers, but had switched her uniform shirt for an embroidered white blouse with mother of pearl buttons. Her soft brown hair, usually pinned up in a twist when on duty, giving unruly suspects less to grab onto, was brushed out and hung loose, down around her shoulders. Without speaking, we strolled through a vine-covered arbor flanked by painful photographs of Holocaust history, past an eternal flame, and entered a dark and lonely tunnel.

It led us out into the light, where the outstretched arm reached for the sky. We lingered in silence, then passed a long black granite wall etched with victims' names, similar to the Vietnam War Memorial.

"Doesn't this place give you the heebie jeebies?" Francie whispered.

"Nope," I said, scanning the familiar rows of names. The sun felt good on my skin as we settled on a stone bench, facing the lily pond. "In fact, I like to come here."

"I'll never understand why," Francie said, squinting, and slipping on her sunglasses.

"It's hard to explain, but it's a comfort, like church, or coming home. On our jobs we see people brutalized and killed every day. It happened yesterday, it's happening today, and it'll happen tomorrow, over and over. They die alone and are forgotten. Statistics. But not these victims." I gestured at the scene around us. "Nothing could be worse than to face what they did and be forgotten. But they weren't. They weren't simply swallowed by time.

"People read their names over and over. That keeps them alive. I think that as long as somebody remembers you, you're never really dead."

"I see your point," Francie said slowly. "So many of the victims we see are forgotten two weeks later. Like they never existed."

"Exactly. Nobody even knows or cares that they lived or died. That's why I love to write about old, unsolved murder cases whenever I can, to make people remember. Speaking of work, how's the job?"

"Are you kidding? It's getting harder and harder to be a cop in this town." Her small face looked sad. "Sometimes I'm almost embarrassed to wear the uniform. You stop a motorist on traffic and they say, 'What are you gonna do, beat me to death?' Strangers make remarks on the street. People are afraid to open their doors to us, even when we're trying to help them. The streets are hostile. I've never seen it this bad. Morale is at rock bottom. You hear about the fight the other night?"

"What fight?"

"I'm glad you're sitting down, Britt."

"Not another black versus white incident?"

"You got it."

"Oh no."

"But this time there's a twist. It wasn't cops brutalizing civilians. The cops were brutalizing each other."

"What the . . .?"

"The midnight shift comes on, and Connery, a white patrolman and a redneck from way back, is assigned to ride with a female partner. His usual partner was suspended in the latest scandal. The female is Jessie St. Juste, a Haitian who takes no shit from anybody. Connery is not crazy about it and neither is she, with all that's been going on, but the sergeant gives them a pep talk after roll call and all goes well—until they get out to the parking lot to pick up their patrol car."

"What happened?"

"They both insist on driving. She's got the keys, he grabs them, she snatches them back and starts climbing into the driver's seat. He drags her out by the hair, and they get into it. Major fistfight, rolling around on the ground, a free-for-all. She winds up with a gash on her forehead, his front teeth are loosened."

I remembered Jessie St. Juste, a tall, muscular woman who had never driven until she came to this country. She had totaled a patrol car in training. In a way, I could see Connery's point. "Who won?"

"A draw, though she almost bit off his trigger finger. It took seven of us to drag them apart. She kicked him in the crotch, and he was going for his gun."

"They were in uniform at the time?"

"Yep."

"Jesus, what a story that would have been if they'd wound up shooting each other."

"Thanks a lot, Britt. The department is crumbling around us, and you're thinking great story."

"You know what I mean. What happened to them?"

"Both relieved of duty. Under investigation, probably will wind up with short suspensions. They're trying to keep it quiet. The brass is afraid it will further erode public confidence in the police department if the story gets out. But it surely would have leaked anyway, without me telling you. The Miami Association of Women Police has filed a grievance, so did the Anglo officers' group and the Black Police Benevolent Association. Did you hear, the Puerto Ricans have dropped out of the Hispanic Officers Association to establish their own group? They don't want to be associated with the Cuban faction any longer. And the Haitian officers have splintered off from the black association."

"This is all so crazy."

"I know, I know." Francie sighed. "How's the trial coming?"

"I won't see Janowitz's story for the street until I get into the office. Why do you think they're all still lying about a BOLO that night?"

Francie frowned. "Personally, I don't think they're lying. I think there was one, but I can't say that I remember hearing it myself. I've tried to think back, but it wasn't important to me at the time. I was on another call."

"How can you say that, Francie? If there was one, it would have been on the tape. It's not there."

She frowned.

"All transmissions are on the tape, right?"

"No. Only communication between the dispatcher and officers in the field. Car to car isn't on the tape."

Something stirred in the pit of my stomach. "Then anybody out there with a police radio could issue a BOLO, and there would be no record of it?"

"They could, but it's not done. It's not procedure. According to proper procedure," she said, "anybody who wants a suspect stopped or picked up gives it to the dispatcher, who broadcasts the BOLO."

"But what if somebody didn't follow proper procedure and put it out on the radio himself?"

Francie shrugged. "Then the troops on that frequency would hear it, although it would have bypassed dispatch and wouldn't be on the tape. But that's not supposed to be how it's done."

I was excited now. "But Francie, what if it *was* done? That would explain it."

"That would explain it," she echoed, looking thoughtful. "But who . . ."

"If somebody did it, why haven't they come forward? There's no excuse for Hudson's death, but it sure would make the officers look a little less culpable. It could explain why they went after him. It would prove that it wasn't just because he was a black man in a nice car; it would show that they really had some reason to think he was armed and dangerous. Otherwise, they just look like racist hoodlums."

"Maybe that's what somebody wanted them to look like," she said.

"You mean they were set up?"

"Things are so crazy in the department," Francie began slowly, then stopped and shook her head. "But it's all too far-fetched. Why would anybody do that?"

"Unless it was somebody who was setting up D. Wayne Hudson, not the cops."

"He didn't seem like a man with those kinds of enemies. And it had to be somebody with access to a police radio—who knew our frequencies, unit numbers, and procedures."

"So it had to be somebody on duty that night, right?"

"Not necessarily," she said. "A lot of officers, and all of the brass, have their own radios. It wouldn't have to be somebody who was actually working. But why, Britt?"

"Maybe just a bad practical joke. One that got out of hand. They didn't realize that D. Wayne would get thumped."

"But who?"

"You've got me, Francie, but you have to admit it's a possibility."

"Yeah. Let's think about it." She took off the sunglasses and folded them, her eyes speculative. "Strictly personal, Britt, and far more pleasant, I hear you're seeing Kenny Mac, one of the homicide guys."

"That's around the station?" I raised my eyebrows.

"I heard him taking a razzing."

"God, Francie, cops are worse than, than . . ." I groped.

"A bunch of little old ladies," she said, finishing my sentence for me. "I felt sorry for the guy, given the current state of police-press relations."

My face felt hot, remembering that first night with McDonald, and our post-coital banter about the police and the press.

"This is serious! You're blushing, Britt!"

"I don't blush," I said. "It's the sun."

She laughed as we stood to walk back to our cars. "He's a nice guy, gorgeous eyes, a real hunk, too. Hope it works out for you. By the way, I also heard about your encounter with Major Alvarez awhile back."

"I figured. Gossip travels with the speed of light at police headquarters."

"The man is nuts, Britt, totally unpredictable. I try my best to stay out of his way. He's got a short fuse."

"Don't I know it." I nodded and rolled my eyes, remembering.

"I'm serious. His wife manages one of those walk-in clinics in Little Havana, the one at Ninth Street and Twelfth Avenue. She's an RN. We've had a couple of calls out there in the past. Some kid broke in one night, looking for drugs. I heard Alvarez not only caught the kid but beat him half to death."

"There was never a beef?"

"The kid came in through a skylight. Alvarez claimed he fell. The kid's a junkie. He's a major, with political clout. Who's going to challenge his story?"

I drove back to the paper, my mind abuzz with the possibilities in the Hudson case, and wondering why McDonald never mentioned being teased about our relationship.

I scanned Janowitz's story from Atlanta. Only one black selected for the jury, and he was an alternate. The fate of the Hudson cops would rest in the hands of an all-white panel. Our daily nuts-and-bolts coverage was thorough, but not front-page stuff. On television, however, everything was front page.

Night after night, we saw stills of D. Wayne Hudson, photogenic and smiling, with his beautiful wife and children. Footage of him in action on the football field, to the roar of a cheering crowd. Footage of his funeral. And once testimony started, with cameras in the courtroom, tape of the most damning moments presented by the prosecution. Dr. Duffy, the assistant medical examiner, on the stand, using a pointer to detail each injury on photos shot in the morgue.

Carpenter demonstrated how he helped smash the lights on Hudson's car, then push it into the ditch. An officer witness demonstrated the blows that rained onto the head and body of the handcuffed victim. All were shown and reshown over and over again.

It certainly looked bleak for the defense. But I knew there are no guarantees with a jury, and the jury was not watching TV. If you read Janowitz's copy carefully, the squadron of defense lawyers seemed to be making some points that might stick.

The Blackburns and the bodybuilders insisted that Hudson violently resisted arrest, that he never appeared seriously injured. That hospital personnel may have been responsible for the death by failing to recognize, diagnose, and treat his injuries sooner.

Meanwhile, I put out feelers by phone, since most cops did not want to be seen conversing with reporters, and even pumped McDonald about who might have broadcast a BOLO that night, either as a prank or for more sinister reasons.

Dan Flood proved more helpful than McDonald, who had actually talked to me more freely about cases when we were strangers. Now that we were lovers, he wouldn't tell me a damn thing.

"It wouldn't be ethical to tell you," he responded to my simple question about an open homicide case one night on our way to a movie.

"I hate men with ethics."

"It's not so much ethics," he said. "It's known as covering my ass."

"You're overreacting, and it's unfair to me," I pouted. "This is reverse discrimination."

"Ha, now you know how it feels. It's just that if I'm accused of talking to you about police business, I want to be able to truthfully deny it. I don't like being labeled the leak in the department," he grumbled.

"Oh you poor baby," I joked. "Sticks and stones . . ."

He didn't laugh. He parked the Cherokee in the lot facing the Byron-Carlyle Theater, and we strolled across the street toward the box office. Suddenly, McDonald took his hand off my shoulder and spun away. "Be cool. Meet you back at the car," he murmured, then went back to the curb and returned to the Cherokee via a circuitous route. He did not look back.

I wasn't sure whether to follow, wait for him, or go ahead and buy the tickets. The movie would start in less than five minutes.

He must have seen something, I thought, looking wildly around; a suspect, or a missing car that homicide had been looking for. Nothing looked obvious to me. Annoyed, I marched straight back to the Cherokee. He stood beside it, trying to appear casual. "Walk on around the corner," he said in a low voice, without looking at me. "I'll pick you up there."

"What *is* this? What's going on?" He made a quick, impatient gesture. Feeling foolish, I trotted dutifully around the corner and stood waiting in front of a closed dry cleaning shop. The Cherokee came gliding around the block a few minutes later. He glanced furtively around as I climbed in. "What the heck is going on?" I demanded.

"We almost walked right up on them," he said.

"Who?"

"You didn't see them?"

"Who?"

"Lt. Simmons and his wife. They were waiting in line at the box office."

"So what?"

"You know it's not a good idea for us to be seen together right now."

"You don't want to be seen with me!"

"You know how things are at the department."

"Yes, but this is ridiculous. Does this mean we have to sneak around like illicit lovers, as though we're each married to somebody else?"

"That," he said, grinning, "would probably be simpler than our current situation."

"*This* is why we've been staying home a lot," I said accusingly. "Am I dumb. I thought you just liked being alone with me."

"That's a bonus." He squeezed my knee.

"What about the movie? The lieutenant and his wife are probably already inside."

"We'd probably bump into them on the way out."

"And maybe we could go have a cup of coffee with them, like normal people."

He cut his eyes at me and turned right, onto Indian Creek Drive, toward my place. "Things aren't normal right now. Let's just rent a movie tonight."

I sighed out loud. "I didn't know whether to scream, cry, or eat a banana when you just walked away and left me in the middle of the street. That's why you were so eager to go all the way across state to Sanibel, isn't it? That explains that awful, dark Italian restaurant that's suddenly your new favorite."

"I'm sorry, Britt. But I'm studying hard for the lieutenant's test next month, hoping to make the list. Being seen with you can't do me any good. You know how cops are."

"You can just tell them that we don't talk business! God knows it's true." His face had darkened and looked set. "Are you really taking that much heat?" I asked more gently.

"If you must know, yes," he said finally. "Check the glove compartment."

I did. Atop the owner's manual and car papers was a name plate, neatly lettered and constructed of heavy cardboard. Somebody had put a lot of effort into it. The name and the title had been carefully stenciled and filled in with a black felt-tip marker. JIMMY OLSON, Boy Reporter. I couldn't help but whoop with laughter.

"Found it on my desk," he said, controlling his temper with obvious difficulty.

"When?"

"Right after you broke that story on the fight in the parking lot."

"I didn't get that tip from you."

"Nobody in the department believes that. Every time you write a story," he shook his head, "everybody looks at me."

"That's ludicrous. I had sources before we started seeing each other. You were one of them," I sniffed. "I still have the others. It's not fair."

"Tell me about it."

The evening was not a total loss. Our lovemaking was passionate. The frustration of our situation only made me want him more. In fact, behaving like strangers in public and uninhibited lovers behind closed doors lent a clandestine sense of excitement to the relationship.

But when it came to talking shop, he was a sphinx. Thankfully,

Dan Flood was back on the job, his speech still a bit clipped, but feeling fine, thank you, and looking good, having lost almost twenty-five pounds while unable to eat. We chewed on the question of who could have put out the BOLO, chatting on the unrecorded homicide line.

"What you have to consider, Britt, is why. If it was someone on the force, who would stand to gain by polarizing the department, by this scandal, by the guys being on trial?"

"I dunno," I said puzzled.

"I don't either," Dan said. "But anybody could have. Uh oh, my partner, a guy you know, is getting pissed at me for spending too much time on the phone. Gotta go. But why don't you check out the Thursday night poker players? See if they know anything."

"The who?"

"For the past twenty years, a bunch of the guys have been getting together for a game. Whitaker, Alvarez, O'Rourke, and Duran are some of the founding members."

"Who else plays?" I reached for a pencil and began to scribble on the notepad next to the phone as Flood rattled off names.

"Tell your partner hello," I said, trying to sound casual.

"Sure thing, toots."

I got the distinct impression that he did not use my name because he did not want to be accused of talking to me. He didn't even want McDonald to know.

I shook my head, hating all the secrecy and being treated like I was contagious. The names of the poker players were all familiar; they were cops who had been around for a long time. A few were old-time hard-liners who did not deal well with the press. I knew three of the others, Duran, O'Rourke, and Salazar, well enough to have their unlisted home phone numbers. Over time, as they ascended in rank, many cops became less paranoid about giving out their numbers. Two were lieutenants, another a captain.

They're all buddies, I thought; if I use a shotgun approach and start peppering them with questions, word will quickly get back to all of them. I had to think this through and try to hit pay dirt on the first call.

I sat and studied the names. Lt. Sean O'Rourke's jumped out at me. He was a smart man, good cop, loud and often boisterous, a bit of a drinker, and somewhat of a maverick. That had to be the reason he had not climbed higher in rank. I had called him at home a few times on breaking stories, and even relatively early in the evening his words had been slightly slurred, though he remained articulate. His dad had been an assistant chief on the New York City Police Department, a fact he was proud of. He loved police work, but exuded a sense of bitterness at the direction the department had taken. I knew he was eligible for retirement and thinking about putting in his papers. I had never known him to lie, which was why he often got in trouble with the brass. He hated politics and those who played it, loved the truth, and spoke out, often to the detriment of his career. He would loudly castigate his own men when they screwed up, but never allowed anyone else to criticize them. He was a real cop's cop.

O'Rourke was beefy, with a chubby face, pale eyes, and a growing gut. I also knew that he'd been divorced a few years earlier after a long-term marriage, and had a son in college, studying engineering. Always alone at the functions I had covered, he was either carrying a torch or awkward about reentering the single social life. The times I had called him at home, he seemed to be alone and enjoyed talking, keeping the conversation going far beyond what I needed for the story. I glanced at the accursed cuckoo clock. If I catch him at home, I thought, he'll probably have had a few drinks by now. Loose, alone, maybe eager to chat.

"I need to talk to you," I told him.

"Where've ya been, Britt?" His words seemed more than slightly slurred. "What's up?"

"I wanted to talk to you about the Hudson case." Nothing like getting right to the point.

There was a pause. I heard him breathing. "I was wonderin' when you would catch on. This whole trial, it's a crock of shit. Those poor bastards."

"What do you mean?" I said, trying not to sound too eager.

"Where are you calling from?"

"Home."

"You know we shouldn't talk like this over the phone."

"I doubt there's any risk . . ."

"Never say anything over the phone that you don't want your mother to hear when it's played at your trial."

"I could come there. Is that okay? What's the address?"

He told me. "Jus' come south down the Palmetto, get off at SW Twenty-fourth, hang a right at the fourth light. Don't park in the driveway."

"I'll leave it down the block," I promised, my pulse pounding in my throat. "I'll be right there."

NINETEEN

I drove through the night with a growing sense of excitement at what lay ahead. I had no trouble finding the address; cops give good directions. I worried that maybe I was being set up. But O'Rourke had never lied to me, or anyone as far as I knew. He had a stubborn Irish sense of honor and decency that never helped him advance his career. More realistically, I worried that he might keep drinking and be incoherent by the time I got there. Or that he might sober up and, thinking clearly, decide against talking to me.

I carefully parked the T-Bird a block away from the house. It was about 10 P.M., and I saw no one out on the street.

The door opened on my first ring of the bell. In his hand was a nearly empty glass, with melting ice cubes. His broad face was ruddy and red-veined.

"Didn't take you long," he said. "Come on in. Want a drink?"

"Club soda?"

He frowned.

"A wine spritzer?"

"Sure."

I trailed him through the living room out into a screened-in patio, half-covered by an overhang. Baskets of well-tended orchids and stag horn ferns hung from a pipe that seemed to be part of the screening. "Wonderful house," I told him.

"Been here twenty-two years," he said. "Built this addition myself." He was obviously proud of the place. Everything was orderly, with almost a military spit and polish.

A wet bar faced the pool and a brick barbecue. I could picture years of evening meals and family gatherings here. He moved comfortably behind the bar, fixing my drink. "I shoulda told you to bring a swimsuit."

"It's a little nippy for me," I said. I love swimming in the ocean when the water is languid and steamy, like a warm bath.

"Peanuts?" He reached down to a shelf and came up with a vacuum-packed can. "I've got some right here." He turned a key, opened the can with a whoosh, sprinkled the contents into a bowl, and pushed it in my direction. Music came from behind him, a stereo tuned in to an oldies station, playing hits from the fifties.

He stood behind the bar, lonely master of all he surveyed. I sat on a rattan stool in front of him. He had been drinking, but probably no more than he drank here alone every night. His usual refrain was the sorry politics, the ethnicity, the leadership, or lack of it, in the department. His father had been highly decorated in New York. "The job had some honor to it then," he was saying, about the early days when he was an eager, ambitious rookie and Miami was a sleepy southern resort city.

I could see that O'Rourke wanted to play host a bit longer, but I was impatient to address the reason for my visit.

"Have you been reading the trial coverage?"

O'Rourke looked glum. "Those poor bastards." He shook his head.

"What about D. Wayne Hudson, that poor bastard?" I said, taking a handful of peanuts.

"It could be a homicide," he blurted, staring bleary-eyed into his glass. "Cold-blooded, premeditated, first-degree murder."

"But they didn't even know who he was, much less have time to premeditate killing him."

"Not them." O'Rourke looked me straight in the eye, swaying slightly on his feet. "I have suspicions of my own."

I felt chilly, despite my long-sleeved shirt.

"What do you mean?"

"This is strictly confidential, Britt. You can never, ever, use my name, or even hint that any of this came from me. We never spoke. I'll deny it."

I looked him square in the eye. "I never give up a source. You know that about me by now."

He nodded and dropped fresh ice cubes into his glass. He poured a healthy slug of Jack Daniels over them.

"I've never been a rat no matter what they've done," he muttered. "But seeing those guys—on trial, like common criminals. I'm not saying the Blackburns are heroes, and the department is better off without the Machados and Estradas, but I have a strong feeling that they shouldn't be on trial, at least not on murder charges."

"You believe somebody put out a phony BOLO?"

"It's the only explanation."

"Who could it have been?"

"Alvarez. He had the opportunity, and the motive."

My mind raced, suddenly remembering. "Alma told me he was at the meeting with D. Wayne Hudson that night! It would have been simple for him to watch Hudson leave, then radio a description of his car and report it as stolen, driven by an armed and dangerous suspect. But why?"

"He wants the chief's job so bad he'll fuck over anybody to get it." O'Rourke's pale eyes looked haunted. "I've worked with the man for more than twenty years, Britt. He is without conscience. Totally amoral. Ambition can be an overpowering addiction. He'll do anything for power. People like him would turn in their own mothers to make a rank." As his voice rose, his fingers tightened around his glass until I was afraid it would shatter.

"Wait a minute." He was getting carried away, and I was still confused. "Why would he believe that putting out that BOLO would land him the job?"

O'Rourke gulped a deep breath. When he spoke again it was in a lower register. "We've all played poker once a week over the years since back when Hector was a pup. We rap, we brainstorm, we relax. Over the years we all came up together through the ranks, and we all were pretty well disgusted when they brought the new chief in from out of town. It should have been somebody from inside. One of us. Nobody wanted it more than Alvarez. We all pretty much pissed and moaned when they brought in an outsider. Especially this chief. I swear, the man can't count past twenty with his fly up. We all despise him, never cut him a break. We talked about it incessantly every week, hoping he'd screw up bad enough to get fired or forced out."

O'Rourke leaned heavily across the bar, on his elbows, his jowly face open and sincere. "Alvarez knows that if this chief goes, he is next in line for the job. He's front runner."

I nodded, not wanting to slow him down.

"But as time went on, the goddamn chief seemed to be more and more entrenched. The son of a bitch has been weathering it, even with nobody giving him a break. Hell, he could be here for another ten years." He rolled his eyes. "We'd all be long gone by then. Somewhere along the line, a running joke started among us about how to get rid of the man. Sheer speculation, just bullshitting. I said it myself one week, 'What the hell do we have to do to get rid of the mother-fucker, put a bullet in his head?' Scuze my French."

I nodded and sipped my drink. In the distance a dog barked and somebody's car alarm yelped. The oldies station played something throbbingly sweet and sentimental, meant for the occupants of back-seats in lovers' lanes, back in the days when young sweethearts could frequent lovers' lanes without being robbed or raped, or worse.

He leaned closer. "The night I said that, Alvarez said, 'No, you're wrong. He's not the one we have to kill.' He said it matter of fact, like he'd been thinking about it. Somebody asked what the hell he was talking about, and he made a little speech about how it's better for a cause to kill a good man than to kill a bad one."

I frowned. "What does that mean?"

"You know how these Latins scheme, how they love intrigue. You understand it better than anybody; hell, you're one of them."

"Only half-Cuban," I said.

O'Rourke studied me as if, even cold sober, I was too dense to comprehend simple English. He spoke carefully, like a drunk will do when trying to be certain he is understood.

"Simple. The catalyst needed to get this department cleaned out from the top would be a high-profile brutality case. If that wild bunch on midnights killed a well-known, highly respected black man, the community would be howling for the chief's head."

I gasped, a peanut slid sideways down my throat, and I erupted in a paroxysm of coughing. "You can't be serious," I sputtered, eyes tearing, my voice choking.

"You all right?" He patted me on the back with his big hand.

"Yes, yes," I gasped, wanting to ask a dozen questions, unable to catch my breath.

O'Rourke took a long pull on his drink, watching me, then spoke slowly again. "He said when you kill a bad man nothing changes, but kill a good man and people react. They would kick the bad one out. His regime would topple. The chief would have to resign or be fired."

"Which has almost happened," I said, my voice still gravelly. The impact had hit me like a painful punch in the solar plexus. Had D. Wayne Hudson died to make Alvarez top man in the department?

"The funny thing is," O'Rourke said ironically, "we laughed, we all said it made sense. We thought it was just the drinks talking." He stared glumly into his glass, then refilled it.

"So he set up Hudson *and* the cops? But how could he know what they would do?" It seemed too farfetched.

"You have to remember," O'Rourke said, "that Alvarez is the man who transferred most of those guys to midnights. He knew their propensity for violence, their reputations. He must have had a pretty good idea that they'd pile onto Hudson. If they didn't, fine. It was worth a shot."

"But he couldn't know they would kill him."

"Maybe they didn't."

My eyes locked onto his, waiting for his words.

"I've always thought it pretty strange that nobody, not the guys at the scene, rescue, or the doctors considered Hudson's condition critical. Then all of a sudden, he's brain dead. Just too damn convenient."

"It happens." I shrugged. "But you're saying . . ."

"No way to ever prove it," he warned. "Sheer speculation on my part, but what if after hearing Hudson was going to be okay, somebody made sure he wouldn't be?"

Murder. I stared at O'Rourke. "Was Alvarez at the hospital that night?"

"Not on paper. He's not mentioned in any reports. For all we know he went right home after the meeting."

My mind was reeling. "If D. Wayne was murdered in the hospital, how? There would have to be medical evidence."

O'Rourke shrugged. "Whatever it was, the medical examiner didn't find it, did he? I told you Britt, this is all just speculation, my own theory, with holes in it big enough to drive a truck through."

"The doctors who tried to revive him would have spotted any fresh injuries," I said, thinking aloud. "You think he could have been smothered, with a pillow or something?"

O'Rourke looked skeptical, shaking his head.

"Wait a minute!" I said. "Alvarez has access to drugs . . ."

"How do you figure that?"

"His wife operates a clinic in Little Havana. I just heard something about it the other day. She's a registered nurse. He could have gotten anything he needed right there."

He shrugged. "But why didn't the ME find something? If you pursue this, Britt, you have to make everybody think you figured it out by your lonesome."

I nodded, and drained my own drink, heart pounding.

"Those poor bastards, on trial for murder." He poured himself another, then sloshed wine into my empty glass.

"He's dangerous, Britt. Alvarez is as crazy as hell. When the trouble the chief is in was brought up at the last card game, he just grinned. He thinks he's gonna take his place. Looks like he will."

"The chief has no idea?"

"Not a clue. As far as I know, he thinks it's all just bad luck."

I thought back over everything that had happened. "But why was Alvarez so infuriated when I showed up on the fifth floor? He had no reason if I'd served his purpose by writing about the attack on D. Wayne."

"He bragged about that later, he really enjoyed hosing you down. Maybe he did it for effect, maybe it really did piss him off to see you up there. He's always hated reporters. Without the media, he thinks he would have been chief long ago."

"If you suspected all this, why haven't you gone to homicide or internal affairs?"

He shook his head. "I told you, I'm out of it, Britt. There's a big difference between having a gut feeling and proving something happened. My word against his. If it doesn't stick, where do I stand? I don't even know if any of the other guys have given it a thought. Besides, I wouldn't piss on the chief if he was going up in flames. Those poor dumb bastards up there on trial, even *they* think they're guilty."

It all fit, in a crazy, evil way. A native of this city where anything could happen, I was still stunned. I left O'Rourke the way he was when I arrived, standing alone at the door, a half-empty glass in his hand.

Once home, I called the hospital. On the third try, I finally got through to Rico, at a nurses' station in ICU. "I need your help," I said. "It's really important."

"What do you mean?"

"I need you to think back to the night D. Wayne Hudson came in."

There was a pause. "Let me call you right back on another phone."

"No problem." I fidgeted for nearly ten minutes before the phone rang.

"Okay," he said. "You didn't leave any messages around for me with your name on them, did you?"

"No, you know better than that."

"What do you need?"

"Remember that night?"

"If you recollect, I was the one who called you."

"Right. Remember the blue uniforms. The Miami cops who were there?"

"Yeah?"

"They were mostly patrolmen, the ones involved in the chase. I need to know if one of the brass was there. Maybe later . . ."

"Frankie Alvarez?"

I caught my breath. "I didn't know you knew him."

"Sure, he's been around for years. His wife used to work here, in the unit, before she got involved with some clinic, over there in Little Havana."

"Was he there that night?"

"Sure. He showed up. I saw him out there on the floor, alone."

"Do you know when it was?" I tried to keep my voice calm.

"The exact time, no. The other cops were long gone." He thought for a moment. "It was before all the excitement, the code. Before D. Wayne went sour on us."

"Didn't anybody think it unusual? Could he ever have been alone with Hudson?"

"Without a doubt. What are you getting at, Britt? Nothing unusual about cops being in and out of here. I figured he just wanted to get a look at the patient. Him being a celebrity and all."

"Thanks, Rico." I was trembling.

"Whatever it is, we didn't talk."

TWENTY

The newsroom was building up steam early the next morning. So was I. Final arguments were scheduled in Atlanta, and the case would probably go to the jury by the end of the day. With five defendants, there was no telling how long deliberations would take. This was Thursday, and we could have a verdict by the weekend. Reporters were at work on backgrounders and poised to do reaction stories.

I called the chief medical examiner first. Dr. Duffy had performed the autopsy on Hudson, but he was still in Atlanta, on the chance he would be recalled to the stand for rebuttal. I hoped he would not be offended that I went straight to the top. The chief had been out of town when Hudson was killed.

He didn't hem and haw around, or give me any wishy-washy crap about it not being his case. He had been chief for three decades now. He was the man in charge; every case was his case.

"I have information, from a usually reliable source," I told him, "that D. Wayne Hudson's injuries were not critical when he reached the hospital. That he may have been deliberately murdered afterwards."

The chief was cool. After more than a hundred thousand corpses, there was nothing he hadn't seen. He did not react.

"What are you looking for? The man was badly beaten."

"I think some kind of drug or drug combination could have been administered," I said. "How can we find out?"

"Let me review the case file, the toxicological findings, and see what we come up with."

"The file's not in Atlanta?"

"No, Dr. Duffy took a copy of the autopsy report with him. The original records are kept here. Did your source have any information on what drug we would be looking for?"

"No," I sighed, realizing how vague this sounded. "The person allegedly responsible has access to a clinic."

"Hummm. How long was Hudson hospitalized before he was pronounced?"

"Twenty-four hours. He was a donor, so they kept him going to harvest the organs."

"That's what I thought I recalled. We would not have run a blood test at autopsy after doctors had medicated him for that long. All it would turn up would be therapeutic, what the doctors had given him. We would have been interested only in whatever chemicals he had on board before he was injured."

My heart sank. There was no postmortem tox screen to review.

"If my memory is correct," the chief was saying, "our tests were run on blood drawn when he first arrived at the hospital. All we came up with was a small amount of alcohol."

"Right, it showed something equivalent to a drink after dinner, no drugs. So it's too late now and there's no way to tell?"

"Sure there is." His voice was as confident and well modulated, as always. "The gray-top tube."

"The what?"

"The gray-top tube. What we have to do now is go back and check the gray-top tube. We preserve a vial of blood from every autopsy we do, whether it's a fresh case or somebody who was in the hospital for six months. That's one of our policies, in case something should ever come up later, something like this."

I asked a stupid question, forgetting how precisely coded everything is at the medical examiner's office. "Why is it called the gray-top tube?"

"The red-top tubes come with nothing, the purple-top tubes contain anticoagulants, the green-top tubes have heparin, another anticoagulant, the gray-top tubes have sodium fluoride, a preservative, the striped-top tubes are used for separating . . ."

"I get it," I said. What a meticulous and brilliant man, I thought. Miami is so lucky to have him.

"We keep them in the autopsy room. When each body is admitted, a morgue attendant enters the name and case number into the computer, which automatically prints out labels for all the necessary containers. In every case there is a label for the gray-top tube."

"So you still have a sample of D. Wayne Hudson's blood, taken after his death?"

"Oh yes."

"How long will it take to test?"

"Under the circumstances, we could probably have enough done this afternoon to tell us something."

"Shall I call you at noon?"

"Two o'clock is more realistic."

I dialed Major Alvarez at police headquarters and asked his secretary for an appointment to see him later in the day.

Perky when she answered, she now sounded vague and doubtful. "He's very busy," she said. "He, uh, has meetings all day."

"I need twenty minutes of his time," I said urgently, "for an important story."

"Why don't you call the public information office?" she asked brightly.

"This story is sensitive, it concerns him personally. I think he would much rather speak directly to me." That was tipping my hand, I knew, but I couldn't resist, and he might be curious enough to bite the bait.

She said she'd get back to me later in the day.

Restless and on edge, I wanted to escape the office. Onnie's temporary job had ended; I'd heard about a job prospect I wanted to talk to her about, and it would give me a chance to see Darryl. I called her number.

"It's me," I said. "In the mood for a *media noche?* I'll stop at La Esquina, and be right over."

"Don't come, Britt." I could hear Darryl playing in the background. Her words failed to register at first.

"Don't come, I said."

"Onnie? What's wrong?"

"It's too dangerous." Her voice was a low whisper; I could scarcely make out the words.

"Has something happened?" Unconsciously my own voice dropped to a whisper. For a moment I was afraid that Darryl's father had tracked them down.

"It's the streets," she blurted. "They're about to boil over. You're not safe in this neighborhood, Britt. Don't come."

"Come on," I said, exasperated. "I know things are hot right now, but I've been over there a million times and nobody looks at me twice." Hell, I thought, it's not the greatest neighborhood, but if Onnie and Darryl can live there, I can certainly visit.

"Not the way it is now, Britt. Don't you dare try to come here. No white face is safe in this neighborhood today. I mean it." Her voice shook. She was serious.

"Oh, Onnie. I'm so sorry. But it's gonna be okay, I promise."

"The jury is out, Britt. We'll wait and see what happens." The words sounded ominous.

"Give Darryl a kiss for me, and yourself a hug."

"Be careful, Britt."

Shit, I thought savagely, what the hell is going on in this town?

I called the medical examiner's office. Nothing yet. I had hoped to have the ME results first, but decided to fill in Fred Douglas and Mark Seybold. Fred's office was empty; he'd gone to lunch. I called O'Rourke; but he was out of his office, too.

Too uptight to eat, even though I'd skipped breakfast, I drank some Cuban coffee from the machine in the third-floor cafeteria, probably the last thing I needed since I was already about to cartwheel off the walls. I sat alone for a few minutes at a window table reserved for the pressmen whose clothes usually leave the plastic chairs smeared with low-rub ink. I drank in the strong brew along with my favorite view, the spectacular panorama of vivid bright blue bay and a cerulean cloud-swept sky, soothing, as always.

Gretchen was in when I came back to my desk, and I tried to avoid her eyes. I didn't want to have to explain to her what I was working on. This story was far too important to trust to her judgment.

She and Ryan were chatting amiably up at the city desk. They had been getting along famously since their triumph with his rafting story.

I dialed the ME again. The chief took the call immediately.

"You were right," he said.

"What was in the gray-top tube?" I said breathlessly.

"Barbiturates, a lethal concentration. We've gone back to check his hospital records. It took about an hour to pull the file out of the record room and send somebody for it. Barbiturates are sometimes used in head injuries to decrease metabolism and oxygen demands, decreasing damage to the brain. But this concentration is far in excess of any therapeutic use. We double-checked our own lab to see whether we made an error, or used the wrong tube, and I also talked to the donor people to see if they might have done something they didn't chart as part of the harvesting procedure. We found nothing that changes the bottom line."

"Would a lethal dose of barbiturates damage the harvested organs?"

"No, only the brain."

"How do you think it was administered?"

"Most likely injected into his IV."

"So that, not the head injuries, caused the fatal brain damage?"

"Correct. Somebody almost got away with it. We're about to contact the state attorney's office. It certainly changes the complexion of the trial."

"Too late," I said. "It's gone to the jury."

He paused and I heard a long sigh. "It'll certainly be grounds for reversal—should there be a conviction. I think homicide and the state attorney's office will want to talk to you, Britt."

"I'm writing the story now. All I have to do is talk to one more person."

Excited, I spun around in my chair after hanging up. "Ryan, you won't believe this . . ." As he looked up, my phone rang, and I answered impatiently. "Britt Montero." No one seemed to be there. "Hello?"

"This is Francisco Alvarez."

I nearly dropped the telephone, taken totally by surprise. I had planned to park outside of his office if necessary. I had never expected him to personally return my call.

"My secretary said you wanted to talk to me."

"Yes, Major," I felt flustered. "Can I come over now to see you?"

"I don't have time for reporters. Call PIO."

"Wait a minute, Major." I was afraid he'd hang up. "You will want the chance to answer some of the questions in this story. It's about you."

"What about me?" Was it my imagination, knowing what I did now, or was his voice sinister? It sounded slick, deep, and dark, like the man. The hair on the back of my neck prickled.

I had to push him into saying something quotable, even if it was only an angry denial. Without his comment I had no legitimate way to publicly link him to Hudson's death, only hearsay from sources who would not, could not, be quoted.

"Your involvement in the D. Wayne Hudson case."

Silence. I was afraid he had hung up. "Major?"

"I'm still here."

"I would like you to respond to the accusations."

Silence. "Major, I know about the BOLO, the one you broadcast that night." Silence. The emptiness on the line seemed to project something—was it fear, or indifference? "I know about your visit to the hospital, with the barbiturates."

Silence. "I'm writing the story now," I bluffed. "Whether you respond or not." He was too shrewd to say anything. His silence chilled my spine. I would have welcomed threats, curses, or angry denials.

"Major . . ." the line went dead.

Damn! I hit the button, got a dial tone, and began to punch in his office number. Had he not taken me by surprise, perhaps I could have approached him in a more effective way.

"Not guilty!" The cry echoed in choruses across the newsroom, repeated by everyone who heard it. Janowitz was on line, a bulletin was crossing the wire.

The jury had returned a verdict in less than an hour, forty-nine minutes to be exact. All had been acquitted. Not guilty. I put down the phone. Not guilty. Knowing what I knew now, I didn't know whether to laugh or cry. Not guilty. Dazed, I thought of Ted Ferrell and Betsy, thought of Estrada and Machado, and the Blackburns, back in uniform. There would still be administrative charges, but if they fought, they were likely to win back their badges. One of the blessings of my job is that there is never time to think about it.

Gretchen appeared at my desk. "We need reaction for the state edition, Britt. Get the police chief, the mayor, and any of the city commissioners you can find."

"We may have some trouble on the street, Gretchen. I probably ought to get out there." Her uncomprehending eyes stared, and her brow began to furrow under the shiny bangs.

"Trouble?"

I nodded, gravely.

"Well, do the reaction story first." She flicked an invisible speck off the shoulder of her sleek mustard-colored suit and strutted back to the city desk.

The police chief took my call. His reaction? "The jury has spoken. There is nothing more I can say. We have to have faith in our system of justice." Discussing whether the men would be reinstated was premature at this time, he said. He expected no problems the department would be unable to handle.

The politicians' comments followed along the same lines. I batted out the story, then joined the growing group at the city desk. Fred Douglas was coordinating the coverage.

"Britt can go out into the black neighborhoods to pick up reaction there. Take a photographer," he said, turning to me.

"I'm up," offered Lottie, who had joined the crowd from the photo desk.

"Okay, let's go," I said.

She glanced at her watch. "We better huggle-de-buck. I'll catch you downstairs."

Gretchen interfered. "I think a man should go with Britt and Lottie. For their protection. Britt says there might be trouble out there."

"We don't need anybody else," Lottie and I chorused.

Fred looked preoccupied.

"Ryan," Gretchen said, summoning him from his desk. "You go with Britt and Lottie."

Lottie and I exchanged glances. "We'll be okay, just the two of us," I said.

"Yeah," Lottie quickly added. "We don't need protection."

"Ryan," Gretchen ordered. "Go with them."

"He's got no street smarts," I said quietly, so Ryan, bounding eagerly from his desk, could not hear. "We'd have to look out for him."

"None of this silly feminist rhetoric. This is not the time." Gretchen sighed aloud at our foolishness.

We looked to Fred Douglas for help, but he was engrossed in the first copy from Atlanta, which had just appeared on his editing terminal. Janowitz was filing directly from a portable laptop computer right outside the courtroom.

We read for a moment over his shoulder. Members of the all-white jury had jovially lined up to pump the defendants' hands after acquitting them.

"Jesus," Fred said, shaking his head. He looked up, "You guys get going. We need more reaction and art for the state."

"I have to talk to you as soon as we get back. It's important," I said urgently, "and we'll need Mark Seybold to sit in. I've got one hell of a story."

"Okay, okay," he waved us off.

"Hell's fire, do we have to take Ryan?" Lottie mouthed, looking disgruntled.

"Fred, we don't need another reporter . . ."

"Will you guys just go?" He pointed impatiently toward the elevator. "Do as Gretchen says for a change."

Gretchen looked smug. "Watch out for them, Ryan," she called after us.

"Sure thing," he responded.

Fortunately, neither she nor Ryan could see us rolling our eyes.

It got worse. "I'll take the keys," Ryan said manfully, when we got to Lottie's Chrysler under the building.

"No, Ryan," she said. "This is my company car. I drive."

"I'm the man, I drive."

"Oh no!" we shrieked.

"Look Ryan," I said, "Lottie and I have both had police combat driving courses."

"Which is exactly why I'm going to drive," he said. "I know what happened to your other cars."

"It was only one, and it wasn't our fault! Ryan, that rafting experience has made you crazy!"

"I'd like to see you survive a week at sea." Pouting, he folded his arms and leaned stubbornly against the driver's door.

"You've become macho," I cried. I thought of Jessie St. Juste. "I swear I'll bite off your finger!"

"What?"

"Oh hell, Britt." Lottie had unloaded the camera equipment she needed from the trunk. "We're wasting too much time as it is. Give him his way. I can shoot pictures, you can take notes." She tossed him the keys and looked him sternly in the eye. "Damage this car, Ryan, and you are a dead man."

He grinned. They piled into the front.

"Lottie," I said, settling in the backseat, amid all her packets of pictures, "you should have let me bite off his finger."

"Hell, Britt, you don't want to do that. He's not a policeman. And he needs them all to count."

We rolled out from under the building into the brilliant afternoon air.

"It's nice to get out of the office for awhile," Ryan said happily, as if on a pleasure jaunt. "Where to, girls?"

Lottie and I stared at each other.

We stopped to interview several people at a Liberty City bus stop. All had heard the verdict. Radio and TV news bulletins had swept the city. Even older women, on their way home from day jobs, seemed wary and hostile. A lanky youth approached us, angry and jabbing his finger. "The pigs," he cried, his eyes wild and wet with rage. "They beat up on the easy targets, they let the bad people go! They're dead!" he shouted, referring to the defendants. "They're dead!"

We thanked him and moved on.

"Ryan, lock your door, and be careful," I said.

"If we yell *go,* you floor it," added Lottie. "Okay?"

"Sure, sure." He was smiling, enjoying this. "How about them?" He nodded toward a corner bar with a small knot of men outside.

"No point in trying to open a dialogue with a bunch of drunks."

Lottie agreed. "No point in stirring 'em up."

They shouted, raising fists as we passed.

We stopped at a small corner grocery, where there were women and kids. Ryan pulled to the curb. Lottie and I stepped out and approached a small group of people. "We're from the *News,* have you heard about the verdict in the Hudson case?" I said.

"You better get outta here," a heavyset woman said. Her eyes slid back to the store. I took a step toward the door, hoping to interview the owner.

Two men lurched from inside, shouting. "White mothafuckers," one screamed. One lunged for Lottie's camera, arm outstretched as though he was a baseball player diving for a line drive.

"Go, Ryan!" we yelled, scrambling back into the Chrysler. He had switched off the ignition, which we had warned him not to do. He fumbled with the keys. "Go!" I screamed, engaging in a tug of war with one of the men over my car door. I finally yanked it closed as the man beat on the window with his bare fists.

"Go!" Lottie yelled. She had managed to slam her door. The man after her camera spat on the window, then dropped his eyes, scanning the gutter. We knew what he was looking for, something heavy enough to break glass.

"Go!" we screamed.

Ryan floored it, first in reverse, throwing us forward, then he slammed it into drive, grinding gears, hurling us back into our seats and screeching through a stop sign.

"That's it!" I said. "I'm driving."

"Dad blasted right," Lottie said, rolling down her spit-streaked window and leaning out to shoot a picture of the shouting group on the corner we had just escaped.

Ryan looked shocked. "Why didn't you just tell 'em that you're the one who broke the story, Britt? Those cops wouldn't have been arrested if it hadn't been for you."

"You try telling them," I said. "I doubt these people are our subscribers, Ryan."

The smell of smoke hung on the air, and I vaguely wondered where it came from. A bottle smashed in the street in front of us. Ryan swerved and hit the brakes.

"Don't stop," I yelled.

"Keep going, keep going, keep going," Lottie said.

"Don't panic," Ryan said. "I'm driving."

I rolled my window down an inch. "Did you hear that?"

"Yeah." Lottie's face was taut.

"What, what?" said Ryan.

"Those loud pops. That's gunfire. Must be a sniper." I scanned the upper floors of the buildings around us.

Ryan gripped the wheel. Black smoke up ahead, cascading down the street. For a moment it cleared and we saw what was burning. A late-model car in flames, overturned and totally engulfed.

"Man oh man," Lottie was muttering. I heard the click and whirr of her shutter.

Ryan stomped the brake, face stunned. Two crumpled bodies were sprawled in the street near the flaming car. Between them and us was a mob of about thirty or forty people, some carrying weapons.

Lottie kept shooting. "Sure don't like their looks," I said, scribbling notes.

"Great stuff." Lottie reached for another camera. "Let's move."

"See that!" I cried. Something kicked up powdery dust and shattered pavement in the street next to us and in front of us. Sniper fire from high in one of the apartment houses we were passing; or maybe the roof.

"Time to go." I spoke calmly. "Make a hughie, Ryan."

As he swung the wheel there was a thud as something hit the car, rocking it slightly. About ten men and boys were in the street behind us, about half a block away, coming up on us fast. The larger mob advanced from the front.

Lottie was shooting pictures. My hands itched for the steering wheel. "Go through 'em Ryan," I warned. "Don't stop."

Something hit the windshield, rolled and bounced off the hood.

"Son of a bitch!" Lottie muttered, still shooting. "They better not damage this car!"

Too late. Cracks cobwebbed across the glass. I scribbled notes. "Lean on the horn and go, Ryan," I said quietly. He floored it.

"Noooo!" Lottie and I screamed. Instead of heading back down Twelfth Avenue, he turned and swerved into an open-ended alley between Sixty-first and Sixty-second Streets.

"Don't worry," he said confidently. "I'm taking evasive action."

"Never let yourself get trapped in an alley!" Lottie cried.

"Get on the radio," I yelled. The local community center was at the far end of the alley. There would surely be more people and more violence there. The car bounced against garbage cans and trash in the alley. Rocks and bottles crashed onto the trunk and roof from behind us, dense smoke up ahead. Running figures passed the mouth of the alley. Ryan hesitated, taking his foot off the gas.

"Go! Go! Go! You can't stop now," I said, glancing at the mob behind us.

We emerged onto the open street over the crunch of broken glass; shattered store windows. People were running. A man, his face contorted in rage, grabbed the door handle on my side and hung on, half running, half dragging alongside for a few moments. Ryan was yelling, "Mayday! Mayday!" into the radio mike.

"Give them our location!" I shouted.

"Where are we?" His voice was panicky.

I screamed the answer. Lottie was shooting pictures again. The service station on the corner was in flames. I realized now what had struck me as so odd. With all the smoke around us, there were no fire engines, no fire fighters.

The car was being pelted from every direction now. Newspaper racks, bus benches, and garbage cans had been hurled into the street ahead. Suddenly I saw something coming and gasped. Lottie ducked. A huge piece of concrete crashed through the windshield and hit Ryan square in the face.

Blood flew, spattering the windows from the inside. We were all screaming, and in that terrible moment of chaos and panic, bombarded from all sides, I thought of D. Wayne Hudson and knew what the last conscious moments of his life had been like.

Then survival instinct took over. Ryan was slumped to the side, both hands to his head.

"I'll drive," I yelled, and somehow scrambled feet first over the seat to grab the wheel. Lottie had Ryan in her arms, dragging him out of my way, toward her. I couldn't see if he was still conscious or not.

Four or five men were converging on the car from behind us. I threw it into reverse, and screeched back toward them, as they scattered in surprise, then floored it, trying to see through the shattered windshield, weaving, trying to avoid the deadly barrage of flying missiles.

Lottie was on the radio to the city desk. "We're under sniper fire, at Sixty-first Street and Thirteenth Avenue, being rocked and bottled. Ryan is injured. We need a rescue unit. I repeat, Sixty-one Street and Thirteen Avenue. We have an injury. There are also two bodies back there in the street, overturned cars, and a gas station burning."

The idiotic voice of Gretchen responded, a dubious pitch to her words. "Is that you, Lottie? Repeat that please. What did you say is going on?"

If I survive this, I vowed, swerving at top speed around a burning garbage can in the street and a man swinging a baseball bat, I will kill that woman. The thought gave me comfort.

We were gallumping along on rims now, with at least two flat tires. Up ahead, thank God, I saw police barricades. They had blocked off the street. Too late, I thought, for the motorists trapped inside.

We pulled up there, and I got out. Nobody came rushing to our aid. Too much was going on. The car looked as though it had rolled sideways down a steep hill and seemed to be leaking both gas and oil. I managed with difficulty to open the battered trunk lid, snatched out Lottie's first-aid kit and some towels, and ran around to the passenger side. Ryan lay slumped across Lottie's lap. I wiped his face with a hand towel. It didn't look as bad as I had feared. His bloodied nose didn't seem broken, but the ragged gash across his forehead would definitely need stitches. At least he was conscious, mumbling, "I'm sorry, Britt"; a good sign. I folded a towel into a compress, placed it across the wound, and told him to hold it there. Lottie was squirming out from under him to shoot pictures of the police barricades.

We ignored Gretchen's voice bleating shrilly from the radio, demanding to talk to Ryan.

"Look," I told Lottie, "I don't know how long the car will keep running. Drop Ryan at the emergency room and get your film back to the paper so it can be processed for the state."

"You ain't comin'?" She gave me a long look.

"Hell no, I'll stay out on the story until it's time to write for the final. I'll stick with these cops and use their barricade as a base. Get us another car and meet me back here."

She nodded. "Watch yourself." She crouched, focusing her camera on the cops manning the barricade, then a long shot down the street we had just escaped. Then she stepped back and took one of the car.

"Lordy," she said. "Look at this wreck. We're in trouble now."

"It wasn't our fault." We both looked at Ryan, who groaned. "You're okay," I told him. I patted his cheek, made sure his fingers and toes were all tucked into the car, and closed the door.

Lottie took off, the car lurching along on its two good tires.

TWENTY-ONE

I t was too late to stop it—the juggernaut was rolling over our city. I could hear it on the radios of the cops assigned to the perimeter. Sections of expressway that cut through black neighborhoods had been shut down as unsafe for motorists. An angry radio personality had urged people to gather at the courthouse for a candlelight vigil. More than 2,000 were there within an hour, but they didn't bring candles. They brought guns, piled out of their cars, and began shooting at the building. Employees and a few court liaison officers with a limited amount of ammo were barricaded inside like the defenders of the Alamo. Fires and looting had broken out as far south as Goulds and in Coconut Grove. I told police at the barricades about the people we had seen lying in the street. They might still be alive. The cops said their orders were to remain where they were, and keep motorists from entering the area.

Except for a few drops of Ryan's blood splashed onto my yellow cotton sweater, I was in pretty good shape, glad I was wearing slacks and comfortable shoes.

Prevailing police strategy seemed to be to avoid confrontation, pulling back the perimeter whenever necessary, letting the mobs take the neighborhood. The tactic took me by surprise at first. While

I watched rioters torch an auto parts store, the police around me swiftly pulled out. After I became aware of this and took off down the block after them, two cops in a squad car picked me up and let me ride with them. They seemed to find it funny that I had found myself alone, on foot, in a riot zone. I wondered if McDonald had been called in and where he was in all this.

With the perimeters constantly changing, it would be tougher to team up with Lottie again. I decided not to worry about how to get back to the paper until the time came to go. More press was arriving. I saw a TV crew broadcasting live from high up on an overpass; a perfect place to shoot from and still keep their expensive equipment intact.

I heard via police radios that another station's TV news car had been lost, attacked, and burned on Thirty-fifth Street. There were injuries.

Acrid smells of fear, smoke, gunpowder, and panic filled the air. Blood-drenched motorists in shattered cars continued to pull up to the safety of the barricades, where fire rescue men now waited to render first aid.

The new perimeter was at an intersection with two liquor stores on opposite corners. The owners had had no time to board up before fleeing. The establishments had already been broken open, and the burglar alarms were ringing. When the time came to pull back again, I heard a lieutenant ask on the air what he should do about the package stores. "Use your own judgment," he was advised.

He directed his men into the stores and I tagged along, to watch. Wielding riot sticks and clubs, the officers cleared the shelves, smashing bottles into showers of broken glass. The only thing worse than an enraged mob, presumably, was a drunken, enraged mob. The smells of spilled booze mingled with smoke and cordite made me queasy, and my knees shook. I wished now I had eaten some lunch, or breakfast.

Police radios erupted with reports of looting at a big Zayre's department store, just three blocks south. I jogged along the sidewalk, arrived just after the first police unit, and stood, stunned, near the patrol car. Hundreds of people had smashed the store's front doors and windows, surged inside, and were in the process of taking the place apart. The parking lot was a sea of shopping carts with legs. You could not see the upper bodies of the people pushing them because the carts were stacked so high with merchandise of every description. Men, women, and children of all ages, shapes, and sizes were hauling their booty in all directions.

A young cop in the first unit radioed for help. "We need policemen here." The crackled response was that five or six officers would be dispatched.

"No," he responded, "we need fifty or sixty!"

Undermanned and ill-prepared, the cops were as disorganized as the chaos mushrooming around them. There was no way to arrest everybody, or anybody, at that point. A handful of frustrated cops finally snatched baseball bats from a display inside the front door. Unable to escape out the steel-reinforced back door, the thieves were forced to run a gauntlet of policemen swinging nightsticks and baseball bats.

Two officers snatched cans of spray paint from toppled displays and sprayed LOOTER and THIEF on cars backed up to the store.

Across the street, several officers dove for cover and began returning fire at a burning convenience store, thinking they were being shot at by someone inside. An angry captain ordered them to hold their fire, pointing out that no gunmen could be alive, much less shooting from within the inferno. They were engaging in a gunfight with soda cans and mayonnaise jars exploding in the heat.

Some of the looters torched storerooms at the rear of the big Zayre's store. Sprinklers went on and lights flashed. Black smoke began streaming out the back of the building. The lights kept flashing on and off. The entire scene was surreal. My thoughts raced as I tried to follow what was happening. Sniper fire in the street was interspersed by the occasional boom of a shotgun and the crashing of broken glass.

I returned to the action at the command post. More cops were showing up, brought in from home and other departments. Several, mostly military veterans, volunteered to man a rescue mission into the riot zone to save any survivors among motorists who had been dragged from their cars and brutalized. They had brought up a paddy wagon and were stripping the bench seats from inside. I pushed my way up to the coordinator, Sgt. Randy Springer, a tough, rock-hard, middle-aged veteran.

"I saw two of them," I said. "In the street near an overturned car that was burning. That was a couple of hours ago. They weren't moving, I couldn't tell if they were alive or not." I paused to collect my thoughts. He watched my face intently, a shotgun in his hand. "There was sniper fire, lots of it. At least one shooting from a rooftop in the middle of the block on the west side of Twelfth Avenue, between Sixtieth and Sixty-first." He nodded and they took off in the paddy wagon, a crew of five: Springer and another man poised to go into the streets for victims, two riding shotgun, and a driver. "Good luck," I whispered.

I held my breath as they swooped down a street littered with rocks and broken glass, under a late-afternoon sun that glowed eerie orange through dense smoke and lengthening shadows.

The sniper fire and shotgun blasts picked up as they disappeared into no man's land, straight into the screaming mob. Onnie, you were right, I thought, praying that she and Darryl had stayed safe inside their little apartment.

The wagon seemed to be gone forever. My watch said it was sixteen minutes before the lumbering truck reappeared like an apparition emerging from the smoke, dented and bullet-torn, headlights shot out. They brought back eight maimed and badly injured men and women, four dead motorists, and half of another body, found in the street.

Firemen worked on the survivors as I approached Springer. Under the streaked soot and perspiration, his face looked gray.

"We just grabbed bodies and threw them in the paddy wagon, Britt. My guys covering us kept firing over the mob right down to the last shotgun round."

"You think you found them all?"

"Jesus, Britt." He paused. "I hope so." His eyes were wet. I pretended not to see his hands jumping and shaking. He stared down at them himself, his expression odd, as though the quirky appendages belonged to someone else. "I was shot in Vietnam," he whispered, "but I never saw anything like this." He shook the tears out of his eyes, gulped, and looked away. "We needed air support," he said shakily.

I fought the urge to hug him. I couldn't, because I am a professional, but I knew he needed a hug. I needed one, too.

A woman police officer shared an orange with me, which I accepted gratefully. Feeling slightly better, I hiked back to see what was happening at Zayre's. I had filled my notebook, and was now using the backs of the used pages, still taking notes. The fire continued to burn at the rear, in a storeroom area. The place looked as though it had been totally cleaned out. Alarms were still ringing. The sprinklers seemed to have stopped. I wondered if anyone was hurt inside. I stepped through the shattered front door and felt sucked in by the building's hot smoky breath.

Dark shapes and shadows materialized on the floors between the aisles. Were they people who had been overcome, or mannequins? I took a few more steps inside. The empty, smashed display cases and bare shelves yawned in eerie abandonment. A broken doll lay discarded on the floor. Water dripped somewhere. I wondered what the cost in dollar damage would be, the stolen stock as well as the building, and scribbled a note to myself to check with company officials when I got back to the office. The loss has to be well into six figures, I thought.

A sudden sound startled me, and my heart hammered a triple beat. With nothing left to steal here, newly arrived looters would probably turn ugly. With relief I saw that a patrol car had pulled up close to the front entrance. Glad to see a uniform approaching the door behind me, I resolved to stick closer to the cops from now on. I hoped this one didn't think I was a looter.

I turned and called, "It's only me, trying to come up with a ball-park figure on the damage. What do you think?"

The man in uniform kicked a piece of debris out of his way and stepped closer, moving out of the shadow until I could see his face. He smiled, and my heart lurched into my throat. Francisco Alvarez. I hadn't even thought of him during the last few hours. Yet I should have. All of this was his doing. I swallowed hard.

"They really cleaned the place out, huh?" I said, and moved to step by him, heading for the door.

"You really think you're going somewhere?" He spoke slowly.

His words and tone were so passionless, so calm, yet so chilling that, without thinking, I broke into a run. He caught my right arm as I passed, throwing me off balance and spinning me around. He drew me close, his face looming large over mine.

"You were so anxious to see me, *chica,* remember?"

"That was before all this happened. I'm on deadline now. I don't have time." I tried to sound firm and businesslike and shake myself loose, but his grip was iron.

His left hand groped between my legs. He was smiling. "I hear you like to screw cops."

"No, I don't," I panted, my blood turning to ice water. "Let me go!" I said angrily.

I shot a glance at the door as though expecting someone. "The field force unit will be here any minute."

He reacted with a smirk. "I command the field force unit."

"My editor, the medical examiner, and the state attorney's office all have the story. I told them everything." My voice seemed to be coming from underwater.

He hesitated for a moment, glaring into my eyes. Then he put his left hand tightly around my throat, bruising my chin and drawing my face even closer to his. He smiled, baring his teeth in a look that dissolved my bones into icy dust. "I don't think so. I know a bluff when I see it."

He let go of my arm, reached under my sweater, and twisted my right breast. "Like that?" he said. I whimpered. Shouts sounded out in the street. He reacted by spinning me around, right off my feet, twisting my arm behind my back, and kicking me forward. "Let's go," he said, "where we can be alone."

I heard him unsnap the handcuffs from his belt. "Major," I said, fighting panic, trying to sound rational, "you can't do this. This is ridiculous. I'm sure we can talk, outside somewhere." I made a slight movement in the direction of the door, but he jerked me back.

"No," he whispered softly, almost seductively, into my ear. "First we'll have some fun, and then you won't talk to anybody. No more stories for you."

"This is not worth your career," I said, coughing from the smoke that wafted from the back of the building. My eyes stung.

"No, it isn't," he whispered. "And never fear, *chica,* it won't be."

He was marching me back toward what had been the women's clothing department. Curtained dressing rooms lined the wall. "Excellent," he whispered, shoving me inside one and turning me to face him. "Now," he said briskly, "on your knees." His eyes glittered, his expression expectant. I got the distinct impression, as his body pressed against mine, that the man had an erection.

As he snapped the cuffs around my left wrist, I chopped his adam's apple with my right hand, kneed him in the groin with all the strength I could muster, and was off and running.

He followed, amazingly fast for someone I thought I had just disabled. I had hoped to be outside before he recovered; but I heard the crunch of his footsteps on broken glass behind me.

"Halt, or I'll shoot," he shouted, hoarse and gasping.

I dove down behind a counter, next to a cash register broken open on the floor. The metal cuffs still dangled from my left wrist. "I have a gun, *chica.* I will if I have to, but I would prefer not to shoot you."

No, I thought, skittering on all fours to the cover of another counter, he would rather make it look like rioters killed me. No ballistics in beating deaths. I would be a statistic, another casualty of this huge disaster, lost in the numbers. I held my breath.

If I could make it out the door, the barricades were not far away. Once in sight of other cops, he wouldn't dare.

I strained to listen, ears wide open, unsure of exactly where he was. The unfought fire was slowly spreading, smoke swirling around me. I got closer to the floor and tried not to cough. Only one thing was clear—I had to get out of there. I raised myself up to a crouch, like a sprinter at the starting line, breathed deeply, counted to three and bolted.

I heard his surprised grunt from somewhere to my right, but concentrated on moving fast and keeping my footing on the littered, slippery floor. Ten feet from the door I heard the shot and the tinkling sound of glass shards falling as the slug jammed into a window frame ahead of me. I kept going and burst out the door, moving as fast as I ever have in my life.

Hesitating an instant to catch my breath and bearings, I broke for the barricades, only a short distance away. But as I ran and my eyes began to focus, I became disoriented, overwhelmed. Tears stung my eyes. The barricades, the perimeter was gone. They had moved out again, pulled back, without me. This was no man's land now, abandoned to the mob, no cops in sight.

I had no idea how far they had withdrawn, or in which direction. A glance over my shoulder accelerated my heartbeat. Alvarez, running powerfully, was gaining, his gold-plated gun in his hand. A stitch stabbed my side, but the pain was nothing, I thought, compared to what would happen if he caught me. I forced myself to keep up the pace.

Skidding up to the corner, I looked wildly up and down, not knowing which way to run. No sign of cops or barricades or help, only smoky streets. I thought I was going crazy, because I smelled blood and the faint odor of tear gas.

I saw the source of the blood, a butcher shop on the far corner, ransacked, windows broken, raw meat littering the street. The distant sound of grinding metal, a car crash, drew my eyes to the west and a glimpse of the golden sun, setting serenely on a horizon that glowed purple and red. Panicked and almost sobbing at the sound of Alvarez's footsteps pounding behind me, I ducked into a liquor store.

The alarm rang maddeningly. Smashed bottles lay in glittery heaps amid golden puddles tracked with crimson. Would-be looters, perhaps some of them barefoot or in flipflops, must have cut themselves on broken glass trying to salvage intact bottles from the mess. I hid behind the counter, scrabbling about, searching for a weapon. Most liquor store operators keep a gun, but this one must have taken his with him; either that or a looter owned it now. I thought bitterly about my revolver, in the glove box of my car, parked safely back at the newspaper.

A shadow fell over the sparkling diamonds of debris: Alvarez, breathing hard in the doorway. He stepped inside cautiously, like a man crossing thin ice, the gun in his hand, barrel pointed at the ceiling.

If I die, I thought, my mother will believe she was right. I should have sold dresses. I thought of McDonald. Where was he? Cops are never around when you need them. I pictured my father's face. He would never surrender; he never did.

"Britt! Come out, now." The commanding voice was one accustomed to obedience. No telling how many shots in that automatic, probably fifteen or eighteen, I thought. He only got one, maybe two, off at the store. He probably had another clip. Whatever, there was little chance he would run out of ammo.

A door hung ajar at the far end of the counter, possibly to the stockroom or a bathroom. It might lead to a back door or a window, or trap me at a dead end. I tried to remember the outside of the building. It was freestanding, with a small parking lot at the rear. Whatever, I had to try for it, or else stay here to be shot like a fish in a barrel. Alvarez seemed to be checking the aisles from a command position near the front door. At any moment now he would look or vault over the counter. Thanks to the sounding burglar alarm, I could crawl toward the mystery door without him hearing my progress, if I was careful.

Broken glass shredded my slacks and ground into my knees and the palms of my hands. I'd reached the door and was inching it open a little wider when I heard him cry out and rush toward me. Staggering painfully to my feet, I dove through the door and slammed it behind me. There was a simple bolt; I knew it wouldn't hold. A short hallway ended at the back door. There was a windowless stockroom on one side, a bathroom with a small, shuttered window at the other. I threw myself against the back door, made of steel and dead-bolted, as Alvarez kicked the door between us. It almost gave. Another kick would do it. The steel door wouldn't open; it needed a key.

I scrambled into the bathroom, slammed the door, and locked it, another simple throw bolt. The wooden shutter creaked open easily, but the window had long been painted shut with many coats. I snatched up the small round wastecan, stood on the toilet, and broke the glass, just as I heard the outside door crash open. The bathroom door rattled. I took off my sweater, wrapped it around my arm, cleared the frame of the sharp remaining shards of glass, and hoisted myself up and out. I dropped six feet to the ground as Alvarez shot the lock off the bathroom door.

My ankle and knees hurt when I got up, but I pulled my sweater back over my head and started to run across the parking lot. I glanced back at the window: nothing. Then I saw him charge around the side of the building. He'd run back through the store and out the front door rather than try to squeeze his bulk through that small window.

He had a clear shot at me now. I tried to weave from side to side, stumbling, as I ran. Several people emerged through the smoke. Men and youths, shouting, armed with clubs, pieces of broken furniture, and pipes. "Help me!" I cried, waving my arms, handcuffs catching the light.

Alvarez still came, focused on me. Other figures loomed behind him.

"There's one of them! Get 'em! Get 'em!" somebody shouted. "Pig, motherfucker!" Cries went up. "Hey, look what we got here!" one man shouted. "A policeman! A goddamn policeman!" I stood, frozen, as the mob surged forward, then past me. Alvarez, gun in hand, boldly began to shove his way through, and reached for my arm. I yanked it away.

"She's my prisoner . . ." he said, as a man hit him from behind. Another lunged for his gun. The gold-plated automatic went flying, scooped up in somebody's hand. I backed away.

Alvarez went down on one knee, his eyes still on me as they swarmed over him. I ran. I looked back once, but all I saw was flailing elbows, knees, and feet. One man was kneeling, stabbing with what looked like a screwdriver, over and over and over. Then I heard gunfire: the gold-plated automatic.

Blindly I ran, running forever, stumbling, lungs in spasms, until I thought I heard my name. A patrol car, flasher spinning, screeched to a stop ten feet away. I kept running, thinking somehow that Alvarez had come back to life to kill me.

The officer jumped out, clumsy in bulky riot gear, wearing a visored helmet with a Plexiglas face protector, and a gas mask strapped to her leg: the most beautiful sight I had ever seen.

"Oh Francie, Francie," I gasped in relief. "Thank God!"

"Britt! How the hell did you get out here?" She reached for me. "Are you okay?"

"He tried to kill me," I sobbed, slumping against her and her car. "He tried to kill me."

"Who?" She stepped away and looked around, hand on her holstered gun.

I lifted my left arm, handcuffs dangling. "Major Alvarez. He's dead. I'm sure he's dead. The mob got him. He did it, Francie! He put out the false BOLO. He went to the hospital and killed D. Wayne Hudson!"

Her blue eyes widened. "You sure you're okay?"

I knew I sounded hysterical. "Come on," she said gently, then scanned the streets around us. "This is a war zone, they're burning down the whole damn town. We have to get out of here—until the Guard comes in to back us up. The perimeter has been pulled back again."

Shots, crashes, and breaking glass resounded from the next block. A bonfire roared in the street, rippling heat waves rising into the darkening sky. Francie looked and sounded exhausted, her pale face streaked with perspiration.

"This gear is as hot as hell," she said. "It weighs more than I do. My T-shirt is soaked."

"Have you seen Lottie?" I said. "I've gotta get back to the paper." Shots sounded close by.

"Get in the car." She reached for my arm. "It's too dangerous for us to . . ." Her hands flew to her throat.

"Francie? What is it?" Spurts of bright red arterial blood suddenly pumped from between her fingers. I watched in horror as she crumpled to the pavement.

"Oh my God, Oh my God," I cried. I knelt beside her, looked up, and saw another bright flash from a building across the street. A bullet ricocheted off the bumper of her patrol car. "Oh my God! Francie." She moved her lips, trying to say something, but made only terrible sounds. Blood bubbled and was everywhere. I unfastened her helmet strap, pushed it back, and tried to stop the flow. But the hole was too big, and if I applied pressure to her throat, she would choke. She was already choking, drowning in her own blood. I pulled her into my arms and cradled her, weeping, not knowing what to do.

"You'll be all right. You'll be all right," I repeated, over and over. Her body began to convulse, arms and legs jerking. I held her until the shaking stopped.

When a car horn blared, I looked up. A yellow taxi cab, a black man at the wheel, skidded to a stop. "Come on, come on!" he yelled. "You the lady reporter, right?"

"Yes." I felt foggy, about to wake from a bad dream.

"Come on, get in. We'll get outta here."

It took a moment to begin to compute, then I stood up and tried to drag Francie toward the cab, my hands under her armpits. My fingers kept slipping in the blood. Her heels dragged in the dust.

Something bounced by me and rolled to a stop under her patrol car. A bottle. A Molotov cocktail. It ignited in a whoosh, bathing the undercarriage of the cruiser in flames.

"Sheeet," the cabbie said. "Come on! Come on! Leave her be." He looked around wildly, one foot out, his door half-open. "Leave her here. She's dead. She's gone."

"No," I whimpered, well aware that he was right.

He swung the back door open. "Come on, Come on. I can try to get you out of here."

I let go of Francie and went to the cab, my hand on the door. "No, wait!" I cried.

"Sheeet!" he yelled, as I turned and ran back to the patrol car. The door handle was hot to the touch and flames crept up around the chassis.

"It's gonna blow!" he yelled. "Git away from it!"

I yanked it open, scorching my palm. She was crouched on the floorboard in the front.

I reached out and Bitsy crept into my arms. I ran back to the cab and scrambled inside. He took the corner squealing, on two wheels, as I heard the muffled blast behind us.

"Get down. Stay down," he said. I fell to the floor, my cheek pressed against the carpet, sure I would never get up again.

"Where you want to go?" he asked after a time.

"The newspaper."

"You sure you want to go there?"

The question surprised me. Where else would I go?

TWENTY-TWO

They tried to send me home, but I stayed, washed up as best I could in the ladies' room, changed to the clothes in my locker, and worked through the night on the riot coverage. My clearest recollection was a moment I wish I could forget.

As we pieced together the stories of destruction, terror, and confusion, the managing editor emerged from his carpeted office in shirtsleeves, smiled at me, nodded and said, "Good work, Britt."

I sat there numb as he walked away. But his words stayed with me. Exhaustion, deadlines, and breaking stories suppressed my conflicting emotions and feeling of guilt for a time. My landlady, Mrs. Goldstein, took care of Bitsy, while Lottie and I camped out at Onnie's place the following night. Police had imposed a curfew, and there was no other way for reporters to have access to the riot zone after dark. While there, of course, I had to keep up a good front for Darryl.

Not until the third day, after the National Guard had restored order, did the full impact hit. McDonald arrived at my door, also exhausted, still wearing a uniform that smelled of smoke and tear gas, after forty-eight hours on duty. We fell into each other's arms. He held me and listened to everything that had happened. Spilling the story to him was little comfort. Bruised body and soul, sore and sick,

I had trouble sleeping. Neither sleep nor sex nor long hot baths restored me. That's when I made up my mind and told him I was quitting. I called the city desk to make it formal, but McDonald reached past me and hung up the phone.

"Don't do it," he said. "You would only regret it the rest of your life. I know exactly how you feel, but this is no time to make a major decision."

"You don't know how I feel! How could you possibly?" I said irritably, pulling my bathrobe tightly around me and hugging my scabbed knees, which were drawn up to my chest.

His face worked, as though summoning up secret thoughts, unpleasant ones. "You know I killed a man once?"

I nodded. "Justifiably."

"Sure, he was armed and loco and dangerous. He tried to kill me, but I managed to get him first. That doesn't make taking a life any less traumatic. It was a numbing, shattering experience." His eyes clouded in recollection. "But when I got back to the station, I was congratulated and backslapped, and told by everybody from the chief to the guys in the locker room what a great job I had done.

"I shook their hands and accepted their congratulations. But I knew that what had happened was not something to be congratulated for. It was a tragedy, something painful that I had had to do. I went home and bawled like a baby."

I leaned against him, he put his arm around me and stroked my hair. "That's something else we have in common, Britt. Our jobs are a lot alike. We're going to hurt people, and they're going to hurt us. Sometimes they're strangers, sometimes they're the people we work for. That's sad, but that's what happens in this business. Lord knows my life would be easier if you chose some other line of work. But we both care about our jobs, do them the best we know how, and go on in spite of it when these things happen. We're not quitters."

He was right.

Francie will always be alive in my heart. Not a day passes that I don't think of her. How could she be gone? Not Francie. I still have not come close to accepting it. Her nearest relative, a cousin from Tampa, wasn't interested in taking Bitsy. After seeing what a good dog she was, Mrs. Goldstein agreed to let me keep her until I found a suitable home. "If Billy Boots can deal with it, so can I," she said. I didn't want a dog. They are so much more needy than cats. But I guess I have one. How could I give up Bitsy, already uprooted and bewildered, to a stranger?

As soon as the riot coverage ended and the city was under control, I began putting together my story about the truth, what really happened. I worked hard on it, for two days. It explained everything. It was never published.

After I turned in the story, there was a solemn meeting among editors, lawyers, the mayor, the city manager, the police chief, and black leaders.

"They believe you," Fred Douglas told me, when he called me into his office later. "We believe you. But there is no sure way to prove Alvarez was guilty. No way a dead man can defend himself against allegations."

"But we have to expose the truth about what happened." I couldn't believe what I was hearing. "The public has a right to know."

"Britt, you know as well as I do, the black community would never believe that those officers who were acquitted did not kill D. Wayne Hudson."

"They didn't."

"But they did commit a crime. They beat him, and then tried to cover it up. The chief has agreed to tighten supervision on the midnight shift and investigate the practices that led to some of the bad cops being there in the first place. The people who run this city and this newspaper agree it's time to put this case to rest. More accusations, stirring up more controversy, won't solve a thing."

I understood what he was saying. The city had already been through a terrible trauma. Its image, along with that of the police department, had been cruelly wounded. The quicker the healing process and rebuilding began, the better for all of us who lived here. My story would bring no one to justice and would only further polarize a divided community. For those reasons, the most important story I ever wrote was never read.

The final toll was fourteen civilians and two police officers dead, hundreds of people injured, and millions of dollars in damage.

McDonald was right: I love my job, and the city, and want to be part of the recovery process. But it isn't easy.

Despite, or perhaps because of, the reforms, the police department was colder and more paranoid than ever after the riot. When I called for simple information on a homicide, I was told that the chief had issued an order. Any officer I contacted for information was instructed to refer me to the PIO, and then write a memo on when and why I called. Cops hate paperwork, so relations with many of my sources were effectively chilled.

The department was making it tough on both me and McDonald. That became more clear than ever when he showed up unexpectedly at my door one night with Chinese food, a bottle of Dom Perignon, and a need to talk.

He wore a handsome new sports jacket, a shirt the color of his eyes, and the silk briefs I had given him for Valentine's Day. He had good news and bad news. He had scored among the top ten on the lieutenant's test and was elated. I thought I knew what was coming. "There is one thing that would reduce my chances right now to less than zero," he said. "You know what it is?"

I nodded and put down my champagne glass, sorry now that I had lit the candles for atmosphere.

"If we should be seen together," he said.

"Well we're not exactly gamboling naked up Flagler Street," I said. "Where would anyone see us?"

"If I was just spotted coming out of here . . ."

"So now they are spying on the private lives of would-be lieutenants?"

He shrugged, slightly sheepish. "You never know what IA and those guys assigned to background checks will do. This means a lot to me. And I know you don't like sneaking around like this."

"Oh, so this is for my benefit?" I didn't like the sound of my own voice, but I said it anyway: "Ambition can be overpowering."

He looked pained. "Things change, everything is cyclical." He reached out across the table and chucked my chin. "We just have to cool it for awhile, Britt. It's not forever. The brass changes, things blow over. Better times will come."

He wanted to stay longer, but I saw him to the door and kissed him lightly on the cheek. "It's been real," he said softly.

"Very real," I said miserably.

There was one plus. I ripped the damn cuckoo clock off the wall and let Billy Boots and Bitsy have at it until they killed the cuckoo and the Tyroleans. Then I gave it to Goodwill Industries.

With all the truly important and tragic events in life, I refused to let myself be too bummed by a busted romance. After all, I told myself, I am sick of buying my dating clothes in the lingerie department. It would be nice to someday actually date a man who was unconcerned about taking me out in public, who might even be proud to be seen with me. It would be nice someday, though I wasn't quite ready yet.

Work, as always, was my solace. If I stayed busy enough, there was no time to think. There were rewards from communicating with vast numbers of readers, even if you couldn't communicate well one on one, up close and personal.

And things did change. Working late one night, finishing a story about a snorkler attacked by a shark, my phone rang. A wail from the jail: Pete Zalewski, as gloomy as ever. "I'm worried about my mother," he began.

"Well Pete, all of us lucky enough to still have them worry about our mothers. I worry about my mom too. Nobody ever gets any younger . . ."

"The SWAT team has her trailer surrounded."

"What?"

"She just shot my stepdaddy with a shotgun, blasted him right out the screen door."

"Are you sure?"

"Yeah, just talked to my cousin Frankie," he whined. "I'm afraid the cops are gonna shoot her, Britt."

"Hold on."

I grabbed Ryan's phone and called Miami PIO. He was right. Pete's mother had been holding off SWAT for four hours. They hadn't even been able to get close enough to drag her dead husband off the doorstep.

"You're right, Pete. What should we do?"

"If I could just talk to her. She must be off her medication again, or drinking. Booze don't mix with it. I could always communicate with her better than anybody in the family. I've always been her favorite, Britt."

I wondered darkly what her least favorite child was like.

"Does she have a phone?"

"No, just a pay phone at the manager's office."

"Okay, give me that number. I'll try to get hold of the cops at the scene."

I called and asked for the homicide sergeant in charge.

He got on the phone. I told him who I was.

"Call PIO," he said, and hung up.

I dialed back. He snatched up the phone. "Goddamn it, stop tying up this line and call PIO," he said.

"Look," I said tersely. "I didn't call to ask you anything. I called to tell you something. Something you may find helpful."

"I'm listening. I got to write a goddamn memo now anyhow."

"The woman under siege in the trailer, I have her son, her favorite son, on the other line. He can probably talk her out of there without anybody else getting hurt."

"How quick can he get here?"

"Well, sergeant, that's the problem . . ."

Lottie and I were in a hurry to get out to the trailer park. The infernal newsroom elevator took forever. "What we really need," she said, jabbing the button viciously, "is to have 'em install a fire pole so we could just slide right down to our cars in the parking lot." Sounded good to me.

We arrived at the SWAT scene just a few minutes before a squad car pulled up with Pete. He was happy to see us, happy for a break in his dull jail routine, and happy to see his mama, even under the circumstances.

The cops wouldn't let him enter the trailer, for fear they'd have two murder suspects holed up. But when she heard Pete was outside, she quickly agreed to drop the shotgun and came out, stumbling over her late husband, still sprawled on the doorstep, in her haste.

The mother-son reunion was sweet. Lottie got great pictures. The cops were so touched they let the two of them ride back to jail in the same patrol car, so they could catch up on family news.

Danny Menendez was there. He was on call, and would be writing the press release. He looked friendly for a change. "Nice work, Britt. Homicide told me how you helped them out. Changed your mind about cops, huh?"

"Do you hear that?" I muttered to Lottie as we climbed into the car. "Cops!"

"To them, you're either for 'em, or against 'em," she said, "no middle road there."

"It's like they've never heard of such a thing as objective reporting."

On the way back to the office, we talked about my love life, or lack of it. The split with McDonald, I tried to convince myself and Lottie, was actually a blessing. "Neither of is likely to change jobs. He was right about that."

"Maybe it only tasted so sweet because it was forbidden fruit," she said.

"You may be right. If we had been free to see each other in public and talk openly about everything, including our work, maybe there would have been no magic."

"I know you've been burned," Lottie began carefully. "But I do have good news. Don't ask me why, but Steve and Larry are still interested. They want to take us to the opera, the opening night of *Carmen,* at Gusman Hall. With Marilyn Horne!" She whistled under her breath. "You know how hard it is to get opening-night seats? People actually leave them in their wills. They stay in families for generations. Opera patrons sit in the same seats their mamas and daddies sat in years ago."

"How did Larry and Steve ever get tickets?"

"Some client of Larry's is going to Houston for heart surgery and owes him a big one. Cain't you just see us now, all gussied up and in high cotton, mingling with everybody who's anybody?"

"I really don't think so . . . ."

"Look, it's high time somebody took you out and showed you off in public. This is big time, the place to see and be seen."

"Damn straight," I said, suddenly buoyed by the idea. "Okay, let's go." Maybe it was the euphoria, the exclusive story and pictures we had just aced, thanks to Pete. "Sure, I'm game. Larry is a nice guy."

"Hallelujah! And remember, this is it. Our last chance. World War III can break out, but nothing is gonna make us cancel. We don't show up this time, and we can forget these guys."

"You're right," I said, warming up to the idea. "They have been pretty understanding. Let's be there with bells on!"

We spent the rest of the ride back to the office conspiring about what to wear.

Larry was in black tie when he picked me up on the big night. He looked pretty spiffy, except for the pale blue cummerbund. Steve was waiting in the car. As he drove his BMW, Larry squeezed my hand and explained the difference between term and whole-life insurance so well that, for the first time, I actually understood it. I may have been too enthusiastic, because he continued on into annuities.

Lottie met us at the box office. She had had to work that day, so she dressed at the paper and drove over. She looked great, her red hair ruly for a change, and swept up. It was one of the few times I have seen her in high heels instead of cowboy boots. She wore green velvet and long, glittery earrings that swept her freckled shoulders, and carried a dainty little evening bag.

Larry and Steve were taking us dancing at Regine's at the Grand Bay afterwards. I wore a bright pink satin evening skirt with a big blousy white top with a wide collar and a matching jeweled belt and evening bag, courtesy of my mother's professional discount.

Our seats were great, up front in Row D. I have always loved Gusman Hall, smack in the heart of downtown Miami. My mother saw Elvis perform there when she was a teenager in the fifties.

The place opened in 1926, when theaters were built like palaces, and it is a grand and gaudy piece of Miami history, with marble floors, gilded gates, and travertine walls. A philanthropist who had made his millions in condoms saved the place from demolition in the seventies, and converted it to a concert hall named after himself.

The interior resembles a courtyard in Seville. An archway frames the stage, stars twinkle, and clouds float across a deep blue ceiling. It was the perfect setting for *Carmen,* a story that was right up my alley, a Spanish tale of love and violence.

The audience settled down as the Prelude began, a happy, bustling tune that set a sunny scenario for the brooding action to follow.

By the time the impertinent Carmen was conning the hapless Don José into helping her escape instead of hauling her off to jail, my beeper had begun to chirp. I knew I shouldn't have brought the darn thing. Force of habit. I caught Lottie's warning eye, reached into my evening bag, flicked the switch to off, and left it that way.

During Carmen's fiery gypsy song in the next act, Lottie's beeper sounded. I was surprised she even had it with her. Our dates exchanged concerned glances, and an elegantly dressed couple in the row in front turned to give us cold stares. Lottie turned it off and made no move for a telephone. This was our night. Larry put his arm around me and I smiled, as Don José pleaded piteously with Carmen, who stamped her foot angrily and insulted him.

At intermission we strolled out to the lobby, mingled with the beautiful people, and drank champagne. Several of Miami's ten best-dressed women, in all their finery, greeted Lottie with glad cries, as though she was an old friend. We hurried back to our seats as the lights flashed.

The musicians stamped their feet and the maestro readied his music, but the curtain was briefly delayed. The lights came back up, setting the audience abuzz as the elegantly garbed general manager of the Greater Miami Opera stepped on stage.

"A short announcement," he said. "The police and fire department have asked us to advise members of the audience to avoid south Biscayne Boulevard when they exit this evening." Out the corner of my eye I saw Lottie, who had been whispering intimately in Steve's ear, straighten in her seat. Her eyes looked alert and wary, like those of a startled deep woods creature.

"It seems there's a little problem at the port," the manager continued. "A fire out of control and the possibility of explosions due to the fuel storage tanks there."

Lottie and I exchanged glances.

"So motorists who intended to take the MacArthur or Venetian Causeways home are advised that both bridges will remain closed, and that they should detour west to I-95 and take 112 back east to the Tuttle Causeway. Now," he gestured expressively, "back to Bizet's *Carmen.*" He stepped offstage as the lights went down and the curtain rose.

Carmen contemptuously told Don José to go home. She was about to have her cards read, her fortune told. The future would not look good.

I leaned foward slightly, looking across Steve to sneak a peek at Lottie. Our eyes met in a meaningful glance.

"Excuse me. Powder room," I whispered to Larry, who stood to let me by. People behind us murmured in annoyance.

Lottie emerged from the auditorium two minutes later, eyes sweeping the lobby for me. Elegant and ladylike we minced to the Flagler Street exit, glanced over our shoulders to be sure we were out of sight of the audience and our dates, and broke into a run.

"Where's the car?" I panted.

"Across the street in the parking garage, first level."

She paused at the curb to pull off her high heels. "Dang it, these dadblasted things were killing me."

"Can you shoot color for the front page?"

"Yep, I've got color negative PPC film in the car. I can push it two stops in the processor."

She tossed me the keys, and I slid into the driver's seat of her new white company Chrysler.

"Watch out for this car, Britt. You know all the heat that came down on us about the others."

"It wasn't our fault."

She nodded, and slammed her door. "Larry and Steve," she mourned, as I threw it in reverse. "They will never understand this."

The tires whined down the curving ramp to the street.

"They weren't our types anyway."

"You're right, Britt. Wow! Will you look at that!" Flames were clearly visible at the port, towering into the night sky, reaching for the moon. As I turned onto Flagler, we could still hear the strains of the orchestra mingled with the music of sirens converging from all directions. An engine company honked its air horn, roaring by us on the wrong side of the road. My pulse quickened.

"Looks like the county and the Beach are responding too, under the mutal aid pact," Lottie said. She slipped off the long, glittery earrings, tossed them into the backseat, and checked her cameras. "I'll radio the city desk and let them know we're on it."

"They must have put out a general alarm." I hit the gas, trailing in the wake of an aerial truck roaring straight across the bridge to the port. "Find out how much time we have until the final."

"Right," she said.

I caught my own image in the rearview mirror, the flames and flashing lights reflected in my eyes, and I smiled.

"You know, Lottie, you were right. It really did me good to get out."

ACKNOWLEDGMENTS

I had a little help from my friends. I am grateful to Dr. Steve Nelson and Dr. Joseph H. Davis; to Ann and D. P. Hughes; to Miami's finest: Sergeants Jerry Green and Roberson Brown, Lieutenant Robert Murphy, Major Mike Gonzalez, and Officer Lori Nadelman; to the Miami *Herald*'s library staff, *Herald* attorney Sam Terilli, and *Herald* writers: Liz Balmaseda, Arnold Markowitz, Lisa Getter, Joan Fleischman, and Fabiola Santiago; to the Rev. Garth Thompson; my sharp-eyed compadres: Marilyn Lane, Cynnie Cagney, Lloyd Hough, and Marshall Frank, and, especially, to the talented Leslie Wells, an editor you can trust.